UNEXPECTED RESPONSES

Sinjun closed the distance between them and pulled her into his arms, crushing her against him in an onslaught of lust so startling that she felt him shaking from it. "Everything about you pleases me," he whispered against her lips. "I wonder..."

Christy's thoughts scattered. The feel of her husband's arms around her and the heat of his body affected her strangely. She hadn't expected to feel any kind of response for the hedonistic man that St. John Thornton had become. Her personal agenda was to seduce him quickly, and assure Glenmoor of an heir.

"What do you wonder?"

"I wonder if you know how very much I want you."

A TASTE of SIN

CONNIE MASON

LOVE SPELL   NEW YORK CITY

To my brother-in-law John MacDonald,
whose Scottish heritage was the
inspiration for this book.

LOVE SPELL®

July 2006

Published by

Dorchester Publishing Co., Inc.
200 Madison Avenue
New York, NY 10016

ISBN 0-505-52681-6

The name "Love Spell" and its logo are trademarks of Dorchester Publishing Co., Inc.

Printed in the United States of America.

Visit us on the web at www.dorchesterpub.com.

A TASTE of SIN

Prologue

Scottish Highlands
Glenmoor Castle, 1747

"You know why you have to do this, don't you, Sinjun?"

"I know, but I don't like it, Father," young St.John Thornton replied.

"We do what the king asks of us," Roger Thornton, fourth earl of Mansfield, said.

Fourteen-year-old St.John Thornton, marquis of Derby, looked as if he'd rather be anywhere but standing in Glenmoor Castle's guest chamber dressed in his best velvet breeches and waistcoat.

"Why me, Father? Julian is your heir, let him marry that wild Scottish hoyden."

"Come now, Sinjun, you know Julian has been betrothed to Lord Sinclair's daughter since the day she was born. They will wed when she turns eighteen."

"I am fourteen, Father, and the Macdonald heiress is but seven."

"Think you I don't know that?" Roger said with asperity. "We're not talking about bedding here.

You have but to marry the chit and then you may return to England until she comes of age. You can go to the university like you planned and sow your wild oats while Lady Christy is growing up. When the time comes, I trust you to do your duty by her."

"I can't bring myself to like her, Father." He wrinkled his aristocratic nose. "When we arrived, I saw her playing in the courtyard with her kinsmen and mistook her for a dirty beggar child. Her face was smeared with mud and she was barefoot." He shuddered. "Can't the king find someone else to marry her? She looks like a witch with her tangled red hair and white skin."

" 'Tis the king's plan to demoralize rebellious Highlanders by placing their lands into the hands of loyal Englishmen. After Culloden, every one of Scotland's orphaned aristocratic daughters were married to men of King George's choosing. The king trusts none of the surviving Highland lairds. Old Angus Macdonald wields great power over his clan, and his granddaughter will become laird after his death.

"Christy's father, Gordy, as well as both her brothers, died at Culloden," Roger continued. "And old Angus, Christy's grandfather, became her guardian. Angus leaves no male heirs, all were slain at Culloden. Marriage will gain you both Christy and stewardship of Glenmoor into perpetuity. Through your wife you can control the clans who swore fealty to old Angus Macdonald."

Sinjun tossed his head of dark hair and glared sullenly at his father. "I don't care about any of that. I like nothing about the Scottish Highlands. 'Tis a desolate land, fit only for wolves and savages."

"The king does us great honor, Sinjun," Roger

chided, exasperated at his son's lack of gratitude. "Thorntons are loyal subjects of the crown. We have been honored by numerous titles and land grants. The Macdonald holdings are vast. Through this marriage you gain the kind of power and wealth that will make the Thornton name one to be reckoned with in England. 'Tis a great opportunity, Sinjun, not to mention the honor. Taxes and rents from your lands will keep you in luxury the rest of your life. You should appreciate what King George is doing for you and our family."

Sinjun's full lips, which ladies one day would describe as sensual, turned downward into a scowl. "I suppose, since you put it that way, Father, I will have to marry the girl. But I will not lie, I do not like Christy Macdonald."

"I'm not telling you to like her. All you need do is marry her now and return briefly to Glenmoor when she is old enough to consummate the marriage. After that you can do what you like with your life. Keep in mind, however, that when Christy's grandfather dies and she becomes laird, you will wield great power in the Highlands through your wife."

"What if I wish to stay in England, as far away from Christy as I can?" Sinjun asked.

"You can hire a bailiff to oversee your Scottish estates, and your wife can remain safely sequestered at Glenmoor. But you have plenty of time to decide what you want to do."

Lord Mansfield regarded his son with a critical eye. The boy was tall for his age, with shoulders nearly as broad as his own. Sinjun was a handsome young devil, and he knew it, Mansfield thought. Too handsome for his own good, and far too knowledgeable in the ways of the world for his tender age. He pitied the women who would try to capture his son's heart when he was old enough to catch their attention. And the young devil would attract women by the droves, and probably lead them a merry chase. How could women not fall under the spell of his dark, brooding eyes and dashing smile? The young maidservants at Thornton Hall were beginning to look upon him with favor, and Roger wondered if his son had already sampled what they had to offer.

Sinjun knew exactly what he wanted to do with his life, and it did not include forsaking London and rusticating in the Highlands with a wife obviously as wild as the land she lived in. He would go to the university, of course, and embark upon life's adventures. Even at the tender age of fourteen he'd learned to appreciate women. Polly, an upstairs maid just a few years older than he, had taken him under her wing and shown him how to enjoy himself in bed with a woman. The lessons had been fascinating, and he couldn't wait to spread his wings and practice with other women.

When he'd been told he was to marry a young Scotswoman, he'd rebelled, but his protests had been ignored by both his father and the king. Very well, he would marry Christy Macdonald, but he did not have to like her, nor did he have to live with her.

Now Sinjun waited on the steps of the village kirk for his seven-year-old bride to arrive. Flanked on either side by his father and the minister, there was no escape. The Macdonalds and their allies were all present, none of whom appeared pleased with the marriage of one of their own to an Englishman. One Scotsman about his own age was particularly fierce in his disapproval, sending Sinjun menacing looks.

A frown darkened Sinjun's brow when he saw Christy coming down the hill with her grandfather. It appeared he wasn't the only one reluctant to marry. Christy was digging her heels in and protesting loudly as her grandfather dragged her to the kirk. She wore the Macdonald plaid though it had been forbidden, and in the background Sinjun heard the slow dirge of bagpipes, also forbidden by order of the king after Culloden. Her flaming hair did nothing to enhance her pale complexion, and it was so wild and disorderly that Sinjun wondered if she had even tried to tame it.

Angus Macdonald finally reached the kirk with his wildly resisting granddaughter and pushed her toward Sinjun. She stomped her little foot and glared up at Sinjun, her chin tilted pugnaciously. Sinjun nearly laughed aloud at her belligerent expression. She didn't want to marry him any more than he wanted to marry her! Well, too bad, he thought. As far as he was concerned, this marriage was ill-conceived and would never amount to anything.

The minister opened the book, cleared his throat, and began the ceremony. His words flowed over Sinjun like water. He glanced at his older brother, his father's heir, with envy. Julian still had several years before he had to marry. Julian grinned at him, and Sinjun had the unaccountable urge to stick out his tongue. As the minister droned on, Sinjun's mind wandered to pretty Polly, wondering if she missed him. He was brought up short when the bride-to-be kicked him hard in the shin.

A gasp of pain escaped from between his teeth.

"What did you do that for?" he hissed, pinning her with a hard look.

"Yer an Englishman," Christy hissed.

"Hush!" Angus warned from somewhere behind them. "Pay attention to the ceremony."

Sinjun glared daggers at his pasty-faced bride, wondering what in the world he'd ever done to deserve such an unjust punishment. His stomach churned and he wanted to retch when the minister pronounced them husband and wife. He turned to his bride and was stunned by her expression. Her scorching green gaze blazed with hatred as she stuck out her tongue at him. How could his father do this to him? he lamented as he quickly turned away. Wed at fourteen to a redheaded firebrand who obviously possessed a temper to match the ugly color of her hair.

As if to reinforce his unfavorable opinion, Christy kicked him again. He howled in outrage and made a grab for her, but she was too quick for him. She turned on her heel and fled back to Glenmoor as fast as her little legs could carry her.

Chapter 1

London, 1762

A hush fell over the crowd as St.John Thornton, marquis of Derby, entered the ballroom.
" 'Tis Lord Sin," a young man whispered in an aside to his friend. "I wonder what brings him out into such mundane company tonight."

His companion, Lord Seton, sniffed disdainfully. "I say, Renfrew, he must be slumming. He rarely attends public functions."

"The moniker Lord Sin fits him so well, you know," Renfrew returned. "Why, there isn't a more dissolute rake in all of England." He sighed enviously. "His escapades with the ladies are legend. Look around you. There isn't a lady here tonight who wouldn't fall into his bed if he but asked."

"He's married, you know," Renfrew confided. "Since he was fourteen."

"So I've heard, but one would never know it."

" 'Tis common knowledge," Renfrew said.

"Where does he keep his wife hidden? The way he carries on, you'd think he was footloose and fancy free."

7

"Ha! And so he is. I had it directly from one of his confidants that he actually likes the idea of being married. Marriage places him off limits to matchmaking mamas trying to find husbands for their marriageable daughters. Or from being eyed as a prospective husband by marriage-minded young misses. His wife is safely tucked away in Scotland, don't you know? What she doesn't know won't hurt her. Lord Sin takes his pleasure where and when he finds it without fear of entanglements or repercussions."

"Lucky bastard," Seton said.

Renfrew leaned close. "Believe it or not, Lord Sin hasn't seen his Scottish wife since their marriage was ordered by George II fifteen years ago. 'Tis rumored the marriage was never consummated. Can you imagine? The woman is laird of some wild Highlander clan."

Seton gave a hoot of laughter. "Lord Sin might not have consummated his marriage with his bride, but he certainly has cavorted with enough women to make up for the lack. Don't know how his brother the earl puts up with his shameless debauchery."

"Lord Mansfield seems preoccupied these days. Don't see him around much. Damn shame about his betrothed dying before their wedding."

"Shhh, here comes the notorious Lord Sin now," Renfrew hissed as Sinjun and his friend, Rudolph, Viscount Blakely, approached.

"What a crush, Sinjun!" Blakely said as he shouldered his way through the crowd. "Don't know why you insisted on coming out tonight. I'm accustomed to your avoiding these public gatherings."

Sinjun Thornton and his good friend headed directly for the card room. Dressed to the nines in modified riding clothes, which had recently become all the rage, Sinjun, more commonly referred to by the *ton* as Lord Sin, wore tight black breeches with tall boots over them, pristine white shirt and stock, purple brocade waistcoat, and black dress riding coat cut high up and double-breasted, with wide lapels in the front and long-tailed in the back.

"Boredom, Rudy, sheer boredom," Sinjun said, surveying the crush of people with a jaundiced eye. "So far I've seen nothing here to interest me."

"Not even the lovely Lady Violet?" Rudy asked, calling Sinjun's attention to a striking brunette wearing a thin gauze gown with minimal stays and dampened to show her extraordinary figure to the best advantage. "Brace yourself, she's seen you."

"Drat!" Sinjun muttered beneath his breath. "I was hoping to avoid her tonight."

"Trouble in paradise?" Rudy guffawed.

Sinjun shrugged. "Our affair has run its course."

"Obviously the lady doesn't think so."

Sinjun nodded to his two acquaintances, Renfrew and Seton, as he pulled Rudy through the thick of the crowd. But it was not to be. Lady Violet honed in on him and finally caught him.

"Sinjun, I hoped you'd be here tonight. What happened to you last night? I waited ever so long for you."

"Your husband was home, Lady Fitzhugh, or have you forgotten?"

"Whenever did that make a difference?" Violet challenged. "Besides, Fitzhugh always finishes off a bottle of port before he goes to bed. He wouldn't have heard a herd of elephants were they to stampede up the stairs."

Rudy coughed, reminding them of his presence.

"I'll leave you two to your . . . er . . . conversation. I'll catch up with you later, Sinjun."

Sinjun tried to stop Rudy from leaving, but Lady Violet had other ideas. "Let him go, Sinjun. Will you come to me tomorrow night? Fitzhugh is leaving in the morning for his hunting lodge in Scotland. He expects to be gone a month or better."

Sinjun tried his damnedest to be polite, but Lady Violet was making it difficult. She didn't seem to know when something was over. And as far as he was concerned, their affair had ended the night he met Lord Stanhope sneaking around to the back door as he was leaving by the front. When he took a lover he liked to think he was the only one, but now that the affair was over, it no longer mattered how many men she took to her bed. So tonight he was at loose ends, seeking new diversions.

Sinjun was preparing to tell Violet they were through when a ripple of excitement captured his attention. Everyone seemed to be looking toward the entrance, and he followed their gaze. He inhaled sharply when he saw what, or rather who, had everyone agog. Sinjun was positive he'd never before seen the woman poised just inside the entrance, for he would have remembered her.

"Who is she?" he asked, thoroughly intrigued by the exceptional beauty who had just graced the ballroom with her auspicious presence. "I can't recall seeing her before."

"She's new to town," Lady Violet said coolly. "From Cornwall, I understand. No one seems to know much about her except that she's married to some elderly viscount who conveniently remained behind in Cornwall." She sniffed disdainfully. "She has shown up without a proper escort at three of the last four public social events. She stays a short time, then disappears. Had you attended some of those events you would have seen her. Strange," Violet mused, "but I'd swear she is looking for someone."

"Her name. Tell me her name," Sinjun demanded. "She's a rare beauty."

"Her name is Lady Flora Randall." She gave the mystery lady a disparaging glance. "Her husband must be as understanding as your wife."

Sinjun stared at the young beauty, struck speechless by an indefinable sensation that nagged at his memory. For the life of him he couldn't recall ever meeting Lady Randall before. Though she could not in any sense of the word be described as a redhead, her hair was a striking color, somewhere between cinnamon and copper, with just enough gold thrown in to make an interesting contrast.

She was small-boned and petite but had a presence about her that made her seem taller. As she lingered near the entrance, every unattached man in the room gravitated toward her. Sinjun's legs moved unerringly in her direction.

"Where are you going?" Lady Violet asked shrilly.

"To see what I've missed by not showing up at the other social events these past weeks," Sinjun threw over his shoulder as he strode purposefully toward Lady Flora Randall.

Sinjun pushed his way through the tight ring of smitten men, admiring the way the lady handled the young dandies of the *ton*. The young fops must have realized who was pushing them aside, for Sinjun heard someone whisper his name. Immediately a path was cleared for him, allowing him into the inner circle. Then he was standing before her, staring into the perfect oval of her flawless features.

Her eyes were green, he noted, as green as sparkling emeralds. Her lips were full and red, her lashes long, dark wings that curled upward at the edges. Her glowing, sun-kissed complexion surprised him. Ladies of the *ton* religiously avoided the sun. Yet everything about the mystery woman was exquisite.

She wore a green gauze gown that, though not dampened, revealed every curve of her lush figure. Sinjun seriously doubted she wore even light stays beneath her chemise. Though her décolletage was not severe, it revealed enough of her magnificent breasts to make staring worthwhile. And he'd wager he wasn't the only one who thought so. Sinjun felt himself harden and was shocked to the core. Bloody hell! He wanted her and he didn't even know her!

"I believe this is my dance," Sinjun said in a sensual drawl that would normally send most women into a veritable swoon.

Slowly she raised her eyes to his, and Sinjun was struck by the strangest feeling of déjà vu. He searched his memory and came up blank.

"Do I know you, my lord?" Flora said in a slightly husky voice that teased Sinjun's senses and made him aware of other more prominent places on his body.

"No, my lady, but 'tis easily remedied," Sinjun said. "I am St.John Thornton, Lord Derby. My friends call me Sinjun." Sinjun thought he saw something stir in the clear depths of her eyes, but it was too quickly gone for him to be sure.

"His friends call him Lord Sin," someone nearby whispered in an aside loud enough for the lady to hear.

Flora's elegant brows inched upward. "Lord Sin?"

"Pay them no heed, my lady. You may call me Sinjun. And you are—"

"Lady Flora Randall," she said, offering her hand.

Sinjun clasped her small, warm hand and placed a kiss on her knuckles. Then, giving her a bewitching smile, he turned her hand, drew her glove back, and kissed her wrist. He felt a shudder go through her and drew her forward. "Ah, a quadrille is just beginning. Shall we join in?"

Before she had a chance to protest, he led her out on the dance floor.

"So you are the Lord Sin I've heard so much about," Lady Randall said as the opening strains of music filled the room.

"My friends exaggerate," Sinjun demurred. "Pay them no heed, my lady. Is this your first time in town?"

"Aye, and I admit it's far different from what I'm accustomed to."

The dance steps separated them, and when they rejoined, Sinjun asked, "Is that an accent I detect, my lady?"

"Just a country accent, my lord," she murmured.

Christy Flora Macdonald, laird of the Macdonald clan since the recent death of her grandfather, stared at the man she hadn't seen since their marriage fifteen years ago and nearly choked on her anger. Truth to tell, she wanted Lord Derby no more than he wanted her. But circumstances had changed. Her English husband had raised rents and taxes to unconscionable levels, and her clansmen, especially the Camerons, had insisted that she seek an annulment in the English courts and wed Calum Cameron.

Christy liked Englishmen no better than her clansmen did, and she resented the fact that after the Battle of Culloden disaster her family's holdings had been confiscated, and she had been forced to marry a hated Englishman. But she had no desire to marry Calum Cameron. Nor did she have any intention of obtaining an annulment. She had her own reason and a private agenda, and she was determined to succeed.

Christy liked her life the way it was. Having an absentee husband allowed her to do as she pleased without restrictions. She didn't want a husband making decisions for her. Everything had been perfect until Calum and his kinsmen had decided the time had come to make changes, citing the fact that an unconsummated marriage was no marriage at all.

"You're very quiet, my lady," Sinjun said, recalling her to the present.

"What would you have me say, my lord?"

"Tell me about yourself."

"I'm married."

"Where is your husband?"

"In Cornwall. Though he is not well enough to travel, he insisted that I come to town and enjoy myself. He . . . is much older than I," she lied.

"Ah," Sinjun said with a wealth of understanding.

Christy studied Sinjun from beneath long, feathery lashes. She saw a tall man, large but lean, loose-limbed and sleekly muscled. A superbly put together figure. He had always been handsome, even as a lad, but maturity had given him a certain edge other men lacked. Oh, aye, maturity agreed with him. His shoulders had broadened and his chest had deepened. His exquisitely tailored jacket fit him like a glove, and his tight breeches left little to the imagination.

She searched his face and decided that no one had a right to be as devastatingly handsome as Lord Sin. He wore his shiny black hair long and unpowdered, tied back with a thong. Even though she hadn't seen him in fifteen years, she'd know him anywhere by those dark, mesmerizing eyes. They weren't black, nor were they brown. More like deep midnight blue. His full, sensuous lips and languorous smile gave mute testimony to his hedonistic nature.

She couldn't blame him, however, for not recognizing her. In fact, she had counted on it. The last time he'd seen her she had been a seven-year-old hoyden who played at wooden swords with her cousins, rolled in the mud, and had garish red hair that had miraculously darkened into the rich copper hue it was now.

Sinjun's wicked reputation and womanizing ways were legendary. Rumors of his romantic intrigues and excesses had reached her even at remote Glenmoor. Society called him a notorious rake, a connoisseur of beautiful women who savored his conquests to the fullest. She'd heard he liked women, enjoyed the chase and capture, but stayed with none of them long enough to form a lasting relationship.

"You have beautiful green eyes," Sinjun said when the dance brought them together again.

Christy blinked up at him, forcing herself to concentrate on her reason for coming to London. She had a mission, and if she hoped to succeed she had to focus on making Sinjun believe her lies. Failure was unthinkable.

"Thank you," she said, smiling demurely.

The dance ended. Moments later Christy was surrounded by eager young men vying for her attention. Sinjun bowed and left her to her admirers, but his gaze remained riveted on her as she danced the evening away with a variety of eager partners. It wasn't conceit that told Sinjun she wasn't unaffected by him, for her overt glances gave mute testimony that she was as interested in him as he was in her.

Rudy found him leaning against a pillar, a slight frown pulling at the corners of his mouth.

"I saw you dancing with the mysterious Lady Randall," Rudy said. "Is she to be your next conquest?"

"Tonight, if I have anything to say about it," Sinjun said, sending him a determined grin. "I don't know when I've been so taken with a woman, Rudy."

Rudy rolled his bright blue eyes heavenward as he tapped a finger against his lips. "Let me think," he said dryly. "Not since Lady Violet. Or perhaps Lady Scarlet. Or was it Lady Ellen? Nay. I think it was Lord Dunsley's little parlor maid you dallied with a few weeks ago. If I recall correctly, you couldn't wait to get her into your bed. That affair lasted no longer than any of your other affairs of the heart."

Sinjun's frown deepened. "Look at her, Rudy. Do you think Lady Randall favors young Fairfield's suit? Or that bounder Crumley? Now she's dancing with Overton, the rotter."

"My God, you *are* smitten!" Rudy exclaimed, grinning from ear to ear. "Poor Lady Randall. She doesn't stand a chance with Lord Sin in hot pursuit."

"I'll have her, Rudy, she can't escape me."

"You don't have to convince me, old chap. If you'll excuse me, I'll leave you to your games. You're not the only one in need of female companionship tonight. Lady Grace is at loose ends. Her husband is out of town and she's consented to favor me with her company for a few hours."

Sinjun laughed. "Be careful of that one, my friend. She's a man eater. You'll be lucky if you can hobble out of her bedroom when she's finished with you."

Rudy returned his grin. "I'm quite looking forward to it."

Sinjun returned his attention to Lady Flora and spotted her descending the staircase, probably going to the ladies powder room. He pushed himself away from the pillar and followed at a discreet distance, determined to intercept her on her way back to the ballroom. He concealed himself in a shadowy corner and waited for her.

While he waited, Sinjun spent a pleasant few minutes considering the places best suited for an assignation. There were several curtained alcoves off the ballroom, but they were not private enough for what he had in mind. Nor were the upstairs rooms where couples sometimes met in secret. He had used them all at one time or another, but somehow they didn't seem right for the exquisite Lady Randall. Then he remembered the elegant garden on the grounds, with the gazebo situated at its center, and he smiled.

Perfect.

Sin's patience was rewarded when the lady in question came out of the powder room alone. She started violently and uttered a small cry of fright when he stepped from the shadows.

"Lord Derby, you startled me."

"I've been waiting for you, my lady."

Christy frowned. "Whyever for, my lord?"

His dark gaze flowed over her face and settled on her bosom. "I think you know."

The sound of voices near the staircase forestalled Christy's answer.

"We can't talk here," Sinjun said as he grasped her hand and pulled her down a dark passage.

She resisted. "Where are you taking me?"

He gave her one of his charming smiles, put off not at all by her token resistance. "Where we can have some privacy. There is a rear exit. It leads to the garden."

"I cannot, my lord. We just met. What will people think?"

"I don't give a damn and neither do you."

He found the exit and pulled her out into the star-studded night. It was warm for May, exceptionally pleasant for what he had in mind. The garden was rich with foliage and redolent with the smell of spring flowers and wet earth. As he inhaled the heady scent and felt himself swell with anticipation, Sinjun couldn't recall when he'd last been so excited. He led Christy unerringly to the gazebo. It was unoccupied, and he whispered a heartfelt thanks to the goddess of love, for if any night was made for *amour*, it was this one.

Christy had heard about her husband's madcap escapades with women, but until this moment she hadn't realized how finely honed his talents were. He ushered her into the gazebo and kicked the door shut. Moonlight filtered through the shutters, starkly etching Sinjun's intense features, and

Christy inhaled sharply. There was a predatory set to his mouth and dancing flames in his eyes. As if nothing occupied his mind but seduction. Her seduction. She took a deep, steadying breath. Was she ready for this? She hadn't expected it to go so fast. Still, she didn't intend to make this easy for him. Husband or no, he was still an Englishman and an enemy.

"We should return to the ballroom, my lord," she whispered.

"Don't try to deny that you've had your eye on me all night, for I won't believe you. You've bewitched me, my lady, and well you know it."

"That's a powerful statement, my lord."

"My name is Sinjun. May I call you Flora?"

"If it pleases you."

He closed the distance between them and pulled her into his arms, crushing her against him in an onslaught of lust so startling that she felt him shaking from it. "Everything about you pleases me," he whispered against her lips. "I wonder . . ."

Christy's thoughts scattered. The feel of her husband's arms around her and the heat of his aroused male body affected her strangely. She hadn't expected to feel any kind of response for the hedonistic man that St.John Thornton had become. Her personal agenda was to get herself with child quickly, thus assuring Glenmoor of an heir.

"What do you wonder?"

"I wonder if you know how very much I want you."

She lowered her eyes. "We just met."

He pressed his open mouth to her cheek, her hair, her neck, her chin, and finally her lips. "Have you never heard of destiny?" he whispered against her lips. "The moment I looked at you I knew we were meant to be together."

Oh, he was good. Very good. Did he say that to all potential lovers? "I understand you're married."

He shrugged. "So? You have a husband. Neither one of us is looking for permanency in a relationship. I have not seen my wife since the day we were wed. Ours is a marriage of convenience. What else do you wish to know? Do I love my wife? How can I love someone I haven't seen in over fifteen years?"

His callous words had a chilling effect. "How very cold-blooded you are, my lord."

He smiled. "Not really, just practical. The marriage works exceedingly well for both of us. As for being cold-blooded, I intend to prove tonight that my blood runs hot, not cold."

Christy stared at him. His features, defined in shadows and angles, were sharp with desire, almost feral, a predator who has singled out his prey and is ready to move in for the kill. Now she knew how a snared rabbit felt.

His eyes were golden pinpoints of light as he pressed his open mouth against hers. The sudden bolt of sensation shocked her. She could feel his body heat mingling with hers, and it was not an unpleasant feeling. His mouth was warm and soft, his lips pliant. The musky scent of his arousal overwhelmed her, his taste a powerful aphrodisiac that sent her senses reeling. This wasn't what she wanted from her husband.

His kiss seemed to go on and on, stealing her breath and turning her legs to rubber. Her husband was said to be a master at seduction, but in her innocence she'd thought she could resist his seductive wiles. Obviously her experience with rakes left much to be desired. In fact, she knew nothing about men like Lord Sin, or what drove them to behave as they did. She considered herself lucky to have been spared his attention these past fifteen years.

Beneath Sin's expert tutelage, her lips softened and she felt herself opening to him, returning his kiss with an exuberance that defied explanation. When she grew dizzy from lack of breath, Sinjun abruptly released her lips and stared at her, a puzzled expression marring his brow.

Christy dragged in a sustaining breath. "Is something wrong?"

"You kiss like an innocent."

She flushed and looked away. "I'm sorry if I displease you."

"You do not displease me. I'm merely curious." He led her to a padded bench, eased her down, and sat beside her. "Tell me about your marriage."

Christy lowered her gaze to her lap. She had never been a good liar and feared her eyes would give her away. "My husband and I live quietly in a remote corner of Cornwall."

She could feel his dark eyes boring into her. "Yet he let you come to town. Rather strange," Sinjun mused. "You said he was elderly. Just how old is he?"

Christy considered her answer carefully, reflecting on ages between fifty and eighty to assign to her fictitious husband. She finally settled on eighty, for surely a man of eighty was too old to maintain sexual relations or father a child.

"He's quite elderly," Christy said. "He was eighty on his last birthday."

"Eighty!" The word exploded from Sinjun's lips.

"What kind of parents would force a young woman to marry a man of eighty?"

"Does it matter?"

"I suppose not."

He caressed her face with his knuckles, then slowly slid them down her neck, to where the décolletage of her dress met the rounded tops of her breasts. She sucked in a startled breath. No man had ever touched her there. But it didn't escape her that if Sinjun was to become her lover, he would be touching her in far more intimate places.

"Do you like that?" Sinjun asked in a sensual purr.

She thought a moment, then nodded jerkily.

"Let's see if we can get this dress off of you. Then I'll show you the difference between an eighty-year-old man and one in his prime. Have you had other lovers?"

"Other lovers?" Christy squeaked. "N . . . no, no other lovers."

Sinjun gave her a feral smile. "I'm honored, my lady. Why have you chosen me to be your first?"

Because you're my husband! she wanted to shout. Aloud, she said, "Because I heard you're a man without principles, one who won't demand more of me than I'm willing to give."

Sinjun stilled, apparently stunned by her harsh appraisal. "Who told you I am without principles?"

She shrugged. "Am I wrong?"

He chuckled mirthlessly. "Perhaps you're right, my lady. Giving pleasure is my forte. If you want more, you will be disappointed, for I can offer neither marriage nor permanency in a relationship."

What a conceited oaf, even for an Englishman,

Christy thought. "Since I already have a husband, I'm not interested in permanency."

Sinjun grinned, pleased that they both wanted the same thing. "Then we're of one accord. You're a pleasure seeker, just as I am. You have chosen wisely, even if I say so myself. I will not disappoint you, my lady. No one cares more about a lady's pleasure than I. I foresee a long and mutually beneficial association. Now," he drawled, turning her away from him so his nimble fingers could undo the tiny buttons marching down the back of the dress, "about that dress. It will have to go, along with everything else you're wearing."

"Wait!" Christy choked out.

Her words crept through the red haze of his lust and struck a discordant note. His brow furrowed, for he was annoyed at the interruption. "What's wrong? Not having second thoughts, are you? It's a little too late for that. Never tell me you're a tease who enjoys leading men on."

"No, it's not that. There . . . there's something you should know before . . . before we . . . begin."

He nuzzled her neck. "I know all I want to know. You're soft and sweet-smelling and willing. And I want you. What else is there to know?"

"I'm a—" Her words skidded to a halt, and she glanced furtively toward the door. "Someone is coming."

A curse exploded from Sinjun's throat. "Bloody hell! What rotten luck."

He grasped her hand and pulled her through the door into the dark garden, scant seconds before another couple appeared on the path. They hid behind a row of hedges as the couple disappeared into the gazebo.

Sinjun glanced at Flora and suddenly knew a

physical yearning so deep he was literally shaking from it. She was standing so close he could feel her body heat through their layers of clothing, and his reaction was somewhat startling for a man of jaded appetites. Sinjun couldn't remember when a woman had affected him so profoundly. He blessed the darkness, for he had grown hard as stone, and his tight breeches would have hidden nothing.

"We can't do it here," he whispered. "There isn't enough privacy. I want to take my time with you. You deserve to be loved properly. Where do you live?"

She was so long in answering that Sinjun feared she was going to refuse him. "I rented a house in Belgrave Square."

Though Belgrave Square was less fashionable these days, it was still respectable. "Is that a problem for you?" Sinjun asked. "Would you prefer to come to my bachelor lodgings in Grosvenor Square? We can't let this end this way."

He turned her into his arms and pressed her snugly against his loins. He heard her draw in a shuddering breath and was surprised by the ragged edge to his own breathing. What in the hell was wrong with him? No woman, and there had been many, had skewered his restraint like Lady Flora Randall.

"No," Christy whispered. "It cannot end like this."

She couldn't return to Glenmoor without Lord Derby's bairn inside her. Birthing her husband's child was the only way to convince her clansmen that her marriage had been consummated and that she could assure Glenmoor of an heir. Thus far she'd managed to maintain order within the clans, but it had been difficult. The Camerons and other clansmen wanted a male laird. They wanted Calum Cameron. After her grandfather died and she became laird, some of her clansmen were clamoring for her to annul her unconsummated marriage and marry one of their own. Even though Lord Derby had stewardship of Glenmoor, Christy was still laird of the Macdonalds, Camerons, Ranalds, and Mackenzies, a position Calum Cameron coveted.

But Christy wanted nothing to do with Calum Cameron, the most vocal of her suitors. She had grown accustomed to running her own life and didn't want to answer to a man's authority. As far as her clansmen knew, she had come to London to seek an annulment, but her actual mission was to get herself with child by Sinjun, hoping that the consummation of her marriage and a bairn would appease the most vocal of her clansmen.

And she intended to accomplish this without Sinjun being aware that he was bedding his own wife. Sinjun didn't want to be bothered with a wife and she didn't want to be bothered with a husband. Lord knows she had no love for Englishmen.

"Flora," Sinjun whispered, interrupting her thoughts, "please don't keep me in suspense. Where can we meet? I have to see you again."

Shoving aside the uncertainty battering her, Christy gave the only answer possible. "Tomorrow night. Number forty-six Belgrave Square. I'll be waiting."

She slipped out of his arms and disappeared into the shadows. For better or worse, it was done. She had set the course of destiny, and, come what may, she had to live with the results.

Chapter 2

Christy's hands fumbled as she inserted the key into the door of her rented townhouse. The door swung open, and she stepped inside. She closed the door and leaned against it, dragging in several sustaining breaths. She'd had no idea that meeting her estranged husband would be such a traumatic experience. Though she was safely at home, she still felt the heat of his aroused body, the strength of his personality, the intensity of his dark gaze, and the daunting power of his lust.

Nothing she knew or had ever heard concerning her husband's sensual nature had prepared her for Lord Sin. Before arriving in London she'd feared that attracting him might be a problem, but apparently she had worried needlessly. With a single-mindedness that stunned her, he had begun his pursuit the moment he had set eyes on her. Pushing herself away from the door, Christy wondered how many hapless women had been the recipient of Lord Sin's sensual charm. Too many to count, she was sure.

Damn the man! He was married. Had he no conscience? No morals? Was seducing women a game with him? Obviously, for he was so good at it. She picked up the candle left in the foyer to light her way and started up the stairs. When she reached the top landing a door opened, revealing a strapping young woman clutching a wrapper to her ample breasts.

"You didn't have to wait up, Margot," Christy said as she drew abreast of the woman.

"I heard ye come in. Did ye see him? Is that why yer so late tonight? What happened? Did ye recognize him? Did *he* recognize ye?"

Christy didn't want to talk about her encounter with Sinjun, but she owed her cousin a full disclosure of what had happened tonight. Margot had been in on her plan from the beginning, though she had serious misgivings.

"Come to my room, Margot. I'll tell you about this evening while you help me undress."

Margot followed Christy into her room, her eyes wide with curiosity. "Does Lord Derby live up to his reputation?"

"Every bit and more," came Christy's muffled reply as Margot lifted the dress over her head. "He didn't know who I was, if that's what you're wondering."

"Did ye speak to him? Did he seem interested in ye?"

"More interested than I could have hoped for. Oh, Margot, he's every bit as handsome as we heard. I remembered so little about him except for his dark eyes. Those I will never forget."

"I recall that ye kicked him during the wedding ceremony and stuck out yer tongue at him. And at the dinner following the ceremony, ye refused to sit beside him. Ye called him a murdering Englishman."

Christy groaned. She had forgotten that part. No wonder he'd never returned to Scotland to consummate their marriage.

"Sinjun actually pursued me tonight," Christy confided as she climbed into bed. "I suppose it was because I was a new face, someone ripe for seduction."

"Did he believe yer lies?"

Christy nodded solemnly. "I have every reason to believe he did."

"So, when does it happen?" Margot asked sourly. "He wants to see ye again, doesn't he?"

Christy flushed, unable to conceal the tide of emotions racing through her at the thought of what would happen between her and Sinjun tomorrow night.

"He's coming here. Tomorrow night. Aye, he wants to see me again. He's a creature driven by lust. A hedonist who lives for pleasure. Everything we heard about him pales in comparison to the man himself."

"Are ye sure this is what ye want?" Margot asked uncertainly. " 'Tis not too late to hie ourselves back to Glenmoor."

Christy shook her head, sending a wealth of rich copper curls swirling about her head. "Nay. 'Tis far too late to turn back now. Would you have me wed Calum Cameron?"

Margot blanched. "Nay, I would not."

"If I petitioned the English courts for an annulment, they might deny my request. I'm not even sure Sinjun would let our marriage end, for he seems to enjoy his marriage of convenience."

"Oh, aye," Margot said with a hint of sarcasm. "And he grows rich from our sweat."

"An absentee husband is better than a husband

who would rule me with an iron hand. At least Sinjun ignores me and allows me to do as I please."

"What about love, Christy? What if ye find someone to love?"

The glow seemed to leave Christy's face. "Love. I know not the meaning of the word. 'Tis unlikely I'll find love at Glenmoor, and I wouldn't have another Englishman on a silver platter."

"So that's it then," Margot said, apparently unconvinced that Christy's course was the right one.

"Aye. My marriage will finally be consummated, and no one, not even Calum, can argue the fact when I return with Sinjun's bairn in my belly."

"So be it," Margot said as she let herself out of the chamber.

Christy's bravado departed with Margot. Though she had gone over this countless times in the past months, she still wasn't convinced she was doing the right thing. It wasn't as if she were committing a sin, for Sinjun was her legal husband despite the fact that there had been no bedding. The bedding would make it legal and binding. And Glenmoor needed a Macdonald heir.

Those thoughts led her into dangerous territory. To thoughts of Sinjun, and what would happen tomorrow night. That remorseless rake had made no secret of the fact that he wanted her, that he would pursue her until he had what he wanted from her body.

Sinjun's kiss had been her first, and she couldn't deny that she'd liked it. Too much, maybe. She'd had to remind herself that he was English, that the English had murdered her father and brothers and stolen her land. Christy's unrelenting fear was that Sinjun would claim more than her virginity. The only way to resist his charm, she told herself, was to keep reminding herself of Lord Sin's unsavory reputation.

Sinjun returned to his townhouse shortly after Lady Flora disappeared into the dark regions of the garden. He'd searched for her both inside and out and wasn't too surprised when he failed to find her. He had to forcibly restrain himself, however, from following her to her lodgings. Had she not agreed to an assignation the following night he would have thrown caution to the wind and barged into her house uninvited. That's how much he wanted her.

What a rare beauty she was, Sinjun thought as he sat in his library sipping brandy from a crystal goblet. She was everything he admired in a woman. More importantly, she was married and would make no demands upon him. She looked so damn innocent and untouched that he found it difficult to believe she was a married woman who had tasted passion.

He chuckled to himself. Foolish man. Of course Lady Flora hadn't tasted passion. How could an eighty-year-old man possibly satisfy a healthy, vibrant woman? After she'd admitted she had taken no lovers, he was determined to be the first. That thought brought an immediate and violent reaction. He groaned and shifted uncomfortably, his breeches suddenly too tight, too confining. Tomorrow night couldn't get here fast enough for him.

Rarely did Lord Sin have to wait for his pleasure, and he didn't like the feeling. He should have taken Lady Flora in the garden, but for their first time he wanted more than a quick coupling. Before she returned to her husband he wanted to give her enough pleasant memories to last a lifetime. And if she took another lover after him, he wanted to be the one she remembered when she was old and gray.

He was still hard, still throbbing when he tossed down his brandy and sought his bed. He undressed quickly and flopped down on his stomach, groaning when his erection refused to be quelled. It was going to be a long night and an even longer day, he predicted.

He was right. That night her image haunted his dreams, and the following day it teased his waking hours.

"What shall I wear?" Christy asked as she riffled through her wardrobe. "Oh, Margot, he'll be here soon. I'm so nervous I can hardly think."

Margot crossed her arms over her ample bosom and tapped her foot against the floor. "Wait for him in bed, naked, and I'll show him up to yer bedchamber," she said with asperity.

Christy sent her a censuring look. "Be serious, Margot. Help me pick something subtle, but not too subtle. I want to dazzle without seeming over-bold."

Margot sent her a sharp look. "Ye truly *are* excited about this, aren't ye?"

Christy flushed and looked away. "Nonsense, Margot. You know me better than that. I'm anxious, that's all. This has to work. If I'm not pregnant in three months, my future doesn't bear thinking about. You know Calum won't rest until he controls the clans who swore fealty to grandfather and me. Sinjun's bairn will foil all his plans for me."

"Very well," Margot sighed. "Wear the white gauze with a sheer shift and no stays. White makes ye look young and innocent. It might be a good idea to dampen it. Ye *did* say ye wanted to make an impression, didn't ye?"

Christy grimaced. "Aye. Sinjun thinks I'm like him, a pleasure seeker. I might as well live up to his image of me. I fear I was rather shameless with him last night. I would have let him take me in the gazebo had we not been interrupted."

Margot stared at her. "Mother of God, lass, that would have been a mistake. After he had his way with ye he would have lost interest. Ye were wise to hold him off. Yer going to have to use all your feminine wiles to keep the rake coming back until he gets ye with child."

Margot helped Christy don the white dress, then left. Christy was glad for the time alone. Her stomach fluttered with apprehension and she had these strange, unsettling feelings that seemed to ebb and flow whenever she thought of her husband. And if those discomfiting sensations weren't bad enough, there were more. She had a disconcerting premonition that Sinjun was more man than she had bargained for. Unfortunately her experience with men was sadly lacking. Sinjun was altogether too daunting. She recalled his kisses and remembered the potently male taste of him. He was too vibrant, too charming, an unrepentant rake.

Christy sat down at her dressing table and ran a brush through her hair until the golden strands nestling amid the coppery tresses gleamed brightly in the candlelight. She decided to let it hang loose tonight, instead of binding it up in an elaborate coiffure. At home she normally plaited her hair, letting the braids swing loose around her hips. But tonight was special. Tonight she would become a woman. She had to cast aside the restrictions by which she had conducted her life and act the part of wanton for her husband.

Christy glanced at the clock, saw it approaching ten-thirty, and felt a surge of excitement rush through her. Too nervous to relax, she began to pace, silently rehearsing the lies she must tell Sinjun in order to maintain her deception.

When Sinjun heard the clock strike eleven-thirty, he drained the last dregs of brandy from his goblet and shot to his feet. He'd intended to wait until midnight, but the interminably long day had worn him down. He'd tried to go about his business, but his mind had been on other things. Things like the delectable Lady Flora and the pleasure awaiting him in her bed. His manhood jerked in response to that thought, and he hastened his steps to the front door. Pemburton, his butler, appeared with his hat and cane.

"Don't wait up, Pemburton," Sinjun said, dismissing the servant with a nod. "I'll probably be quite late."

"Your carriage is waiting, milord," Pemburton intoned dryly.

"Very good. Good night, Pemburton."

"Good night, milord."

Pemburton turned and walked away, his tall, upright figure disappearing into the dark reaches of the house.

Eager now to reach the woman who had invaded his dreams and made his day unbearable, Sinjun opened the door and stepped outside. He cursed beneath his breath when he saw Viscount Blakely strolling toward him.

"Ah, Sinjun, going out, I see," Rudy hailed. "I'm just in time. White's was damn dull tonight.

Thought we might make the rounds of fleshpots in the seamier sections of town."

"Not tonight, Rudy," Sinjun said with an uncustomary lack of patience. "I have an ... appointment to keep."

Rudy's sandy eyebrows shot upward. " 'Tis no wonder you're the envy of the *ton*. Who is it tonight? Lady Violet? A new conquest?"

When Sinjun remained uncharacteristically silent, Rudy slapped his thigh and crowed, "By God, 'tis Lady Flora, isn't it? I wondered where you'd gotten off to last night. You both disappeared at the same time." He leaned close, though no one was around to hear. "How was she? A veritable tiger in bed, I assume, else you wouldn't be wasting your time."

Sinjun stiffened. For some reason he didn't want to discuss Lady Flora with anyone, not even his good friend. His thoughts were too private, his conquest too new to share.

"The nature of my engagement tonight is private," Sinjun said. He reached his carriage, then turned to inquire of Rudy, "Shall I drop you off someplace?"

Rudy laughed. "I do love a mystery. I hope you tell me about it one day, Sinjun. Very well, drop me off at Brooks. Perhaps I'll join in a card game and increase my wealth a bit."

"Or lose more than you can afford," Sinjun muttered as he tooled his matched bays toward Pall Mall, where most of the gentlemen's clubs were located. He pulled up at Brooks on St. James Street. The moment Rudy stepped down onto the sidewalk, Sinjun flipped the reins against the bays' backs. A grinding spin of the wheels, and he was off.

There were few carriages on the street to hinder his progress as Sinjun headed for Belgrave Square. He found Lady Flora's house with little difficulty and spent an indecisive moment deciding if he should leave the carriage in the street or drive around to the carriage house. The carriage house, he decided as he drove the team to the end of the street and into a rear alleyway. A brawny stableman loomed up out of the darkness, holding a lantern aloft. He looked Sinjun up and down, a sneer curving his lips.

"I'll see to your rig, milord," he said, eyeing Sinjun with what could only be described as loathing. Sinjun couldn't recall having encountered the man before and wondered at his surliness. When he noted a Scottish burr in the man's speech, he dimly wondered where Lady Flora had found the Scotsman. Since Culloden, most Scotsmen held Englishmen in contempt.

Abruptly he shoved his mental musings aside as thoughts of the woman waiting for him inside the townhouse took their place. Perhaps, he thought, this *affaire de coeur* would prove more diverting than others he had conducted in the past. Though he was loathe to admit it, flitting from affair to affair was becoming a burdensome chore. But changing his lifestyle at this point in his life seemed rather senseless. Nor was he ready to claim his Scottish wife, who doubtlessly despised him. No, he wanted nothing to do with his wife, though he appreciated the fact that he was able to use his marriage as an excuse to maintain his lifestyle.

Meeting the mysterious Lady Flora had been an invigorating experience, Sinjun decided. Beating the competition, the thrill of pursuit, the excitement of the capture, the bedding, all combined to put a fine edge to the game.

Sinjun reached the front door, mounted the steps, and knocked discreetly. It was opened almost immediately by a tall young woman Sinjun assumed was a maid. She held a branch of candles, the light illuminating her face and figure, and Sinjun couldn't help gawking at her ample breasts, bright red hair, and wealth of freckles sprinkled liberally across her nose. She said not a word as she motioned him inside and started immediately up the staircase, looking over her shoulder once to make sure Sinjun was following.

To his dismay, Sinjun felt himself harden in anticipation of the pleasurable hours he intended to spend in Lady Flora's bed. The thought that she had chosen him to be her first lover was empowering, and his virility had never been more potent.

The maid reached the top landing and continued down the hall, stopping before a closed door. She knocked once, nodded at Sinjun, then turned and disappeared into another room, plunging the hallway into darkness. Sinjun's hand curled around the doorknob. He twisted, and the door swung open. He entered immediately and closed the door behind him.

His hooded gaze searched the room for the lush figure he remembered so well from the previous night. He could see nothing beyond the circle of light provided by a flickering candle placed on the bedside table. His gaze settled on the empty bed, turned down invitingly. His nostrils twitched as he caught an intriguing whiff of her perfume—the same scent he'd noticed last night when he'd held her in his arms and kissed her into submission. Roses, with a subtle underlying hint of something that belonged solely to the woman herself.

"My lady? Where are you?" His voice was husky with grinding need, the kind he hadn't felt in far too long.

She stepped into the puddle of light, and Sinjun exhaled sharply. She was a feast for the eyes, dressed in something white and gauzy, demure yet highly erotic, so sheer he could see through both the gown and shift beneath.

Her nipples were plainly visible, two dark peaks cresting creamy mounds more tempting than the finest wine. His gaze roved downward, past the incredibly tiny waist, over sweetly curved hips, and down pale, luminous thighs to trim ankles. Suddenly his gaze jerked back to her thighs and the dark triangle sheltering her woman's mound. The groan began deep down in his belly and rumbled through his chest.

"My God! You're lovelier than I dared hope." His hand slid below his waist. "I've been rock hard all day just thinking about tonight." He opened his arms. "Come to me, goddess."

Christy conquered the sudden onslaught of fear and stepped into his arms. She'd thought of nothing all day but what tonight would be like, and it couldn't compare with reality. This was her wedding night, whether Sinjun realized it or not. Then his arms closed around her and her initial fear was swamped by other, more potent feelings. She lifted her eyes to his, to meet the challenge of his gaze, and her breath caught in her throat. Her eyes fell, and wordlessly, she lifted her face, offering her lips.

He took them, framing her face with his hands as their lips fused. Boldly he pressed his loins into the cradle of her thighs. His hands slid lower, brazenly outlining the contours of her bottom. He filled his hands with her flesh and kneaded gently. She stiffened, then relaxed as she remembered her reason for being here and what Sinjun intended to do to her. Heat spread, flushing her skin as their bodies meshed into one.

She felt the rigid proof of his desire, felt his heavy member pressing against her belly. He held her against him a long time, kissing her, slowly awakening passions she never knew existed. She closed her eyes and sank beneath another wave of sensation as his tongue surged deeply into her mouth. She was panting softly when he broke off the kiss and lifted her into his arms, so flustered she could barely think, much less string coherent words together.

Struggling to collect her wits, Christy remembered that she wasn't supposed to enjoy this, but her body betrayed her as Sinjun took her mouth again. The evocative caress of his tongue, the unhurried possession of her mouth sent molten heat surging through her veins. It settled hot and heavy in her loins. The force of their combined desire stunned her. Moments later she found herself lying fully clothed on the bed with Sinjun leaning over her, his features dark and predatory, his eyes seething pools of liquid fire. A heady languor weighted her limbs, slowed her senses.

She didn't resist when Sinjun gently turned her, his nimble fingers making short work of the fastenings holding her dress together. He was very good at this, she thought dimly.

A master of seduction.

The unspoken words reverberated through her head, returning her abruptly to reality. Lord Sin was a remorseless rake, and she must remember that she was just another conquest to him. A woman to bed and then discard after she had lost her heart to him, or he tired of her, whichever came first. But Christy had resolved beforehand to protect her heart against Lord Sin's seductive charm. What she wanted from Sinjun had nothing to do with her heart, and she had no intention of losing it along the way to obtaining her goal. Allowing Sinjun to seduce her was necessary, she reminded herself. Definitely not something she should enjoy. Unfortunately her body refused to listen to her mind.

Christy was achingly aware of the muscled hardness of his body. Of her nipples pressed against his chest. Of his tightly controlled passion waiting to be unleashed. She should have been frightened, but she wasn't.

Christy started violently when Sinjun peeled the dress from her upper body and pulled the tape holding her chemise together. The moment the edges loosened, he pulled both gown and chemise down to her waist and stared at her breasts as if they were the first he'd ever seen. A nervous giggle slipped past her lips at the incongruity of that thought.

Sinjun's gaze slid upward from her breasts to meet hers. A smile teased the corners of his mouth. "Do I amuse you, my lady? Do you find me clumsy?"

"Oh, no, my lord," Christy protested. "You are neither clumsy nor amusing."

His eyebrows shot upward. "I hope, before our association ends, you will find me fascinating. I'd hate to be remembered as a bore."

She gulped. Lord Sin a bore? The moon would fall to the earth before anyone would think Lord

Sin a boring fellow. "You do not bore me, my lord." She was more than a little stunned to realize that she actually meant it.

He touched her breasts, molding his hands around them. "My name is Sinjun."

She felt her breasts swell and tauten as his fingers closed around them. When he lowered his mouth to a ruched nipple, already excruciatingly sensitive, and sucked it into his mouth, a sigh hissed through her teeth. His tongue swirled around the hardened crest, creating an ebb and surge that battered her senses.

"Oh . . ."

"Do you like that, sweet Flora?"

"I . . ." Like it? She adored it. "Aye, I like it."

"Does your husband arouse you like this?"

She flushed and looked away. "He's very old."

"I need to see all of you," he said as he tugged her gown and chemise down past her hips.

Heat surged through her as he tossed her clothing to the floor and gazed at her body, now naked but for her white silk stockings held in place above her knees with white ribbons. She could tell he liked what he saw, for his eyes darkened with an intensity that made her heart beat faster and harder. Then he removed her shoes and peeled both stockings down her legs.

Sinjun felt his control shatter. The remaining shreds had been removed and tossed aside with her stockings. He felt like an animal cursed with the instinctive need to mate, fevered with it, desperate. His body was rigid, tense with excitement, eager to partake of the feast temptingly arrayed before him. With a growl of impatience, he threw off his coat, undid his neckcloth, and unbuttoned his shirt with such haste that buttons flew in all directions. His boots hit the floor, and his breeches and stockings followed in short order. He turned back to Flora, frowning when he saw that her eyes were tightly closed.

"There is nothing to be frightened of, love. I know I'm probably bigger than your husband, but I swear I'll not hurt you."

Christy's eyes opened slowly, oh, so slowly, then closed quickly, oh so quickly. What she had seen in those fleeting moments was more thrilling than frightening. Sinjun was abundantly endowed every place she looked. His sleek body was thickly muscled in all the right places. Wide chest, narrow waist, slim hips, corded thighs. Though she'd tried not to look at that place where his manhood rose from a tangled nest of wiry dark hair, she could not turn her eyes away. He was magnificent. Everything she'd ever imagined a man should be and more.

"Flora, open your eyes." His voice, a seductive purr, slammed through her with devastating effect. Her eyes flew open.

"Look at me, Flora. I'm not an old man. I'm young and vigorous and fully capable of giving pleasure. That *is* the reason you invited me to your bed, isn't it?"

Incapable of coherent speech, Christy nodded. That was all the encouragement he seemed to need as he knelt on the bed and leaned over her. Dark hair spilled over his forehead, adding to his rakish appeal as he lowered his head and licked her nipples. The pure pleasure of it caught her by surprise, and a moan slipped past her lips. She tried to remember that she wasn't supposed to enjoy this, but her mind was too befuddled to think.

Her moan must have pleased him, for he raised

his head and gave her a predatory grin. Then he kissed her. His kiss was rough, sharp-edged with need. His lips were hard, devouring, plundering hers and demanding a response. She tried to crush her enthusiasm, aware that she was just another woman in Sinjun's long list of conquests, but the man was too persuasive, too experienced to allow her to remain passive. Without conscious thought her arms crept around his neck and she opened her mouth to the subtle probing of his tongue. He tasted of sin, of danger, of dark pleasure.

Her heart pounded, roared in her ears, drowning out reason. After an eternity his lips left hers and roved downward, seeking more intimate territory. She crooned a soft melody, certain she'd never heard those sounds that came from her throat. His kisses blazed a fiery path down her breasts, then he paused to rest his head low on her stomach. When she felt his breath close to her private place, she lurched sharply upward.

"Sinjun, no!" His hot breath stirred the gleaming curls protecting her mound. Frightened of the feelings he was arousing in her, she tugged on his hair. He raised his head and grinned at her.

"Do you like that?"

"I . . . I've never done . . . I mean . . ."

"I understand. This is new to you. Very well, I'll stop if you insist. But I swear you'll soon beg me to taste you more fully."

Christy released a shaky breath. She hadn't prepared herself for the kind of pervasive intimacy Sinjun demanded. She knew what happened between men and women, how the sex act was accomplished, but what Sinjun wanted was sinful, wicked, unthinkable.

Christy's relief was short-lived as Sinjun lowered

his head and kissed her there, between her legs. She felt a jolt of something so intense it defied description. Then just as quickly he moved his body upward, until he rested fully against her. Breast to breast, thigh to thigh, his staff probing ruthlessly between her legs.

She shifted uncomfortably as he inserted his slick head into her tight passage and pushed relentlessly. She clamped down hard on her tongue to stifle the groan of pain that rose unbidden to her lips. He shoved himself deeper, then suddenly went still, his eyes narrowed, his expression arrested.

"You're a virgin!"

She knew he'd notice. A man of Sinjun's experience would know everything there was to know about a woman. "Aye, does it matter?"

Sinjun thought about it for a moment and decided it didn't matter to him if it didn't matter to her. But she did owe him an explanation. Not now, however. He was too hard, too needy, too hot to waste time on lengthy explanations. His answer was to flex his hips and break through the membrane shielding her innocence.

She cried out and lurched upward, her fingers digging into his shoulders. "I'm sorry, but there is no other way," he whispered, gentling her with his voice. "I promise it will get better soon."

He moved his hips slowly, giving her time to adjust to his size. Never in his wildest dreams would he have guessed he was to deflower a virgin—not that it didn't please him to be the first with her. He withdrew, flexed, and seated himself more deeply inside her. His control was badly battered, his restraint desperately taxed. But he'd promised her pleasure, and Lord Sin always deliv-

ered. He had never in his life left a woman wanting.

Sinjun sent up a prayer of gratitude when he felt
Flora's first tentative response. Perspiration dotted
his brow and dripped into his eyes. His teeth were
gritted so hard that his jaw ached, and he was so
close to the edge he feared he would tumble over.

"Ah, sweetheart," he encouraged. "That's it.
Move with me. Feel it, live it, flow with it."

He thrust hard and was rewarded with the subtle movement of her hips. There was no holding
him back now. Thrust and withdraw, in and out,
again and again. She was responding beautifully,
every bit as passionate as he had imagined. Her
small, enthusiastic cries were music to his ears, her
short, gasping breaths a gift from the gods.

He was losing control. His body tingled with the
beginning of his climax. He looked down at the
woman straining beneath him and was deeply
gratified when he saw she was nearly there. Her
eyes were glazed over, and short, small gasping
sounds escaped from her open mouth. He bared
his teeth and concentrated on the goal within their
reach.

"Come to me now, sweetheart. You're almost
there. Don't hold back. Oh, God, I'm . . . I can't . . ."

He heard her call out his name, felt her body
contract, felt her tight passage squeeze around him,
and he spewed forth his seed. He came in a great,
gushing upheaval of body and spirit so intense that
it defied description. He'd always enjoyed the
games associated with sex—the chase, the seduction, the ultimate possession—but nothing this
earth-shattering had ever happened before.

Did Lady Flora Randall possess mysterious powers that transcended simple earthly pleasure?

Nothing as sublime as what he had just experienced could be considered mundane. If he were a poet he'd describe it as an affair inspired by heaven.

Chapter 3

Her eyes were closed. Her head rested on his shoulder. He stared at her curiously. What was there about her that seemed so familiar? Nothing about the mysterious Lady Flora made sense. He had enjoyed her immensely and knew he had given her pleasure despite her innocence.

Why was she, a married lady, still a virgin?

It mystified him, but he didn't let it deter him from his course. There was so much he wanted to teach her. He looked forward with relish to all the nights to come, when they would explore every nuance of sexual pleasure together. That thought brought an instant resurgence of lust, and a groan slipped past his lips.

She must have felt him harden against her, for she blinked up at him. He gave her an owlish smile. "The night is still young and I'm ravenous."

"You're hungry? My maid has gone to bed, but if you'd like, we can raid the kitchen."

His grin widened. "You truly are innocent, aren't you? I usually prefer experienced women, for they rarely demand things I can't or am not willing to give, but you're a refreshing change. Why didn't you tell me you were untouched? Has *everything* you told me been a lie? Is there truly a husband?"

"Aye, there is a husband. He . . . he's impotent and cannot perform in bed or produce a child. He needs an heir and approves of what I am doing. He insisted that I come to town, find a man to my liking, and . . . well, he knows having a child would make me happy and he cares about my happiness."

Dismayed, Sinjun stared at her. Did the kind of man Flora just describe really exist? Could a man be so anxious for an heir that he would encourage his wife to let another man impregnate her? If *he* were Flora's husband he would *never* allow her to bed another man, no matter how old and decrepit he became or how desperately he wanted an heir.

"How very cavalier of him. I would not be so generous were you my wife. On the other hand," he said, drawing her against him, "I'm deliriously happy with the choice you made. I'm curious to know why you chose me. Dare I hope I'm the only man who appealed to you?"

"You may hope anything," Christy said with asperity. "As I explained to you last night, I heard you were a man without principles, so I assumed you wouldn't make demands upon me should I bear a child from our association. It didn't hurt, however, that I found you physically attractive.

"And you're married," she continued, "just as I am, and therefore not interested in commitments or lasting relationships. When I return to my husband, as I must, I know you will have no trouble finding another mistress. Men like you are interested only in casual affairs. Am I not right?"

"This conversation is beyond the pale," Sinjun groused. Her description of him made him sound callous and shallow. "In all my days I've never met a woman, and there have been many in my life, who became my lover for the reasons you just specified. I think I've just been insulted."

"I thought I was speaking the truth. Besides, I want the terms of our affair clearly understood."

Sinjun stilled as her insult sparked his anger. "What exactly are those terms, my lady? Besides wanting to take my child back to Cornwall with you and passing it off as your husband's? What we just shared tonight indicates that we are remarkably compatible.

"You have a passionate nature, whether you realize it or not, and if you want to become pregnant, who am I to discourage you? If you're serious about what you just told me, I want you for myself. I want you for my mistress."

Christy regarded him solemnly. This relationship was progressing faster than she had expected. A perverse devil inside her made her ask, "Will you remain faithful to me during the length of our association?"

"Is that what you want?"

"Those are my terms." If Sinjun stayed faithful to her during the three months she remained in town, she suspected it would be three months longer than he had *ever* been faithful in his marriage.

"Very well, I accept your terms. But the same holds true for you. I will be your only lover for the duration of our alliance, and you will take no other man to your bed. Shall I rent a house for you, or will yours do? I'll expect you to accompany me to social events, of course. And to let me visit whenever I feel the need."

He grinned at her. "And speaking of need..." He grasped her hand and brought it to his loins.

"See what you do to me? I can't recall when I've been so quickly aroused by a woman. You're deliciously different from any woman I've every known, my lady."

Christy took his words with a grain of salt. A notorious rake like Sinjun probably said that to all the women he bedded. He oozed charm from every pore; she suspected he could charm the wallpaper off the walls and women out of their petticoats simply by flashing that devastating smile of his. Her thoughts scattered when he lowered his head and kissed her.

He nudged her lips with his tongue and she opened eagerly to him, meeting his tongue with her own, finding herself helplessly drawn into the web of his seduction. With a sigh of capitulation, she gave herself up to his loving.

Christy learned volumes about her husband that night. She learned that he was a perfectionist when it came to sexual matters. Nothing was left half done. He gave of himself with enthusiasm and passion and expected no less from her. She couldn't have held back if she'd wanted to, for Sinjun wouldn't have allowed it. With hands, mouth, and tongue, he gave her more pleasure than she had ever thought possible. And during the long hours before dawn, he taught her to please him in ways she'd never imagined.

When night faded into a new day, Sinjun slipped out of bed and dressed in the gray dawn of morning.

"The Ravensdale ball is the first big event of the Season," Sinjun said. "Wear something fetching tonight. I want to show you off to the *ton*. I'll be the envy of Londontown when I walk into the ball with you on my arm."

"You are always the talk of Londontown," Christy observed dryly. "I'll go masked, of course."

"If it pleases you. I suppose most women will wear masks, since it's all the rage." He bent and brushed her lips with his. "Just remember, you belong to me and I guard my possessions jealously."

Christy stiffened. What an arrogant lout, she thought dispassionately. He was possessive of all his women except one. His own wife. It was no more than she'd expected from an Englishman. She hoped she could put up with his arrogance for the time it took to get with child. As for his lovemaking, though she hated to admit it, she could put up with that forever. She hadn't wanted to enjoy it, but what red-blooded woman could remain unmoved by a man as sensual and accomplished as Lord Sin? Though her experience was limited, she seriously doubted a man existed who could challenge his reputation as a fabulous lover.

"I'll pick you up at ten," Sinjun continued when the silence grew between them. "I hope you're not planning on dancing till dawn, for I doubt I can wait that long to have you again."

Christy gulped back a tart reply and forced a smile. "You need not worry, my lord. I'm yours . . . until the day we part."

"Aye," Sinjun replied in a voice made husky with desire. "As you said, my lady, you're mine." He brushed his lips against hers again. Then he filled his hands with her breasts and kissed each pert nipple.

His eyes were dark and hot, his face tautly drawn over the sharp contours of his cheekbones. His hungry, predatory look stunned her. Were all men as sexually charged as her husband? Did they all want but one thing from a woman? Many men had looked upon her with lust, but nothing she'd experienced compared with the potency of Lord Sin's ravenous gaze. She felt devoured by it, as if her bones were melting. How naive she'd been to think she could walk away from this escapade without sustaining serious damage to her heart.

"Farewell, sweet Flora," Sinjun whispered against her lips. "Until tonight."

"Aye, until tonight," Christy choked out.

With a jaunty wave, he let himself out of the room. She waited until she heard his footsteps descending the staircase before bouncing out of bed. The moment her feet hit the floor she regretted her haste. Every bone in her body ached, though not unpleasantly, and the soreness between her legs attested to the success of her plan to seduce her husband. Only one thing troubled her. Had she been the seducer or the seducee?

Her head was still reeling with that thought as she pulled on a wrapper and hurried to the window. She threw back the drapery in time to see Sinjun tool out of the alleyway and guide his high-stepping matched bays down the street.

She turned away from the window just as the door opened, admitting Margot. Margot's narrowed gaze slid over Christy, assessing her condition with a practiced eye.

"Are ye all right, lass? He didn't hurt ye, did he? If he did, I'll have his balls on a platter."

Christy suppressed a grin. She loved her kinswoman dearly, but at times she tended to smother her. Though only a few years older than Christy, Margot had been with Christy since both women had lost their fathers and brothers on the battlefield at Culloden. Margot's mother had died shortly afterward, and old Angus had taken Margot in and raised her with Christy. Together, Christy and a somewhat cautious Margot had conceived the plan that had brought them to London.

"Sinjun didn't hurt me, Margot. Quite the opposite. I am sore, though, and a hot bath would not be amiss."

"I'll see to it," Margot said. "Rory can carry up the buckets for ye. He may as well make himself useful while he's here. Lord knows there's little enough for the lazy lout to do in the carriage house."

"Complain all you want about Rory, but I'm glad he agreed to come with us. We couldn't have made the long trip from Scotland without him. He's a trustworthy lad."

"Ye are the laird and he'd do anything for ye. He'd better," Margot added, "if he knows what's good for him. I've promised to become his bride when we return to Glenmoor. Rory likes English swine no better than any true Highlander. He'll go along with whatever ye choose to tell the clan when ye return to Glenmoor. I'll go rout the lout out from the carriage house now."

A short time later a scowling Rory carried in the wooden hip bath and set it before the hearth. It was obvious to Christy that Rory was upset about something and she thought it best to get it out into the open.

"What's bothering you, Rory? Are you upset with me?"

"Och, 'tisna for me to tell our laird what to do, but entertaining Englishmen is beneath ye, Christy Macdonald. Yer a married woman."

"A married woman whose husband doesn't even know what she looks like," Christy retorted. "I know what I'm doing, Rory. One day you'll understand, but until then, I ask that you trust me."

"What about the Englishman?" Rory growled.

Christy sighed. There was no help for it. Rory must be told enough to keep his loyalty. "The Englishman is my husband, Rory. He doesn't know me and I'm not going to tell him."

Rory stared at her until he finally seemed to grasp what she had told him, then he smiled. "Yer bedding yer own husband! Here I thought . . ." His eyes narrowed. "I smell something foul."

" 'Tis nothing for you to worry about, Rory, everything will be fine. When we return to Glenmoor I intend to have Derby's heir growing in my belly. That should stop the talk that I end my unconsummated marriage and wed Calum Cameron."

"There are those who say yer marriage to the Englishman isna legal, lass."

Christy's chin rose defiantly. " 'Tis no longer true. My marriage is legal in every sense of the word, whether or not Lord Derby realizes it."

"Yer not going to tell him," Rory said, giving her a slow smile. "Serves the bastard right."

"As far as Sinjun is concerned, I'm Lady Flora Randall from Cornwall, wed to an elderly viscount who cannot sire an heir and has given his wife leave to get herself with child. Now that you know, can I trust you with my secret, Rory Macdonald?"

"Och, ye can trust me with yer life, lass. 'Tis why I offered to come to London with ye and Margot." His chest swelled. "Margot is to be my wife, I couldna let her wander about the wicked city alone, now could I?"

"You have my gratitude, Rory. With luck we'll be back at Glenmoor before snow flies."

"It canna be too soon for me," Rory mumbled as

he let himself out of the bedchamber to fetch water for the tub.

"Nor for me," Christy muttered to herself. She'd been so sure she could handle a man like Sinjun, but she'd been wrong. No woman could possibly be prepared for the sensuous, wickedly charming rogue known as Lord Sin.

His kisses took her breath away. His talented hands made a shambles of her resistance, and his endearments, though they held little truth, made her wish for things that Sinjun was unwilling to share with any woman. Things that only a husband could give to his wife.

Sinjun didn't want a wife, however. As long as she remembered that, she would be safe. But the moment she forgot that Sinjun had bedded countless women during the years of their marriage, she was in danger of losing her heart to him.

Sinjun returned to his bachelor quarters, bathed, and ordered a breakfast that could easily feed three healthy men. He couldn't recall when he'd been so ravenous this early in the morning. He finished off the last bite of kidney and eggs, drank his coffee cup dry, and sat back, replete. Then, since he had nothing pressing to do this morning, he returned to his room to take a nap. He'd had bloody little sleep last night, and tonight, if he had anything to say about it, promised to be just as sleepless.

He closed his eyes and imagined Flora as she had been scant hours ago. Men waxed poetic about beauty such as hers, and she had gifted him, of all men, with her innocence. He'd never encountered a married virgin before and he had to admit it had stunned him. As jaded as he was, he found Lady Flora's innocence incredibly arousing.

He frowned when he remembered exactly what it was she wanted from him, but he shoved the thought aside. Why should he let his conscience bother him when it never had before? If her husband was willing to pass his child off as a Randall, should she conceive, so be it. If last night was any indication, his association with the lady was going to be immensely satisfying for both of them.

With delightful thoughts of his new mistress dancing in his head, Sinjun fell soundly asleep. Hours later he was rudely awakened when someone barged into his room without knocking and shook him awake. Sinjun reared up, disoriented, searching for his pistol to dispatch this unseen enemy.

"Damn it, Sinjun, wake up!"

Sinjun shook his head to clear away the last dregs of sleep and frowned at the man looming over him.

"Bloody hell, Julian, what's wrong with you? It's not polite to burst into a man's bedroom and scare the living hell out of him."

"As long as I'm the head of the family I have the right to do as I please. Besides, it's the middle of the day." Concern worried his brow. "Are you ill? Why are you still abed?"

Julian Thornton, Sinjun's older brother and fifth earl of Mansfield, was every bit as handsome as Sinjun. Whereas Sinjun rarely met a man he didn't like or a woman he couldn't love, Julian was more reserved, more discerning in his tastes. He took his duties as head of the family—namely, Sinjun and his younger sister Emma—seriously, and his duties to his country even more so.

Julian was a mystery to his peers. He disappeared for long periods of time and told no one where or why he went. Since Sinjun's own life was full and rewarding, he rarely questioned his older brother about his mysterious comings and goings. He merely accepted it as part of his brother's private life, though he did worry about Julian. Despite Julian's gruff manner, there was a closeness between the siblings others admired.

"I'm in perfect health, thank you," Sinjun said as he leaped naked from bed and threw on his dressing gown. "To what do I owe the pleasure of this visit? Not going off on one of your jaunts again, are you? I don't imagine Emma is going to like that. She's too much alone these days."

"I'm not going anywhere for the time being," Julian said. "It wouldn't hurt if you paid Emma more attention yourself. Only the good Lord knows the kind of trouble she gets herself into when I'm away. She's too old for a governess and too young to go about without a proper chaperone. I've hired a maid to accompany Emma about, but she flouts my authority at every turn. I'm at my wit's end with her."

"Is that why you're here? You're the head of the family. You have more authority over Emma than I do."

"No, Emma isn't the reason I'm here, though we should discuss her. Emma is going to need your guidance when I'm called away again."

Sinjun laughed. "Are you sure I'm the one to see to our sister's welfare? As I recall, you don't approve of my lifestyle."

Hands clasped behind his back, Julian started pacing. A scowl darkened his brow, and he appeared upset as he stopped abruptly and whirled to glare at Sinjun. "Your excesses are the talk of the town, Sinjun. No woman is safe around you. Fetch your wife from Scotland. 'Tis time you settled down."

Sinjun sighed. "Who complained this time? How much will it cost me? I swear, Julian, I don't dally with innocents, and to my knowledge I've left no bastards with any of my mistresses."

He thought of Lady Flora and flushed. She wanted to conceive his child and return to her husband. For the first time that thought made him uncomfortable. He'd always been careful not to release his seed inside his lovers. But if Flora did conceive, the child wouldn't be a bastard. It would become heir to a title and be much loved. Did that make everything all right? Why in the hell did his conscience have to kick in now?

"Thank God for that," Julian said, raising his riveting dark eyes heavenward. "The reason for my visit is important, Sinjun, but this time it has nothing to do with your dissolute lifestyle. This morning I received a missive from your bailiff at Glenmoor, along with his quarterly report. There is unrest among the clans loyal to The Macdonald. They have refused to pay the quarterly taxes and rents. Sir Oswald says he's afraid to approach them about payment, for they have threatened his life."

"Bloody hell! What am I supposed to do about it?"

" 'Tis your land, your wife, your people. You've enjoyed the profits all these years, go up there and see what's going on. I've always considered the rents and taxes quite reasonable."

Sinjun thought of Lady Flora and felt disinclined to leave her so soon after finding her. He was too blissfully happy with her to abandon her to another.

"Perhaps I will, Julian, but not now. I . . . damn

it! If you must know, I've taken a new mistress and simply don't want to leave her just yet. She's . . . I can't explain it, but Lady Flora is . . . special. There's never been another like her."

Julian gave an exasperated snort. "You said that about your last three mistresses. I tell you true, Sinjun, if you don't see to your holdings you're going to be sorry. Soldiers have been keeping the Highlands under severe military rule for seventeen years and resentment runs high. 'Tis time you claimed your wife and consummated your marriage. You should have done it years ago."

"You want me to bed that redheaded, freckle-faced hellion!" Sinjun exclaimed. "Surely you remember what a rude little baggage she was. I want nothing to do with her, Julian. Let King George's army handle her rebellious clansmen. That's what his army is for."

"They wouldn't be rebellious if you'd put in an appearance from time to time to collect your own rents and remind them that you're their laird's husband."

"You're probably right, Julian, but I can't tear myself away just yet. You'll understand once you meet my new mistress. Maybe after a few months I'll feel differently."

Julian cocked a dark eyebrow. "Given your history with women, I predict you'll tire of her within a fortnight."

"Don't act the prude with me, Julian. You're no angel. After your betrothed died you showed no interest in settling down to marriage with another woman. Your name has been linked with at least a dozen women, from innocent maidens to lonely widows. You just don't stay in one place long enough to settle down with one of them. What dangerous games are you playing, Julian? Your mysterious comings and goings worry me. And I know Emma is concerned. I don't wish to become an earl, you know, so take care of yourself."

Julian gripped Sinjun's shoulder. "Don't worry about me, Sinjun. 'Tis you I'm concerned about. I care what happens to you. Will you at least promise to go to Scotland when you and your latest lightskirt part?"

Sinjun stiffened. "Flora is no lightskirt. She's a lady, a virgin, until she gave herself to me. And, aye, I promise to see to my affairs after Lady Flora returns to her elderly husband."

Julian looked astounded. "A married virgin? I'll bet that's a story worth hearing. If that's the best I can expect from you, then so be it."

"Will you be attending the Ravensdale ball tonight? Everyone who's anyone will be there."

"Aye, I'm escorting Emma. You can introduce me to your new lover."

"Very well, if you promise not to charm her away from me."

Julian laughed. " 'Tis unlikely any woman would prefer me over you. I'm far too uninteresting." He went to the sideboard and helped himself to the brandy.

Sinjun sent him an assessing look. "If you weren't so bloody somber you'd have women falling at your feet."

Julian raised his glass to Sinjun. "One rake in the family is all the *ton* can handle." He tipped the glass to his lips and drained it. "Well, I must be off. I'm to meet Lord Finchley at the Stock Exchange. I'll see you tonight."

Sinjun stared after his brother, wondering why Julian didn't marry and settle down. He certainly wasn't lacking in the looks department. There was something dark and dangerous about Julian that attracted women. Needless to say, Julian wasn't a man Sinjun would like to have as an enemy. But as a brother there was none better.

The rest of the day progressed far too slowly for Sinjun's liking. He couldn't wait to see Flora again, nor could he recall when he'd been this excited about a woman. Something he couldn't quite put his finger on set her apart from other women of his acquaintance.

That evening Sinjun ordered the coach bearing the Derby coat of arms to be brought around. He wanted everything to be perfect for his first public appearance with his new mistress. As the coachman drove him to Belgrave Square, Sinjun was already wishing the evening over. He couldn't wait to have Flora's sweet body all to himself.

For tonight's outing Christy chose a gown fashioned of gold tissue, deliberately shunning dampened gauze, which many of the other ladies would be wearing. The gown, fitted at the waist, had drop sleeves that bared her shoulders and allowed a tempting peek at the creamy tops of her breasts. A hooped petticoat worn beneath her gown added fullness to the skirt. Christy had never worn anything so fine and thought the coin well spent. At home her usual attire consisted of the Macdonald plaid and homespun.

"Yer a vision," Margot sighed, putting the final touches on Christy's hair. "Yer sure to dazzle that scoundrel ye married. Make him fall in love with ye, Christy. 'Twould serve the devil right."

"I don't want Sinjun's love," Christy argued. "Just his bairn."

Margot sent her a sharp look. "Just make sure *ye* dinna fall in love with *him*, lass."

"Fear not, Margot. My heart is well guarded against the likes of men like Lord Sin."

Margot left shortly afterward to await Sinjun's arrival. When Christy heard the rumble of Sinjun's voice below stairs a short time later, her heart did a curious flip-flop. She had anticipated his arrival all day, and now that the moment had come she felt all aflutter with excitement. She wasn't supposed to feel anything for Sinjun, she berated herself. The rake had tupped half the women in London without a thought for the wife he had deserted.

Then the door opened and Margot stepped inside the room. "He's here, Christy. Are ye ready?"

Christy dragged in a sustaining breath and nodded as she moved past Margot into the hall. She saw Sinjun waiting for her at the bottom of the stairs, looking so breathtakingly handsome she forgot to breathe. She saw the swift appraisal and fierce look of desire that hardened his face and knew she pleased him. When his sensual mouth curved into a smile, she renewed her vow to harden her heart against him lest she lose it.

Apparently not content to wait for her at the bottom of the stairs, Sinjun sprinted halfway up to meet her. He offered his arm, and they descended together. When they reached the bottom, Christy gave a squeal of surprise when he pulled her into his arms and kissed her soundly. After thoroughly exploring her mouth, he set her away from him and gave her a cheeky grin.

"Sorry, sweetheart, I couldn't wait. I've been thinking about kissing you all day." He threaded her arm in his. "Do you have a wrap?"

Margot appeared from the dark reaches of the house with a fringed shawl and half mask. Sinjun draped the shawl over her shoulders and handed her the mask. Then he ushered her to his carriage and handed her inside. He sat beside her, so close that his masculine scent enveloped her in a sensual haze. She sniffed appreciatively of his cologne and that underlying musky odor she remembered so well from the previous night, and knew it would linger in her memory long after they parted.

"You look good enough to eat," Sinjun whispered, pulling her into the curve of his body. "Tonight I'm going to taste you all over. You're the most tempting morsel I've ever had the privilege to meet, sweet Flora. I predict a long and mutually satisfying association."

"Until I return to Cornwall," Christy reminded him. "I cannot stay in town forever. My . . . husband expects me back home."

"Aye, with a babe in your belly. We'll cross that bridge when we come to it," he murmured, brushing his lips against her cheek.

Christy offered no response. Fortunately there was no need, for the coach had pulled up in line to let them out at the Ravensdales' spacious townhouse. Christy put on her mask and waited for the coachman to lower the stairs. Sinjun exited first and helped her down.

"I can't wait to show you off," he murmured as they entered the commodious hall and ascended the stairs to the ballroom. "I'll be the envy of the *ton* tonight."

They paused in the doorway. Christy felt like a fish out of water as everyone stopped what they were doing to stare at her. Discreet, and some not so discreet, whispers followed them as Sinjun introduced her to their host and hostess. Christy had attended several public dances since arriving in town, but this was her first event given by members of the *ton*. Just being in the same room with so many English swine stuck in her craw. How she wished she were back home at Glenmoor, roaming the hills and glens and riding free and wild into the wind on her favorite mare.

Unfortunately she couldn't conceive an heir for Glenmoor in Scotland. And in order to meet and seduce Sinjun, she had to travel in the same circles.

Sinjun led her out onto the dance floor, and afterward they joined the throng of people at the buffet table.

"There's Julian," Sinjun said, waving to a tall, handsome man who had just entered the room. "Lord Mansfield is my older brother. He's rather dour but a likeable sort." Christy stared at the man rapidly approaching them and felt a moment of panic. She would have fled had she not been so conspicuous. If he recognized her, all was lost.

"Sinjun, I feared I wouldn't find you in this crush of people."

"Where's Emma?"

"She and Amelia Ravensdale went off together to exchange gossip. Will you introduce me to your ... friend?"

"Of course. Julian, meet Lady Flora Randall. Flora, this is my brother, Lord Mansfield. Don't mind his scowl, he always looks like that."

Head bowed, Christy dropped a curtsey. She remembered Sinjun's brother very well. She prayed he wouldn't recognize her with her mask on. "My lord."

Julian's scowl deepened. "Do I know you, my lady? Something about you is vaguely familiar."

"I'm sure we've never met, my lord."

"Odd that you should say that, Julian. I had the same feeling the first time I saw Lady Flora."

"Please excuse me, my lords," Christy said, anxious to escape Julian's intense scrutiny. She touched Sinjun's arm. "I wish to repair my hair." She hurried off toward the powder room.

"She certainly is a beauty," Julian said, staring after her. "There's something about her—"

"I thought the same thing, Julian, but I would have remembered had I met her before. Besides, this is her first visit to town."

"Don't introduce her to Emma," Julian warned. "It wouldn't be proper."

"Don't worry, Julian. I know what's proper and what isn't. I wouldn't dream of introducing Emma to my mistress."

Christy entered the powder room, relieved to find it empty. Appearing in public as Sinjun's mistress was devastating to her ego. He should be introducing her as his countess, not his lover. But she had made her choice and must now accept the consequences.

Chapter 4

C hristy removed her mask and rubbed her temples. Meeting Sinjun's brother had been nerve-wracking. She'd wanted the evening to end so she could go home. Heaving a sigh, she realized she couldn't hide in the powder room forever. But as she settled her mask in place, the door opened, admitting two young women, one blond, one brunette. They were laughing and giggling like schoolgirls, loudly lamenting the lack of attractive, mature men and commenting on the Season's offering of young suitors who had little to commend them.

Suddenly the brunette spied Christy and sent her a brilliant smile. Christy sucked in a startled breath, for the lovely young woman had the most remarkable violet eyes she had ever seen.

"I don't believe we've met," the brunette said, offering Christy her hand. "I'm Emma Thornton, and this is my friend, Amelia Ravensdale."

Sinjun's sister! Though Christy realized she was treading in dangerous waters, she couldn't help responding to the young woman's friendly overture.

"I'm Chris, er, Flora Randall."

Emma's eyes widened. "Lady Flora Randall! I've heard of you but never had the pleasure to meet you. You're very beautiful. Amelia and I came out last year," she revealed. "We were just discussing the paucity of interesting men this year." She sighed. "I suppose I compare all men to my brothers, and none of them can hold a candle to either Julian or Sinjun. Do you know them, Lady Flora?"

Christy felt certain Emma had no idea she was here tonight as Sinjun's mistress. She'd be content if Emma never found out. "I believe I've met your brothers."

"Are you here with your husband, Lady Flora?" Emma asked.

Was there no end to Lady Emma's curiosity?

"I . . . no, he's not well. If you and Lady Amelia will excuse me, I must return to my . . . friends."

"Perhaps we'll run into each other again," Emma said.

"Perhaps," Christy replied, having every intention of avoiding Sinjun's sister the rest of the evening. She adjusted her mask and left the powder room.

Sinjun was waiting for her. He wasn't alone. "Ah, there you are," he said, grasping her arm in a proprietary manner. "I don't believe you've met my friend, Lord Blakely. Rudy, this is Lady Flora Randall."

Rudy gave Christy an arrested look, then bowed over her hand. "Though we haven't met, I've heard nothing but praises about you from Sinjun."

I'll bet, Christy thought. " 'Tis a pleasure to meet you, Lord Blakely."

"Would you allow me to dance with your lady, Sinjun?" Rudy asked.

Sinjun frowned. "Perhaps another time, Rudy. I

was just about to lead Flora onto the dance floor myself. If you'll excuse us . . ."

Though the words weren't meant for her ears, Christy heard Rudy whisper to Sinjun, "Lucky dog. Lord Sin always keeps the best for himself."

Christy tried not to let the words affect her, for she knew Lord Blakely wasn't alone in believing she was simply an adornment on Sinjun's arm. Being paraded around as a mistress and not a wife was degrading. But Christy knew it was her penance for lying to Sinjun.

Sinjun's patience was wearing thin. Every man in the room was staring at Flora as if she were a sweetmeat waiting to be devoured. He couldn't wait to get her alone. Flora was going to be devoured, all right, by him. His need for the copper-haired beauty was consuming every minute of every day. It left him reeling, without direction, and it wasn't a feeling he enjoyed.

After the midnight buffet he suggested that they leave. His eyes darkened with irrepressible desire when she appeared as eager to leave as he.

"Wait here," Sinjun said as he retrieved Christy's cloak and draped it over her shoulders, "while I summon the coach."

Sinjun was gone only a few minutes, but when he returned to usher Lady Flora outside, he saw Julian and Emma approaching. He knew how Julian felt about introducing his mistress to his sister, so he tried to hurry Flora out the door and into the coach. It wasn't to be, however. Emma hailed Sinjun before he could hand Flora into the coach.

"Sinjun! Were you going to leave without greeting your sister?" She sent Julian an exasperated look. "Why didn't you tell me Sinjun was here?"

Sinjun cursed beneath his breath. There was no help for it. He had to stop and speak to Emma despite Julian's blistering scowl.

"Hello, Emma. You look ravishing tonight."

She dropped a curtsy. "Why, thank you, kind sir. And you are far too handsome for your own good."

"Come along, Emma," Julian said, attempting to push her toward their own coach.

Emma shrugged free. "I'm not through talking to Sinjun." Her gaze slid around to Christy. "Why, Lady Flora, we meet again. I didn't know you were here with my brother. Why didn't you tell me?"

Sinjun's eyes narrowed as he swung around to confront Christy. "You know my sister?"

"Of course," Emma said, forestalling Christy's answer. "We met in the powder room. I must say, Sinjun, your taste is improving. Lady Violet wasn't at all your style."

"That's enough, Emma," Julian said reprovingly. "It isn't proper for unmarried young ladies to be so outspoken."

"Oh, pish, Julian. If you weren't so serious all the time you'd be as popular as Sinjun."

Julian rolled his eyes. "God forbid. Nevertheless, I insist that we leave now. Perhaps Sinjun will come around for a visit soon." It was a direct command, one Sinjun couldn't ignore.

"Of course I'll visit soon, Emma," Sinjun said, "if I can wade through the throng of suitors beating down your door."

"Forget the suitors," Emma said. "I don't give a hoot about any of them. Please come soon, Sinjun. And bring Lady Flora."

"He'll come alone," Julian said sternly.

Sinjun cursed beneath his breath. The meeting

was unfortunate. Emma was a mischievous little imp, and far too inquisitive. He should have known she'd find a way to meet his new mistress.

"I'm sorry," Sinjun said as he handed Christy into the coach. "Julian considers himself the family's conscience. He didn't want Emma to meet you. You *do* understand, don't you?"

"It's all right, my lord. I understand. Emma must be protected from Lord Sin's excesses. I suspect Emma knows more than either you or your brother give her credit for. Lord Sin's exploits are the talk of the *ton*. How could she not know?"

Sinjun flinched. Though true, Flora's words gave him pause for thought. She considered him unprincipled, a man without morals. He wouldn't call himself a model of decorum, but he did have morals, dictated by his own personal code. Perhaps his decadent ways *were* common knowledge, but why should he change when his lifestyle fit him perfectly?

"Forget Emma," Sinjun said as the coach lurched forward. "Do you know how very much I want you? I'm not sure flaunting you in public is a good idea. There wasn't a man present tonight who didn't wish he were in my shoes."

He pulled her against him, smiling when she dutifully raised her head for his kiss. He stared a moment at her full lips, then took her mouth with his. She tasted so sweet he couldn't stop the groan that rose in his throat. Never had a woman gotten under his skin so quickly. He couldn't wait. He wanted her, and he wanted her now. His hand slid beneath her skirts, raising them high as his hand skimmed along her leg.

"Sinjun! What are you doing?"

"What I've wanted to do all evening. Don't

worry, I told the coachman to take the long way home. Spread your sweet thighs for me, sweetheart. I need to touch you."

Christy's breath seemed suspended. She couldn't move her eyes from his face. She could almost hear her blood pounding through her veins; every sense seemed intensified, and yet she was aware of little beyond the small, enclosed place that held the two of them. Sinjun required things of her she'd always considered wicked. She knew he was wild, hedonistic, unpredictable, but making love in a traveling coach was beyond anything she had imagined. Closing her mind to the very improper behavior Sinjun demanded of her, Christy realized a mistress would be eager to acquiesce to her lover's whims, no matter how improper. She spread her thighs.

Sinjun's hand slid up her stocking-clad leg past the garter. His hand found her, and she jerked in response. Something very strange was happening, and once again she felt the disorienting sensation of losing control of her senses. It was not at all what she was supposed to feel for her womanizing husband.

"You're already hot and wet for me," he whispered against her lips. "I have to have you, Flora." He raised her skirts to bare her thighs and shifted away to release his rigid staff. His member sprang free, and he pulled her astride him. "Ride me, sweetheart."

Christy rose slightly and impaled herself; the feeling of him sliding inside her was pure bliss. She arched her body and took him deeper. He gripped her bottom, his hands kneading, caressing, urging her to take even more of him. Her body drifted apart from her mind, lost in a sensual haze of pleasure. Excitement raced through her. A sudden jolt of sensation wrung a strangled cry from her lips, brought forth from deep inside her by the man who didn't know he was her husband. Then she knew no more.

When her wits reconnected with reality, she found herself lying on the seat with Sinjun leaning over her, his dark eyes inscrutable.

"You're incredible," he whispered as he hastily pushed down her skirts to cover her legs. "We're almost home."

With Sinjun's help, Christy straightened her dress and patted her hair into place, relieved that Margot wouldn't be up to remark on her dishevelment.

Sinjun exited the coach and handed her down. She wasn't sure he intended to go inside until he followed her to the door and held his hand out for the key. She handed it to him and stood back while he opened the door. A moment later she found herself being swept up into his arms and carried up the stairs. He entered her room and slammed the door with his boot heel. Then he set her on her feet, undressed her slowly, and made love to her again. Christy thought she had given her all in the coach, but their loving was as fierce as any storm, battering her senses and leaving her breathless. Afterward, she was more confused by her feelings than ever.

She was enjoying this far too much.

The following days and nights were surprisingly full. Since Sinjun never left until the sun rose high in the sky, Christy slept late. Sometimes he took her to the opera or theater, or riding in the park, but always they ended up in her bed. They ran into Julian a time or two. Stiff with disapproval, he usually acknowledged them with a cool nod but rarely spoke to them. She saw Emma only from afar, for Julian was careful to avoid them when he escorted his sister about.

Christy thoroughly enjoyed the operas and plays, even the rides through the park, but she abhorred the balls, routs, and dances. Sinjun seemed to recognize her reluctance to attend private functions and honored her unspoken wishes by escorting her upon occasions to public affairs.

Christy could not fault Sinjun's attention to her. His faithfulness never wavered, which surprised her. Sinjun wasn't known for his fidelity. As for herself, what she feared most was happening. Making love with Sinjun was the greatest pleasure she had ever known. She awaited his arrival each night with breathless anticipation, no matter that he had left her bed scant hours before.

Lust was a powerful emotion.

Christy knew Sinjun wasn't the kind of man a woman could depend on. His very nature precluded a lasting relationship. Had he wanted a wife, he would have consummated their marriage years ago. Had she wanted an Englishman for a husband she would have done something about it long before now. What she wanted was freedom to do as she pleased without an interfering husband. And she wanted an heir for Glenmoor. If she were clever enough she could have everything she wanted. *But at what cost?* a voice inside her asked. Would her heart survive Lord Sin?

A month sped by. Then another. At the end of her second month as Sinjun's mistress, Christy had every reason to believe she was pregnant. She had missed her monthly flow by two weeks and there was still no sign of it. But to be absolutely certain, she decided to remain until the end of the third month, just as she had originally planned. As her deadline approached, it became apparent to Christy that if she didn't remove herself mentally from Sinjun she wouldn't be able to leave at all. That night, after they returned from the opera, Christy attempted to separate herself from her body's response to Sinjun's loving.

After Sinjun had made love to her, he looked at her strangely and asked, "Are you not feeling well tonight?"

Had she been that obvious? "I feel fine. Why do you ask?"

"You seem distracted. Tiring of me already?" His voice was light and teasing, but his expression was intense.

" 'Tis almost time for me to leave," she reminded him.

She felt him stiffen. "Leave? No!" He went very still. "Are you increasing?"

"Do you really want to know? Let's just say 'tis time I leave London and return to my husband."

"Bloody hell! I'm not ready for you to leave. If you were honest, you'd admit you want to stay."

"It doesn't matter what either of us wants," Christy said in a hushed voice. "I gave my word. Lord Randall expects me home."

"Promise you'll give us more time together," Sinjun pleaded.

Christy couldn't believe her ears. Lord Sin begging? That was likely to be a first. "I cannot," she said on a sigh. "Please do not ask it of me."

Sinjun made a growling sound deep in his throat and pulled her beneath him. What transpired next was so savage, so utterly devastating, that it left her feeling bruised and more than a little frightened of her growing desire for her husband.

Two weeks after their conversation Sinjun felt fairly certain that Flora had abandoned her plan to leave London any time soon. In fact, the subject had not been broached again. Their coupling, as always, was wildly passionate and immensely satisfying for both of them; parting now was unthinkable. There was so much more he wanted to know about Lady Flora Randall. He knew her shapely, responsive body as intimately as his own, but she remained a mystery in every way except sexually.

During his latest visit to White's, Sinjun learned that a wager had been placed on the betting books as to the date Lord Sin would end his association with his current mistress. It probably would happen, Sinjun supposed, but his passion for Lady Flora was still too powerful to let her slip away.

He began his campaign to keep her in town by giving her emeralds to match her eyes. Next he presented her with a diamond bracelet, then a tiara. Nothing was too expensive for her. The pleasure with which she accepted the gifts warmed his heart, but a certain wariness in her green eyes made him uneasy.

There were no lights in the windows of Flora's rented townhouse when Sinjun arrived to escort her to the opera one night about three months into their passionate affair. A feeling of dread crawled up his spine as he pounded on the door. When no answer was forthcoming, he turned the knob. The moment the door opened beneath his hand he knew that she was gone. He detected no spark of life, only emptiness, as if the heart had gone out of the house. Unwilling to accept the only plausible answer, Sinjun took the stairs two at a time. The rooms were cold and lifeless. He flung open the wardrobe. Empty. His curses echoed hollowly in the barren chamber when he spotted the gifts he had given her lying in full view on the nightstand. He scooped the jewels into his pocket and stormed out of the house.

Gone! She had left without a word or proper good-bye. Damn her! What kind of woman was she? Did she care nothing for his feelings? Had he not been generous enough with her? His other mistresses had received less from him and hadn't complained. But the weight of the jewelry in his pocket banished the uncharitable notion that Flora was greedy. It was the old man she was married to, Sinjun thought angrily. Though they had never discussed feelings, the thought that she loved her elderly husband more than she enjoyed his company battered his ego.

Determined to forget the callous Lady Flora, Sinjun headed to White's, where he proceeded to get roaring drunk and gamble as if his pockets had no bottom. He was well into his cups when Rudy spotted him in the card room.

"Sinjun! I haven't seen you alone in months. Have you and your mistress parted ways already? I'd be happy to take her off your hands."

"If you can find her, she's yours," Sinjun muttered as he slammed down another losing hand and rose unsteadily. "Good night, gentlemen. It seems the cards are trying to tell me something."

Rudy grasped his arm to steady him. "I'll be damned! You're foxed. This isn't like you, Sinjun."

Sinjun shoved him away. "Go to hell, Rudy."

"Come on, Sinjun. Let me help you."

"I don't need your help."

"The hell you don't. You can barely stand. Where is your carriage?"

"S-s-sent it home," Sinjun mumbled, slurring the words. "I'm afoot."

"I'll take you in my rig," Rudy said, guiding him out the door. "You can tell me what's wrong while I drive."

"Not a damn thing wrong that a few drinks and a hot woman won't cure. Drop me off at Violet's townhouse. I hear her husband is still in Scotland."

"You wouldn't do Violet or yourself any good in your condition," Rudy chided. He picked up the ribbons, and his team lurched forward. "What happened?"

A tense silence followed, then Sinjun growled, "Flora left. Gone without a word."

"So what? Since when did Lord Sin let a woman disrupt his life? You've never had a problem moving on before. You knew she had a husband waiting for her in Cornwall." He sent Sinjun an incredulous look. "Don't tell me she stole your heart."

Mellowed by drink, Sinjun admitted to something he wouldn't have had he been sober. "Flora was different, Rudy, and that's all I'm going to say."

"Bloody hell! You *are* smitten. 'Tis not like you, my friend. What are you going to do? Will you pursue her?"

Sinjun's reputation was at stake. He'd never chased after a woman in his life and wasn't about to start now. So what if he felt at loose ends and without direction? So what if his ego had been battered? There were plenty of other women to take her place, should he want one.

"Hell no! Her husband is more than welcome to her."

Following Flora's departure, Sinjun embarked on a path of self-destruction even more dissolute than usual. Though he didn't take another mistress, he was seen with various women of the *ton* as well as ladies of easy virtue. Lord Sin's excesses grew even more unpredictable and wild as he tried to purge Lady Flora from his mind and heart. It wasn't like him to obsess over a woman, and he reacted by embarking upon a life of debauchery that made his previous excesses seem tame by comparison.

Ultimately his libidinous conduct reached Julian's ears. He stormed into Sinjun's townhouse one morning about a month after Christy's departure and pulled him from bed at the ungodly hour of noon. Sinjun glared at his brother through bloodshot eyes.

"I'm not in the mood to be lectured, Julian."

"You're going to listen whether or not you like it. You can't go on like this, Sinjun. Your excesses are getting out of hand, even for a man of your unsavory reputation. Is your parting with Lady Flora the reason you're hell-bent on self-destruction?"

"I don't wish to discuss Flora," Sinjun groaned as he sat on the edge of the bed and cradled his aching head in his hands. "She's gone. Left a month ago without so much as a good-bye."

Hands behind his back, Julian began to pace. "The lady is married, Sinjun, what did you expect? What's gotten into you? Mistresses come and go. What makes this affair different from the others?"

"Dammit, Julian, you have no right to question me. Perhaps you're more discreet than I, but your own affairs aren't above reproach. For instance, where do you disappear to several times a year? Everyone thinks you have a woman stashed away somewhere; someone not fit to meet your peers. What is she, a Gypsy? Or someone even worse? At least I'm more forthcoming than you are."

"More forthcoming and more debauched," Julian muttered irritably. "We're not talking about me, we're talking about you."

"Come back later. I'm not fit company."

"I'm leaving tomorrow. I'll be gone several weeks. That's another reason I wanted to speak to you. You've been avoiding Mansfield Place, I had to come to you."

"Does Emma know you're leaving?"

"Of course. I've asked Aunt Amanda to move into Mansfield Place to look after Emma during my absence. I expect you to escort them about while I'm away."

Sinjun sent his brother a disgruntled look. "Where are you off to this time?"

"I'm afraid I can't divulge that information. I'll expect you to control your excesses when you're with Emma. The girl is willful enough without your example of debauchery."

"You've got a lot of nerve, Julian," Sinjun blasted. "I'll do as I damn well please."

"A word of advice before I leave," Julian said. "Go to Scotland and fetch your wife. With all the talk of unrest in the Highlands, Christy needs to know she has a husband she can count on."

"The hell with Christy Macdonald," Sinjun muttered. "I was forced to marry against my will, but I don't have to live with her."

"Is that why you've wasted your life on useless pursuits? I knew you were bitter about your marriage, but I never suspected you would rebel by embarking upon a wastrel's life. Wake up, Sinjun. You're not the only one forced to wed unwillingly."

"Don't preach, Julian. Why should I fetch my wife when I'm satisfied with the way things are now? She will only complicate my life."

"I can see I'm wasting my time," Julian said with a hint of regret. "Just remember, I love you too well to see you waste your life. Don't let your behavior shame Emma. I'll talk to you when I return."

"I love you, too, Julian, but you can't run my life." Shaking his head, Julian quietly left the room.

Frustrated, Sinjun flopped down upon the bed. He knew he was out of control, but he couldn't seem to stop. He kept himself drunk because sobriety hurt. When sober, Flora consumed his thoughts. He relived each moment with her, recalling her sweet kisses, the way her body responded to him, her passion, the bliss he'd found in her arms. Despite the constant ache of missing her, he hated her for leaving him at loose ends.

Bewilderment and battered pride were making him bitter. Were Flora to return, he couldn't predict how he would react. Flora had left him without a word of good-bye, and his confusion regarding his feelings for the heartless chit was disconcerting. He didn't want to feel anything.

Though Julian's lecture had made him uncomfortable, he knew his brother was right. He had never before drunk himself to oblivion, or spent so much time in gambling hells, or paid women of easy virtue he'd picked up in Covent Gardens. Even Rudy had expressed disgust at his excesses, and Rudy was no angel.

Julian's words continued to weigh on Sinjun's

conscience. To please Julian and keep Emma's regard during Julian's absence, Sinjun resolved to make a concerted effort to behave around his sister. On those nights he wasn't required to squire Emma and Aunt Amanda to various functions, he was free to indulge himself. It wasn't as if he enjoyed waking up the next day with a big head, wondering how much money he'd gambled away or which friend he'd insulted; it was just that he had this compelling need to prove to the world that Flora had been nothing more to him than a passing fancy.

Julian returned to London a month later. The note he sent Sinjun requested his immediate presence. Wondering what Julian had heard about him now, Sinjun removed himself to Mansfield Place with undue haste. Julian received him in the library, his face a study of concern.

"What is it now, Julian?" Sinjun asked as he flopped into a comfortable chair before the hearth. "I did what you asked. Emma found my conduct as an escort quite satisfactory."

Julian thrust long, tapered fingers though a fine head of dark hair, clearly upset about something.

"Spit it out, brother. Is it my behavior again?"

"Not this time, Sinjun. This concerns your wife."

"Christy Macdonald?"

"Aye. A message from your bailiff at Glenmoor awaited me when I returned home. There's trouble. Sir Oswald reports that the crofters have refused to pay the current levies. I've been handling your business because you professed to have no head for it, but 'tis time you accepted responsibility and took charge."

"I told you before," Sinjun repeated, "tell the

king to send his soldiers to set them straight."

" 'Tis more serious than that, Sinjun. I don't know how this is going to set with you, but Sir Oswald heard rumors that your wife is expecting a child."

Sinjun leaped to his feet. "What! Has she no shame? No honor? How could she do this to me?"

Disgust colored Julian's words. "How can you expect her to honor her marriage vows when your own conduct is less than noble? You've flaunted your mistresses without a thought for your wife's feelings."

" 'Tis different for men," Sinjun claimed. "Christy Macdonald is not a courtesan. Those kind of women are sought after by men for their beauty and experience. Christy is a Highland lass, neither beautiful nor experienced."

Julian's fine eyebrows arched sharply upward. "How do you know what she looks like? You've not seen her since she was a child of seven. I'd say her patience wore thin waiting for you to claim her."

"Don't preach, Julian. If the rumors are true, Christy is no better than a whore."

"You have no choice now, Sinjun. You'd best hie yourself to Scotland and straighten out this mess."

"Aye," Sinjun allowed. "But before I leave, I intend to obtain a writ of annulment from the courts. If Christy is indeed increasing, I'll present the document for her signature, assuming she can write."

"You were given stewardship of Glenmoor into perpetuity, and that stewardship included a wife. Both are your responsibility."

"Glenmoor belongs to me and my heirs, I know that. But I will not have a whore for a wife. An annulment is inevitable if I find Christy carrying another man's child.''

"I've asked Sir Oswald to return to London to make a full report on the situation in the Highlands.''

"I can't wait for his return,'' Sinjun said, determined to confront his wife with her infidelity. For many years he'd enjoyed the freedom marriage granted him without being burdened with a wife, but Christy's behavior went beyond anything he could condone. No bastard was going to bear the Thornton name if he had anything to say about it.

Julian's intervention helped Sinjun obtain a speedy writ of annulment that required only Christy's signature.

Sinjun left London within the month. In a way he was grateful for the distraction for it served to keep thoughts of Flora from overtaking his life.

He traveled in his own coach, staying at posting inns along the way. When no inns were available, he found accommodations with English nobles eager to provide a night's lodging to Lord Mansfield's brother, a man whose reputation had preceded him. Lord Sin's exploits had been the talk of the *ton* for years.

After two weeks of exhausting travel over nearly impassable roads, Sinjun spied the aging turrets of Glenmoor.

Chapter 5

Perched on a bluff overlooking the loch, Christy folded her legs beneath her, pulled her cloak closer around her narrow shoulders, and stared out across water that reflected the color of the gray clouds scudding overhead. Christy loved this land. The heather-topped moors, the craggy mountains, even the mist that clung to the ground and hung over the loch. She heaved a heavy sigh as her thoughts wandered back to London and Sinjun. Two months had passed since she'd left him but it seemed like an eternity.

It hadn't been an easy two months. The weather hadn't cooperated, and the coach ride home had kept her in a constant state of nausea. Rutted roads mired in mud had made the journey perilous, and the situation she'd returned to at Glenmoor was explosive.

Calum Cameron had been stirring up trouble in her absence. When she'd explained that she and Sinjun had reconciled and arrived at an amicable agreement concerning their marriage, he had been livid. He had expected her to return from London a free woman and take him as her husband.

Telling Calum and her clansmen that she was expecting Sinjun's bairn hadn't been easy. There had been an outcry of disbelief and disappointment. Clearly no one wanted to believe she was carrying an Englishman's child.

"I thought I'd find ye here."

Christy started violently, surprised to see Calum bearing down on her. "Calum, you shouldn't sneak up on a person like that. You frightened me out of my skin."

Calum, a hulking giant of a man with shaggy brown hair and bulging muscles, hunkered down beside her. Instinctively Christy scooted away. She wasn't exactly afraid of Calum, but the look in his blue eyes unnerved her. He would make a powerful enemy.

"We need to talk."

"About clan business?" Christy asked, pretending to misunderstand his meaning.

His cold blue gaze raked her figure, intense with loathing. "Nay, about us."

"There is no us, Calum. I have a husband. I've been married nearly three quarters of my life."

"Ye know yer clansmen dinna accept that English swine as yer husband. We canna forget that our land has been taken from us and our freedom denied the day our fathers were defeated at Culloden. Yer own father and brothers died that day. Lord Derby shames us all by his lack of interest in his wife and lands."

"I told you, Calum, Lord Derby and I are no longer estranged. I carry his bairn."

Calum's expression turned fierce. "Where is the bastard, then? Why is he not here with ye? Yer lying, lass. There is no bairn, no reconciliation. No Englishman is worthy of ye."

His heavy hand came down hard on her shoulder. She flinched but made no other concession to his strength. "Ye know I want ye, lass."

"You want to be laird," Christy charged. " 'Tis all you've ever wanted. The Highlands will never be ours again in our lifetime if the English have anything to say about it."

"The clan needs a man to lead the fight against oppression and the unfair levies that line Lord Derby's pockets."

Christy bristled. "What can you do that I haven't already done? I've verbally protested to Sir Oswald. We've even withheld the quarterly levies."

"A man would lead a rebellion. *I* would lead a rebellion," he said, his massive chest swelling with pride.

"What good would that do us?" Christy challenged. "Lives would be lost, innocent lives, perhaps even those of women and children. Did you learn nothing from Culloden?"

"I learned not to trust Englishmen, lass. Ye forget, I lost loved ones that day, too. Why dinna ye tell me the truth, Christy? Ye never saw yer husband, did ye? Yer not expecting a bairn, are ye?"

Christy sighed. There was no help for it. It was time to prove she hadn't lied about her condition.

"Give me your hand, Calum."

"Why?"

"Just give me your hand."

He held out a callused paw, and Christy guided it to the swelling beneath her waist. Though not large, it was hard and round and could be mistaken for nothing but what it was, a bairn growing beneath her heart. Calum's blue eyes grew as hard as diamonds and he jerked his hand away, as if scalded. His expression was so fierce that Christy feared he would strike her.

"Damn ye to everlasting hell, Christy Macdonald! Why did ye do it? Why did ye play whore to an English swine?"

Christy raised her chin defiantly. "Sinjun and I are married. We reached an agreement, Calum. Since he prefers to remain in London and I at Glenmoor, we agreed to live apart. He gave me leave to rule Glenmoor as I please. There *will* be a Macdonald laird to take my place after I'm gone," she vowed, touching her stomach.

"What if yer bairn is a lassie?"

"So what if it is? Am I not my grandfather's heir? The sex of the bairn will make no difference."

"Yer grandfather did ye no favors," Calum said sourly. "He should have made me his heir."

Christy bristled indignantly. "You still don't understand, do you? The land is no longer ours to claim. It was taken from the clan as punishment for their support of Prince Charles, the pretender to the throne. Wouldn't you rather have an absentee landowner than one who rules you with an iron fist? One day my bairn will become laird. He will inherit Glenmoor from his father and a Macdonald will once again own the land."

"Englishmen owning Scottish soil is an abomination," Calum muttered darkly. "Ye were supposed to ask yer husband for an annulment and demand that he reduce the high levies we pay him. But what did ye do? Ye fell into his bed like a mare in heat. Have ye no shame, Christy Macdonald? Yer husband is a debaucher of women, a rake, a man without morals or scruples. He cares nothing for ye."

Christy winced. Calum's words held more truth

than fiction. Doubtless Sinjun had forgotten she existed hours after she'd disappeared. She held no fear that Sinjun would come to Glenmoor. Should he by chance try to find her, which she seriously doubted, he would look to Cornwall, not Glenmoor.

Christy tried not to think of Sinjun with other women, but it was impossible to imagine Lord Sin without a beautiful woman on his arm or in his bed. Would he return to Lady Violet? Or would he find a new mistress to flaunt before the *ton*?

"Perhaps what you say is true, Calum, but an annulment is no longer an option. I *am* carrying Lord Derby's child. Nothing you can do or say will change that."

Calum surged to his feet. "We'll see about that, lass. The clansmen are awaiting ye at Glenmoor. Macdonalds, Camerons, Ranalds, and Mackenzies. They've come to protest the excessive levies. Ye'd best come along and try to placate them."

The weather that had been merely threatening earlier suddenly turned dark and foreboding. Before she reached the ancient fortress where she had been born, the skies opened up.

Glenmoor was a desolate place, Sinjun thought as his coach clattered down the nearly nonexistent road to the fortress. The weather had turned raw, and rain pelted the land.

"Abominable country, rotten weather," Sinjun muttered, cursing his willful wife who had brought him to this inhospitable land. Had he not been required to travel to the Highlands to learn if the rumors about Christy were true, he might have gone to Cornwall to find Flora. He'd tried to tell himself he didn't care about her, but deep in his heart he knew better. God, he remembered every little detail about her. The silky texture of her skin, the way her nipples peaked at his slightest touch, the moist tightness of her body as he sheathed himself inside her.

He groaned and adjusted his breeches to accommodate his growing arousal. Just thinking about her made his shaft hard as a pike. He'd thought a return to debauchery would turn his thoughts away from the woman who had captured his fancy so completely, but he'd been wrong. He'd been angry, was still damn angry. Flora had made him care about her, and he didn't know how to handle rejection. Never again would he allow himself to care for a woman. He wasn't a violent man, but he was so furious with Flora that were he to see her now he wouldn't be responsible for his conduct.

The coach pulled up before the stone steps of Glenmoor. Sinjun leaped down, instructing John Coachman to take the horses to shelter and present himself in the kitchen for a hot meal. Then he made a dash up the steps. He flung the heavy wooden door open and encountered pure chaos. The main hall was packed with men, women, and children. A cacophony of angry voices bounced off the walls. Curious, he moved closer. No one noticed him as he paused just inside the hall to listen.

"Our people canna survive the winter if we pay the levies demanded of us!" one man loudly proclaimed.

"Our children will starve," a woman interjected. "What kind of monster would condemn innocent children to death?"

"Lord Derby, that's who!" another man roared as he jumped onto a table to be better heard. "The English have raped our land, married the orphan daughters of our noblemen, and left us with nothing but our pride. When the tax collector comes around again we must defy his authority."

"Sir Oswald has returned to England," a man exclaimed. "And good riddance."

"He'll send the king's soldiers," a woman said on a sob. "Lord save us all."

"What the clan needs is man to lead them," the Highlander standing on the table charged. "The Macdonald is too weak to lead the clan."

As if on cue, people began to shout, "Calum! Calum! Calum!"

Calum held up his hands for quiet. "Aye, tell The Macdonald who ye want for laird. The English lord hasna set foot in Glenmoor since he was wed to The Macdonald."

"Calum! Calum! Calum!"

Sinjun watched in astonishment as Calum jumped down and lifted a woman onto the table where she could be seen. Her back was to him as she confronted her angry clansmen. So this was his wife, he thought dispassionately as she raised her hands for quiet. Then she spoke, and a roaring began in his ears.

"I am The Macdonald," Christy said when the angry chanting subsided. "We must not lose our heads. 'Tis not the time for rebellion. There will be bloodshed. Women will lose their men, perhaps their own lives. Children will be without fathers and mothers. As long as I am laird, there will be no rebellion."

"We canna support the high levies," a man shouted.

"Are you willing to sacrifice your life, Donald Cameron?" Christy challenged. "Your wife and children will go hungry should they lose your support."

" 'Tis easy for ye to say," came Donald's angry reply. "Ye have an allowance from yer husband. Ye dinna have to pay taxes or rent. I say we set aside The Macdonald and choose another laird from our ranks."

"Listen, all of you." She touched her stomach. "I carry the Macdonald heir. He or she will be your protection for the future. For now, all I can say is that Lord Derby has promised to look into the unfair levies."

Sinjun sucked in a startled breath. He knew that voice! Little by little he recognized other things about The Macdonald. The shimmering waves of copper-colored hair, the trim curves, the regal bearing. Bloody hell! Flora. No, not Flora, but Christy Macdonald, his very own wife, and she was carrying *his* child! His fists clenched at his sides and his face grew mottled. How *dare* she do this to him! How *dare* she plot behind his back!

Everything she'd told him had been a lie. Who she was, where she lived, her elderly husband. She had a husband, all right, but he was neither old nor senile. Had he wanted to impregnate his own wife he would have done so long ago, but to be tricked like this was unconscionable. And more than a little disturbing.

He stared at her in silent fury. His eyes froze into chips of ice, and his gaze raked her from head to toe. Did she have to look so beautiful? A length of Macdonald plaid was slung over her shoulder. Her copper hair was plaited into a single braid, and her head was topped with a chieftain's cap adorned with a single feather.

He felt used, helpless, as if he'd lost control of

his life. He wanted to storm through the throng of people and shake her until her teeth rattled. The conniving little witch had gotten under his skin as no other woman ever had. When he recalled how distraught he'd been after she'd left him his anger intensified. Her hasty departure had left him bereft and suddenly in possession of a conscience, something Lord Sin had managed to avoid during his lifetime.

Suddenly Christy spun around, as if sensing his presence. He saw her eyes widen, saw her mouth his name. A hush fell over the hall as his presence became known. Someone whispered his name, and it traveled through the room like wildfire. But Sinjun heard nothing, saw nothing except Christy, who teetered dangerously on the tabletop.

The crowd parted as he started forward, his face unable to mask the seething rage in his heart. He was halfway there when Christy swayed perilously close to the edge of the table. He spit out a curse and broke into a run. He snatched her to safety scant seconds before she pitched to the floor.

"Where is her room?" Sinjun bit out to no one in particular.

Margot stepped forward. "Follow me, yer lordship."

Suddenly Calum stepped in his path. "Ye are Lord Derby?"

"Aye. Let me pass, man."

"What about the levies? Ye have raised them until we canna pay them without our families suffering."

"We will discuss it later," Sinjun said, shoving past him. "Lead the way, Margot."

Margot hurried up a winding stone staircase and opened the door to a large chamber at the top. Sinjun carried Christy to the bed and eased her down onto the feather mattress. Then he stepped back and stared at her through shuttered lids.

"Does she do this often?" he asked Margot.

"Nay, yer lordship, never before. Seeing ye at Glenmoor was a shock."

"I shouldn't wonder," Sinjun said dryly. He sent Margot a censuring look. "You were her conspirator in this ruse."

Margot stiffened. "Aye. 'Tis the only way Christy could keep Calum and the others in line. They wanted her to petition for an annulment and marry a Scotsman. Calum was so determined to become laird that Christy feared he would . . . force her and seize power for himself."

Sinjun's brows rose sharply. "Force her to bed him?"

"Aye. 'Tis the way of the Highlands." Her voice hardened. " 'Tis all yer fault, yer lordship. Ye should have consummated yer marriage years ago."

"So you and Christy plotted to trap me into getting her with child," Sinjun charged. "Quite a story you two hatched."

"Aye, we did. We had to do something to keep Calum from taking her by force, or the clan from choosing another laird. She hoped having your child would settle things once and for all."

A movement from the bed brought Sinjun's attention back to Christy. Her eyes were open, and she was staring at him.

"Why did you come?" she choked out, struggling to rise.

"Lie still," Sinjun said, pushing her back down. "Leave us, Margot."

"Nay. I willna leave ye alone with her."

"I won't strangle your mistress, though I must confess the urge is great."

Margot hesitated.

"Go!" Sinjun roared.

Margot turned and fled.

"You didn't have to frighten her," Christy complained.

"Nothing could frighten that one," Sinjun scoffed as he perched on the side of the bed. "Are you feeling better?"

Christy pushed herself up against the headboard. This time he didn't stop her, but his fierce scowl did little to comfort her. "I'm fine."

"You have some explaining to do," Sinjun said harshly.

He was looking at her as if he hated her, and Christy's heart sank. How could she ever make him understand? "I know you must hate me," she began.

"To say the least," Sinjun snarled. "You can't possibly know how I felt when I realized Flora and Christy were the same woman. I felt used, and the feeling is not one I enjoyed. You lied, and I, like a besotted fool, believed you."

Christy searched his face and realized she was happy to see him despite his anger. Her heart beat faster, and excitement danced through her veins. Her skin felt tight and hot and the flesh beneath aching. This wouldn't do, she chided herself. She clamped her lips together and hardened her heart against him. A man like Lord Sin would only bring her grief.

"Why are you here? You would have never known who I was had you remained in London."

"I've come because I heard that my *virgin* wife was expecting a child," he spat. "I should have questioned you more closely in London. What a fool I was to accept that cock-and-bull story about a husband unable to produce an heir. I should have known it was all a pack of lies, no husband would give his wife leave to cuckold him. And to think my conscience bothered me after you left."

Christy reeled in the face of his rage. "Do you think we Highlanders are ignorant of what goes on in London? Lord Sin's reputation reached me even in far-flung Glenmoor. Visitors to London delighted in regaling me with your exploits. When I learned the kind of man you'd become I had no regrets about lying to you. Would you have made love to me had you known I was your wife?"

"That isn't a fair question!"

"You have never been fair to me, Sinjun," Christy defended. "Why should I care about Lord Sin when he was having the time of his life, wallowing in debauchery and flitting from mistress to mistress while I tried to keep the clan from open rebellion? You cared nothing about Glenmoor or our problems. You've raised the levies to unconscionable levels in order to support your vices."

"If the levies were increased, I had nothing to do with the decision. Julian takes care of those things for me."

Christy swung her legs off the bed and lurched to her feet. "Do you always shirk responsibility?"

"Damn you!" Sinjun railed. "Until you walked into my life things were relatively peaceful. Julian handled all aspects of family business and legal matters."

Christy faced him squarely, hands on hips. "Which left you more time to indulge your excesses, I'm sure. Unlike you, I have responsibilities and own up to them. There were times I needed a husband's counsel, but where were you? Either gambling away Glenmoor's hard-earned money or squiring your current mistress about. Not once since our unfortunate marriage did you think about me. You're a rake with all the instincts of a rutting stallion."

Sinjun's eyes glinted dangerously. "I let you rule Glenmoor as you pleased."

"And I would have continued to do so had you not decided to arrive at a most inopportune time."

He stared pointedly at her stomach. "My bailiff heard rumors that Christy Macdonald was carrying a child, and I hied myself up here to learn the truth for myself. I even brought a writ of annulment in case I needed to rid myself of a faithless wife should the rumor prove true."

She gave a mirthless laugh. "Did it hurt to think that your wife was following in your footsteps? What a hypocrite you are."

"It's different for a man," Sinjun maintained. Abruptly he changed the subject before Christy could ridicule his faulty logic. "Tell me the truth, Christy. Is it my child you carry? Or is some other man's babe growing in your belly?"

"English swine!" Christy blasted. "Of course the bairn is yours. How can you doubt it? Oh, how I rue the day I became your wife."

"No more than I," Sinjun muttered darkly.

"Unfortunately an annulment is no longer feasible," Christy advised. "Our marriage has been consummated, and I'm carrying the future Macdonald."

"You're carrying a Thornton. He'll bear one of my lesser titles until he inherits mine."

Christy bit her lip to keep from screaming her frustration at Sinjun. Her bairn would remain in

Scotland with her no matter what he decided about their marriage. The future Macdonald belonged in the Highlands, among his own people.

"Fine," Christy bit out. "Now you can turn around and leave. I don't need you."

"I'll be the judge of that."

Appalled at Sinjun's arrogance, Christy couldn't wait for him to leave. Or so she tried to tell herself. How could she have fancied herself in love with the impossible rogue who cared for nothing but his own pleasure?

"I don't want you here."

Sinjun scowled at her. "I'll leave when I'm good and ready and not before. Your clansmen appear upset with you. I think I'll stick around a while. Perhaps I can be of some help. 'Tis time I took an interest in my land."

"I can handle my clansmen without your help," Christy maintained.

"What if the English garrison at Inverness learned of the unrest at Glenmoor? They would crush the uprising before your clansmen could arm themselves."

"I can handle them," Christy persisted.

He stared at her stomach. "Can you? When I arrived I heard you tell your clansmen that you had discussed lowering the levies with me. Strange, I don't recall that conversation."

"I had to tell them something. I intended to write a letter of protest."

Sinjun frowned. "I wonder why Julian never mentioned the increase in levies. Glenmoor is mine, after all."

"How nice of you to remember," Christy mocked. "How do you intend to help starving villagers?"

Sinjun flinched. It hurt to know she thought so little of his ability to accept responsibility. He groaned inwardly, recalling those times in London when he'd spoken disparagingly of his Scottish wife and holdings. She must have bitten her tongue to keep from lashing out at him.

Sinjun searched Christy's face, as if trying to unlock the secrets of her soul. Her glittering green eyes presented a challenge he could not ignore, and her full lips provoked and lured at the same time.

He recalled how those same lips had opened sweetly for him. How his tongue had explored all her tantalizing secrets. How she had deftly drawn him into her web of lies. She'd let him think he had seduced her, and he was amazed at how easily he had fallen under her spell. He had gobbled up her lies, every single one. God, what a fool he'd been! Lord Sin, the master of seduction. What a laugh.

His hooded eyes raked over her, finding her just as beautiful, just as desirable as he remembered, and his anger intensified. He wasn't supposed to know about this child, and that incensed him even more. He'd always been careful to withdraw before giving up his seed, but Flora had all but asked for a child, and he'd wanted to draw out the pleasure until every last drop was drained from him.

Damn her! He saw her watching him, her eyes wary, her body tense. What did she expect him to do? Attack her? His eyes lingered on her lips, and suddenly he knew what he wanted to do. She *was* his wife, wasn't she? As if reading his mind, she retreated a step. He reached for her.

She darted away. "What do you want?"

Sinjun smiled as his arm snagged her waist, bringing her against the unyielding wall of his chest. "Aren't you going to welcome your husband properly?"

Her eyes blazed defiantly. "Why should I?"

"You liked me well enough in London. We were lovers. I have explored every inch of your body and you mine. I know when I please a woman, and you enjoyed me every bit as much as I enjoyed you. Deny it if you want but you'd be lying."

"Of course I wanted something from you," Christy defended. "Don't you understand? I needed an heir for Glenmoor. Calum would have taken me against my will had I not tricked you into consummating our marriage and giving me a child."

"No one takes what's mine," Sinjun said savagely, surprised by his vehemence. For years he hadn't spared a thought for his wife. Scotland and Christy were only a dim memory. But now, after having her in his bed for three months, just thinking about another man making love to her sent him into a veritable rage.

"Let me go, Sinjun."

"No. You wanted a husband and now you have to suffer one."

A low growl rumbled from his chest as he brought his mouth down to hers. *Let her deny it now*, he thought. She could play the unwilling bride all she wanted, but he knew better. She was a hot little wench, as eager for him as he was for her. His mouth battered hers, his lips hard and punishing. He intended for his kiss to be bruising enough to teach her a lesson in obedience, but then her scent enveloped him and he forgot everything but the warmth of her body, the sweetly curved lips beneath his, and her arousing essence that had pursued him in his dreams.

He parted her lips with his tongue and tasted the sweetness of her mouth. She fought him, dammit. To the credit of her unrelenting pride, she tried to push him away. He held her tighter, savoring the unique taste of her. Memories of their explosive passion pierced through him like lightning. Her breasts, so perfect for his hands, the tight sheathing of his shaft, the way she arched up against him as he moved inside her. The steamy nights in her bed, their sweat-slicked bodies moving together in perfect harmony, all these he remembered with mounting ardor.

Suddenly Christy gave a mighty shove and backed away from him, trembling, her eyes wide and troubled. She was panting, her chest rising and falling with every quick breath she took.

"No! I won't let you do this to me!"

Sinjun stiffened, his mood shattered. "Do what, wife? 'Tis nothing we haven't done before."

"I was a different person then. You want a wife no more than I want a husband. Let us part on friendly terms."

Sinjun muttered a curse. "You carry my child. It takes more than friendship to make a baby. Why pretend we've never been lovers?"

"Because it's over, Sinjun," she said bluntly. "I got what I wanted and you had a willing mistress for a time. No one need ever know about our bairn if you don't want them to. I'll never return to London and I know how much you hate the Highlands. Should you someday find another woman you wish to marry, you can divorce me. Lord Mansfield's influence should clear the way for you."

Bloody hell! Why did she have to sound so damn cold-blooded and logical? "The first thing I'm going to do is send a message to Julian concerning the increase in levies. Sir Oswald should be back in London by now. A few questions about the increases should clear up the matter. Meanwhile, I have to do something to calm your rebellious clansmen. Do you feel well enough to accompany me to the hall?''

"I'm fine. 'Twas the shock of seeing you at Glenmoor that made me faint. I'm healthy as a horse."

His gaze lingered on her face. "You certainly look healthy enough. Glowing would be a more accurate description." He offered his arm. "Don't think for a minute this is settled between us, Christy. I'm angry. Damn angry. You took something from me you had no right to."

Christy accepted his arm with ill grace. Sinjun thought she had been properly chastised until she delivered her parting shot. "Did you have some other woman besides your wife in mind to bear your bairn?"

Sinjun refused to be goaded. She had already chewed him up and spit him out. How much more could he take? No woman had ever treated him as shabbily as his own wife. He had known Christy Macdonald was trouble the first time he'd laid eyes on the seven-year-old hoyden. He'd never expected her to grow into a provocative beauty with a body that would tempt a saint. And the good Lord knew he was no saint.

He had become infatuated with his own wife. What a bloody coil. But he was finished with playing the dupe. His feelings had cooled considerably after discovering exactly whom he had made his mistress in London. What he felt now was rage for being lied to and used. Unfortunately, though he was loathe to admit it, he still wanted her.

* * *

They found Christy's clansmen milling around in the hall, muttering among themselves and drinking a powerful Scottish brew made from barley, which could put a strong man under the table within an hour. Conversation halted when he and Christy entered. The mood was still volatile, the people sullen and withdrawn.

Sinjun felt a prickling sensation along his spine and instinctively knew he had no friends here. That thought rankled, and suddenly something shifted and changed within him. This was his land, dammit! Responsibility was a concept so utterly foreign that it took him a moment to digest his newfound sense of loyalty to these Highlanders whom he had disdained most of his life. Conscience was something he thought had died of neglect years ago.

"Did the blackhearted sinner hurt ye?" Calum asked as he shoved through the crowd to Christy.

"I'm fine, Calum," Christy assured him. "It was a shock to see Lord Derby here so soon after I left him in London, that's all."

Calum sent Sinjun an ominous glare. "Since yer here, yer lordship, ye should know how we feel."

"I'm listening," Sinjun said, bracing himself.

"I am Calum, chieftain of Clan Cameron," Calum said with importance. "The Macdonald is our laird, and her clansmen are concerned for her welfare. Ye have been no proper husband to her. We dinna want ye here. Go away and leave us in peace."

Sinjun went on the defensive. "Glenmoor and its domain is mine. And like it or not, I am your laird's husband."

A knot of disgruntled Scotsmen gravitated around Calum. Camerons, lending him support.

They were all big, intimidating men, but Sinjun was no coward. He stood his ground, his body tense, his hand on the hilt of his sword.

Calum's grin did not reach his narrowed eyes. "Accidents do happen, yer lordship. 'Twould be easy enough to rid Christy of a husband she doesna want."

Sinjun sent Christy a shuttered look. "Are you sure she doesn't want me? Perhaps you should ask her. Kill me and I guarantee that Glenmoor will be swarming with the king's soldiers," he warned.

A tense silence followed as the Highlanders mulled over Sinjun's words.

"Listen, all of you!" Christy shouted into the strained atmosphere. "There will be no talk of killings, Calum Cameron. Sinjun is my husband, and I carry his bairn. Go home, all of you. There is nothing more to be discussed."

"Wait," Sinjun ordered. "There is something more I wish to say. I don't know why your levies were increased, but I certainly intend to find out."

" 'Tis not just this year," Donald shouted, "but the year before, and the year before that!"

Sinjun frowned, wondering not for the first time why Julian hadn't mentioned the fact that he'd been raising levies on his holdings. He usually discussed business matters concerning Glenmoor before acting on them.

"I don't have the answer, but I will find out. When my coachman leaves for London tomorrow he'll carry a message to my brother, asking him to look into the matter. Meanwhile, no one will be required to pay levies this quarter. Furthermore, I will personally visit your homes to see what can be done to improve living conditions."

His speech was met with cautious approval, despite open hostility from the entire Clan Cameron.

"I'll wait and see how much yer fancy words are worth before I pass judgment," Calum growled, apparently unappeased.

Then he turned and stormed from the hall. The crowd quickly dispersed after that, leaving Sinjun and Christy alone.

"That was generous of you," Christy said, a hint of acerbic approval in her voice. "But can we trust the word of an Englishman?"

Chapter 6

Christy locked Sinjun out of her bedchamber that night. After turning the air blue with profanities, he followed a silently gloating Margot to an unoccupied room, cursing Christy Macdonald and Flora Randall and any other name she chose to use. He didn't need this. He'd been happy and carefree in London, maintaining his reputation and using his God-given talents to pursue his hedonistic lifestyle. He wanted to leave these cursed Highlands, but how could he? Christy was carrying his child, and he had the compelling urge to remain long enough to see what he or she looked like.

Sinjun found his belongings piled against the wall in the chamber assigned to him. Two trunks and a small bag. He didn't know how long he'd be required to stay, so he'd brought nearly his entire wardrobe. He'd also had the foresight to bring a small casket of gold sovereigns, and another with silver coins, hidden inside one of the trunks.

Before retiring that night he spoke with John Coachman about the return trip to London early the following morning. He had composed a letter to Julian and gave it to John to deliver to his brother. Weather permitting, the letter should reach Julian within a fortnight. That meant it would be at least four weeks before he received Julian's reply, which he hoped would clear up the mystery of the increased levies. If things continued as they were, a rebellion would result. Christy wasn't strong enough to control the Cameron chieftain.

Yet he had to admire Christy for the way she'd held her clan together since old Angus's death two years ago. It had never occurred to him that she might have needed him. He'd left her on her own, thinking he was doing them both a favor, while in reality he had left her to deal with things that needed a man's firm hand. When he compared Christy's problems to the profligate lifestyle he enjoyed, he felt inadequate and shallow. And he didn't like the feeling.

For the first time in years, Sinjun had a glimmer of what Julian had been trying to drum into him. When he'd heard about his nickname, he'd actually been pleased. Lord Sin. Delightfully wicked, marvelously decadent, and he'd spent his adult life living up to its promise.

Lord, what an absolute ass Julian must think him.

The following morning, after a night of intense introspection, Sinjun saw John Coachman off and went to the hall in search of food. Christy was already breaking her fast with Margot and the young man he recognized as Christy's London coachman.

"You remember Rory Macdonald, don't you?" Christy asked, nodding toward the sullen young man who was regarding him with resentment.

"I remember the face but not the name," Sinjun said, taking a seat beside Christy. Immediately a short, round woman came in from the kitchen. She paused beside Sinjun, scowling unpleasantly.

"Do ye want something to eat, yer lordship?" she asked curtly.

"I'm sure Lord Derby is hungry, Mary," Christy said reprovingly. "Bring him what we're eating."

Sinjun grimaced at the oat gruel Christy was spooning into her mouth. He didn't like pap. "I'd prefer eggs and steak," he said, smiling at Mary.

"Ye dinna want oats?" she asked, clearly affronted.

Sinjun shook his head. "I don't like oats."

"Did ye hear that, Christy? The mon dinna like oats. All Scotsmen worth their salt eat oats in the morning."

"Bring Lord Derby steak and eggs, Mary," Christy said on a sigh. " 'Tis his home, he can have what he wants for breakfast."

Mary sent him a disgruntled look, then, with a swish of her skirts, stomped back to the kitchen.

"I trust you slept well, my lord," Christy said.

"So I'm 'my lord' now, am I?" Sinjun replied, scowling. "I'm your husband, remember? You used to call me Sinjun."

Color pinkened her cheeks. "Your coach left this morning without you, Sinjun. We have a few spirited horses in our stables, perhaps you'd prefer to ride one of them back to London."

"Why are you so anxious to be rid of me?" His face darkened. "Is there another you would prefer to call husband?"

Her reply was forestalled when Mary appeared with Sinjun's steak and eggs. He jumped when she banged the dish down in front of him. "Dinna choke on the steak, yer lordship," she said sweetly. Then she whirled and marched back to her domain.

Neither Margot nor Rory did anything to hide their amusement. "Enjoy yer breakfast, yer lordship," Margot said, rising. "Duties await me." She sent Rory a speaking glance. "Are ye coming, Rory?"

Rory scraped back his chair. "Aye."

"Wait," Sinjun said around a mouthful of steak. "Since there are horses in the stables, I'd like to inspect my land and perhaps ride through the village today. I'll require Rory's assistance. Can you be ready in an hour, Rory?"

Rory slid an inquiring glance at Christy before answering. It galled Sinjun that Rory needed Christy's approval when he was the lord of the manor. But he supposed it would take time for the Macdonalds, Camerons, Ranalds and Mackenzies to accept his authority as landowner. Winter was swift approaching and he doubted he'd be traveling until spring thaw made the roads passable again. According to his calculations, Christy would deliver his child sometime in March. He still had several months yet in which to decide what his future would hold where Christy and the child were concerned.

"I'll go with ye, yer lordship," Rory said, sounding pleased despite his scowl. "I'll saddle the horses and meet ye outside in an hour."

Rory left immediately. Sinjun devoted his attention to his food. His healthy appetite surprised him. In London he rarely rose before noon. Since his stomach was never at its best after a night of carousing, he ate sparingly during the early part of the day. Dinner was usually very late, possibly a midnight buffet at some social event or other. He couldn't explain his appetite this morning, unless it was due to his enforced abstinence during his trip to the Highlands. He hadn't touched a drop of anything stronger than ale since he left London.

"How long do you intend to honor us with your presence?" Christy asked as she pushed her empty bowl aside.

"Be careful, *wife*, I'm still bloody angry at you. I'll let you know when I decide to leave. Did it ever occur to you I might want to learn more about my holdings?"

"No. That thought never occurred to me," Christy said bluntly. "You're staying to punish me."

His gaze raked her. "Don't flatter yourself. I'm staying because 'tis time I took an interest in my holdings."

"Damn interfering Englishman," Christy muttered beneath her breath. "I don't need you. I've never needed you."

Sinjun dropped his fork, his anger mounting as he scraped his chair away from the table. "You needed me for one thing, madam." He gazed purposefully at her stomach.

Christy faced him squarely, fists clenched, chin firmed, eyes blazing hotly. "Aye, my lord. Had I not wanted something from you I would never have debased myself. Do you know how embarrassing it was to play your whore? I'm your *wife*! Such subterfuge wouldn't have been necessary had you been a proper husband to me. You wore me like a trophy upon your sleeve for the benefit of your friends. All of London whispered about Lord Sin's latest mistress. God, how I hated it!"

Her outburst stunned Sinjun. She sounded as if she were the wounded party. Didn't she know he had cared for her more than any other woman of his acquaintance? Had that been her plan all along? Make him care, then leave him to wonder why she had abandoned him? Was that to be his punishment for ignoring her all these years?

"You used me!" Sinjun charged.

"I took nothing that wasn't rightfully mine," Christy contended. "Is your pride wounded, Sinjun? Perhaps it was time a woman gave you your comeuppance. Lord Sin. Bah! Lord Decadence more aptly describes you."

Rage seethed through Sinjun. He didn't lose his temper often, but Christy was sorely trying him. It took all his willpower to keep from exploding. Mouth taut, expression stiff and cold, he turned his back on her and walked away.

Damn him! Christy silently ranted. Why couldn't he have remained in London? She had already set her mind to live the rest of her days without Sinjun. Then he'd barged into her secure life, bringing turmoil, along with painful memories of the man who had made a woman of her and taught her passion.

Her clansmen were more than a little disturbed over Sinjun's arrival. Calum had even threatened his life. Why had Sinjun come alone, without guards or soldiers? He was but one Englishman among scores of Highlanders who hated the English passionately.

Christy sighed. She knew Sinjun would never forgive her for lying to him, and she really couldn't blame him. But, oh, he made her so angry. The world didn't revolve around Lord Sin. Had he expected her to welcome him into her bed last night? She grinned as she recalled his colorful curses when he'd tried to enter her chamber and found the door locked. What really galled was the knowledge that she had had to force herself to lock him out of the room. From the moment he'd entered

Glenmoor, she'd hungered to touch him, to get close enough to inhale the male muskiness of his scent, which had haunted her dreams. The need had been so compelling that she'd had to force her anger to keep from surrendering to him.

If Sinjun had wanted her because he loved her, she would have welcomed him into her bed and into her heart. But Sinjun wasn't a man easily satisfied by one woman. She might satisfy him while he remained at Glenmoor, but when he returned to London, Lord Sin would continue his wicked ways.

Her hand went to her stomach, where his bairn grew. He might not want the child, but she did, fiercely. The future Macdonald. He or she would inherit Glenmoor and give the clan back its pride, its heritage. Sinjun's heir was the clan's salvation, its destiny. More importantly, the child would be a part of Sinjun, someone to love after he was gone. It would be so easy to give Sinjun her heart were he of a mind to remain faithful to one woman. She vowed to raise her bairn to live up to the potential Sinjun himself would never attain.

Sinjun's mount delighted him. He had no idea Glenmoor possessed a stable of such fine horseflesh. His stable, he reminded himself. Everything he'd just seen—the land upon which he rode, the village, the church, the fat sheep being driven down to the valley for the winter, was his. His chest swelled with a pride he hadn't felt in a very long time. He'd never liked the wild, windswept Scottish Highlands, or its savage inhabitants, but now, a strange sense of peace, of possessiveness, made him see it differently.

"The moors are nay so beautiful this time of year, yer lordship," Rory said by way of conversation. "In the spring they are covered with heather. 'Tis a wondrous sight."

Sinjun thought the hills and moors rather desolate this time of year, but no less beautiful. It was a different kind of beauty. Stark, comfortless . . . compelling. The trees had lost their leaves and the air was crisp with the promise of winter. He could hear the rush of water in the nearby loch and feel the salt spray upon his cheeks. It was so invigorating that Sinjun wasn't surprised to discover he was hungry again.

Sinjun loved horses, and he rode in the park daily for exercise, but loping over leagues of open land, beneath a sky so blue it dazzled the eyes, was exhilarating. He wondered now why he'd taken such a strong dislike to the Highlands.

"Are those Glenmoor sheep grazing in the valley?" Sinjun asked.

"Aye. Clansmen tend the sheep for ye and receive a portion of the profit when the wool is sold. Some of the sheep will be butchered for meat and shared with the crofters."

"Were the shepherds paid after the shearing this year?"

"Aye, but Sir Oswald said the market wasn't good and they received less than they had expected. Then rents and taxes were raised. 'Twas what started talk of rebellion. The Cameron urged everyone to protest by withholding the quarterly dues, and we all agreed."

Sinjun mulled that over for a while, until they reached the village perched on a hillside below Glenmoor. There couldn't have been more than two dozen stone cottages clustered together haphazardly. It was a poor village, Sinjun noted. The thatched roofs of nearly every cottage were badly in need of repairs.

People stopped what they were doing to stare at him. Their silent animosity was so potent that Sinjun was glad Rory was riding at his side. He stopped often to converse with the people, but most turned their backs and refused to acknowledge him.

"Not a very friendly lot, are they?" Sinjun said.

"Can ye blame them?" Rory replied. "An Englishman now owns them and the land they once called their own. The Macdonald does all she can to ease their suffering, but their children are still dying from starvation." He sent Sinjun an aggrieved look. "And ye wonder why we hate Englishmen. When the land belonged to us we only fought amongst ourselves. We stole our neighbor's livestock and they stole ours, it was a way of life. But we never went hungry."

Sinjun took a closer look at the cottages and decided that something would have to be done before first snowfall.

"Can men of the village make the necessary repairs to the cottages?"

"Aye, but there isna enough thatch to go around and the homeowners canna afford to buy material. Many will die of ague when the winter snows come."

"I will pay for repairs and give the workmen a decent wage," Sinjun said, grateful for the gold sovereigns in his trunk. "Can you arrange it?"

"Ye want to pay for repairs out of yer own pocket, yer lordship?"

" 'Tis what I said." A passel of ragged children stopped their game of tag to stare at him. Sinjun was appalled at their lack of proper clothing. Some even wore animal skins fashioned into tunics and breeches. He made a mental note to speak to Christy about the situation in the village.

"This village is the Macdonald stronghold, yer lordship," Rory said. "Would ye like to visit the Cameron, Ranald, and Mackenzie strongholds?"

"Tomorrow, Rory, I've seen enough for today. Let's head back to Glenmoor. I'm hungry enough to eat a horse."

"Why dinna ye say ye were hungry?" Rory asked as he reached into the bag he carried at his waist and pulled out a bannock. "Have a bannock, yer lordship. Nothing like an oatcake to stave off hunger pangs. I never leave home without a few in me vittles bag."

Sinjun accepted the oatcake with misgiving. He'd never liked oats in any form, considering it food fit for horses, not for humans, but he was too hungry to argue. He paused but a moment before biting off a chunk and chewing. Though somewhat dry, the taste wasn't at all bad. In fact, he finished that and accepted another as they rode back to Glenmoor.

"Did ye mean what ye said about repairing the cottages?" Rory asked, as if unable to credit Sinjun's generosity.

Sinjun sent Rory a sharp look. "What made you think I was lying?"

Rory shrugged. "Yer English," he said, as if that explained everything.

Sinjun chewed that over for a moment, then said, "You don't like me, do you? I sensed that in London."

"Ye've given me no reason to like ye, yer lordship."

"You knew what Christy intended, didn't you?"

"Not at first. She told me after I spoke out about yer visits to her townhouse in the middle of the night. I dinna like it, but 'twas not my place to question the laird. Margot and I are handfasted, she would have had my hide if I betrayed the laird."

"Tell me about the Camerons," Sinjun said.

"They're warriors, not sheepherders or farmers, though 'tis how they earn their keep. They've been angry ever since old Laird Angus made Christy his heir and successor. Calum Cameron has been plotting ever since to cast Christy aside and make himself laird of the clan."

"Could he have done that?" Sinjun asked.

"He needed the Macdonalds, Ranalds, and Mackenzies behind him. Fortunately, most, except maybe the Mackenzies, are loyal to Christy and thwarted Calum's efforts. Then Calum decided he would become laird through marriage to Christy. But he couldna convince Christy to seek an annulment. Then the quarterly levies were raised again and those originally opposed to Calum agreed with him that the clan needed a male leader. They wanted a warrior who would fight for their rights. That's when Christy and Margot hatched the plan to seek ye in London. Ye know the rest, yer lordship."

"Indeed," Sinjun said dryly.

Though he understood Christy's motives for pursuing him in London, he had a hard time forgiving her for lying. She had tricked him to get her with child, and that hurt his pride. She had wanted him for only one thing, while he had truly desired her. It had all been a clever ruse, and he had landed in her bed. Well, things had changed. He was at Glenmoor now, and whether Christy liked it or not, he was going to make damn sure she and her clansmen knew he was in control.

Sinjun breathed deeply of the cold, crisp air, rather enjoying the outing. His mount was spirited, the company wasn't bad, considering his lack of popularity among these Highlanders, and Christy was waiting for him at Glenmoor.

Christy was sweeping the cobblestones in the courtyard when Sinjun and Rory returned. As Rory led the horses away, she leaned on the broom, watching Sinjun. Her eyes narrowed thoughtfully when she saw him gaze intently at Glenmoor's ivy-covered walls, as if assessing their worth. She knew Glenmoor meant nothing to him, but to her it was everything. She still couldn't conceal the surge of pride she felt for her ancestral home.

He saw her then, and she walked over to join him. His negligent posture in no way concealed the tension in his coiled muscles, or the way he looked at her, like a predator focusing on his prey. Her steps slowed as she recalled the intimate details of their affair in London. She sighed expansively, remembering how the crisp hair on his chest teased her naked breasts, the way the taut muscles of his buttocks flexed beneath her hands, his hard, hair-roughened thighs. Nothing had prepared her for Lord Sin's devastating charm. For three wonderful months she had known both desire and fulfillment. And now she knew despair. Sinjun hated her, and she had to harden her heart against him before she yearned for things that could never be.

"Did you enjoy your ride?" Christy asked when Sinjun continued to stare at her with a curious glint in his eye.

"Aye, most enlightening. Rory made an excellent

guide." He stared at her breasts, then let his gaze wander down to her stomach. "Are you well?"

"Very well, thank you."

"Come inside with me." It was more an order than a request.

"Now?"

"Now," Sinjun said. "We need to talk. Your chamber will do."

Christy had to run to keep up with him. "Can't we discuss whatever it is you wish to talk about in the hall?"

"No." He started up the stairs and didn't stop until he reached her chamber. He opened the door and waited until she went inside. Christy's heart began to pound. Being alone with Sinjun was dangerous. His potent sensuality had led lesser women than her to perdition.

She walked to the window and gazed out over the land that had been in her family for generations. Sinjun came up to stand beside her. She felt his heat, sensed his anger even before he spoke.

"You locked me out of your chamber last night."

"You were angry. Did you expect me to welcome you?"

His voice was clipped, taut with tension. "I liked Flora better."

Christy shrugged. "Flora was a myth. I gave you what I thought you wanted and . . ." Her words fell away.

". . . I gave you what you wanted."

Her jaw firmed. "Aye. I won't deny it. I'm sorry if it distresses you, my lord, but do not concern yourself with the child. Our bairn will not lack love."

"A child needs a father," Sinjun said. She saw his clenched fists and wondered what he expected from her. Not love, obviously. The world was filled with countless women Sinjun had yet to meet and love.

"I . . . assumed you wouldn't want to be bothered."

"You assume wrong. I intend to be at Glenmoor for the birth of my child. Then perhaps I'll take him to London, where he'll be raised among civilized people. I daresay Julian will stop carping at me if I become a family man."

Christy gasped and flung herself at him, her eyes wild, fierce, her small hands beating against his chest. "No! You can't do that! I won't let you."

"Cease!" Sinjun said, grasping Christy's flailing wrists. "We'll discuss this when you've calmed down. I'm probably stuck here for the winter anyway. Come spring, I should have a better understanding of the unrest I've witnessed at Glenmoor."

"I warn you, Sinjun," Christy hissed, "take my bairn and you'll live to regret it."

An elegant brow shot upward. "You should have considered the consequences before you hatched your scatterbrained plan to become pregnant."

"You were never supposed to know! Or care," she added.

Still holding her wrists firmly within his grasp, Sinjun pulled her against him. He felt her heat, inhaled her tantalizing scent, and his shaft jerked in response. The hard little swelling below her waist intrigued him. He wanted to see her naked, to touch the place where his child grew. Her breasts were larger than he remembered, and the need to explore them was so urgent that he released her wrists and cupped them. He felt her nipples pebble beneath his palms, and his eyes darkened with desire.

No matter how angry he was at her for deceiving him, he couldn't stop his body's response to her soft, fecund curves. As swiftly as it had come, his anger dissipated. He ached to push himself into her tight sheath, to taste her sweet passion, and to give them both what they so obviously needed.

Christy must have read his mind, for moments before he would have swept her into his arms, she pulled away, her face set in stubborn lines.

"No! I won't let you do this! I'm nothing to you but a warm body. You've never wanted a wife or family. What kind of man are you? If you recall, you agreed to my terms to end the affair when the time came for me to leave. Whether or not I became pregnant during that time was a problem I would handle alone.

"I cannot count the times you told me how well your marriage suited you because your wife made no demands upon you. All I wanted from you was an heir for Glenmoor, and someone of my own to love." She touched her stomach. "Through your bairn, a Macdonald heir will regain ownership of Glenmoor."

"Damn you!" Sinjun snarled.

"No! Damn *you*! You lied to me."

Sinjun could find no fault with Christy's logic. He had indeed agreed to her terms. He'd wanted her so badly he would have agreed to anything. It was a devil's pact he'd made. He remembered thinking that her husband had even less morals than he did. His conscience had pricked him, but lust had won out. He realized too late his thinking had been faulty.

Sinjun's introspection was interrupted when

Christy fled through the door. Muttering to himself about the failings of women, he followed her down to the main hall, where he found Rory waiting for him.

"When do ye want the workmen to begin the repairs?" Rory asked.

"As soon as possible," Sinjun replied. "I understand winters in the Highlands can be harsh."

Rory nodded and left the hall. "What repairs?" Christy wanted to know.

"I'm paying for repairs to be made to the cottages in the Macdonald stronghold. There is much to be done and the need seemed urgent. I haven't visited the Camerons, Ranalds, or Mackenzies yet, but I'll get to them as soon as I can."

"There is no coin for building materials," Christy demurred.

"Let me worry about that." He sniffed appreciatively of the tempting aroma coming from the kitchen. "I'm hungry. What time do we dine? Will I have time to bathe?"

"We eat early, but there's sufficient time for a bath. I'll send the kitchen boys up with the hip tub and hot water. Excuse me, I'll see to it now."

Sinjun caught her wrist. "I'll need help bathing. I left my valet behind."

"Everyone at Glenmoor helps themselves," Christy informed him.

"Will you scrub my back? 'Tis no more than any husband would expect of his wife."

He watched her face turn red and hoped she wouldn't refuse. Her answer, when it came, was grudgingly given. "Aye. I'll ask Mary for the stiff wire brush she uses to scrub pots."

Her parting shot brought a shout of laughter. No matter how angry he was at Christy he knew she would never bore him. More to the point, he didn't know how long he could keep his hands off her. After experiencing Flora's uninhibited passion, he couldn't wait to discover if a difference existed between Flora the mistress and Christy the wife.

After his initial anger had dissipated and calmness prevailed, he saw no reason why he and Christy shouldn't enjoy one another in the same way they had in London.

He wondered how long it would take him to persuade Christy to let him share her bed. He chuckled to himself. It wasn't going to be easy, but nothing worth having was ever easy.

Chapter 7

Sinjun's mind drifted as he leaned his head back against the rim of the tub and waited for Christy. He wasn't certain she would come, but the thrill of anticipation was worth the wait. Pregnancy hadn't dimmed her beauty. If anything, it had enhanced it. And to think he had avoided Christy all these years because he'd remembered her as a nasty, red-haired hoyden with little to commend her. No, that wasn't entirely true. He hadn't wanted a wife intruding upon his lifestyle. He'd wanted freedom.

It was hard to imagine himself as a father. The idea was going to take some getting used to. But the longer he thought about it the more it grew on him. A son and heir or a daughter who looked like Christy. He hadn't mentioned in his letter to Julian that Lady Flora and Christy Macdonald were the same woman. He thought he'd save that for when he could tell Julian in person. Wouldn't his brother be surprised? And Emma. She'd be ecstatic to learn she was going to be an aunt.

A knock on the door brought a smile to Sinjun's sensuous lips. Christy. She'd come. His shaft gave an involuntary jerk, and he wondered how long it would take him to coax Christy into his bed.

"Come," he called.

His smile faltered when Rory entered the chamber. "Where is Christy?"

"Entertaining Camerons. She sent me to tell ye they await ye in the hall."

"Did they say what they wanted?"

"Nay. With Camerons ye can never tell. Christy invited them to share our meal."

Sinjun spit out an oath. "Tell them I'll be right down."

Disgruntled at the untimely interruption, Sinjun entered the hall a short time later. Christy, Margot, and Rory were seated at the table with Calum, Donald, and an assortment of Camerons.

"I understand you wanted to speak with me," Sinjun said, seating himself beside Christy.

"Aye," Calum said. "We understand ye were nosing around Glenmoor village today."

"If you call inspecting my property nosing around, then, aye, I was doing just that. I intend to visit the Cameron, Ranald, and Mackenzie strongholds in the coming weeks."

Calum's furious gaze rested on Christy a moment before returning to Sinjun. " 'Tis true, then. We heard ye were settling in at Glenmoor for the winter."

Knowing it would annoy Calum, he placed his hand over Christy's. "Aye, 'tis my intention to remain for the birth of my child."

Calum's ruddy features grew mottled, and Sinjun tensed, waiting for the expected outburst. Mary and her helpers chose that moment to carry in trays of food. Calum dismissed Sinjun with an angry glare and fell upon the food with gusto.

Ravenous, Sinjun devoted the next hour to his stomach. He sampled oyster soup, roasted mutton, poached trout, hare, boiled root vegetables drenched in butter, and the inevitable bannocks. Dessert consisted of pudding made from apples. Sinjun ate generous portions of everything set before him, amazed at his appetite. At this rate he'd lose the slim figure the *ton* so admired.

Replete at last, he sat back and waited for the Cameron chieftain to air his grievances. He didn't have long to wait. Calum pushed to his feet and said, "Shall we continue our conversation in private, yer lordship?"

"Fine with me," Sinjun replied, scraping his chair back.

Christy rose. "We can converse right here." Immediately the hall cleared.

Calum sent Christy a disgruntled look. "What I have to say is for his lordship's ears. 'Tis no concern of yers."

Christy squared her shoulders. "As laird of the clan, 'tis my right to hear whatever it is you have to say to Lord Derby."

"Christy, I'm going to speak to Calum alone," Sinjun said, brooking no argument. "Let me handle this."

He could tell from her expression that his words upset her, but it couldn't be helped. She was pregnant; she didn't need the aggravation of Calum's anger. He was better equipped to handle Calum than a woman carrying a child.

"Don't tell me what to do, my lord," Christy hissed. "I have handled problems without your help before and will continue to do so after you're gone. My condition makes me no less capable."

"I'm here now, wife," Sinjun said, putting starch

into his words. " 'Tis my understanding that our marriage gives me authority to handle clan matters."

"I am still laird!" Christy charged. "You are here but one day and already you are trying to take over."

"Nevertheless, I will speak to Calum privately," he said, determined to persevere. " 'Tis been a long day. Go to bed."

He felt the scorching heat of her anger and tried to control his own. Didn't she know he was trying to help? He had shirked his duty to her for years, and while he was here he intended to make himself useful. After he returned to London she could do what she damn well pleased.

Sinjun remembered the study from his visit to Glenmoor for his wedding and thought it a good place for privacy. "The study will do," Sinjun said, motioning for Calum to follow.

Once inside, he lit a brace of candles and turned to face Calum. Though nearly of the same height, Calum was broader and more muscular.

"What is it that cannot be said in front of others?" Sinjun challenged.

"We want ye to leave the Highlands."

"Do you speak for the Ranalds, Mackenzies, and Macdonalds?"

"I believe they'll fall in line with the Camerons."

"I'm not going anywhere, Cameron. Not yet, anyway. This is my land. I've decided to take a hand in its management for as long as I'm here. I've already undertaken repairs in the Macdonald stronghold. What can I do to improve the Camerons' lot?"

"We want nothing from English dogs."

Sinjun's eyes narrowed. "What else have you come to say? Spit it out, man."

"Yer not wanted here. Christy should have wed a Highlander."

"A man like you?" Sinjun scoffed.

"Aye, a man like me. Ye care nothing for Glenmoor, ye never have. Ye collected yer dues and lived like a king on our sweat. Things were different when old Angus was laird. Then he died and Christy became his heir. Many of us wanted Christy to annul her marriage and wed me. The marriage was unconsummated, it would not have been difficult to end it. She told us she was going to London for that purpose. Instead she returned with a bairn in her belly. She says the bairn is the answer to our future."

"Perhaps she's right," Sinjun allowed. "One day my child will become the new laird."

"Och! The bairn is a Thornton, not a true Scotsman."

"Christy is a Macdonald," Sinjun reminded him. "She carries my child; there can be no annulment."

Calum's cold smile and threatening words gave ominous warning of his intent. "There are other ways to get what I want."

"You don't frighten me, Cameron. Christy is mine, you'll never have her."

"Yer staying then?"

"Aye, for the time being."

Calum's eyes narrowed. "Dinna say ye weren't warned, yer lordship. Highlanders havena forgotten their losses at Culloden. 'Tis a dangerous place for Englishmen. I'm giving ye fair warning. Protect yer back."

"Are you threatening me, Cameron?"

"Take it any way ye like," Calum growled.

"Good night to ye, Lord Derby." He stormed from the chamber.

Sinjun remained in the study, mulling over Calum's threats, long after Calum collected his kinsmen and left Glenmoor. Calum was a dangerous man, one who bore watching.

"Sinjun, are you still in there? Calum left a long time ago."

Sinjun started at the sound of Christy's voice. "Aye."

She walked into the chamber. "What are you doing?"

"Thinking."

"What did Calum want?"

Sinjun chose his words carefully, so as not to upset Christy. "Nothing that would interest you."

He could almost see the wheels in her brain working as she came to the correct conclusion. "He threatened you, didn't he?"

"He doesn't frighten me."

"He should. Calum is a vindictive man. He's never gotten over the fact that Grandfather chose a woman as his heir."

Sinjun pulled Christy into his arms, gratified when she didn't resist. "Don't worry about it, Christy. I can take care of myself. I've not wasted my entire life in useless pursuits. I took fencing lessons and boxing lessons and know how to protect myself."

"Not against the Camerons. They don't fight in gentlemanly ways. You're not to go anywhere without Rory. He'll protect your back."

"You worry too much," Sinjun said lightly as he grasped Christy's hand and led her back to the hall.

Rory and Margot were sitting beside the hearth, talking quietly, when they entered.

"What's amiss?" Rory asked, glancing from Sinjun to Christy. "What did Calum want?"

"Nothing important," Sinjun said.

"He threatened Sinjun," Christy contended. "You're not to let Lord Derby out of your sight, Rory. Do whatever is necessary to protect him. Calum is destroying the clan with his jealousy and threats."

"Ye can depend on me, Christy," Rory proclaimed. "I'll keep yer husband alive for ye."

"You are all taking Calum too seriously," Sinjun argued. "But I'll be glad for your company, Rory."

"So be it," Rory said. "Come along, Margot, 'tis late."

"Do ye need me tonight, Christy?" Margot asked.

"No, go to bed, Margot. Rory is right. 'Tis late."

"I'll give Christy whatever help she needs," Sinjun said. Margot gave him a startled look before she turned and accompanied her handfast husband from the hall.

"Good night, Sinjun," Christy said. "I can manage just fine by myself."

"It would please me to help you undress."

"But not me," Christy muttered beneath her breath.

Ignoring her, Sinjun swept her into his arms and strode up the stairs.

"Sinjun! Put me down."

Christy could do little but cling to him as he negotiated the narrow stairs. When he finally did put her down, they were inside her chamber. He let her slide down his body, giving her the full benefit of his aroused body. Christy smothered a moan.

Didn't he know what he was doing to her? How could she possibly resist Sinjun's seduction if he continued to batter her senses?

His hands went to the fastenings on the front of her gown. "I'm rather good at this, if you recall."

She recalled every moment she'd ever spent with Sinjun. Too well, unfortunately. She shoved his hands aside. "I don't need help."

Sinjun's heated gaze shifted from her face to her stomach. "I want to see you. I have a right. I am your husband."

"How nice of you to remember." Her words dripped with sarcasm. "Too bad you didn't know that when you made me your mistress. Or when Lord Sin was having a grand time earning his reputation."

Sinjun scowled. She made him sound like a man without any redeeming qualities, a man she didn't admire. Hell, he didn't even admire himself these days. What had happened? He had as much reason as Christy to be angry, if not more. "You should have told me who you were," he shot back. "I want you, that hasn't changed."

"Are you offering me forever, Sinjun?" Christy challenged, her voice trembling with emotion. "Will you be around to guide our bairn to adulthood? Will you be faithful to me? Will I ever be more to you than a convenience? A woman to warm your bed until you return to London and your decadent ways?"

"I honestly don't know," Sinjun said bluntly. "I could say you'll always be the only woman I'll ever want, but, dammit, I don't know. In fact, I feel that way right now, but Lord Sin doesn't have the best reputation when it comes to matters of the heart. Can you accept me on those terms?"

Tears clogged Christy's throat. Didn't he know how much she wanted him, how she ached to hear him say he loved her? Why couldn't he be the kind of man she needed?

"I thought you were angry with me."

"I was, but 'tis difficult to remain angry at the woman who is carrying my heir. Lying to me was wrong, we both know that. But after careful consideration, I see no reason why we should deny ourselves something we both want and enjoy."

Christy stiffened. "How do you know what *I* want? You never so much as thought about me until I came to you in London." She touched her stomach. "I already have what I wanted from you." She turned away.

"Dammit, don't turn away from me!"

He pulled her against him. He kissed her nape. His heat scorched her. She absorbed his musky scent through her pores and felt herself softening. She knew she shouldn't, but when he touched her, her bones melted and her resistance wilted. Succumbing to Sinjun's seduction would not be in her best interest, but sweet Virgin, the temptation was irresistible. She was not made of stone.

His hands were on her breasts, cupping them, stroking her nipples. She flushed when she felt them pebble against his palms and knew Sinjun felt it too, for she heard a chuckle rumble from his chest. His sex stirred against her bottom, and she had to forcibly restrain the urge to press backward into the hard ridge of his desire. When his hands splayed across her stomach, she went utterly still as he explored the mound where her bairn grew.

"I want to see you naked," Sinjun whispered against her ear. "I want to see where my child is growing."

His hands returned to the fastenings on her gown. He undid the first button, then a second. She watched his clever hands manipulate the fastenings and remembered how swiftly he had undressed her in the past . . . and how eager she had been to undress him.

"You can look," she said, "but nothing more. I can't risk having my heart torn from me when you leave."

His hands stilled. "What about me? Did you ever consider what your leaving did to me?"

She shook her head. She hadn't thought it would have mattered to Lord Sin. She assumed he would have had another woman waiting to take her place.

"Damn you!" he cursed, turning her roughly in his arms. "I wondered if you were carrying my child and didn't like the idea of another man claiming him. I drank to forget, lost money in the seediest gambling hells in London and haunted Covent Gardens for a woman I hoped could make me forget you. Nothing helped." He gave her a gentle shake. "Nothing, do you hear me? Julian carped at me constantly about my excesses. You did that to me, Christy. You! What do you think of that?"

Christy blanched. It hadn't occurred to her that Sinjun would miss her as much as she missed him. Not Lord Sin, a man who avoided commitment and shunned responsibility.

"I . . . had no idea. I didn't like myself much for what I did to you, but I feared you'd avoid me like the plague if you knew I was your wife. You forget, Sinjun, I was privy to your thoughts during our time together. You didn't mind being married as long as your wife remained where she couldn't interfere in your private affairs. You weren't about to mend your wicked ways."

"Did you care for me at all? Or was everything about our affair a lie?" Sinjun asked.

How can he be so dense? Christy wondered. Were all his experiences with women so shallow that he couldn't tell when a woman truly cared? "I cared, Sinjun, too much. 'Tis why I can't let you seduce me. Were I to care for you more than I do now, 'twould tear me apart when you leave me. That's why I asked if you were ready to settle down and be a husband to me and a father to our bairn. Without assurances, I cannot let myself love you."

Something inside Sinjun stirred. Conscience? Suddenly he wanted to become the kind of man Christy needed. "I can try, sweetheart. We have all winter. Give me a reason to change my ways. Let me love you. Give me a chance to be what you want."

She stared into his eyes. They were utterly black, utterly determined. With a cry of exultation, he swept her into his arms.

The feel of her warm flesh forced the tightening in his groin into full erection. The front of her dress was gaping open, and he jerked it down over her shoulders, then yanked the tape holding her shift. Her breasts were larger, her nipples darker. He lowered her to the bed and followed her down.

He kissed her eyelids and the tip of her nose, while he caressed the smooth white flesh of her breasts. Moments before his mouth claimed hers, he looked into her eyes and read eagerness and mounting desire. He prodded her mouth open and wrote love notes with his tongue. He was starved for her taste, her sweetness. He kissed her until she was trembling beneath him. When he lifted his mouth and stared into her eyes, he saw his own reflection, and something else. Something he'd never seen, nor looked for, in the eyes of women he'd bedded. It was so stunning, so unexpected, that he feared to give it a name.

"Christy . . ." There was something he wanted to say, but he couldn't find the words.

He groaned when she dug her hands in his scalp and brought his mouth down to hers again. He kissed her long and passionately, sucking her tongue into his mouth and then giving her his. She sighed when he broke off the kiss. Sinjun merely smiled and slid his mouth down to her breasts. He licked her sensitive nipples, and she whispered his name, arching her back to offer more of herself.

"Too damn many clothes," he whispered as he raised his head from her breasts and made swift work of her clothing. When she was naked, he sat back on his heels and stared at her.

She tried to cover her stomach with her hands, but he pushed them aside. "No, don't try to hide yourself from me." Reverently he ran his fingertips over her distended stomach. She wasn't large enough, he thought, and vowed to make her eat more for the sake of their child.

"The bairn is small yet," she said shyly. "She will grow during the next four and a half months."

Sinjun's elegant brows shot upward. "She?"

"I'm hoping for a daughter."

Did he detect a hint of challenge in her voice? He spanned her hipbones, shaking his head in dismay. "You're too narrow. I'm a big man. Are you sure you're capable of birthing this child?"

" 'Tis rather late to question my ability to deliver. I'm determined to have this child."

"Aye, I know. You're beautiful. More beautiful than the first time I saw you." He lowered his head and kissed her stomach.

She appeared surprised. "I don't disgust you? Most men can't stand the sight of their pregnant wives."

"Do I act like you disgust me? Your body is lovelier than I remember. I'll be careful. Let me know if I do anything to hurt you."

"Why are you being so nice? When you arrived you acted as if you couldn't stand the sight of me."

"Each in our own way, we must bear the burden of guilt for our past actions."

"I have little faith in you, Sinjun. I warn you, I'm not letting you steal my heart; you cannot be trusted with it. Come spring, Lord Sin will hie himself back to his decadent life in London."

Sinjun supposed he deserved that, but it still hurt to have his sins laid bare before him. "I can't promise it won't happen just as you say, but I can say with complete honesty that you are the only woman in my life right now."

"There has *never* been another man in my life," Christy whispered against his lips.

He kissed her hard, then rose quickly and began pulling off his clothing, ignoring the flying buttons and ripped material in his haste to render himself as naked as Christy. Then he covered her with his body, gazing intently into her expressive green eyes.

She wrapped her long legs around him, groaning in frustration when he made no move to enter her. Instead, he trailed his mouth down her throat to her breast, sucking a ripe nipple into his mouth.

Then his mouth moved lower, to her waist, her belly, trailing burning kisses down her trunk until he found her center. A jolting thrill of pleasure danced through her body, searing and shocking and wonderful. She gasped, arching upward into his caress.

When his tongue stroked her there, she moaned and thrashed wildly against the heat of his mouth as waves of sensation rocketed through her. His tongue parted her, explored the moist folds, dipped into her heat. The tension that had been building inside her uncoiled in a burst of ecstasy, the explosion rendering her mindless and boneless.

When she floated back to reality, she saw Sinjun leaning over her, gazing into her unfocused eyes. "Open for me, sweetheart." His eyes were so dark, so drenched in desire, that she felt herself drowning in them. Her legs parted, and he pushed inside her. "Tell me if I hurt you."

Hurt her? The pleasure of having him inside her again was so incredibly wonderful that she nearly swooned. She wrapped her arms and legs around him, meshing their bodies; nothing had ever felt so right, so complete. His hardness filled her, possessed her, enchanted her. Her hips rose upward to meet his slow, deep thrusts, drawing him deeply inside her.

She heard him whisper her name, heard his long drawn out sigh, and felt him grow and throb within her. And it began again, that feeling of helplessness, that swiftly gathering heat that drained the strength from her limbs and scalded her body, that sweet, intense feeling she couldn't contain.

"Christy, come now, love . . . now." His voice sounded hoarse, as if his throat were raw.

She felt his body convulse, felt his sex expand and contract inside her, and her body shattered around him.

"Christy, are you all right?"

She was floating, lost somewhere in that blissful

void where pleasure had taken her. She heard his voice as if from a great distance.

"Sweetheart, was I too rough? Forgive me. I didn't hurt the baby, did I?"

Somewhere in the fog of her mind she registered Sinjun's concern and smiled. He sounded as if he truly cared about her and her bairn.

"Thank God," Sinjun said when she opened her eyes.

"You weren't too rough," Christy said on a sigh. "It's been so long . . ."

He gave her a disarming grin. "Much too long. No other woman makes me feel like you do."

Christy stared at him, stunned. "No other woman?" He must have had dozens. "Surely you jest. You've had scores of women more experienced than I."

"Scores," Sinjun agreed, kissing the tip of her nose.

"Men aren't interested in their wives that way."

"True."

"Why are you being so agreeable?"

"I'm an agreeable fellow."

"Sinjun, be serious. Tell me why you're helping the crofters."

"Now?"

"What better time?"

"I want to love you again."

"Now?"

He threw her words back at her. "What better time?"

He loved her slowly, with such tender care that Christy felt truly cherished. His thrusts were slow and measured, his excitement carefully banked, and then Christy's patience snapped. Grasping his hips, she pulled him deeper, showing him without words what she wanted from him. Only then did he unleash the full potential of his passion, thrusting them both to completion. Afterward, she spooned herself against his back and dozed.

She was nearly asleep when she felt a tiny fluttering in her abdomen. An unmistakable movement. She cried out, waking Sinjun. He reared up, his eyes wild as he sought the reason for Christy's alarm.

"What is it? Are you ill?"

"Feel," she said, grasping his hand and bringing it to her stomach.

"Feel what?"

"Wait."

The bairn moved again. Sinjun must have felt it, for his hand tensed and his eyes widened with pleasure.

"Is that what I think it is?"

"Aye. Our bairn. 'Tis the first sign of life I've felt."

The flutter came one more time before the baby settled down. Christy thought it appropriate that her child's father was with her the first time she felt life. She wondered if he was as awed as she by their bairn's first feeble movement.

"Sinjun."

"Aye."

"I know you don't want this child as desperately as I do, but I hope you won't close your mind against her."

Sinjun was silent a long time. Then he said, "I never gave it much thought. Lord knows I'm not the best person to preach responsibility, but when you hatched your plan to carry my child, was it because you truly wanted a child or because you needed an heir for Glenmoor?"

Christy stiffened. Sinjun had come too close to the truth for comfort.

"The truth, Christy," Sinjun prodded.

How could she explain that his bairn was the clan's future without sounding cold-blooded? Before she'd met Sinjun and fallen in love with him, giving Glenmoor an heir and thwarting Calum had been her primary goal. But the moment she learned she carried Sinjun's child, everything had changed. She loved Sinjun's bairn. Fiercely. She wanted the babe. Desperately. Her bairn would be a part of Sinjun. The only part she would ever have. How could she explain that to Sinjun?

"I cannot lie. At first, having your bairn was something I needed to do for the clan. To save Glenmoor for future generations. Later, your child became very real to me and I realized I wanted it for myself."

Sinjun chewed that over and realized he had acted irresponsibly in London. He bore half the blame for making a baby. He could have taken precautions instead of agreeing to the terms Christy had set forth for their affair, but at the time he'd been crazed with lust and would have agreed to anything Christy wanted.

"Don't worry, Sinjun," Christy said, rushing into the void left by his silence. "Your bairn will never lack for love. Nor will I make demands on you, if that's what you're concerned about. We don't need you. You can leave Glenmoor without regrets."

Bloody hell! Hearing that he wasn't needed did nothing for Sinjun's deflated ego.

Chapter 8

❧∽◡◯◯◡∼

Sinjun was up at dawn. Christy was sleeping peacefully, so he tried not to awaken her as he tiptoed from her chamber and returned to his own room to wash, shave, and dress. Rory was already in the hall when he arrived. He seated himself at the table just as Mary bustled in with Rory's oats. She glared at Sinjun, her usual cheerful mood replaced by a sour look.

"What will it be this morning, yer lordship?"

Sinjun eyed the oats Rory seemed to be enjoying and swallowed his distaste. "Perhaps I'll try oats this morning, Mary. And maybe a couple of eggs to go with it."

Mary's mouth twitched suspiciously, but she left too quickly for Sinjun to tell if she had actually smiled.

"Ye made Mary happy this morning, yer lordship," Rory said between mouthfuls of oats.

"If we're to work closely together, Rory, perhaps you should call me Sinjun."

" 'Tisn't right," Rory muttered.

"It's right if I say it is."

138

"What is right?" Margot asked as she slid into a seat beside her husband.

"His lordship asked me to call him Sinjun," Rory explained.

She eyed Sinjun with a healthy dose of suspicion. "Why would ye do that, yer lordship?"

"All this 'your lordship' is daunting. My friends call me Sinjun, or Derby, and I'd feel more at home if both you and Rory called me Sinjun."

"If ye say so, yer . . . Sinjun," Margot said, clearly uncomfortable using his name. "Where is Christy? She's usually down before now."

Sinjun assumed an innocent look. "Still abed. She must have had a restless night."

Margot and Rory exchanged knowing looks, then Margot shot to her feet. "Perhaps I should go up and see if she's all right." She rushed off in a flurry of petticoats.

Sinjun was all too aware of Rory's censuring look. "Spit it out, man. If you've anything to say, get it off your chest."

"Verra well, yer lordship, I mean Sinjun. We all love Christy. None of us wants to see her hurt."

Sinjun saw Mary approaching. He waited until she set his bowl of oats and plate of eggs before him and marched away before answering. "Christy carries my child. What makes you think I'd harm her?"

"I ken how angry ye were with her when ye arrived at Glenmoor."

"I've forgiven her for tricking me. Perhaps I deserved it. Ask Christy if you don't believe me."

"Ask me what?"

Sinjun swiveled around at the sound of her voice. She and Margot had entered the hall so quietly that he hadn't heard them. She looked tired but radiant nevertheless. Pregnancy agreed with her.

"I'm having the devil's own time convincing your kinsman that I mean you no harm."

"Sinjun isn't going to hurt me, Rory," Christy said. "At least not physically," she added in an undertone that didn't reach Rory.

Sinjun heard and decided to ignore it. Instead, he lifted a spoonful of gruel to his mouth and swallowed before he had time to think about it. Though the taste almost gagged him, he managed to keep it down.

"Sinjun! You're eating oats," Christy exclaimed, clearly amused. "I thought you didn't like oats."

"Sometimes one has to swallow things one doesn't like," he said as he choked down another spoonful of gruel. Somehow he managed to finish the entire contents of the bowl, washing it down with generous gulps of ale. Then he attacked the eggs, which were more to his liking.

"I thought we'd inspect the sheep today," Sinjun said, eager to enjoy the fine, brisk day. It had been a long time since he'd risen early and ridden for the pure joy of it in so invigorating an environment.

"Bring something along to eat in case we don't make it back in time for the noon meal, Rory," Sinjun added as he scraped his chair back.

"Dress warmly," Christy advised. "And watch your back for Camerons," she added.

Sinjun sent her a cocky grin. "I have my bodyguard, remember?"

The hills and moors were white with frost; Sinjun's breath hung in the air like heavy mist. The day was dismal with the promise of snow, but Sinjun's exuberance couldn't be dimmed this morning. Christy had spent the night in his arms.

They found the sheep huddled together in a sheltered valley. Sinjun reined in his horse and took pleasure in watching them. Though he'd had nothing to do with their care, pride swelled his chest. The flock was a large one, several hundred, he estimated, and each and every one wore a thick coat of wool. Come spring and shearing, profit from the sale of the fleece would be substantial. Sinjun had paid little heed to business in the past, but he did know that the price of wool hadn't slackened in several years and wondered why Sir Oswald had said otherwise. It just didn't make sense. Somewhere in the far reaches of his brain he began to suspect that Sir Oswald might be lining his own pockets while robbing the estate and its shepherds of their fair share.

Sinjun made an effort to speak with the shepherds. They answered his questions readily enough but appeared wary of his interest. He learned that not all the sheep belonged to Glenmoor. Some were owned by clansmen and tended along with Sinjun's flock. After he'd seen how well the flock was being cared for, Sinjun decided to visit the Ranald stronghold.

"The Ranalds are loyal to Laird Christy," Rory explained. "They accepted Laird Christy without question. Tavis Ranald, the clan's chieftain, and old Angus Macdonald had been fast friends. Except for a few of the younger, more militant Ranalds, they are farmers and sheepherders, unlike the thieving Camerons, who make their living stealing their neighbors' livestock."

"I thought the Camerons were your allies," Sinjun said. He would never understand these Highlanders and the workings of the clans.

"Aye. They are our allies but we know better than to turn our backs on them. 'Tis no secret that Calum Cameron expected to become laird when Angus left no male heir except for some distantly related Macdonalds like myself. They complained bitterly when Angus named Christy their overlord. There was even talk of joining the Campbells, our sworn enemies. But nothing ever came of that."

"Forget the Camerons," Sinjun said. " 'Tis the Ranalds I'm interested in now. Is that their village up ahead?"

The Ranald stronghold consisted of an assortment of stone cottages not far from the Macdonald stronghold. As Sinjun expected, his appearance caused quite a stir. A sturdy old man who, Sinjun imagined, would have been a force to be reckoned with at one time, stepped out of his cottage to greet his visitors.

He nodded to Rory before directing his words at Sinjun. "I am Tavis Ranald, chieftain of Clan Ranald. What business do ye have with the Ranalds, yer lordship?"

"You know who I am?" Sinjun asked.

"Aye. I was at Glenmoor the day ye arrived. We heard ye were staying. Is it true?"

There had been so many people gathered in the hall the day Sinjun had arrived he hadn't had time to sort them out yet. Besides, he'd only had eyes for Christy that day. "I'm staying for the time being," Sinjun allowed. "I wanted to thank you for defending Laird Christy when the Camerons tried to force a rebellion."

"I wouldna flout Angus's wishes. Laird Christy is his granddaughter and that was good enough for Ranalds."

Sinjun had made a hasty inspection of the cottages as he'd ridden in, and he'd noticed they were in no better repair than those at Glenmoor village.

"As I speak, workmen are repairing the cottages at Glenmoor village. I couldn't help noticing that some minor repairs wouldn't be remiss here. After the work is finished at Glenmoor I could send the workmen here, at my expense, of course."

Tavis's eyes narrowed. "Why would ye do that, yer lordship? To my knowledge, ye have never cared for yer wife or yer holdings. Why the sudden change of heart?"

Sinjun knew these Highlanders had no reason to trust him. The Crown had taken their land, forbidden them to wear kilts or play the bagpipe, and married the daughters of their noblemen to Englishmen. He knew he had instilled scant trust in these Highlanders throughout the years. He had ignored his Scottish wife and taken little interest in his holdings.

"Let's just say it's time I devoted some attention to my holdings."

"Did ye mean what ye said about the quarterly levies? 'Twould ease our burden considerably if we didna have to pay them."

"I meant every word, Tavis Ranald. I've asked my brother to look into the recent increases. I'm beginning to suspect there is more involved than meets the eye. I intend to adjust the future levies as soon as I hear from Lord Mansfield."

"Would ye and Rory like to take a bite with me and me wife, yer lordship? We'd be pleased to have both of ye share our meal. Nothing fancy, but Meg is a good cook."

"What say you, Rory?" Sinjun asked, pleased with Ranald's invitation. It was the first tenuous sign that he might find acceptance among his tenants.

"My stomach is touching my backbone. A bite to eat wouldna be remiss," Rory said, grinning. "Meg Ranald is the best cook around. Dinna tell Mary I said that"

Sinjun laughed. "Mary wouldn't believe anything I said. I don't think she likes me."

The meal was simple but ample and well prepared. Cold mutton, coarse bread, boiled potatoes. Everything tasted so good, that Sinjun embarrassed himself by cleaning his plate and asking for more. He supposed the cold air had sparked his appetite.

Before Sinjun and Rory left, Tavis agreed to let Sinjun finance repairs to the cottages. They parted on friendly terms, considering he was an Englishman.

After they left the Ranald holdings, Sinjun decided to visit Glenmoor village. Repairs were well underway when they arrived. Rory was greeted with enthusiasm, and Sinjun, with cautious optimism. A few shy smiles were directed at him by the ladies whose homes would receive new roofs and other amenities, and Sinjun considered that a very good beginning.

On impulse, Sinjun dismounted, hefted a bale of thatch over his shoulder, and carried it up a ladder to one of the workmen. When Rory saw what Sinjun was doing, he joined in. They didn't leave until the first glimmer of darkness fell over the land. Then, tired, aching in every muscle yet feeling a sense of accomplishment he'd never felt before, Sinjun returned to Glenmoor.

A contingent of Camerons was waiting for him in the hall. Sinjun groaned aloud. Camerons were the last people he wanted to see right now. He wanted to soak in a tub, eat, then make love to Christy. His loins stirred and his breeches suddenly felt too tight. Thinking about Christy always brought the same heady response, and he wondered why Lady Violet, or any other woman of his acquaintance, had never affected him in the same way.

"Ye visited the Ranalds," Calum charged when Sinjun strode into the hall. Sinjun's nostrils flared with jealousy when he saw Calum sitting beside Christy. Nor did he like the way Calum looked at Christy. Too possessive, for one thing.

"Aye, does that bother you?"

"Yer turning our clansmen against the Camerons."

"I don't recall mentioning the Camerons in the course of my conversation with Tavis Ranald. Is there something else you wanted to discuss?"

"Dinna come snooping around the Cameron stronghold," Calum warned. "We dinna want ye there."

"Aren't the Macdonalds, Camerons, Ranalds, and Mackenzies allies? Isn't Christy your overlord?" Sinjun asked.

"Aye, 'tis true enough. 'Tis yer lordship we feel no kinship with. We want nothing from ye, Derby. Highlanders are a proud breed. We want no reminders of our defeat at Culloden."

"That was fifteen years ago, Cameron," Sinjun reminded him.

"We have long memories," Calum retorted. "The day our land is returned to us is the day we'll stop hating Englishmen."

With a nod to his clansmen, Calum stormed from the hall. Sinjun glanced at Christy, saw her troubled look, and went to her.

"What did he say to you?" he asked. "If he threatened you in any way—"

"Nothing has changed. He wants power and is angry because I didn't seek an annulment in London. He considered an unconsummated marriage no marriage at all and was prepared to take me by force. With me as his wife, Calum would be in a position to lead an uprising. He never dreamed I would return with your bairn in my belly. Your heir is a threat to his ambitions."

"Forget Calum. The Ranalds are still your allies. You have nothing to fear from Calum."

"You don't know Calum, Sinjun. You should heed his warnings. 'Tis not too late to return to London before snow and ice make the roads impassable."

"Do you want me to go?"

Sinjun held his breath. For the first time in his life he felt needed. Lord Sin was but a distant memory. St.John Thornton was a different man, living in another time and place. Today he'd used muscles he hadn't even known he had, and it felt damn good. Food had never tasted so good, simple though it was, and the air had never smelled so fresh, not even at his country estate in Kent.

Christy stared at him, finding nothing to remind her of Lord Sin, London's darling. What she saw was a man whose face was windburned and ruddy from the cold. He had lost his London pallor, and Christy had never seen Sinjun eat with such obvious enjoyment.

"Ye should have seen Sinjun work today," Rory confided. "He lifted bales of thatch all afternoon. I'll bet his muscles are aching. Mine are, and I'm no stranger to hard work."

Sinjun frowned. "You make me sound as if I

spent my entire life in useless pursuits."

Christy smothered a laugh. "Didn't you?"

A slow smile lit his face. "I suppose you're right, though I did ride, fence, and box to tone my muscles."

"Ye'll be wanting a hot bath, Rory," Margot said. "Come along, I'll see to it."

"Ask the kitchen boys to carry up a tub for Lord Derby," Christy called after them.

"Set it up in Christy's room before the fire," Sinjun added. "And ask Mary if she has any liniment for sore muscles."

Christy cocked an eyebrow at him. "Just because we shared a bed last night doesn't mean we're going to do it every night. I meant what I said, Sinjun. If you can't be the kind of husband and father I need, then I can't let our relationship become important to me."

"Many husbands and wives live apart. 'Tis a way of life."

That wasn't what Christy wanted to hear. "Is that Lord Sin talking?"

"Christy, I'm not going to change overnight. Suffice it to say I'm content for the time being. I love seeing you ripen with our child, and I vow I'm eager to see him enter the world."

"Her," Christy countered, notching her chin upward. "I'm having a lassie."

She had decided long ago that she wasn't going to have a boy. Sinjun might take it into his head to remove his heir from Glenmoor and raise him in England. The thought of being separated from her child was painful.

"If you say so. Shall we go up to your chamber?" Sinjun said, offering his arm. "I can't wait to soak in that tub. I hope Mary is cooking something good, I've worked up such an appetite."

Sinjun's ravenous appetite amazed Christy, as did his penchant for hard work. She'd never known Sinjun to do any type of physical labor in London. Fencing, boxing, and riding had kept his figure trim and athletic, but the kind of work he'd engaged in today could bulk up his body quickly, especially if his appetite remained as sharp as it had been the last few days. She smiled to herself, imagining how the ladies would react to a Lord Sin with bulging muscles and ruddy complexion. They'd adore his newly acquired physique, she decided. He'd be a welcome change to his foppish, pallid peers.

"What's that smile mean?" Sinjun asked.

Christy paused at the top landing to catch her breath. "I just had an amusing thought. It wouldn't interest you."

"Are you all right?" Sinjun asked. "I should have carried you."

"I'm not helpless, just pregnant. You'd best hurry before your bath gets cold."

The tub sat before the hearth, just like Sinjun ordered. Soap, cloths, and towels lay nearby. Christy turned away as Sinjun threw off his clothing and sank into the water.

"Will you scrub my back?"

"I thought I'd go downstairs and see if Mary needs help with supper," she hedged.

He handed her the cloth. "I need you more than Mary does."

Christy sincerely doubted that. "Very well. But I'm just going to scrub your back. You're a charming rogue, Sinjun, and I'm aware of every one of your tricks."

She soaped the cloth and moved behind him. "Lean forward," she murmured.

He complied with alacrity. When she finished, she dropped the cloth into the water, straightened, and, with her hands at the small of her back, stretched her cramped muscles. Sinjun must have noticed, for he became immediately concerned.

"What's wrong? Is it the baby?"

Christy would have given the world to believe Sinjun truly cared about her and her child. "I'm fine. The child grows heavy inside me, and sometimes my back aches when I'm weary."

"Sit by the fire until I've finished my bath. There's something I wanted to talk to you about anyway."

Against her better judgment, Christy perched on a bench in front of the hearth, her eyes carefully averted from the man in the tub.

"I noticed the children in the village are ill-clothed for the winter," Sinjun began.

Her gaze swung around to settle on his face, her surprise obvious. "You noticed that?"

"Aye. That and more."

"I usually provide material for new clothing when I receive my yearly stipend. This year I received less than usual. Sir Oswald said you had cut my allowance. I had to be very careful how I spent the money, and there was wasn't enough left to purchase material."

Scowling, Sinjun surged from the tub, dripping water on the floor as he wrapped the towel around his flanks. "I don't recall cutting your allowance. Julian made sure I was generous with you. It seems Sir Oswald has much to account for." He sent a sharp look at Christy, who was massaging her back. "Does your back still hurt?"

"A little."

"Lie on the bed."

"What?"

"Just do it, Christy. I'm not going to hurt you."

He was so insistent that she didn't argue. She lay on her side, her head resting on her folded hands. "Now what?"

"Just relax."

She felt his hands move down her back, rubbing the taut muscles rising along the valley of her spine. It felt so good that she closed her eyes and moaned with pleasure. He continued to massage away the ache, his hands firm yet gentle upon her, until she was so relaxed she felt as limp as a child's rag doll.

"Don't go to sleep," Sinjun said.

"Of course not," she drawled sleepily. "Shall I rub liniment on your sore muscles?"

"There's only one muscle that needs soothing right now," he whispered into her ear.

Christy's eyes flew open when she felt his hands skim along the outsides of her thighs, drawing her skirts up with them. She jerked reflexively when he bent and placed a kiss on her bare bottom.

"Sinjun! What are you doing?" She rolled over on her back.

"Kissing your bottom."

She tried to sit up, but he straddled her legs, pinning her to the bed. "They're waiting supper for us."

"Let them wait."

He released her legs and lifted her to her knees, kneeling behind her. She choked back a cry when she felt his shaft stroke her buttocks, then dip into the moist crevice between her thighs. She couldn't help herself. Her hips pressed against his loins, and she felt his body respond with an instant, powerful arousal.

"Let me know if I hurt you." His voice was gruff with desire as he opened her with his fingers and slowly entered her. A soft sigh hissed through her teeth. Then he thrust himself to the hilt. She groaned, grinding her hips against his loins.

Suddenly he pulled out and sat back on his heels. She gave a cry of protest and collapsed onto her stomach.

"I'm sorry. 'Tis too hard on you," Sinjun said, panting. "I want you so damn bad I forget you're increasing. Turn around, sweetheart. Let me undress you so we can do this properly."

Dazed, Christy merely stared at him as he skillfully rid her of her clothing. Scant moments later he covered her with his body, kissing her, ravaging her mouth with desperate need. She kissed him back, her arms circling his neck, her legs parting to take him between them.

He covered her breasts with his hands and dropped his lips to her arching throat. His lips slid downward, taking a pouting nipple in his mouth and suckling her.

"Sinjun, please."

"You ask so prettily, how can I deny you anything?" Sinjun said as he placed her legs over his shoulders and pushed himself inside her.

Surrendering completely, Christy gave herself up to loving. She would have flung herself wildly against him if Sinjun hadn't been in complete control of both himself and her.

Sinjun was encouraged by the sounds of her pleasure and the sight of her lovely face glazed with passion. He squeezed her buttocks, suckled her nipples; he couldn't seem to get enough of this complex woman who carried his child. He tried to control his lust but it utterly defeated him as he drove himself deep inside her. He watched her closely for any sign of discomfort and was thrilled to see that she was as lost to passion as he. Her eyes were half closed, her expression suffused with joy. He pistoned his hips against her, clenched his teeth and concentrated on giving pleasure. He heard her cry out, a sharp, piercing sound of ecstasy, felt her spasm around him, shattering his control. Everything he had to give drained out of him into her body. Had it been within his power, he would have given her more.

Long minutes passed before he found the energy to lift himself away from her. She turned toward him, her eyes closed, her face so pale a spear of panic shot through him. "Did I hurt you?"

She shook her head. "No, you didn't hurt me. I'm tired . . . so tired."

He reached down and pulled the blanket over her. "Shall I send a tray up to you?"

"Aye, that would be nice. Tell Margot I won't need her tonight."

Sinjun was quiet throughout supper, and no one seemed inclined to disturb him. He'd seen to a tray for Christy, made her excuses, and proceeded to eat with good appetite. Afterward he didn't linger in the hall. He bid Margot and Rory good night and climbed the stairs to Christy's chamber. He frowned when he saw her untouched tray on the nightstand. But she was sleeping so soundly he didn't have the heart to disturb her. Obviously she needed sleep more than she needed food.

Undressing quickly, he slid into bed beside her and took her into his arms. Without awakening, she heaved a sigh and curled up against him.

The following weeks flew by. Christy wasn't the only one who put on weight. Sinjun found he enjoyed physical activity and joined Rory and the workers nearly every day. His bulging muscles grew apace with his appetite. His torso broadened, his arms strengthened; he had never looked so fit or felt so healthy.

Christy had let out his clothing so many times that he finally had to ask Rory to loan him something sturdy to work in. When the first snow arrived in early December, the cottages were in good repair. Sinjun took great pride in knowing that no villager would suffer because of inadequate housing. Christy had purchased blankets and woolen material from traveling peddlers and distributed them to her clansmen. Since Calum had been so adamantly opposed to accepting anything from an Englishman, the Camerons weren't as snug and warm as the Macdonalds, Ranalds, and Mackenzies.

Sinjun had taken it upon himself to hire additional help for Glenmoor. Each day four young kinswomen arrived at Glenmoor, and each evening they returned to their homes in the village. December arrived on the wings of a fierce snowstorm, and plans for a Christmas celebration were begun. All the clansmen were invited to participate, and Sinjun promised to provide the Yule log.

Though Sinjun still shared Christy's bed, he tried to keep his loving as gentle as possible, and many nights he just held her without making love. Her body was heavy now with his child, and he knew that before long it would be injurious to their child to continue sexual relations.

Christmas Day dawned cold and gray. The Yule log burned merrily in the hearth, holly decorated the hall, and spiced ale was consumed in great quantities, creating a feeling of goodwill. Even the Camerons seemed on their best behavior. Sinjun had a gift for Christy and sought her out toward the end of the evening to give it to her.

She was sitting with Tavis Ranald's wife, and Sinjun motioned for her to attend him. She sent him a puzzled look but rose willingly enough and followed him from the hall into the study.

"Is something wrong, Sinjun?" Christy asked once they were alone.

"Sit down," Sinjun said, handing her into a comfortable chair. "I wanted to give you my gift without everyone gawking."

Christy's eyes lit up. "You have a gift for me?"

"Aye. I bought it in Inverness the day Rory and I went to buy building material." He opened the desk drawer, removed a velvet pouch, and placed it in her hand.

Christy unknotted the cord and spilled the contents into her palm. Her gasp of delight was all the thanks Sinjun needed.

"Sinjun! Emeralds! 'Tis too much." The necklace consisted of a large emerald suspended from a circlet of smaller emeralds.

"I can afford it. They match your eyes, and I wanted you to have them. Will you wear them?"

"Aye. Gladly." She handed him the necklace and turned her back. Sinjun placed the gems around her neck and secured the clasp, then he turned her to face him.

"They look beautiful on you."

"I have something for you," Christy said. "Wait here."

She was gone before Sinjun could reply. He wasn't expecting anything and wondered how and where she had obtained a gift for him. He didn't have long to wonder. She returned a few minutes later carrying a bulky, cloth-wrapped package. Smiling, she placed it in his hands.

"Go on, open it," she urged when he merely stared at her.

Sinjun didn't know why his hands were shaking. He'd received gifts before from beautiful women, but somehow they hadn't meant as much as this crudely wrapped gift from his wife. He set the package on the desk and carefully removed the wrapping. The breath caught in his throat when he saw what was inside—winter clothing fashioned to accommodate his newly acquired muscles. He drew forth woolen breeches, a crisp white shirt, and a woolen waistcoat. Also included was a tunic like the ones worn by the Highlanders. But that wasn't all. Beneath all the fine, warm clothing lay a velvet cloak lined in fur.

Sinjun was stunned. "Did you make these?"

"Aye. I bought the material from a peddler, and Rory trapped beaver for the cloak lining."

"When did you have time?'

"While you were working in the village. Margot helped. You assumed we were making baby clothes. We did make baby clothes, of course, but we made these in our spare time. I seem to have plenty of spare time since you hired extra help."

After that Sinjun couldn't have cared less about the Camerons, their disgruntled looks, or their threats. He couldn't wait to be alone with Christy. Tonight might be the last time they could love without endangering their child. According to Christy, their child would be born in early March. Sinjun knew the child's birth would require some decisions on his part, but he wasn't going to let anything destroy tonight.

Chapter 9

January ushered in a deep freeze. Sinjun spent long hours sitting before the hearth, drinking mulled wine and watching his wife sew the countless little garments that would clothe their child. And he grew restless. He knew Christy must have noticed his unrest, for he caught her staring at him with a somber look when she thought he wasn't looking.

He couldn't help thinking about the Season his friends were enjoying now in London; the fancy balls, the theater, the opera, the galas. It wasn't as if he had been unhappy these past few months, it was just that he didn't know if spending his life in the Scottish Highlands was what he wanted to do. Inactivity had given him too much time to wonder what he might be missing in London.

Shortly after Christmas a message arrived from Julian, hand delivered by John Coachman. After receiving Sinjun's earlier missive, Julian had delved into Sir Oswald's accounts and found that the bailiff they had all trusted had been skimming funds and illegally raising rents and taxes in order to keep an expensive mistress. Julian wrote that the man had been caught boarding a ship for France and was now in Newgate prison awaiting trial, and that he would notify Sinjun when the trial was to be held, for his testimony would be required. Julian also demanded to know why Sinjun had decided to remain in Scotland without a word of explanation.

Sinjun carefully worded his reply so as to reveal as little about Christy as possible. He wanted to tell Julian in person about Christy and his child, to watch his brother's expression when he placed his son and heir in Julian's arms. Despite Christy's desire to have a daughter, Sinjun felt strongly that he was going to have a son.

Sinjun told Julian he intended to remain at Glenmoor until early summer, unless he was needed before that for Sir Oswald's trial. He grinned to himself, imagining Julian's bewilderment when he read the reply. In the past, nothing had kept Sinjun from the gaiety of a London Season.

A thaw occurred in early February, and Sinjun decided he'd had his fill of idleness. He found Rory in the stables and suggested they ride out to see how the villagers were faring.

It felt damn good to have prime horseflesh beneath his thighs and a cold wind clearing the cobwebs from his brain. The sight of sheep huddled together for warmth brought a smile to Sinjun's lips. Months ago he would have scorned such peace and tranquility, if one could call living among volatile Highlanders peaceful.

It was just as they had stopped to watch the sheep that disaster struck. An arrow whizzed past Sinjun's ear. Rory called out a warning and reached for his bow, but the warning came too late. Moments later a second arrow sped from behind a stand of trees, this one lodging high in Sinjun's shoulder. Had he not heeded Rory's warning and crouched, it would have found its mark in his heart. Sinjun grasped his shoulder and hit the ground, his blood staining the dirt-encrusted snow.

The arrows ceased the moment Sinjun fell. The attackers had left as stealthily as they had come. Rory dismounted and crouched beside Sinjun, lifting him to inspect the damage.

Though awash in pain, Sinjun remained conscious. "What happened?"

"Camerons, I suspect. Can ye stand? I dinna want to take the arrow out yet until I ken how much damage occurred. I dinna want ye to bleed to death before I can get ye back to Glenmoor. Hang on, Sinjun, Mary will fix ye up all right and proper."

"Just get me on my horse," Sinjun said through gritted teeth.

Rory helped Sinjun stand, then boosted him onto his horse. The animal seemed to know his cooperation was needed, for he stood absolutely still as Sinjun anchored himself in the saddle.

"We'll take it slow," Rory said, grasping Sinjun's trailing reins and mounting his own horse.

Sinjun recalled little of the trip back to Glenmoor. Blood soaked through his tunic as he swayed drunkenly in the saddle. Though the pain was excruciating, he didn't believe the wound was life-threatening. He'd ducked at the right moment, thanks to Rory's warning. Apparently Calum Cameron was willing to commit murder to get rid of him. He knew Calum hated Englishmen, as did most of the Highlanders, but he never thought it would come to this. He'd begun to believe he had made inroads toward gaining the clan's trust.

"We're almost home, Sinjun," Rory said encouragingly.

Sinjun was beyond speech. He was slumped over his horse's neck, his eyes closed, his teeth gritted against the sharp bite of pain. The next thing he knew he was being lifted from his horse. Their entrance into the hall was greeted by a high-pitched wail. Christy? Then his mind went blank.

Christy saw Rory carrying Sinjun into the hall and couldn't stop the wail of despair that escaped her throat. Her first thought was that he was dead, that Calum had become impatient and killed him instead of waiting for him to leave on his own. She couldn't move, could only stare at the arrow protruding from his body.

Having heard Christy's scream, both Margot and Mary dropped what they were doing and rushed into the hall.

"What is it, lass?" Margot asked worriedly.

"Is it the bairn?" Mary wanted to know.

They saw Rory and Sinjun at the same time. "Lord save us," Mary said, crossing herself.

"What happened?" Margot asked, rushing forward to lend a hand.

"An arrow took him down," Rory said tersely. "Where do ye want him?"

"Take him up to our chamber," Christy said, finally finding her voice.

"I'll fetch me medicines and instruments," Mary said, turning briskly toward the kitchen.

"Dinna worry, Christy," Margot soothed, "ye know Mary is the best healer in the Highlands. She willna let Sinjun die."

"I must go to him," Christy said, waddling toward the stairs. "Oh, Margot, what if he dies?"

"He won't die. Dinna even think it."

Christy negotiated the stairs with surprising agility, considering her ungainly figure. Rory had placed Sinjun on the bed and was removing his boots when she entered the chamber. She hurried to the bed and took Sinjun's hand. He opened his eyes and tried to smile, but it turned into a grimace.

"Don't worry," he gasped. "I'm not going to die."

"I'll kill Calum," Christy hissed.

"Move aside," Mary said, bustling into the room. "Ye dinna undress him," she chided as she set her basket of medicinal supplies on the nightstand.

Rory moved instantly to comply. "Cut the material away from the arrow," she ordered.

While Rory and Christy stripped Sinjun and placed a sheet over his lower body, Mary laid out her needle, thread, salves, and bandages.

"Listen carefully, Rory," Mary instructed. "Dinna pull the arrow out until I tell ye to. Margot, fetch the whiskey." Margot hurried away, returning a few minutes later with a jug.

Mary lifted up Sinjun's head and placed the jug to his lips. "Drink, yer lordship. Yer gonna need it."

Christy watched Sinjun's throat work as he swallowed. Again and again Mary placed the jug to his lips, forcing him to drink, until it dribbled from his mouth and he could take no more. Mary nodded and set the jug within reach should she need it again. Then she nodded to Rory.

Rory grasped the shaft of the arrow and jerked it out in one smooth motion. Christy turned white when she heard Sinjun scream. She closed her eyes, and when she opened them, Mary was pouring whiskey into the raw wound, which was now bleeding freely.

"There's too much blood," Christy whispered, as close to fainting as she'd ever been.

" 'Tis not excessive," Mary replied, calmly threading a needle with fine silk. She handed Rory a pad of clean cloths and told him to press down upon the wound. "When the bleeding slows, I'll stitch up his lordship."

"Is he conscious?" Christy asked, hovering over Sinjun and wringing her hands.

"Aye, and a little drunk," Mary said. "Aren't ye, me fine lord?"

Sinjun opened one eye. It was unfocused. Christy's breath caught in her throat. He looked so comical that if the situation weren't so serious she'd be tempted to laugh.

"I'm gonna sew ye up now," Mary told a barely conscious Sinjun. "Yer a fine braw lad, yer lordship. Ye'll be up and about afore ye know it. Tomorrow I'll make ye a bowl of oats to strengthen ye."

Sinjun grimaced but said nothing as Mary prepared to stitch him up. Christy moved up beside Mary and took his hand. Rory stood on the other side of the bed and grasped Sinjun's shoulders to hold him in place for the first bite of the needle.

To Sinjun's credit, he neither flinched nor moved as Mary sutured his wound with neat stitches. Or maybe he was just too drunk to feel anything. When Mary was finished, she disinfected the wound again with whiskey and spread a salve made of lard and crushed marigolds. Then she swathed Sinjun's shoulder and part of his chest in bandages.

" 'Tis done," Mary said, stepping away. "He's a

lucky mon. Nothing vital was damaged. I'll brew a batch of valarian tea to dull the pain."

"What about infection?" Christy asked fearfully. She knew that wounds, no matter how minor, could become septic and kill. And Sinjun's wound was far from minor.

"Pray, child," Mary said. "Yer man is young and strong and there is no better antiseptic than good Scottish whiskey." She gave Christy a sharp look. "What about ye, lass? 'Tis close to yer time."

Christy gave her a wobbly smile. "I'm fine. I'll sit with Sinjun, I know you have duties."

"Nay, I'll sit with him," Margot offered.

"No," Christy persisted. "I'll call if I need you."

"If ye say so, lass. I'll bring up the valarian tea as soon as Mary brews it. Be sure and call if he starts thrashing around."

"I'll be fine," Christy said, waving Margot and Rory off.

Once they had left, Christy placed a hand on her distended belly and thought of her bairn. She couldn't wait to greet her little lassie. Her pregnancy had gone well. Agnes, the midwife from the village, had examined her and predicted an easy birth. Of course Christy knew danger existed—so many mothers and babies died from unknown causes—but she had every intention of delivering a healthy bairn and keeping her that way.

"Christy?"

Startled, Christy's thoughts shattered at the sound of Sinjun's voice.

"Are you in pain? Can I get you anything?"

"I can bear the pain."

"Mary is brewing valarian tea. That should help."

"Did Rory see who tried to kill me?"

"We think it was Calum Cameron."

"He's not going to get away with this unprovoked attack. When I'm recovered I'm going to report it to the English garrison at Inverness. Does that meet with your approval?"

Indecision rode Christy. She knew Calum was hotheaded and probably an activist in the movement to drive the English from the Highlands, but Camerons had fought side by side with Macdonalds, Ranalds, and Mackenzies at Culloden, and she hated to see Calum hunted down like an animal. Then again, he had tried to kill Sinjun, and that shouldn't go unpunished.

"You must do what you think best, Sinjun," Christy demurred.

The conversation came to an end when Margot arrived with the tea. Christy helped him drink the potent brew, and he fell asleep soon afterward. Christy sat with him far into the night, checking him frequently for fever. But Sinjun remained blessedly cool. Margot appeared in the chamber shortly before dawn, insisting that Christy go to bed. Christy reluctantly complied, dragging her exhausted body to the bedroom Sinjun had used when he'd first arrived at Glenmoor.

Sinjun awakened to pain, and was gratified to find that it was bearable. Gingerly he touched his bandaged shoulder, remembering bits and pieces of everything that had happened after the arrow pierced his flesh. He glanced out the window and saw a weak sun breaking through the clouds. He must have slept through the night. He heard a noise at the door and turned his attention from the window. Christy entered the chamber, and he offered her a feeble smile. Rory followed in her wake, bearing a cloth-covered tray.

"You're awake," Christy said brightly. Sinjun thought she looked tired and wondered if she had sat with him all night. "Mary thought you might be hungry."

Rory set the tray on the nightstand and whisked off the cloth.

"Gruel," Sinjun complained, wrinkling his nose at the glutinous mess. Truthfully, he wasn't very hungry, and the colorless blob filling the bowl killed what little appetite he had. "I think I'll pass."

Christy's frown made him feel guilty. "Could I have toasted bread and tea instead?"

Christy's face brightened immediately. "Aye. If Rory will go to the kitchen and fetch it."

Rory left, and Christy pulled a chair up to Sinjun's bedside. "How do you feel? You slept most of the night."

"I hope you didn't sit up with me all night," he said sternly. Christy's flush told him she had. "You need your rest, Christy. My wound isn't a serious one."

"Perhaps not, but fever and infection are serious. There is no sign of fever, and Mary will be here soon to change your bandage. She'll know if the wound has turned septic."

As if summoned by Christy's words, Mary bustled into the chamber. Rory followed, carrying the toasted bread and tea Sinjun had requested. Hands on hips, Mary wagged her finger at Sinjun and shook her head. "One day ye'll come to appreciate oats, me fine lord. And dinna look at me like that," she added when Sinjun sent her a petulant look. "Let's have a look at yer wound afore ye eat."

Sinjun lay still as Mary removed the bandage,

probed, prodded, and sniffed. " 'Tisn't putrid, yer lordship," she announced as she spread another layer of salve over the wound and applied a fresh bandage.

"I'll be getting up today," Sinjun announced after everyone but Christy had left.

"You're *not* getting up," Christy said firmly.

Sinjun decided not to argue the point. Instead, he mulled over his plans to bring soldiers to Glenmoor, wondering if it was a good idea. If he summoned English soldiers, it was likely to produce more hard feelings and spur talk of rebellion. Damned if he did and damned if he didn't.

"Sinjun, are you all right?" Christy asked. "You're awfully quiet."

"I was thinking," Sinjun said slowly. "When Calum realizes he didn't kill me, he's likely to try again. Or perhaps do something to hurt you."

"We'll talk about this later, Sinjun. You need to rest," Christy said, pulling the blanket up to his chin. "Try to sleep. The faster your body heals the sooner you can make decisions about Calum."

Sinjun took her suggestion seriously, especially since he could scarcely keep his eyes open. Had Mary fed him that damn valarian tea again? A few minutes later he dropped into a sound sleep.

Sinjun made an amazing recovery. Both Christy and Mary had insisted that he remain in bed a full three days. Though he chafed under the inactivity mandated by their stern rules, the bed rest did give his body time to mend itself. By the fifth day he was exercising his arm without experiencing excessive pain. By the seventh day he was able to ride short distances.

March arrived like the proverbial lion, but it

didn't last. All signs pointed to an early spring. Snow was melting on the hillsides, and preparations were being made for shearing the sheep. With the return of his health, Sinjun thought about confronting Calum. The only thing that stopped him was the impending birth of his child.

Christy looked so uncomfortable that Sinjun wondered how she could walk, much less continue to function. He knew her sleep was restless, for she had moved back into his bed after his recovery, and he'd been awakened nearly every night by her tossing and turning. He knew it wouldn't be long now before the birth of their child, and that thought excited him.

A message from Julian arrived two weeks to the day after Sinjun's narrow escape from death. John Coachman had braved bogged-down roads and inclement weather to deliver it. Sinjun sent the exhausted man to the kitchen for refreshment while he read Julian's urgent letter.

"Bloody hell!" Sinjun cursed after he read the first two sentences.

Christy came up beside him and peered over his shoulder. "What does Julian want?"

Sinjun skimmed through the rest of the letter. "Sir Oswald's trial has been set for the last week in March. I'm to return to London immediately to testify."

He heard Christy gasp and cursed his brother's bad timing. Furthermore, Julian's message held a none too subtle demand that Sinjun couldn't ignore. Upon his return, Julian expected Sinjun to report on the situation at Glenmoor, as well as explain why he had delayed his return to London.

"Are you going to go?" Christy asked quietly. Too quietly.

Sinjun felt the weight of indecision bearing down on him. He was needed in London, but he was needed here, too. Though he had often pined for London's social whirl during the long, dreary winter, he wanted to be here to see his child emerge into the world. He searched his mind for an excuse to remain at Glenmoor, one that would satisfy his brother.

Should Sinjun ignore Julian's urgent summons, he felt certain his brother would hear about the attack upon him from John Coachman, for servants were notorious gossips. And knowing Julian, he would get himself to Glenmoor as fast as he could and bring a company of soldiers with him.

Christy stared at him, her eyes watchful. Then she surprised him by saying, "You have to go."

"You *want* me to go?"

"That's not what I said. Sir Oswald has cheated you and caused my clansmen great hardship. He could go free if you don't testify. Is that what you want?"

"No, the man deserves to be punished for what he's done."

"Then you must go."

"But the babe . . ."

". . . will be born in her own good time. Besides, you'll be safer in London."

"Dammit, Christy! I'm not frightened of Cameron. I promised to be here for the birth of our child."

"Do you think I haven't noticed your restlessness this winter? I know you miss London. You've conducted your life as Lord Sin too long to change over the course of a few months."

Sinjun's eyes narrowed. "Are you deliberately goading me? Have I interfered in your life? Are your clansmen more important to you than I am? All you ever wanted from me was my child to ensure Glenmoor's future. He was conceived for only one purpose. To continue the Macdonald dynasty and hold the land for future Macdonalds.''

Her face turned pasty. Oh God, why were they arguing like this? Sinjun silently lamented. They were at each other's throats over old issues that had been resolved long ago. Or had they been resolved?

Christy knew exactly what she was doing. It was in Sinjun's best interest that he return to London. Not just for the trial, which was reason enough, but to find out if he could be happy with one woman. He had to discover that truth for himself. She'd seen the way he'd moped around all winter, those faraway, wistful looks when he thought she wasn't looking. She didn't want him if he was remaining at Glenmoor simply because he thought she needed him.

She wanted Sinjun to love her as much as she loved him. She knew he cared for her, but did he care for her enough to abandon his old life? Returning to London now would give him a taste of what he had been missing and settle the question once and for all.

"Think what you want, Sinjun," Christy said tiredly. Her back hurt, and arguing only made it worse. "For whatever reason, you should return to London. Your brother isn't one to take no for an answer."

"Will you send word as soon as the baby is born? I doubt I'll be back in time for the birth."

"I'll send Rory."

Sinjun nodded. "I'll explain everything to Julian.

Actually, he'll be ecstatic to know I'm to be a father. He's been goading me for years to consummate our marriage and settle down."

Christy gave him a wistful smile. "Time will tell what the future holds for us."

"I'm sorry," Sinjun said. "I don't know why we are arguing. Upsetting you is the last thing I want to do. Forgive me."

Christy had forgiven him before he'd even asked. "Of course. Come along, I'll help you pack. You can boost me up the stairs."

Christy was out of breath by the time she finished negotiating the winding stone stairs. She sat on the bed to catch her breath, watching Sinjun rummage through his trunk.

"I'm only taking a few things in a knapsack," he explained. "I've plenty of clothes in London, though I doubt they'll accommodate the new muscles I seem to have acquired."

"What's that?" Christy asked as an official-looking document drifted from the trunk onto the floor. Sinjun picked up the document, looked at it, and handed it to her.

"I forgot about this. It's the writ of annulment I brought from London for your signature. After I learned Flora and Christy were the same person, and that you were expecting my child, I packed the annulment away and forgot about it. You can do what you want about it."

Christy thought about it a moment. "Put it back in the trunk for now. You might need it one day."

He sent her an inscrutable look and restored it to the trunk. "Thanks for the vote of confidence." He returned his attention to the trunk. "These will do," he said, placing a small pile of clothing on the bed.

"I'll pack your things in the knapsack while you inform John Coachman that you'll be leaving with him tomorrow," Christy said.

He grasped her hands and pulled her against him. "Are you sure this is what you want, sweetheart? I can tell Julian to go to hell."

'Tis what you want, Christy thought. "No, your brother needs you. I'd hate to think that a scoundrel like Sir Oswald could go free without your testimony. He deserves to be punished for what he's done to you and my clansmen."

She felt the warmth of Sinjun's kiss upon her lips and refused to let herself cry. He *would* return, she told herself. And if he didn't, it wasn't the end of the world. She would still have his bairn to love.

Christy slept in Sinjun's arms that night. Making love was out of the question, but they kissed and cuddled until she finally fell asleep. She awoke in the middle of the night with a backache. Her restlessness awakened Sinjun, and he asked what troubled her. She lied and said she was too uncomfortable to sleep.

When morning came, she put on a cheery smile and kissed Sinjun good-bye. She lifted her hand in a halfhearted wave as she watched him disappear over the horizon.

"That's the last we'll see of his lordship," Margot said dryly.

Christy didn't respond. What could she say, when Margot could be right? As she turned away, she felt a twinge in her back and grimaced.

Margot saw and sent Christy a sharp look. "Are ye all right, lass? Ye look like yer hurting."

" 'Tis nothing, Margot. I've been having back pains since yesterday."

"Perhaps ye should tell Mary." She turned Christy toward the kitchen.

"Aye," Christy said, glancing over her shoulder for a last glimpse at Sinjun before following Margot into the kitchen.

Over her pots and pans, Mary studied Christy's face, felt her distended stomach, and asked a few pertinent questions.

"It willna be long now, lass," she predicted. "Why dinna ye tell his lordship afore he left?"

"Sinjun had to leave, Mary. I accepted that. I didn't want him to stay with me for the bairn's sake. You've all seen how restless he's been this winter." She heaved a tremulous sigh. "I never really believed he would be content at Glenmoor. City life has more to offer a man like Sinjun."

Mary clucked her tongue. "Dinna fret, lass. We'll take care of ye. Yer clan needs ye even if yer husband doesna."

Christy took that thought to her empty bed that night. Deep in her heart she wanted to believe Sinjun would return, but she had to be practical. She might never see Sinjun again except for brief visits to see his bairn. It would be painful to live with the knowledge that Sinjun would always have a mistress in London.

A sharp pain in her lower abdomen banished her dismal thoughts. She tried to settle herself into a more comfortable position, but the pain persisted. She suffered in silence until dawn, finally acknowledging that she was in the early stages of labor. She was writhing in agony when Margot found her a short time later.

Both Mary and the midwife were sent for. Mary arrived first and insisted that Christy get up and walk, declaring that it was good for the bairn. So Christy walked while cloths, hot water, herbal preparations, and other paraphernalia were gathered. Then Agnes, the midwife, arrived. She examined Christy and announced that everything was progressing normally.

Christy had no idea what that meant, except that the pain was unrelenting and at times more than she could bear. Hours passed, the pain continued, and Christy wondered if the child would ever be born. Night came. The moon rose high in the sky. Christy walked until a building pressure demanded that she push.

" 'Tis time for my daughter to be born," Christy gasped when the pressure became unbearable.

Agnes nodded agreement, and she and Mary helped Christy into bed. Margot held her hand while Agnes spread her legs and murmured instructions. Through a fog of pain, Christy heard and obeyed. An hour later, just as dawn was breaking, the babe came into the world, loudly protesting its difficult journey.

Utterly drained but jubilant, Christy held out her arms for her child. "Give my daughter to me," she whispered.

Mary gave her a strange look. "Christy. Yer bairn is . . ."

Immediately Christy thought the worst. "Noooo! What's wrong with her? Oh, God, please don't take my bairn."

"Dinna fret, lass," Mary crooned. "Yer babe is as hale and hearty as his lusty sire. I ken ye were expecting a daughter, but God has given ye a fine, braw laddie."

Christy went limp with relief. As long as her bairn was healthy, its sex, though potentially cause for worry should Sinjun take him away, didn't matter. She had hoped for a lassie, but a laddie was just as welcome. Perhaps the next child . . . No, she shoved that thought aside. There might never be another child if Sinjun decided the life he led as Lord Sin held more appeal than a wife and son.

Chapter 10

Christy cuddled her precious son against her breast as he nursed. Gazing down at his dark head, his rosebud mouth sucking vigorously on her nipple, she thought fiercely of how much she loved this child. He was a month old now, and Christy still hadn't sent word of his birth to Sinjun. The first months of a child's life were so precarious that she had wanted to make sure her bairn remained healthy before notifying Sinjun. Babies were known to die for no apparent reason the first weeks after birth.

The tiny scrap of humanity in her arms reminded her strongly of his father. She wondered if Sinjun was enjoying London and if he had resumed his old way of life. Did he ever think of her? Though Sinjun had seemed reluctant to leave, she'd be a fool to believe he preferred simple living to London's pleasures.

The baby's lips fell away from her nipple; he was sated and sleeping soundly. She wished Sinjun had been here to name his son. Strange, they had never spoken of names, and Christy had only names for a lass picked out. For want of direction from Sinjun, Christy had named the boy Niall, after her father.

Christy placed her sleeping son in his cradle in the adjoining nursery and left the chamber to compose the letter to Sinjun she'd put off writing. A month after his birth, Niall was the picture of health, a sturdy replica of his father. She tiptoed from the chamber and ran into Margot, who had come to summon Christy.

"Calum Cameron is here to see ye," she said sourly.

Christy's hand went to her throat. "Now? 'Tis late. What could he want at this time of night? Dear Lord, what kind of trouble has he stirred up now?"

"Perhaps he just wants to offer congratulations on the birth of yer bairn," Margot offered.

Christy knew Calum better than that. He had come to make trouble.

"Yer looking fine, lass," Calum said, his gaze roaming over Christy's newly slim figure with unconcealed admiration. "I hear ye had a fine braw laddie."

A shiver of apprehension slid down Christy's spine. Calum's hulking form seemed to fill the hall with unspoken menace. "You heard right, Calum. Niall is a fine, healthy lad."

"What do ye hear from his sire?"

"Nothing yet. He's only been gone a month."

"I dinna think he will return."

Christy bristled. "You don't know that."

A persistent banging on the door drew Christy's attention from Calum to the front hallway. Two unexpected visitors in one night was rare. Margot opened the door, admitting John Coachman into the hall. He was reeling from exhaustion and nearly asleep on his feet.

"A message from yer husband," Margot said, ushering John into the hall.

"Sinjun," Christy said, eyes glowing. She hadn't expected to hear from him yet.

A travel-weary John Coachman doffed his hat and placed Sinjun's letter into Christy's hand. "His lordship said I should wait for an answer."

"Thank you, John. Margot will take you to the kitchen and see that you're given something to eat and a place to sleep."

Margot led John toward the back of the fortress. Christy wished Calum would leave so she could read her letter in private. But Calum seemed disinclined to leave. She could almost see the wheels turning in his brain as he stared at the letter she held in her hand. Before she knew what he intended, he ripped the letter from her hand and tore it open. She knew he could read, for he'd learned from the same tutor who had taught her to read and cipher.

"You have no right!" Christy raged as she tried to snatch the letter from his hand.

"Dinna fret, lass, I want to see what yer fancy English husband has to say. I'll read it to ye, if ye'd like."

"I can read it myself," Christy snapped, wishing Calum to hell.

"His lordship writes ye on the day after his arrival in London," Calum read aloud. "He says Sir Oswald's trial has been postponed a fortnight." He looked up and gave her a disgruntled scowl. "He says he will return to Glenmoor after the trial." His gaze left the pages and returned to Christy. "Have ye told him about his bairn?"

Furious, Christy snatched the letter from his hand. "Not yet, but I intend to remedy that."

The smile that Calum gave Christy was anything but reassuring. "Tell his lordship ye dinna want him to return."

"What? You're mad. You know Sinjun will want to see his bairn."

"The moment Lord Derby sets foot in the Highlands he's a dead man," Calum promised. "He'll never reach Glenmoor alive. I'm a man of my word, Christy Macdonald. I tried once to kill the bastard and failed, but I won't fail again."

"You wouldn't dare kill Sinjun!" Christy gasped, aware that he would dare anything if it served his purpose. "What would his death gain you?"

"Ye, Christy Macdonald. Through ye I will have the power that should have been mine all along. A woman shouldna be laird."

"I had the blessing of the entire clan," Christy exclaimed.

"Not the Camerons," Calum retorted. "We were outnumbered by the Macdonalds, Ranalds, and Mackenzies. Being chieftain of the Camerons isna enough power for what I have in mind. If it takes Lord Derby's death to have ye and the power I crave, then so be it."

Christy knew with cold certainty that she had to keep Sinjun away from the Highlands. Once Calum's clansmen rallied behind him, Sinjun was in danger of losing his life.

Christy's expression must have given away her thoughts. "I see that we understand one another, lass," Calum said, folding his arms over his massive chest.

"I won't let you kill Sinjun," Christy declared hotly.

"Ye canna stop me. He'll never reach Glenmoor alive. As for his bairn, once we wed, he'll be fostered with a Cameron. 'Tis my bairns ye'll be birthing. One every year.'' Lust-glazed eyes raked over her body. "Ye can depend on it." He turned to leave.

"Calum, wait!"

He halted and glanced over his shoulder at her. "What is it now? Ye canna change my mind, ye know. Derby must die."

"What if Sinjun doesn't return to the Highlands?"

"He'll come. Like ye said, he'll want to see his bairn."

"What if I can convince Sinjun to have our marriage annulled?"

He frowned. " 'Tis too late. Ye have a bairn."

"No, listen to me. When Sinjun first arrived at Glenmoor he had every intention of having our marriage annulled. It could have happened. Sinjun's brother, the earl of Mansfield, is an influential man and would have handled the legalities. The writ of annulment is still here, in Sinjun's trunk. I'm certain I can convince him to proceed with the annulment. I know he'll act upon it when I return the document with my signature in place."

Calum shook his shaggy head. "It willna work. He'll come for his bairn. He can take him away from ye, ye know."

Christy was desperate. Sinjun couldn't return to Glenmoor. He had to live. She racked her brain for a solution that would convince Sinjun to remain in London. The idea that popped into her head was so outrageous she thought it just might work.

"If ye've nothing more to say, lass, I'll be leaving," Calum said.

Christy couldn't allow Calum to leave before she'd laid her plan before him. "Sinjun won't come to the Highlands if I sign the annulment and send it to him with John Coachman," Christy began.

"He'll come anyway," Calum insisted.

Christy took a deep breath, but it did little to calm her jagged nerves. What she was about to suggest was sinfully wrong, but saving Sinjun's life more than made up for it. "Not if I tell him our child died at birth, and that I want to end our marriage and wed you."

Calum's attention sharpened. "Yer smart, lass, I'll give ye that." He stroked his chin. "How will I know ye'll do as ye say?"

"I'll sign the annulment in your presence. And you can read the letter I write to Sinjun."

"How do I know ye willna compose another letter and destroy the first after I've left?"

Calum's suspicious nature was backing Christy into a wall. "I'll send John Coachman off tonight, though the poor man deserves a good night's sleep."

"Sign the document and compose yer letter," Calum commanded as he sat down at the table to await Christy's return. "Ale wouldna be remiss, lass."

Christy grabbed a cup from the sideboard, drew a pitcher of ale from the barrel, and slammed them down before Calum. Then she hurried upstairs, pausing a moment to look in on her sleeping son. Margot was sitting with him, and Christy asked her to stay until she got rid of Calum. Then she entered her own chamber and went to the corner where Sinjun's trunk rested. She raised the lid and sorted through his belongings until she found the annulment document he'd left behind. After collecting her writing materials, she returned to the hall and sat down beside Calum.

"Let me see," Calum said, reaching for the annulment paper. He scanned it quickly and handed it back.

Before she had time to think about what she was doing, she dipped the quill into the ink jar and signed her name. "There, 'tis done," she said with bone-deep sadness.

"Now the letter," Calum directed.

Retrieving a sheet of paper, Christy began to write. Tears streamed down her pale cheeks as she told Sinjun that his child had died at birth. She prayed God would forgive her for such a reprehensible lie, but Calum had given her no other option. She could barely see through the tears when she wrote that she never wanted to see Sinjun again, that she was signing the annulment document and returning it with John Coachman, that she expected him to file it with the courts. She tried to make her letter sound believable. Sinjun was no fool. If she didn't keep the message concise and impersonal, he'd know immediately that something was amiss. When she finished, she handed the letter to Calum.

"If Derby comes to the Highlands after this letter he's more a fool than I gave him credit for," Calum said, nodding his approval. "Summon the messenger. I'll hasten him on his way myself."

Before she could do Calum's bidding, Rory entered the hall through the front door. He saw Calum sitting with Christy and stiffened.

"What brings ye out this time of night, Calum Cameron?"

"I had business with the laird," Calum said, rising until he stood nose to nose with Rory.

"Rory, John Coachman arrived with a message from Sinjun. He's resting in the kitchen. Would you summon him?" Christy asked before the two came to fisticuffs.

"Will ye be all right?" Rory asked, sending Calum a fierce scowl.

"I'll be fine. Hurry. 'Tis imperative that John leave tonight with my reply. And Rory," Christy called after him, "don't mention the bairn."

Rory looked as if he wanted to demand an explanation but Christy's stoic expression must have changed his mind. He strode from the hall with undue haste.

"Yer a smart lass," Calum said. "I want no trouble with the Macdonalds. Dinna tell anyone about our pact. Feuding among ourselves isna a good thing right now."

Christy agreed. She had no intention of telling her clansmen about the terrible lies she had told Sinjun.

John Coachman looked dead on his feet when he entered the hall. He stood before Christy with hat in hand, looking for all the world like he considered Highlanders little more than savages. Christy handed him the packet of folded papers and bid him to leave immediately for London.

"Immediately, milady?" John asked, clearly stunned.

"Aye, John. I know you're tired, but it's imperative that my reply to his lordship's letter reach him without delay."

"Aye, milady," John said wearily.

"Rory, fill John's knapsack with food to take with him on his journey."

"I'll see the man off myself," Calum put in.

While Calum was seeing John off, Rory returned to the hall. "What's the meaning of this, Christy? I smell something rotten. What's Calum doing here?

Margot shouldna have left you alone with him."

"Margot is with Niall," Christy explained.

"What did Sinjun say? Does he know about his bairn?"

"He will as soon as he receives my letter," Christy said cryptically. "But don't look for him to return to Glenmoor any time soon."

Rory gave her a speculative look. "What are ye up to, Christy? I see Calum's fine hand in this. What did he tell ye to make ye send Sinjun's messenger out in the middle of the night?"

" 'Tis hardly the middle of the night," Christy scoffed. "Trust me in this, Rory. I know what I'm doing."

"I hope so, Christy, I surely hope so."

Christy paced nervously, aware that Calum had gone to the stables with John, probably filling his ears with falsehoods about the close relationship between Calum and his lordship's wife.

Mansfield Place, London

"Bloody hell, Sinjun," Julian said, giving Sinjun a thorough inspection. "I hardly recognize you. What have you done to yourself? I've never seen you looking so healthy. Good God, man, your muscles are positively bulging. What have you done to yourself?"

"Working out-of-doors, mostly," Sinjun allowed. "I had to do something to relieve the boredom. New clothing is being made for me as we speak."

"Tell me about the unrest in the Highlands you mentioned, in the only letter you saw fit to send me."

"The Cameron chieftain is preaching rebellion, but I doubt anything will come of it."

"Tell me about Christy. Obviously you found Sir Oswald's claim about your wife's pregnancy false. Doesn't surprise me, after learning the extent of Sir Oswald's dishonesty."

"Sir Oswald was telling the truth," Sinjun said.

Julian's jaw dropped. "The devil you say!"

Sinjun grinned. His explanation was going to shock his brother. Julian had been called away to his country estate on Sinjun's return to London, and he had just returned today. Sir Oswald's trial was to start tomorrow, and Sinjun hadn't had the opportunity until now to tell Julian about Christy and his impending fatherhood. Gleefully he launched into the tale that seemed more fiction than truth.

At the end of the telling, Julian plopped down into the nearest chair and stared at Sinjun. " 'Tis an astounding story, Sinjun. Nearly beyond belief." He shook his head. "Seduced by your own wife."

" 'Tis the truth, Julian, I swear it. Christy posed as Lady Flora in London." He wagged his head. "Can you imagine? I was besotted with my own wife. Christy carries my child. The birth was imminent when you ordered me back to London. I had every intention of telling you to go to hell and remaining at Glenmoor until after the birth of my child, but Christy talked me into leaving."

"You? A father? That's going to take some getting used to. So that's what kept you in Scotland all these months. You could have written," he chided.

"I wanted to surprise you. Besides, the roads were impassable during the winter months. You're lucky your letter ordering me home arrived without mishap."

"What does the future hold for you now, Sinjun? Christy tricked you into giving her a child, can you live with that? You continually surprise me. I would think you'd be as angry as hell."

"I was damn angry . . . at first," Sinjun admitted. "But Christy and I arrived at an understanding. I couldn't remain angry forever, could I? I know the child is mine regardless of how it was conceived. I'm waiting for John Coachman to return from the Highlands, hopefully with news of my child's birth."

"Are you sure you're ready to abandon your sinful life and become a husband and father?"

Sinjun studied his hands. Obviously Julian and Christy harbored the same doubts. "Do you think I'm incapable of settling down?"

Julian pushed his fingers through his hair, his doubts clearly displayed upon his handsome face. "I just don't know, Sinjun. You've shown no signs of settling down in the past."

"I'm going to give it a bloody good try. I intend to return to the Highlands after the trial. I want to see my child."

Julian rose and helped himself to the brandy. He filled two snifters and handed Sinjun one. "What about the unrest you spoke of?"

"I can handle it," Sinjun replied, sipping appreciatively of the amber liquid. "The Cameron chieftain is a troublemaker. He's power hungry."

"By God, you sound like a changed man," Julian said, clapping Sinjun's shoulder—the injured shoulder, the one still bearing a livid scar. Sinjun flinched and cried out. Julian's hand dropped abruptly. "What happened? Were you injured?"

" 'Tis nothing."

"Sinjun," Julian chided sternly. "As head of this family 'tis my right to know these things."

"Did anyone ever tell you you're a meddling fool?"

"You have, plenty of times. Spit it out, Sinjun."

"If you must know, Calum Cameron took it into his head to rid the world of an Englishman. His arrow found my shoulder. Fortunately it wasn't serious. As you can see, I made a complete recovery."

"I don't like this, Sinjun."

"Do you think I do?"

"Why didn't you report the attack to the English garrison at Inverness?"

"I was going to, as soon as I recovered. Then your letter arrived and there wasn't time. I'll stop there on my way back."

"I'll send a few stouthearted Englishmen along with you. No sense taking chances with your life."

"We'll see," Sinjun replied with little enthusiasm.

Emma hurried away from the study door Julian had left ajar, her ears still ringing with what she had heard. Lady Flora wasn't Sinjun's mistress, she was his wife, and she was very near to delivering his heir. The news left her stunned. She'd wondered why Sinjun had gone charging off to Scotland without a word of explanation. She was part of the family, after all, and had a right to know what was happening with her own brother.

She hurried to her room just as the door to the study swung open and Sinjun strode through on his way out the front door.

Sir Oswald's three-day trial went well. Julian's scrutiny of the ledgers, which showed blatant discrepancies, and Sinjun's testimony, which included first-hand knowledge of the levies Sir Oswald had raised to fill his own coffers, provided sufficient evidence to convict him of fraud and theft. He was stripped of his wealth and property and sentenced to fourteen years of hard labor as a bonded servant in the colonies. He was imprisoned on one of the floating hulks in London pool until transportation could be arranged. Everything Sir Oswald owned was given to Sinjun in restitution for his loses.

Sinjun spent several days closeted with Julian and his man of business after the trial. For the first time in his recollection he now had a clear picture of his wealth, and it was considerable.

"Things should run smoothly while I'm gone," Julian said once they were alone.

"You're leaving again? What about Emma? You know I intend to return to Scotland and won't be around to see to her welfare."

"Aunt Amanda has agreed to move into Mansfield Place during my absence."

"She's an old woman, Julian. She's no match for our high-spirited Emma."

"When I made my plans, I counted on you being here to squire them about."

"Must you leave now? What mysterious mission calls you away this time?"

Julian's expression turned deliberately obtuse. "I don't know what you're talking about. There is nothing mysterious about being called away on business. I shouldn't be gone more than a fortnight. How much mischief can Emma get into in a fortnight?"

"You have no idea," Sinjun said, rolling his eyes. "Be careful, Julian. I don't know what you're involved in, but whatever it is, you're not indestructible."

Julian sent Sinjun a sardonic smile. "I'll try to remember. In any event, I'll be around a few days yet."

Sinjun was at his own townhouse several hours later when an unexpected caller arrived. Emma was shown into the house, demanding to speak to Sinjun. When she burst into his chamber without knocking, he knew she was angry.

"I tried to stop her, milord," the long suffering butler said as he followed in her wake.

"It's all right, Pemburton, I'll see my sister."

"Very good, milord," Pemburton said. His tall, thin frame remained rigidly erect as he exited the chamber and closed the door behind him.

"Well, hoyden, what's on your mind? You didn't come alone, did you? You know what a stickler Julian is for propriety."

"I did come alone, Sinjun," Emma said. "What Julian doesn't know won't hurt him. He'd keep me under lock and key if he could. I'm a woman, Sinjun, not a child."

Sinjun's eyebrows quirked upward. He hadn't given enough attention to Emma. Julian had tried to compensate for Sinjun's shortcomings by attempting to suppress Emma's exuberant nature and natural penchant for mischief.

"Sit down, Emma," he invited, "and tell me what's troubling you. Are you angry with Julian?"

"I'm damn angry with both of you," Emma retorted.

"Emma, watch your language," Sinjun warned.

"I can't help it, Sinjun. You don't know what it's like being kept in the dark all the time. I *am* a member of this family."

"What in God's name are you talking about? Are you in some kind of trouble?"

"I'm not allowed to get into trouble," Emma said flippantly. "This has nothing to do with me. Not directly, anyway."

"Why don't you tell me what's bothering you."

"Why didn't you tell me why you went to Scotland? You let me believe Lady Flora was your mistress when she was really your wife."

Stunned, Sinjun stared at Emma. "How did you find out?"

"I overheard your conversation with Julian today."

"You were eavesdropping?"

"How else am I going to learn anything?"

"You've grown up," Sinjun said, suddenly seeing Emma in a way he'd never seen her before.

She was nineteen, deliciously curved and beautiful. He wondered how he had failed to see that she was no longer a child. Like all the Thorntons, her hair was thick and black, her eyelashes long and curly. Her features were classic. If she had a flaw it was her lips, which were full and lush, not at all acceptable by normal standards. Her eyes, especially when she was angry, were remarkably expressive. Unlike both his and Julian's midnight blue eyes, Emma's were a distinctive violet. Vaguely he wondered why, with her looks and generous dowry, she hadn't found an acceptable young man to marry.

"I'm surprised you noticed," Emma said with scathing sarcasm. "In any event, I'm old enough to know about Lady Flora. Or should I say Christy Macdonald? She's expecting your child, is she not?"

There was no help for it. Emma deserved an answer. "Until my recent visit to Glenmoor, I had no idea Lady Flora was Christy, my wife," he began. Then the whole story came tumbling out in a rush of words. Emma listened raptly, and when he was done, she clapped her hands, obviously delighted.

"You love Christy, Sinjun, admit it!"

Sinjun felt as if his world had just tipped. Love? He knew nothing about love. "I truly don't know. I do know that I'm anxious to return to Glenmoor. I wrote to Christy and expect an answer at any time. I told her that I plan to return to her as soon as my business here is finished. I'm anxious, of course, to see my child."

Emma studied Sinjun through a fringe of ebony lashes. "Since I was a little girl, I've heard gossip about Lord Sin, his escapades, and his women. Women swoon at the mention of your name and men envy you. All my friends who visited did so with the hope they would catch a glimpse of you. Christy must be an amazing woman to tame Lord Sin. I know your temper. I'm surprised you forgave her her lies. It wasn't well done of Christy to trick you into giving her a child."

Sinjun surprised himself by blushing. Young ladies weren't supposed to be knowledgeable about sexual matters. "Where did you learn such things?"

"For heaven's sake, Sinjun, I'm not stupid. Julian has never denied me any of the books in his library. I know more than you give me credit for."

"Enough!" Sinjun exclaimed. "I don't want to hear my innocent sister talking like that. 'Tisn't proper."

"Just tell me one thing, Sinjun," Emma said, rising and smoothing her skirts down. "Do you intend to remain in Scotland the rest of your life with Christy and your child?"

"Good Lord, no!" Sinjun blurted out. "I'm hoping to convince Christy to spend at least part of the year in London. I was surprised, however, that I enjoyed the Highlands as much as I did, but I can't see myself staying there forever. I don't want my heir raised among Scotsmen who despise the English. My son is going to have all the advantages I did as a child."

"Thank you for confiding in me," Emma said, heading for the door. "And in the future, try to remember I'm part of the family."

"Lord Derby, John Coachman has returned from the Highlands," Pemburton called through the door seconds before Emma reached it.

Sinjun hurried past her and flung open the door. "Is he still below?"

"Aye, my lord, he's in the kitchen. He's nearly

prostrate with exhaustion. He asked me to give you this." Pemburton handed Sinjun several folded sheets of paper.

"Thank you, Pemburton. Ask John to await me in the kitchen. I'd like to speak to him personally after I've read my wife's letter."

"As you say, milord," Pemburton said, bowing stiffly.

"Oh, do hurry, Sinjun," Emma said. She appeared as excited as Sinjun. "Does it say anything about the baby?"

Sinjun's hands shook as he unfolded the packet. A sheet of paper drifted to the floor, and he let it lay while he devoured the letter Christy had written. Curious by nature, Emma retrieved it, paling when she realized what it was.

"Sinjun, this is a writ of annulment. It bears Christy's signature. What is going on?"

Sinjun's complexion turned as pasty as dough, and he couldn't stop his hands from shaking as he read Christy's letter for a second time. "The baby didn't live," he whispered, stricken. A single tear trickled from the corner of his eye, and he dashed it away.

"Oh, Sinjun, I'm so sorry."

"Christy doesn't want me to return to Glenmoor," he continued, his voice as hard and cold as his frozen heart. "She signed the annulment and asked me to legally end our marriage. She intends to wed Calum Cameron."

"I don't understand," Emma whispered.

"Nor I. But it no longer matters. Christy wants to sever our relationship, and I intend to honor her wishes. 'Tis not the end of the world."

"But you own Glenmoor. It will always be yours no matter who Christy weds."

"True," Sinjun contended. "I can legally remove her from Glenmoor should I so desire."

"Will you do that?"

"I don't know. I need time to think this through before I decide on a course of action. Julian is leaving soon, perhaps I'll wait until he returns to pursue this."

"What if Christy marries this Cameron fellow before the annulment is filed with the courts?"

Sinjun gave her a smile that didn't quite reach his eyes. "That would make Christy a bigamist, wouldn't it? Leave me, Emma, I'm in no mood for company."

Emma's eyes sparked with anger. "Christy must be mad! Why would she want another man when she could have you?"

Despite his grief and confusion, Sinjun sent Emma a wobbly smile. "I'm English, Emma. Highlanders hate Englishmen. Christy is a Highlander." He kissed her nose. "Good-bye, hoyden, try to stay out of trouble."

Sinjun sat in his dark study until the evening was nearly spent, silently mourning his child. He didn't even know the sex of the child and wondered why Christy hadn't told him. When the clock struck midnight, Sinjun shed the cloak of grief, and with it, the man he had tried to become to please his wife. He threw Christy's letter to the floor, placed the writ of annulment in a drawer, and left the house. He had a lot of hell to raise to make up for the months he'd wasted on Christy.

Lord Sin had returned with a vengeance.

Chapter 11

Glenmoor Castle

From the time little Niall was three months old, Calum Cameron began badgering Christy in earnest to take him as her handfast husband. Thus far she had managed to hold him off, but it hadn't been easy. She had insisted that they should wait for word that her marriage to Sinjun had been legally severed. So far she had heard nothing from Sinjun after sending her letter off with John Coachman.

She wondered if Sinjun mourned their child, and she was at once filled with feelings of guilt and remorse. He had forgiven her lies once, but she knew instinctively that what she had done this time was unforgivable. Every day since she'd dispatched John Coachman to London with her letter she'd regretted the injustice she'd done Sinjun in order to save his life.

Pacing her chamber, she tried to imagine his response to her letter but knew her mental image probably fell far short of his actual reaction. He hadn't tried to contact her, so obviously, he believed she wanted to marry Calum. That knowledge brought more pain than she thought possible.

She stopped pacing when Margot walked into the chamber, her arms full of clean linens. She set them down on the bed and wagged her head when she noticed Christy's glum features.

"Moping again, I see. 'Tis not good, Christy. Write to Sinjun. Tell him how ye feel, how much ye miss him. He needs to know that."

" 'Tis too late, Margot."

Margot sent Christy a sharp look. "What have ye done this time, Christy Macdonald? Both Rory and I know ye've been troubled of late. We waited for ye to confide in us, but now I'm demanding ye tell me what is amiss. Ye haven't been yerself since Sinjun's letter arrived. Why isn't he here with ye? And another thing, why is Calum Cameron sniffing around yer skirts?"

Christy sighed despondently. Margot was more than her kin, she was a friend, and she owed her the truth. "Sit down, Margot, you look tired." Margot was carrying Rory's child and hadn't been feeling well. Christy knew that feeling.

"I'm well enough," Margot declared. She perched on the edge of the bed and took Christy's hand. "I willna leave here until ye tell me what's going on."

Christy sighed. "Very well, but you're not going to like it. You recall, don't you, that Calum was here when Sinjun's last message arrived?"

Margot nodded.

"Calum snatched the letter from my hand and read it. When he learned that Sinjun intended to return to Glenmoor, he threatened Sinjun's life and vowed Sinjun wouldn't arrive here alive. He tried once to kill Sinjun and failed, but I feared he'd succeed the next time."

Margot's eyes widened. "Why does he want Sinjun dead?"

"So he can marry me. He's power hungry. He wants to drive the English from the Highlands and needs more power than he has now to rally the clan to his cause. There's more. He wants to foster Niall with his Cameron kin once we are wed."

"The bastard!" Margot hissed. "Wait until Rory hears. Our clansmen willna let that happen."

"You're not to tell Rory, Margot," Christy pleaded. "I took care of everything myself. I found a way to save Sinjun's life without bloodshed."

"And just how did ye do that?" Margot asked suspiciously. "Something tells me I willna like what I'm about to hear."

Christy sucked in a sustaining breath. "When Sinjun first arrived at Glenmoor it was with the intention of ending our marriage. He brought a writ of annulment for my signature. After he discovered that Flora and Christy were the same woman, and that I was carrying *his* child, he changed his mind. I remembered Sinjun had left the document in his trunk when he returned to London and suggested to Calum that if I signed the document and sent it with a letter explaining that I wanted to end the marriage, Sinjun would comply. I was willing to do anything to save Sinjun's life, even if it meant never seeing him again."

"I can't see Calum agreeing to that," Margot argued. "Sinjun would want to see his son no matter what ye said."

"Don't look at me like that, Margot," Christy begged. "I did what I had to do to protect Sinjun."

"And what was that, Christy? There's more, isn't there?"

"I told Sinjun our child had died at birth, and that I no longer wanted to be married to him. I . . ." Her gaze fell, for she was unable to look Margot in the eye. "I told him I wanted to marry Calum."

Margot stared at Christy as if she'd lost her mind. "Christy, how could ye! 'Tis a terrible thing ye did. A mortal sin. If Sinjun ever found out he wouldna forgive ye."

A tear slipped down Christy's cheek. "I know. But it was the only thing I could think of to keep Sinjun in London. Calum is a dangerous man. He'd stop at nothing to see Sinjun dead."

"When is the wedding to be?" Margot said with a hint of sarcasm.

"I've managed to put Calum off, but I don't know how much longer I can delay him. I told him I couldn't marry him until Sinjun sent word that the annulment has been finalized. But Calum is getting impatient. He insists that we become handfast soon. Oh, Margot, I don't know what I'm going to do. I cannot bear the thought of Calum touching me. Not after Sinjun."

"Ye should have told Sinjun and let him handle Calum. Yer husband isna a weak man. He willna be pleased with yer sacrifice."

" 'Tis my fondest hope he'll never know. Oh, Margot, I don't want to marry Calum," Christy wailed.

"We'll think of something," Margot said. "Mind ye, I dinna condone what ye did, for I know ye had yer reasons. If we put our heads together, perhaps we'll think of something to keep Calum out of yer bed."

"Don't tell Rory, Margot," Christy pleaded. "He's going to be a father soon, he'll never understand."

"Ye've got the right of that, lass. We'll keep this to ourselves for a while."

Calum's patience came to an abrupt and jarring end. He arrived with his kinsmen the day following Christy's conversation with Margot, insisting upon a handfast marriage between him and Christy that very day. Calum's announcement was loudly cheered by his kinsmen, who had been pushing to put a Cameron in power.

"I want my babe in yer belly as soon as possible," Calum said when Christy protested the short notice. "Ye've known this day would come."

"We can't be handfast today," Christy declared. Her mind whirled furiously. There must be something she could do to stop this abomination from happening.

He grasped her arm, his fingers biting into her soft flesh. "We can and we will."

Christy sent Margot a frantic look. Rory, who had arrived on the heels of Calum with several Macdonalds in tow, intercepted it and immediately moved up to stand beside her. She was heartened to see Macdonalds lined up solidly behind him.

"What's this all about, Christy?" Rory asked. "Ye canna wed Calum. Yer married to Sinjun."

"Tell yer kinsmen, Christy," Calum demanded. "Tell them the truth about yer marriage."

As much as Christy hated to disappoint Rory and those who had come to admire Sinjun, she owed her kinsmen some kind of an explanation despite their disapproval of her actions. "Lord Derby won't be returning to the Highlands," she said. The crowd fell silent, waiting for her explanation. "Our marriage has been annulled."

Rory looked stunned. "The devil ye say! What about his bairn?"

Christy glanced at Calum, silently begging him not to dispute her lie. "Lord Derby expressed little desire to see his son."

A collective gasp filled the room. People began whispering among themselves. "What kind of man would disown his own bairn? 'Tis no more than I'd expect from an Englishman."

Christy saw Rory's expression turn from disbelief to downright disgust and guilt plagued her. Her lie had turned her kinsmen against Sinjun.

"Do ye truly want to marry Calum?" Rory asked.

"Aye, tell yer kinsman how ye canna wait to become my bride," Calum prodded. His tone implied that he would keep her shameful secret if she fell in line with his plans.

"A word with you in private, Calum," Christy said, pulling him aside. " 'Tis important."

Scowling his displeasure, Calum walked with Christy to the opposite end of the hall. "What is it? Dinna think ye can talk me out of this. I'll take ye by force and ye know it. Ye wouldna be the first Highland bride taken by force and ye willna be the last."

"Give me three days, Calum. Three days to prepare a wedding feast. Besides," she said, forcing a blush as she lowered her head, " 'tis not the right time of month for a wedding."

Calum stared at her, obviously disinclined to believe her. "Yer lying, lass."

"Let one of your kinswomen confirm it if you don't believe me. But I would hope you wouldn't embarrass me in such a manner. My kinsmen might take exception at the disrespect shown their laird. Starting a feud should be the last thing you'd want."

Christy held her breath as Calum mulled over her words. She knew she had won a reprieve when he appeared to accept her advice. "Ye win this time, Laird Christy," he mocked. "But once we are wed ye'll not find me an indulgent husband."

Elated, Christy tried to hide her euphoria. Three days! Anything could happen in three days. Time enough to pack up herself and her son and flee. Her euphoria ended on a sour note when she realized that Calum would come after her. But Christy wasn't one to give up easily. Nothing ventured, nothing gained.

Before Calum left, he announced that he and his kinsmen would spend the three days before the wedding stealing Campbell livestock for the wedding feast. A roar of approval filled the hall as Calum led his kinsmen from the keep.

Christy collapsed into the nearest chair, her relief palpable. Margot hurried up beside her, offering her a cup of ale. "Drink, Christy, ye need it."

Christy took a big gulp, grateful for Margot's unwavering support. "What am I going to do, Margot?"

"Ye knew this day was coming."

"Aye, but I'd hoped I'd find a way to avoid it before it arrived." She bounded out of the chair. "Help me pack. I can't stay here. Niall and I are leaving."

"Calum will follow."

"I'll flee to London," Christy said, warming to the idea. "Calum won't follow me to London."

"What about Sinjun?"

Christy's shoulders stiffened. "We're no longer married, remember?"

"What if he learns ye've lied about Niall, assuming ye can escape without Calum dragging ye back."

"It won't be difficult to keep a small child hidden from public eye," Christy argued. "Sinjun and I don't travel in the same circles. I doubt we'll meet at all."

"I'll help ye pack. Rory can drive the coach and I'll travel with ye."

"No, I won't allow it. You're too far along and I'd be remiss to expect either of you to leave now."

"If ye say so, Christy, but I'd feel better if I went along. If I canna go, Effie Ranald will make a fine nursemaid for Niall, and Gavin, Rory's brother, is young and strong enough to protect ye in London, should God grant ye the fortune to reach England safely."

"They are both good choices," Christy allowed. " 'Tis time to take Rory into our confidence. He should know what I've done and why. I'll leave that to you. Will you summon Effie and Gavin? I'll need to speak with them beforehand."

After Margot left, Christy went to her son's chamber and lifted him out of his cradle. She held him close, crooning softly to him, his smiling face a painful reminder of his father. Her thoughts suddenly turned morose. If Sinjun learned his son was alive, he might take him away from her. What a coil.

She considered fleeing to Edinburgh and discarded the idea immediately. There wasn't a place in Scotland where Calum wouldn't follow. She would rather face Sinjun's fury than wed Calum.

"Don't worry, little one," she whispered softly.

"I'll not let anyone take you away from me. I fought to conceive you and I'll fight to keep you."

Effie and Gavin arrived a short time later. Christy explained her predicament, offering no excuses for the lies she had told Sinjun, and swearing them to secrecy. Both Effie and Gavin agreed to accompany their laird to London even after Christy outlined the hazards of the journey and the possibility that Calum might catch up with them and bring them back.

Effie, a sweet-faced maiden of seventeen, was highly incensed that Calum had threatened to kill his lordship if he returned to the Highlands. Gavin, a handsome young man with a shaggy beard and the same muscular build as his brother, would have rallied the clan against the Camerons had Christy not forbidden it.

"I need you both with me in London," Christy said. "Feuding with our clansmen isn't in our best interest. I haven't heard a word from Lord Derby. At the very least he could demand that I vacate Glenmoor. I'm surprised he hasn't asked it of me before now. If he does, the clan must stick together in order to survive."

"Count on me, Christy," Effie said. " 'Twill be a joy to take care of little Niall in London. I've never traveled farther afield than Inverness."

"I dinna relish living among Englishmen," Gavin muttered, "but I wouldna think of letting ye go alone."

It was settled. Arrangements were made to leave at dawn the following morning. Christy spent the rest of the day packing. She knew money wouldn't be a problem, for Sinjun had left sufficient funds for her use before he returned to London. If need be, she could seek employment. She was an excellent seamstress.

Christy readied herself for bed that night with the sure knowledge that she wouldn't be able to sleep a wink. So many things could go wrong, so many problems to overcome. Calum could find them and bring them back before they reached London. Highwaymen could interrupt their journey and steal her small hoard of money. The coach could break down.

Her disturbing thoughts were swept away by a commotion below. Fear seized her when she heard footsteps pounding up the stairs. *What now?* she wondered. She reached for her robe and flung open the door at the first knock.

"Rory, what is it?"

"Yer wanted below, Christy. Calum sent his brother Donald to fetch ye."

Christy froze. What could Calum want with her at this time of night? Fastening her robe, she hurried down the stairs, skidding to a halt at her first sight of Donald Cameron. Blood was seeping from his head through a filthy bandage, and his arm was in a sling.

"What happened?"

"The Campbells, that's what," Donald said, accepting the cup of ale Rory placed in his hand. "They took exception to our stealing their livestock. Calum was wounded. Took an arrow in his thigh. I'm to bring ye to him so we can keep an eye on ye while he's recovering. He doesna trust ye."

"Look at ye, mon," Rory chided. "Yer dead on yer feet. Go home and let someone see to yer wound."

Reeling from loss of blood, Donald looked as if he wanted to take Rory's advice but didn't dare.

"I promised Calum I'd fetch his intended."

"I won't leave without my son," Christy insisted, crossing her arms for emphasis. "No one here can nurse him."

"Go home while ye can still ride, Donald," Rory urged. "I'll bring Christy to Calum."

Donald looked undecided. But pain was a powerful motivater. "Perhaps yer right, Rory Macdonald," he muttered. "I'll tell Calum that Christy is on her way." He turned around and staggered out the door.

"Hurry," Rory urged. "I'll wake Margot while ye get the wee laddie ready. Ye'll have to leave straightaway, lass. Are yer bags packed?"

"Everything is ready, Rory. I wanted to get an early start tomorrow, that's why I asked Effie and Gavin to spend the night at Glenmoor. God must be watching over me." Giddy with relief, she went to Niall's chamber to prepare him for their journey.

London—Four weeks later

Sinjun entered the Hollingworths' ballroom with a bored look on his face and a beautiful woman on his arm. Not Lady Violet—she had given up on him long ago—but Lady Alice Dodd, Viscount Trent Dodd's beautiful young widow. She was Sinjun's lady of choice this week. More than likely another beautiful woman would take her place next week.

Sinjun's long absence from the London scene had never been explained to the *ton*, but gossip was rife. One rumor had Sinjun's brother sending him away as punishment for his excesses. Another hinted that a woman had lured him away from London, but of course that couldn't be proven. Sinjun's changed appearance alone had been enough to start tongues wagging. His body had grown hard and muscular during his long absence, affording much speculation and many fluttering hearts among the ladies. If Sinjun had been admired and sought after before, it was nothing compared to his popularity with the fairer sex now.

Sinjun was already well into his cups when Rudy intercepted him on his way to the gaming room.

"Where is your new paramour, Sinjun?"

Sinjun stifled a yawn. "Dancing with Lord Welby. I can't seem to manage the intricate steps tonight." He toasted Rudy with his glass and emptied the contents in one swallow.

"Bloody hell, Sinjun, you're foxed again. What's wrong with you? I've never seen you this drunk, not even on your worst days. You're a mess. You go off to God knows where and return more debauched than you were before. Everyone is talking about you. Lord Sin is back, but he's somehow different. There's a rage inside you I've never seen before. You're hard and cynical and no longer fun. What happened to you?"

"Nothing," Sinjun drawled.

"I think there is. I'm your friend, Sinjun, I care what happens to you."

Sinjun slanted him a blurry-eyed look. "You're imagining things, Rudy. In fact, I've never been better. I'm considering asking Alice to marry me."

"Alice Dodd! Bloody hell! She'll take a lover before the ink dries on the marriage license. Her husband was killed dueling for her honor. Besides, if I recall, you're already married."

"My marriage to Christy Macdonald can be ended in short order whenever I wish. As for Alice, she can take all the lovers she wants *after* she gives me an heir. If I have to, I'll chain her to the bed until she quickens with my child."

"Why this sudden need for a child?" Rudy asked curiously. "You've never been eager to become a father before."

Rudy's innocent question hit Sinjun squarely in the gut. He felt suddenly as if the life had drained out of him. He had never thought about children until he saw Christy swell with his babe inside her. He had felt a bone-deep pride he'd never experienced before. He'd loved his unborn child and still mourned its death.

No one, except perhaps for Emma, knew how utterly the baby's death had devastated him. The unexpected death coming on the heels of Christy's request for an annulment so she could wed Calum Cameron had made a shambles of his life. The first time Christy, posing as Lady Flora, had left him, he had embarked on a journey to self-destruction. But that had been nothing compared to what he was doing to himself now.

"Every man wants an heir," Sinjun said lamely.

"You're not an old man, Sinjun. Wait until you find someone worthy of your name. Believe me, 'tis not Alice Dodd."

"Did someone mention my name?"

Lady Alice Dodd's regal bearing, cool blond beauty, and pale blue eyes concealed a passionate nature that attracted a legion of lovers. A Frenchwoman, she'd met her husband while visiting relatives in Dover and had promptly married him. Poor Viscount Dodd had been killed six months after the wedding, dueling over her honor. The first time she'd seen Sinjun she'd selected him as her next husband. Though her friends told her it was hopeless, Alice didn't let that sway her.

"Alice, have you met Lord Blakely?"

"Oh, *oui*," Alice simpered. "So nice to see you again, my lord."

Rudy kissed her outstretched hand and dropped it with undue haste. "The pleasure is all mine, my lady."

Alice flashed him an insincere smile, then blatantly ignored him as she turned her considerable charm on Sinjun. "I'm bored, Sinjun, shall we leave?" Her sexy purr held a wealth of promise. "You said you'd show me your townhouse tonight. There's one room in particular I'm interested in."

Sinjun frowned at Alice, not too foxed to realize she wasn't the woman he wanted. She was very much like the other women in whose arms he'd tried to find comfort.

"If you'd like," Sinjun said indifferently.

He stumbled forward, and Rudy caught his arm. "You're in no condition to show Lady Alice anything but her front door," he admonished. "Go home, I'll see to Lady Alice."

Alice shot Rudy a look that could have boiled an egg. "There's nothing wrong with Sinjun, my lord. I'll take care of him."

"I'm sure you will," Rudy mocked, "but I doubt Sinjun will appreciate your efforts in his condition."

"Bloody hell, Rudy," Sinjun slurred, "who appointed you my guardian?"

"I've done my duty," Rudy said on a long suffering sigh. "I wish you both good night."

"Good night, Rudy," Sinjun said as he wheeled Alice through the crowded ballroom.

"Oh, Sinjun, I forgot to tell you," Rudy called, catching up with him. "Did you know Lady Flora is back in town? I saw her entering a shop on Bond Street."

Foxed as he was, Sinjun whirled around so fast that Alice lost her balance. She would have fallen had Rudy not stretched out a hand to steady her.

"The devil you say! What in bloody hell is she doing in England?"

"I didn't stop to ask. I know you were infatuated with her at one time and thought you'd be interested."

"Do you know where she's staying?"

"I haven't a clue. What if you run into her?"

Sinjun's face hardened, and his dark eyes narrowed into dangerous slits. The pain of betrayal was carved in every line of his harsh features, in the muscle that twitched in his jawline, and in the compression of his lips. He looked so fierce that Alice gasped and backed away.

Bitter words spewed from his throat, raw with barely suppressed anger.

"The bitch! Let's hope I don't."

Chapter 12

Christy bent over her work, adjusting her eyes to the dark velvet she was sewing. After paying the rent on the small house she'd leased in the less than fashionable district south of Bond Street, and hiring someone to do the general housekeeping and cooking, she realized her small hoard of money wasn't going to last as long as she'd hoped.

Effie had offered to find work, but Christy decided that since she had brought Effie and Gavin to London it was up to her to provide for them. Shortly after arriving in London she'd found employment at Madam Sofia's Boutique, one of the better modistes on Bond Street. The work wasn't hard, but the hours were long. The one thing Christy liked about the work was that she could perform her job out of the public eye, unseen by the prestigious clientele that frequented Madam Sofia's establishment.

Christy was hard at work one day when Madam Sofia peeked through the curtain separating the front of the shop from the back and asked her to bring out a bolt of gold tissue she thought one of her customers might fancy. Christy found the cloth her employer wanted, walked through the partition, and set the heavy bolt on the display counter.

"Spread the cloth out, Christy, while I find the fashion doll Lady Thornton requested," Sofia directed. "I won't be gone long."

Christy lifted her eyes and saw Sinjun's sister staring at her with something akin to horror.

"You!" Emma gasped. "What are you doing in London? Haven't you hurt Sinjun enough? Why didn't you stay where you belonged? Wait! I know. Sinjun ordered you to vacate Glenmoor, didn't he?" she said smugly.

"I never meant to hurt Sinjun," Christy whispered, stunned by Emma's animosity. This was exactly the kind of situation she'd hoped to avoid.

"You've already done my brother irreparable damage," Emma charged. "Sinjun isn't the same man I once knew, and 'tis all your fault. He used to be fun, but now there is no laughter in his soul, no happiness, only darkness. When I look in his eyes now, all I see is a man driven by desperation. A man trying to escape his pain."

"I'm sorry," Christy said for want of anything better. She couldn't count the times she'd wondered how Sinjun had reacted to her letter, but Emma's description defied imagination.

"You should be," Emma hissed, her violet eyes seething with condemnation. "I'm sorry about your child, but what you did to my brother was reprehensible. He truly cared for you."

Christy's eyes widened. "He told you about . . . everything? What did he say?"

"I overheard Sinjun telling Julian about you when he returned from Glenmoor. He was so happy about the baby. He intended to return to the Highlands, you know. I was with him the day he received your letter. He was devastated. You're a terrible person, Christy Macdonald."

Christy nearly buckled under the heavy weight of Emma's disapproval. She wanted to blurt out the truth but didn't dare. It had never occurred to her that Sinjun might care for her as strongly as she cared for him. Her only solace was that Sinjun still had his life.

"Leave Sinjun alone," Emma warned. "He's well rid of you. I can't imagine why you would prefer another man when you had Sinjun."

"Is Lord Derby well?" Christy asked, trying to keep the eagerness from her voice and failing.

"If you can call a man bent on destroying himself well, then I suppose he's well enough. I heard that Sinjun is going to marry Lady Alice Dodd. I don't approve of the match, and Julian isn't here to stop him, but if he loves Alice Dodd, then I suppose I can accept her."

Stricken, Christy lowered her gaze. "I wish him well." She wanted to turn and flee, to hug her son close and tell him about the father he would never know. Instead, she said, "Please don't tell Sinjun you saw me. 'Twould be best if he didn't know I'm in London."

"Don't worry," Emma sniffed. "I won't say a word. He hates you as much as I do. I'll never forgive you for lying to him, *Lady Flora*. You've all but destroyed him."

Madam Sofia chose that moment to return from the back of the shop. She sent Christy a sharp look when she noticed Emma's agitation and immediately sought to placate one of her best customers.

"Is something wrong, Lady Thornton? Has my employee offended you in some way?"

"Just the sight of Christy Macdonald offends

me," Emma retorted. "I cannot believe you'd employ a woman of her caliber. I always thought this was a high-class establishment. Perhaps I should take my custom elsewhere."

"I beg you to reconsider, my lady," Sofia pleaded. "I would never knowingly hire someone of questionable reputation, or offend one of my customers. She'll be let go immediately."

Christy's heart sank. This job had been perfect for her. She hated the thought of going out and looking for another. But neither did she wish to offend Emma Thornton. She admired the girl for sticking up for her brother. Under any other circumstances they might have been friends.

"You may leave immediately," Madam Sofia ordered, scowling at Christy. "Come back tomorrow for your outstanding wages."

Christy sent Emma a look of such remorse that Emma had to look away. Though Emma knew Christy didn't deserve her pity, she hoped Christy wouldn't starve because of her. Obviously Christy was in London because Sinjun had turned her out of Glenmoor. She didn't want to think about Christy's lack of home or funds and had to harden her heart in order to remain loyal to her brother.

Nevertheless, as Christy sidled past her, Emma suffered a pang of guilt. There was something about Christy's expression that seemed strangely at odds with the heartless woman Emma had imagined Christy to be. Something was wrong, but for the life of her she couldn't imagine what. She knew what Christy's letter contained, for she'd read it after Sinjun had wadded it up and tossed it to the floor. Was there more here than met the eye?

* * *

Tears clogged Christy's throat. If Emma's words could be believed, and Christy had no reason to doubt them, she had hurt Sinjun terribly. She'd expected him to mourn their bairn, but not excessively. Not Lord Sin. Lord Sin would never deliberately set out to destroy himself, would he?

Firming her chin and dashing away her tears, Christy came to a decision. She had to see Sinjun, to judge for herself how accurately Emma had described his frame of mind. And she had to accomplish it without Sinjun's knowledge.

The following morning Christy asked Gavin to drive her around Hyde Park. During her previous visit to London she'd learned that the *ton* usually rode through the park in the morning, and she hoped to find Sinjun among those trotting along Rotten Row. She swathed herself in a veil and widow's weeds and tried to ignore the curious looks she received. Seeing no reason to deny Niall the fresh air, she brought Effie and her son along on her outing.

Christy saw nothing of Sinjun that morning or the next three mornings. On the fourth day she saw him, mounted upon a magnificent black gelding. He didn't appear unhappy ... only bored.

Christy's hungry gaze devoured Sinjun as Gavin drove the rig past him. That brief glance wasn't enough. She swiveled her head to watch him until her coach turned a corner and she could no longer see him. As if that wasn't punishment enough, Christy returned to Hyde Park later that afternoon, when men often took their ladies riding.

Sure enough, Sinjun was there, handling the ribbons of his high-stepping matched grays with expertise. Sitting beside him was a lovely blond who clung to him with a possessiveness that grated on

Christy. Lady Alice? Jealousy choked her; she couldn't breathe. She paled visibly when the woman leaned close to whisper into Sinjun's ear. He nodded and smiled, but Christy saw nothing in his conduct to indicate his interest. The sunshine had suddenly gone out of the day, and Christy asked Gavin to take her home. She couldn't bear the thought of Sinjun belonging to another woman.

Christy's punishment for the terrible lie she had told Sinjun was to return to the park day after day. Seeing Sinjun with another woman was worse than taking a beating. But if the alternative was never seeing Sinjun, her suffering was worth it.

Sinjun paid little heed to Alice's chattering. He rarely did. He smiled at the right times and murmured something when it appeared appropriate. Most of the time these drives in the park with Alice were pure torture. He didn't know why he put himself through it. He supposed it was to keep himself from being eaten up with hatred for the little Scottish bitch who made love so sweetly while stabbing him in the back.

Thinking of Christy raised his ire another notch and brought a ferocious scowl to his face. If he ever got his hands on her . . .

"Sinjun, whatever are you scowling about?" Alice asked. She squeezed his arm. "One would think you weren't enjoying my company."

"How could I not enjoy the company of so lovely a lady?" he answered with little enthusiasm. "Are you ready to leave? I'm to meet Rudy at White's later."

Alice pouted. "I suppose by evening you'll be too foxed to take me to the opera. I swear, Sinjun, I don't know why I bother with you."

She laid her hand on his thigh. When he didn't respond like she'd hoped, her hand inched upward, stopping just short of his crotch. Sinjun seemed blissfully unaware until her palm cupped him and squeezed.

"Bloody hell, Alice!" he roared, flinging her hand away. "Can't you wait until we're alone? Anyone passing will get an eyeful."

"Since when did Lord Sin care what anyone thought? I want you now, before you get too drunk to do either of us any good. Something always seems to happen to prevent us from being together intimately. I want you to make love to me and remember it the next day, Sinjun."

Her hand crept back up Sinjun's thigh. Sinjun groaned, feeling himself responding. What the hell, he thought as he transferred the ribbons to one hand so he could fondle Alice's small breast with the other. He was about to turn the carriage toward the exit and find the closest bed when a coach lumbered past from the opposite direction. He had no idea what made him turn away from Alice to watch the coach, or why the woman swathed in a black veil and widow's weeds caught his eye. Perhaps it was the small child with her. But if he wanted to be brutally honest, he'd admit his attention had been captured by an all too brief glimpse of a shiny copper curl that had escaped from the woman's veil.

He had no idea why, but that one bright lock of hair triggered waves of intense longing he'd tried to subdue but usually couldn't. He'd had but a fleeting glimpse of the child in the coach but it looked to be about the age of his own child had it lived.

Ever since Rudy had told him he'd seen Christy

in London he'd wondered what he would do should he encounter her. Especially since he now knew that a brief glimpse of a woman he thought looked like her could cause him such anguish.

"Sinjun, you're not paying attention," Alice whined. "I hope you're more attentive after we're married."

Sinjun returned his attention to Alice, suddenly aware that he didn't give a damn about her. Nor had he any intention of marrying her. The sooner she knew it the better off they'd both be.

"There's not going to be a wedding, Alice," he said evenly. "I'm afraid we don't suit."

Alice's face hardened, turning almost ugly as she sputtered indignantly, "What do you mean, we don't suit? I had my heart set on becoming a marchioness."

Sinjun swiveled his head for a last glimpse of the coach bearing the widow and silently upbraided himself for being fanciful. Cursing himself for a fool, he tried to concentrate on Alice. She'd expected to become his wife and he'd let her believe it would happen. Normally he wasn't a cruel man, but since Christy . . . well, it had amused him to let Alice believe he would marry her. Hell, he'd even convinced himself that marrying Alice was what *he* wanted. Until he'd caught a glimpse of a shiny copper curl.

"There won't be a wedding, Alice," he repeated.

Alice's eyes grew positively glacial, and her voice even more so. "I beg your pardon."

"I'm a married man."

He tooled the grays through the gate and into the busy thoroughfare. "You, my lord, are a liar. Everyone knows you are no longer married."

"Everyone is wrong. I neglected to file the annulment document," Sinjun muttered, wanting a drink so badly his hands shook.

She gave him a predatory smile. "I can change your mind. Come home with me now. Let me show you what marriage to me can be like."

Sinjun guided the carriage around the corner and pulled up in front of Alice's townhouse. "Perhaps another time, my lady. I suddenly find myself eager to become hopelessly drunk."

Alice allowed Sinjun to hand her down from the carriage, molding herself against him with wanton disregard for propriety. "You and I aren't finished, Lord Sin," she murmured huskily as she lifted her face and pressed her lips to his. With a laugh and toss of her head, she hurried into the house.

Sinjun climbed into his carriage, Alice already a dim memory. He was going to meet Rudy and drown his anger at a certain Scottish laird in a bottle. If he was still able to stand at the end of the day, perhaps he could sleep without dreaming of Christy in Calum's arms.

Christy knew Sinjun had seen her but felt confident the veil had kept her identity a secret. Still, she couldn't forget the way he'd stared. He didn't look well, she thought. His heavy-lidded eyes sported purple circles, and he appeared to have lost weight. Christy couldn't help but notice where Sinjun's hand had been when they had driven past . . . on the lady's breast. The pain it caused her was like a knife in the gut. Christy hadn't expected Sinjun to remain celibate, they were no longer married, after all, but the searing agony of seeing his hands on another woman sickened her.

At least Sinjun was alive, a voice in her head whispered.

The following day Christy set out to look for work. Spending her days in Hyde Park waiting for a glimpse of Sinjun was consuming her life and making her miserable. Gavin drove her to Bond Street, where most of the fashionable shops were located.

"Return for me in two hours," Christy told Gavin as she surveyed the various shops just opening for business.

A shop called Paris Fashions caught her eye, and she marched determinedly toward the exclusive store, which sported an elegantly arrayed mannequin in the window.

So intent was she on making a good impression that she paid little heed to the man exiting the gentlemen's tailor shop nearby.

"Lady Flora! How wonderful to see you again."

Christy whirled, startled to see Lord Blakely hurrying to catch up with her. She felt the blood rush from her face and she would have given anything to turn and flee. But it was too late. The viscount had already reached her, his smile warmly genuine.

"I caught a glimpse of you a week or so ago but wasn't able to catch your attention. When did you return to London?"

"A . . . a few weeks ago," Christy said, stumbling over the words.

"Is your husband with you this time?"

It took Christy a moment to recall the elderly husband she had invented. "He . . . he died," Christy stammered.

"I'm sorry, my lady. You weren't wearing mourning, so I assumed . . ."

"You've nothing to apologize for, my lord. Before he died, my husband made me promise not to go into deep mourning after his passing. He'd been ill a long time and died shortly after I returned from London. 'Tis why I left London in such a hurry. I was called home to be with him at the end."

"Does Sinjun know you've returned?"

"I . . . no. 'Tis better this way. What Sinjun and I had ended when I returned to . . . Cornwall."

"Then I'm in luck," Rudy crowed gleefully. "May I call on you? Or is it too soon after losing your husband?"

" 'Tis too soon," Christy demurred. "I'm sorry."

Rudy's handsome face mirrored his disappointment. "I was hoping you'd agree to attend the masked ball my grandmother, the dowager duchess of Langston, is giving on Saturday."

"Why me? I'm sure there are scores of women eager for your company."

He gave her a rakish grin. "There are, but I prefer you. Will you reconsider, Lady Flora? Everyone who's anyone will be there."

"Even Sinjun?"

"If he can stay sober long enough to attend. But I won't let him bother you, if that is your wish."

Christy's mind whirled. The opportunity to see Sinjun without being recognized was tempting. She could wear a wig to disguise the color of her hair and a mask that covered everything but her lips. It was unlikely that she would come face to face with him, considering the crush of people who attended a society event. If she did, she would face that obstacle when she came to it.

"I hope your silence means you're reconsidering," Rudy said hopefully.

She'd be crazy to contemplate appearing anywhere Sinjun might show up, she told herself. But after the things Emma had said about him, she *had* to see him, to judge for herself whether Emma had exaggerated his state of mind.

"Actually, I *have* reconsidered," Christy said after a lengthy pause. "I accept your invitation to attend your grandmother's ball."

"Splendid!" Rudy enthused. "Give me your direction and I'll call for you on Saturday."

No, that wouldn't do at all, Christy decided. She would only give out her address if Rudy agreed to certain conditions. "Before I give you my direction, you must promise to give it to no one, including Sinjun. 'Tis the only way I'll agree to go with you. Also, I want my identity to remain a secret."

Rudy frowned. "What an odd request. How am I to introduce you?"

"However you wish, as long as no one knows I'm Flora Randall." *Or Christy Macdonald*, she thought but did not say.

"If that's the only way you'll accept my invitation, then I agree."

"I'm serious, my lord," Christy stressed. "You're not to tell Lord Derby where I live. Your word of honor."

"You have it, Lady Flora," Rudy pledged. "I don't know what happened between you and Sinjun and I don't want to know, but your secret is safe with me."

"Thank you, my lord. You may call for me on Saturday." She gave him her address, and if he was surprised by the less than fashionable section of town in which she resided, he was too much of the gentleman to mention it.

They parted a few minutes later, and Christy

continued down the street. What had she done? she chided herself. Meeting Sinjun, with or without a mask, was asking for trouble. Her instincts had hummed a warning, and she had refused to heed it.

Emma's description of Sinjun's current state of mind had given her so much guilt that she had to see for herself what her deceit had wrought. How she wished she could have explained everything to Emma. She felt certain that Emma would agree that an angry, out of control Sinjun was better than a dead one.

Christy had no luck finding work that day or the next. To Christy's chagrin, Madam Sofia had warned every modiste on Bond Street and beyond that hiring Christy Macdonald would cost them their clientele. Before too long Christy realized that finding work in the fashionable shops on Bond Street was no longer possible. She'd have to go farther abroad to find employment, to the modistes who catered to actresses, mistresses, and high-class prostitutes.

Sinjun no more wanted to attend the dowager duchess's masked ball tonight than he wanted to hang himself from the rafters, but he had promised Rudy he'd attend. He supposed Alice would be there, and he'd have to spend the entire evening avoiding her. He'd been wrong to let her believe he was free to marry when in truth he was still wed to Christy. Not for the first time he wondered why he had dragged his feet regarding the annulment.

Initially he'd decided to wait for Julian to return. But since he had no idea when Julian's mysterious business would bring him home, that excuse was rather lame. Then he'd misplaced the document and just recently found it stuck at the very back of his desk drawer.

As he paced his chamber, waiting for Pemburton to have his bathwater brought up to the bathing room, Sinjun mulled over the startling bit of information Rudy had recently imparted. Rudy had sworn he'd seen Christy in London. The thought of Christy in London had so unsettled Sinjun that he hadn't been himself since, if one could call remaining in a perpetual state of inebriation his usual self.

What was she doing in London? Was Calum Cameron with her? Had they spoken their vows yet? He could think of no reason Christy and Calum would come to London; they both hated anything English. He was more inclined to think that Rudy had seen someone who resembled Christy. Aye, he decided, that's precisely what had happened. For his own peace of mind, he had to believe that Christy was nowhere near London.

A knock on the door disturbed Sinjun's reverie. Pemburton entered upon Sinjun's command. "Your bath is ready, my lord," he intoned dryly. "Shall you require my assistance?"

"Just bring me a fresh bottle of brandy," Sinjun said as he headed toward the bathing room.

Pemburton's eyebrows arched upward. "Before breakfast, my lord?"

"You're not my brother, Pemburton," Sinjun muttered. "Thank God he's not around to flail me with his infernal carping. Just do as I say. I want to be thoroughly foxed before presenting myself at the dowager duchess's ball tonight."

His spine stiff with disapproval, Pemburton left.

* * *

Sinjun's wishes were granted. When he staggered into the ballroom that night, wearing a half mask and resplendent in evening clothes, he was foxed, but not as drunk as he would have liked.

Sinjun made straight for the dowager and bowed low over her hand.

"I wondered if you'd appear," the elegant, white-haired lady said with asperity.

"I promised your grandson," Sinjun slurred. "By the way, where is Rudy?"

The dowager, an erect little woman in her seventh decade, sent Sinjun a reproving look. "Foxed again, Lord Derby? If I didn't like you so well I'd be angry. Rudy will be here directly. He said you would make an appearance tonight, but he has more faith in you than I do. One never knows what Lord Sin might do these days. You simply must learn to control your excesses, Derby," she scolded. "I've known you a long time and I don't like what I've been hearing about you."

Sinjun was spared from further censure when a pair of masked guests came up to greet her. Bowing, Sinjun made a hasty retreat. The dowager's words had sparked a simmering anger inside him. If not for Christy he wouldn't be treading upon the path to self-destruction. His child's death had created an emptiness within him, and he did whatever it took to forget. He hurt, truly hurt inside. Christy had told him so little about his child's death. Had he lost a son? Or had his child been a daughter?

Sinjun wandered aimlessly around the ballroom, encountering no one he cared to engage in conversation, completely unaware of the number of women staring at him with speculation. Before long he found himself surrounded by a bevy of beautiful women eager for his attention. Despite his less than pristine reputation, women still found Lord Sin irresistible. Perhaps it was *because* of his reputation that he was so popular with the opposite sex.

Though his heart wasn't in it, Sinjun ventured onto the dance floor, idly wondering if he was attracted enough to one of his dance partners to bed her. These days he rarely found an interesting woman, and his bed had remained appallingly empty.

Sinjun was resting against a pillar with an empty glass in his hands when he saw Rudy enter the ballroom with a masked lady on his arm. He watched as they joined the promenade around the room, his bleary gaze settling on the woman. She wore a powdered wig, and though her mask covered all but her mouth, Sinjun felt an immediate attraction, as if he were drawn to the mysterious lady by an irresistible force too strong to resist.

He pushed himself away from the pillar, refreshed his drink at the refreshment table, and strode briskly toward Rudy and the masked beauty with him.

"Rudy, what kept you?" Sinjun drawled.

"You're foxed again," Rudy chided. "I don't suppose my grandmother is too awfully pleased with you."

"You suppose right," Sinjun drawled. "Are you going to introduce me to your lady?"

"I don't think so, Sinjun," Rudy said. "I'm not going to lose this one to you."

The sound of Sinjun's voice nearly drove Christy to her knees. She adjusted her mask and clung to Rudy as if he were her lifeline, for Sinjun had never looked so splendid to her. His superbly fashioned evening clothes fitted him like a glove, and Christy tried not to think about the magnificent body that lay hidden beneath those clothes. Without volition she remembered his stunning passion as he'd loved her with his hands, his body, his mouth. She recalled how those sensual lips had explored every inch of her flesh, and she felt herself flush at the memory. She stared at him through the eye slits of her mask, thinking that he carried himself well despite being noticeably foxed.

When she'd walked into the ballroom on Rudy's arm, Christy had seen him surrounded by adoring women, and she wondered how many of the nubile beauties he had bedded since he left Glenmoor.

"What harm can it do to introduce the lady to me?" Sinjun persisted.

"More than you know," Rudy muttered, giving Christy's hand a squeeze.

Sinjun raised an elegant eyebrow. "You're being deliberately cruel, Rudy." He took Christy's hand, turned it palm up, and pressed it to his lips. "I am St.John Thornton, Lord Derby, my lady. My friends call me Sinjun."

Christy felt a shock travel clear up her arms from where his lips touched her palm. "My lord," she murmured in a husky whisper as she quickly withdrew her hand from his grasp. Did Sinjun recognize her?

"Do I know you, my lady?"

"No, my lord, I would have remembered had we met before."

"Your charm won't work this time," Rudy said. "Go find your own lady. Didn't I see Lady Alice a few minutes ago?"

Sinjun shrugged. "Alice and I had a parting of ways."

Christy sucked in a startled breath. Had she

heard right? She thought Sinjun and Lady Alice Dodd were to be married.

"I'm sure you'll find someone to replace her," Rudy said, sounding not at all sympathetic to Sinjun's plight.

"Ah, a quadrille is starting. Do you mind if I dance with your lady?"

"Back off, Sinjun," Rudy warned. "This dance is promised to me."

"Isn't that your grandmother signaling for you to attend her?" Sinjun asked, calling Rudy's attention to the dowager, who was indeed waving at Rudy. "Go ahead, I'll keep your lady company."

"No, I'll go with Lord Blakely," Christy said, edging away from Sinjun.

"Nonsense," Sinjun said, taking Christy's hand and leading her off toward the dance floor while Rudy stood helplessly by, obviously torn between rescuing Lady Flora and attending his grandmother. Then it was too late to intervene as the couple joined the dancers on the floor.

"Who are you?" Sinjun asked when they met during one of the intricate steps of the dance.

"My name is of no import," Christy murmured. "You are exceedingly bold, my lord."

Sinjun gave her a crooked smile. "You must indeed be new to London if you haven't heard of Lord Sin."

"Oh, I have heard of you, my lord. Are all those things they say about you true?"

"Most of them," Sinjun allowed.

The dance parted them again, and when they finally reunited, the last notes of the music faded away. Christy looked for Rudy, saw he was still talking with his grandmother, and started in his direction.

Sinjun had other ideas. "What a crush of people," he said, steering her toward the open French doors. "I find myself in desperate need of air."

"Take your air, my lord, but release me first," Christy demanded. "I must return to Lord Blakely."

"In good time, my lady, in good time."

They had reached the doors. Christy would have loved a breath of fresh air, but not with Sinjun. She couldn't risk being alone with him no matter how she longed for his company.

Gripping her elbow, Sinjun pushed her through the doors onto the veranda. Couples taking the air gazed curiously at them as Sinjun dragged her down the stairs and into the dark garden.

Chapter 13

❧❧❧

"My lord! Stop right now!" Christy demanded, trying without success to pull free of Sinjun's grasp.

Sinjun ignored her. Christy didn't realize how foxed he really was until he staggered drunkenly, nearly spilling them both to the ground. He righted himself and tugged her along with him, until the lights from the house appeared like twinkling diamonds in the distance. Then he pulled her behind some bushes and swung her roughly into his arms.

"Now, my lady," he said raggedly, "I'm going to kiss you. I find you utterly irresistible."

"You find all women irresistible," Christy flung back.

He merely chuckled. Christy's last thought before his mouth slammed down on hers was that this couldn't be, shouldn't be, happening. Then coherent thought fled as his tongue parted her lips and he deepened the kiss. His unique taste, his heady scent, forced a response, and her mouth opened beneath his.

His arms tightened around her; her breasts flattened against his hard chest and her loins meshed with his. She heard him groan; a sound so raw that, had she not known better, would have indicated pain. He whispered something against her lips; she thought it was her name and prayed it wasn't. She had no idea how it happened, but suddenly she found herself flat on her back on the unyielding ground. The pungent scent of earth and male musk lulled her into complacency, until his hands moved determinedly to her face.

"Remove your mask. I want to see your face," he whispered.

Her hands flew upward to stay his hands. "No, please."

He sighed heavily, the sound a combination of impatience and frustration. "I've never made love to a woman whose face I couldn't see. But if you insist . . ."

"I've never made love with a man as foxed as you are," Christy shot back.

He stiffened. "Are you afraid I can't please you?"

"I . . . we are strangers, my lord. Please let me up."

Sinjun went still, his head cocked to one side. "I know you, my lady, I just can't place you. Your kisses, that mouth . . . damn this befuddled head of mine. I'll remember you tomorrow, depend on it."

Christy sincerely hoped not. "I must return to Lord Blakely before he comes looking for me."

"Let him look," Sinjun muttered against her lips. "Serves him right for refusing to tell me your name."

His knee slid between her legs. Panic shuddered through her. "Stop!"

"Tell me your name and where I can find you tomorrow and I'll let you go."

"No, I cannot."

"Nor can I stop," Sinjun said, giving her a lop-sided smile.

Christy tried to push him away, but he was too strong for her. He lowered his body atop hers and pressed his loins into the cradle of her thighs, giving her the full benefit of his aroused sex.

"I'm going to have you, my lady. I may regret this tomorrow, but tonight I'm too foxed to care."

Slowly he raised her skirts, his hands skimming her thighs, stroking, kneading, burning her flesh with his heated touch. Her heart jumped violently, banging against her ribs. This was Sinjun, the man she loved. The man who was no longer her husband. Then her thoughts scattered as he set his hands on either side of her head, holding her still as he leaned down and covered her mouth with his. His tongue drove past her lips, filling her mouth with his taste and scent.

His kiss was neither gentle nor tender. He took her mouth hungrily, almost savagely. Christy moaned into his mouth and kissed him back, passionately, suddenly needing this man as desperately as he seemed to need her. For the first time in months she felt vibrantly alive. Mouths locked together, they rolled on the ground, legs tangling, hands clutching, the friction of their heated bodies wildly arousing.

His hands found her breasts as he dropped his lips to her arching throat. Needing to feel more of him, she tore open his shirt, ripping it downward from his neck and slipping her hands inside. The heat of his bare flesh scorched her palms, the pleasure of it raw and profound. He must have felt it too, for a ragged moan rumbled in his chest. When his lips traveled downward to caress the rounded tops of her breasts, her breath hitched, then hissed from between her lips.

"You're driving me mad," he gasped.

Christy decided it must be the full moon, for she was as mad with desire as he. The only difference was that she knew exactly who he was, while Sinjun had no idea he was making love to his own wife. How ironic, she thought, that they found themselves in the same situation as when they first met. Yet the circumstances were different this time. In the end it didn't matter. Call it moonlight madness, call it insanity, there was no stopping the passion building inside her.

"Bloody hell," Sinjun muttered as he jerked down the neckline of her gown. "Too many clothes."

Christy felt the material stretch, then rip, as cool air kissed her bare breasts. His lips brought back warmth as he drew a sensitive nipple into his mouth. Christy arched against him as liquid fire raced through her. His tongue was a hot brand, searing her nipples with moist heat. And his hands. Oh, God, they were between her legs, his fingers probing, caressing, finding that sensitive nub and rubbing until shock waves racked her body.

Then his mouth replaced his fingers, laving her swollen nub with rough, swirling strokes of his tongue. She gave a frustrated cry when he abruptly lifted his head and grinned down at her. She didn't want him to stop. It felt too good.

"Spread your legs for me, sweetheart. Foxed or not, I've yet to have a lady complain."

The words brought Christy to swift reality. How had she let this happen? Wild, hedonistic, unpredictable, Lord Sin could make a statue want him.

"No, stop!"

Her protest came too late. The engorged tip of his shaft was already probing her passage. He poised above her a brief moment, frowning, as if trying to see the woman beneath the mask. Then he pressed himself down upon her. She arched wildly, trying to buck him off, but his weight trapped her. His legs on either side of hers held her immobile, granting her no relief from the incredible heat building inside her. He flexed his hips and surged inside her, allowing her scant time to catch her breath as he thrust hard and deep, driving his thick length to the hilt.

Christy surrendered to the tension humming through her, rocking against him, arching her back for deeper penetration. Caught in passion's throes, she felt something inside her break free and soar.

His loving was as fierce as a summer storm, battering her senses, leaving her feeling bruised and breathless as her body convulsed. She whispered his name and shattered, surrendering to ecstasy. Moments later she heard Sinjun's exultant shout and felt his seed bathe her womb.

When her wits reconnected with reality, Christy realized this wanton coupling could result in another child. That staggering thought cooled her passion as nothing else could. With a cry of dismay, she shoved him away.

Unprepared for her assault, he fell back, staring at her, his expression a mixture of shock, confusion . . . and sudden knowledge. "Christy . . . my God, it's you!"

Stunned that he had recognized her despite her disguise, Christy leaped to her feet, holding her ruined bodice together at the neckline. She had to flee before Sinjun regained his senses.

He must have surmised her intention, for he suddenly came alive. "Christy, wait! Don't go!"

Her throat clogged with terror, Christy backed away, still shaking from the aftermath of their loving. "I'm not. I'm not who you think," she cried as she turned and raced toward the house. She glanced over her shoulder once and saw Sinjun sitting on the ground, his forehead resting on his knees. When she realized he wasn't going to give chase, she rested a moment against a tree to catch her breath and to think.

Glancing down at her ruined dress, she realized she couldn't go back inside the house without causing a scandal. Tears of anguish slid down her cheeks. How in the world was she going to get back home?

"Flora, is that you?"

Christy spun around, ready to flee again. Then she recognized Rudy coming down the path toward her, and relief shuddered through her. She choked out his name. Then she was in his arms, shaking like a leaf in the wind on an autumn day.

He held her at arm's length and stared at her, his brow furrowed in concern. "My God, what happened to you?"

"I don't want to talk about it," Christy said on a shaky sigh. "Take me home."

Rudy's expression hardened. "Damn Sinjun to hell! He did this to you, didn't he? Look at you, you're a mess. I'll kill him."

"Rudy, no! Just take me home. I'm as much to blame as Sinjun."

"No woman should be treated like he treated you," Rudy railed. "I'll call him out, I swear it."

She pulled on his arm. "I want to leave, Rudy. Please."

"Your wrap."

"Forget it."

"I'll settle you in my coach, then go back for your wrap and make our excuses to my grandmother." He placed an arm around her shoulders and led her off, carefully skirting the puddle of light spilling from the ballroom.

Christy cast a furtive glance over her shoulder, relieved that Sinjun wasn't following. She was in no condition for lengthy explanations, which she was sure Sinjun would demand. She didn't breathe easily again until Rudy returned and the coach pulled away from the townhouse.

She had to have been out of her mind to come here tonight, she scolded herself. But the last thing she'd expected was for Sinjun to recognize her so easily. How had he known?

"Do you want to tell me what happened?" Rudy asked when silence stretched out between them.

Christy dropped her gaze and pulled her wrap closer around her. "I can't."

Gently, he removed her mask. "Did he hurt you?"

She shook her head. "I'm fine, really."

A muscle twitched in his jaw. "You don't look fine."

Her relationship with Sinjun was too complicated to explain. And Rudy wouldn't understand. No one would understand why she had lied to Sinjun about their bairn.

"I'll call on you tomorrow," Rudy said as the coach pulled up before her front door.

"I wish you wouldn't," Christy demurred.

"Soon then. Rest assured I'll bring Sinjun to task for what he's done to you."

Panic rose inside her. "Remember your promise,

my lord. You said you wouldn't tell Sinjun where to find me. No matter what, I pray you will not betray my trust."

Rudy grasped her small, cold hand and kissed her knuckles. "I'd never betray so lovely a lady."

Christy. Still sitting on the ground, Sinjun was too stunned to think beyond the fact that he had just made love to his wife. He'd taken her on the ground like an animal, using her like he would a dockside whore. He was suddenly stone cold sober. As sober as he'd ever been in his life.

Christy. Her name tasted like fine wine on his tongue. He should have known her immediately. Damn his fuzzy head and damn his inability to see beyond her mask and wig. But it hadn't taken him long to recognize her once he'd started making love to her. No other woman in the world made love like the Macdonald chieftain. Her sweet taste, the subtle scent of her flesh, the sweet curve of her lips, the intense green of her eyes. He couldn't pinpoint the exact moment he'd recognized her; perhaps he'd known her all along and had refused to believe what his mind told him.

His eyes darkened with anger when he recalled the cold words of her letter, and how little she'd told him of their child's death. So many questions and so few answers.

Why was she with Rudy? What had happened to Calum Cameron? What in God's name was she doing in London?

Needing answers, he straightened his clothing and stumbled back to the house. The moment he blundered into the ballroom through the French doors he realized he'd made a mistake. Christy wouldn't have returned to the party. Not in her state of dishevelment.

He strode through the crowd of amused faces, aware that he'd become the center of attention. He groaned inwardly and glanced down at himself. His clothing was grass-stained and covered with loose twigs. His neckcloth was awry, his hair messed and his coat unbuttoned. Thank God he'd had the sense to fasten his breeches.

Odd bits of conversation followed him out the door. "A wastrel. Out of control. Shouldn't be allowed in polite society. Debaucher of young women. Blackguard. Scoundrel."

Sinjun paid them little heed as he made his excuses to his scandalized hostess and took his leave. It was imperative that he find Christy.

Sinjun rose early the following morning. His head felt swollen to twice its size and his tongue felt furry, but his mind had never been clearer. He rang for Pemburton, and when the butler appeared with a bottle and glass on a tray, Sinjun waved them away.

"I won't need that this morning, Pemburton. See to my bath. I have urgent business to conduct."

Though Pemburton's long face remained stoic, the twitching muscle in his chin revealed his shock. " 'Tis early, my lord. 'Tis not like you to arise before the sun. Is something amiss?"

"Everything is amiss, Pemburton," Sinjun said shortly. "But it won't be once I speak to Lord Blakely."

"Shall I bring your breakfast, my lord?"

Sinjun's stomach gave a rumble of protest. Yesterday's excesses still plagued him.

"No breakfast, Pemburton. I'll stop at one of my

clubs should I require food later. Have the grays hitched to the carriage and brought around."

An hour later, bathed, shaved, and dressed, Sinjun left the house. The carriage was waiting just as he had ordered, and he waved the driver off as he climbed onto the seat, adjusted the ribbons in his fingers, and drove off down the street with reckless haste.

The carriage had scarcely rolled to a stop before the Blakely townhouse when Sinjun leaped to the ground and sprinted up the stairs to the front door. Several minutes passed before his insistent knocking brought an answer.

"Ah, Carstairs, good morning," Sinjun said, pushing past the startled butler. "Please inform Viscount Blakely that I am here and wish to see him."

Carstairs's eyebrows lifted nearly to his hairline. "Lord Blakely won't be up for hours yet."

"Wake him," Sinjun said as he strode into the study. "I'll wait for him here."

"But . . . but, my lord," Carstairs sputtered, following close on his heels, "the master never arises before noon."

Sinjun rounded on him. "The devil take you, Carstairs, just do as I say."

Shaking his head and muttering something about the impetuousness of youth beneath his breath, Carstairs took himself off to awaken his master.

Sinjun paced impatiently while he waited for Rudy; his friend had much to explain. Sinjun's patience was all but shot when Rudy, his hair tousled and his eyes heavy-lidded with sleep, walked into the room.

"What in bloody hell are you doing here at this

ungodly time of day? You have a lot of nerve, Sinjun. What you did to Lady Flora last night was unforgivable. Name the weapons. I intend to defend my lady's honor."

"Don't be stupid," Sinjun retorted. "Defend her honor my arse. What were you doing with Christy last night?"

"You're still foxed, Sinjun. Go home and sleep it off. I don't know any Christy."

"The devil you say! You escorted her to your grandmother's ball last night."

Rudy's hands balled into fists. "The lady I escorted to Grandmother's ball was *not* named Christy. Foxed or sober, your behavior last night was reprehensible."

"I may have been foxed but I know exactly what I did and to whom I was doing it. Are you going to tell me where to find Christy, or do I have to beat it out of you?"

"I told you, I don't know any Christy."

"Perhaps I should have said Lady Flora Randall," Sinjun bit out. "I may have been foxed last night but my brain was still working. Did you think I wouldn't recognize my own wife?"

Rudy merely stared at Sinjun, his mouth open in silent exclamation, apparently too stunned to answer.

"That's right, Rudy, *my wife*. Flora Randall and Christy Macdonald happen to share the same husband. Me. In case you haven't already guessed, they are the same woman."

"Devil you say!" Rudy said, sinking into the nearest chair. "Why should I believe you?"

"Because I speak the truth. Where did you think I went when I left London? I'd gone to Scotland to confront my wife. Julian heard that Christy was expecting a child, and I went to Glenmoor to get her signature on the annulment document Julian helped me to obtain. I wasn't going to acknowledge another man's bastard. You can imagine my shock when I arrived at Glenmoor and learned that my former mistress, Flora, and my wife, Christy, were the same woman, and that it was my own child Christy carried."

"I don't understand," Rudy said, shaking his head at the unbelievable tale Sinjun had just spun. "I knew you had left England rather abruptly, but then you never were predictable. Tell me about your child? Lady Flora ... er ... Christy never mentioned a child."

"The story is long and complicated," Sinjun replied. "Someday I'll regale you with the details. Right now, there is only one thing I want from you."

"Which is? . . ."

"Tell me where to find Christy."

"Go to hell! I made a solemn vow, and I intend to keep it. You'll learn nothing from me."

"A vow?" Sinjun didn't like the sound of that.

"Aye. Christy, if that is indeed her name, made me promise to tell no one where to find her. She specifically mentioned you. She said you parted on less than friendly terms."

"You're damn right we did. I've been lied to, tricked into fathering a child, and tossed aside for a Scotsman. Christy has much to account for."

Rudy uncoiled himself from the chair, his expression pugnacious. "Perhaps that's why she didn't want you to find her. Did you hurt her last night, Sinjun? If you did, I swear our friendship is over."

Sinjun had the decency to flush. He'd been

rough, but he didn't believe he'd hurt her. Their passion had exploded into a battle of sensual aggressiveness, and he'd been only too happy to assuage her hunger along with his.

"Christy is my wife, I'd never hurt her physically, though she deserves a good thrashing." His expression hardened, his eyes narrowed into slits. "Have you bedded my wife?"

Rudy swung, hitting Sinjun squarely on the jaw. Sinjun staggered backward against the desk. "You deserve that," Rudy said, rubbing his knuckles. "Christy deserves better than you."

Sinjun rubbed his jaw, stunned by his friend's defense of Christy. "Christy left me for another man, for God's sake! What am I to think when I find her with my best friend?" He glared at Rudy for one charged moment, ready to retaliate until he remembered that Rudy was his best friend, maybe his only friend.

"You're making me damn angry, Rudy. Are you going to tell me where to find Christy?"

"Christy doesn't want to see you," Rudy argued. "I promised she wouldn't have to see you if she didn't want to and a promise is a promise, Sinjun. Are you so without honor that you'd have me break my solemn word? Besides, you're angry and might hurt her no matter what you say."

It was all Sinjun could do to keep from hurling himself at his best friend, for all the good it would do him. Fisticuffs never solved anything. Cunning worked better. Sooner or later Rudy was going to call on Christy, and when he did, Sinjun wouldn't be far behind.

Christy wallowed in indecision. Sinjun knew she was in London and she had no idea what to do about it. She could stay where she was and pray that Sinjun wouldn't find her, or she could search for new lodgings. She must have been crazy to think Sinjun wouldn't recognize her.

Christy was sick of pretenses, sick of lying to Sinjun, but she feared that being truthful now would bring unpleasant repercussions. She knew intuitively that Sinjun would neither understand nor forgive her. What if he took her bairn from her? She had no choice. She had to continue this charade to the bitter end. It was her punishment and her penance.

It wasn't until Effie brought Niall to her to nurse the following morning that Christy finally reached a decision.

"Pack our things, Effie, we're going to move," she said decisively.

Effie's mouth dropped open. "Move, Christy? Where will we go? Why must we move?"

"I made a mistake last night," Christy admitted. "Lord Derby recognized me despite my best efforts to disguise myself. I lied about Niall and I fear he'll never forgive me should he find us."

"I dinna think 'tis wise to return to Scotland, unless yer willing to wed with Calum."

"That will never happen," Christy said grimly. "We'll move to a respectable inn until I can rent another place within our means."

"How soon do ye wish to leave?"

"Immediately. I'll look for something today. Tell Gavin to bring the coach around in an hour."

"Perhaps ye should tell Lord Derby about the bairn," Effie suggested.

"No, I cannot. He might take Niall from me, and I couldn't bear it."

She kissed the top of Niall's head, hugging him

against her as his little mouth sucked vigorously at her nipple. When his eyes closed and his mouth slackened, she handed him to Effie and rose to begin her day.

Following at a discreet distance, Sinjun stuck like glue to Rudy, hoping his friend would eventually lead him to Christy. Rudy visited Brooks, White's, the Exchange, and his haberdasher, but not Christy. When Rudy settled in at his grandmother's house for what appeared to be an extended visit, Sinjun gave up in disgust and decided to stop in at Brooks. He was tooling down the roadway when a coach pulling up before the Blue Goose Inn caught his attention. His heart pounded against his ribcage when he noticed that the driver looked familiar. He didn't remember his name, but he sure as hell knew a Macdonald when he saw one.

Sinjun pulled into an empty space behind the coach and waited. He had no idea what was going on, but he was prepared to wait for as long as it took to find out. His patience was rewarded when he saw Christy step down from the coach and enter the inn. The moment Christy disappeared inside, he leaped from his carriage to confront Christy's kinsman.

"You can leave now," Sinjun said, startling Gavin, who obviously hadn't seen him approach from the rear.

"Yer . . . yer lordship, I dinna see ye."

"I know you're a Macdonald," Sinjun said, "but I can't recall your name."

"Gavin, milord, Rory's brother."

"Aye, now I remember. You may leave, Gavin. I'll take care of Christy."

Gavin stiffened. "Nay, I canna do that."

"I insist," Sinjun said sternly. "I'm more than capable of seeing to my own wife."

"Yer wife!" Gavin sputtered. " 'Tis my understanding that ye and The Macdonald are no longer wed."

"Contrary to what Christy thinks, we're still married," Sinjun revealed. "I will assume complete responsibility for her from now on."

Gavin looked unconvinced. "Ye won't hurt her, will ye?"

"The Macdonald is safe with me," Sinjun bit out. "She will be residing with me from now on."

"But yer lordship," Gavin argued, "ye donna understand. There are . . . others to consider."

"I'll take care of everything," Sinjun assured him. "Go home, I'll contact you later, after I've spoken with Christy."

"Verra well, yer lordship, but I dinna like it," Gavin grumbled as he pulled the coach out into traffic with marked reluctance. "Ye'll answer to me and my clansmen if ye harm The Macdonald," he called over his shoulder.

Muttering to himself, Sinjun pulled his carriage into the place just vacated by the coach and sat back to wait for Christy.

Christy knew immediately that the Blue Goose Inn was not the place for her and her small family. From the outside it looked respectable enough, but once inside Christy was disheartened by its disreputable appearance. The Blue Goose was the third inn she'd visited and the third she'd found unsuitable, even for the short stay she had in mind. But she wasn't discouraged. There were least three more inns in good but unfashionable neighborhoods.

Distracted, Christy left the inn, expecting to find Gavin waiting with the coach. The breath slammed from her chest when she saw Sinjun standing beside his carriage, where she had expected to see Gavin waiting with her coach. Sinjun's mouth was twisted into a chilling smile, and Christy felt the first stirrings of fear.

"Sinjun. What are you doing here? Where is Gavin?"

"I sent him home. You're coming with me."

"You had no right!" Christy exclaimed, alarmed by this unexpected turn of events. A confrontation with Sinjun was precisely what she'd wanted to avoid.

"You're my wife. I have every right in the world."

Christy staggered and would have fallen had Sinjun not reached out to steady her. "The annulment . . . ," she began.

"Later," he spat as he grasped her waist and lifted her into the carriage. "Did you think I wouldn't know I was making love to my own wife last night?"

That's exactly what she'd thought. How could her thinking have been so flawed? She couldn't go anywhere with Sinjun. She had a child at home, waiting to be fed. Her breasts were hard and hot, and she could feel milk leaking from her nipples.

"I'm taking you home. My home," Sinjun clarified. " 'Tis where you belong."

"You can't do this! We're no longer married."

"You're dead wrong, and a bigamist if you married Calum Cameron."

Stunned, Christy felt her entire world falling apart. It didn't take a seer to realize that Sinjun was anything but pleased to see her. What would he do when he learned his son was alive?

Stiffening her shoulders, Christy vowed to do whatever it took to keep from losing her son.

Chapter 14

～⌒♡⌒～

"Welcome to Derby Hall," Sinjun said coolly as he handed Christy down from the carriage and propelled her up the front steps.

The door swung open and Sinjun hustled her inside. She shrugged free of his bruising grip and glared at him. Whatever she was going to say died in her throat when she met his fiery gaze. It was like tumbling headlong into a blazing inferno. She'd never seen him so angry, not even that day he'd walked into Glenmoor and recognized her.

His face was set in stone, wiped clean of all emotion, as he stared at her. Suddenly she realized they weren't alone. A tall, gaunt man wearing Derby livery stood at attention beside the door. She gave him a tentative smile. He acknowledged her with a brief flicker of one eyebrow.

"Pemburton," Sinjun began, "I'd like to present to you your new mistress, my wife, Lady Derby."

Pemburton's carefully composed expression went slack with shock. "Your . . . your wife, my lord?" he sputtered.

"Aye. Lady Derby has traveled from Scotland to

join me. Summon the staff. I want them all lined up in the foyer in fifteen minutes to meet their new mistress."

"As you say, my lord," the usually unflappable Pemburton intoned as he disappeared into the dark regions of the house. Though the poor man tried not to appear ruffled, Christy suspected Pemburton had been overwhelmed by her unexpected arrival.

"Why did you tell him that?" Christy demanded. "I'm not your wife and you know it."

"You're wrong, Christy," Sinjun rasped. "I never filed the annulment with the courts. Sorry to disappoint you, but we're still married. If you've already wed the Cameron chieftain, that makes you a bigamist. If you've bedded him, that makes you a wh..."

Rage exploded inside Christy's brain as she drew her arm back and slapped him. "Bastard!" she hissed from between clenched teeth. "How dare you call me names! Misbegotten wretch. Rogue. Wastrel. How many women have you bedded since you left Scotland?"

Sinjun raised his hand to his reddened cheek. "I would advise you not to try that again," he snarled. "You're the one who wanted to dissolve our marriage. You wrote that blasted letter. You didn't even have the courtesy to tell me how our child died." He grasped her shoulders, giving her a rough shake. "Did you think I wouldn't care?"

"Ahem. My lord, my lady. The servants are gathered as you requested."

Christy's face flamed. Arguing in front of servants was not well done of either of them. Not that it mattered what the servants thought of her. She couldn't remain in this house. Not with a husband who hated her and a child who needed her elsewhere. Regardless, Sinjun began the introductions as if nothing had happened.

The plump, bespectacled woman was Mrs. McBride, the cook. Then there were three pert Irish maids, Peggy, Megan, and Bridie. Two young brothers, Jesse and Jerry, helped with odd jobs in the kitchen and drove the equipage when needed. John Coachman, whom she'd met before, had charge of the stables. Pemburton, she learned, ran the household with an iron fist.

When told to select a personal maid from among the three young women, Christy chose Peggy, a saucy brunette with lively blue eyes. After the introductions the staff filed out, leaving Christy and Sinjun alone to continue their argument.

"I'll show you to your chamber," Sinjun said, propelling her up the curving staircase.

Christy waited until they were inside the large, elegantly appointed bedchamber before rounding on Sinjun. "Why are you doing this?"

"You chose to come to London, so I naturally assumed you wished to take up where we left off."

"That's not why I came to London."

"Why did you come, my love?" His gaze traveled the length of her trim form, lingering on her full breasts an unsettling moment before returning to her face. "Having a child changed ... certain things about you," he said. "I don't recall you being so well endowed."

You'd be well endowed, too, if your breasts were filled with milk and ready to burst, Christy thought with asperity.

"I have to leave, Sinjun. Gavin and Effie will be worried about me."

"They know where to find you. What happened

to Rory and Margot? I expected to see them with you."

"Margot is with child." She glared at Sinjun. "Unlike some men I know, Rory wanted to be with Margot for the birth of his child."

"Dammit, Christy! You know why I had to leave. I had every intention of returning, until I received your letter. I had no idea you were so enamored of the Cameron chieftain. Why isn't he with you?"

Christy sought answers to Sinjun's questions and couldn't find it in her heart to tell more lies. "Calum is in Scotland. I . . . we didn't suit."

"So you came to London to win me back," Sinjun accused derisively.

"No! That's not true."

"Why *did* you come to London? Did you think to choose another husband from among my friends? Rudy, perhaps?"

"I don't need a husband!" Unable to bear his false accusations, she started toward the door. "I refuse to stay here a moment longer than necessary." Sinjun was there ahead of her, leaning against the panel, arms crossed over his chest, his smile mocking.

"Tell me what brought you to London."

"I never intended our paths to cross again."

"Liar!" Sinjun shouted. "You wouldn't have attended the ball if you wanted to avoid me."

Christy glared defiantly. "That was a mistake, and that's all I'm going to say. Move away from the door."

Sinjun's temper soared. Never in his life had he been so summarily dismissed by a woman. But despite his anger, his utter confusion, his body stirred with desire. He remembered Christy as she had been last night. Eager, passionate, a flame in his arms. He suddenly felt alive again. The air around them was charged with energy. His body vibrated with a seductive languor that made his breath labored and his senses intensified.

Anticipation quickened the beat of his heart. He needed to be inside her. Desire raged like a wildfire in his blood. The only thing stopping him from stripping her and carrying her to his bed was the knowledge that nothing she'd told him made sense. She had spun so many tales in the past that he was having difficulty separating truth from fiction.

"I want the truth, Christy. I know you're hiding something. What is it? Who are you protecting?"

Christy paled. "I . . . I . . ." Hell would be preferable to what she was going through now.

"How did my child die? Did I have a son or daughter? You owe me answers."

"A son!" Christy blurted out. "He never drew a breath. We buried him the same day."

Sinjun seemed to collapse inwardly, and Christy felt as if her own heart were breaking. It was as if a dam had burst inside her, and suddenly she knew she couldn't continue like this. Dishonesty was a terrible sin. That long-ago lie she'd told Sinjun had compounded until untruths piled one atop another. God would never forgive her. She never considered herself a bad person, but she knew Sinjun would judge her harshly.

"Sweet Virgin! I cannot continue like this. I'm sorry, Sinjun, so sorry."

Tears streamed down her cheeks as she faced Sinjun squarely. Whatever Sinjun thought of her was nothing compared to how she judged herself. "I've lied, Sinjun. So many lies. 'Tis time for the truth. I cannot cheat you of your—"

"Cheat me of what?" His voice was clipped, hard, judgmental. Christy suddenly felt as cold as his voice sounded. Being despised by the man she loved was the worst kind of hell. How could she explain? How could she make him understand that she'd done her best to save his life? Perhaps if he saw his son first he wouldn't hate her so much.

"I owe you the truth, Sinjun, and you shall have it," Christy began. "Allow me to return to my lodgings to . . . get something I left behind, then you'll know everything."

Sinjun gave a bark of laughter. "You must think me a fool. Once I let you out of my sight, you'll disappear again."

Did it matter to him? "Why do you care?" If he had a wee bit of feeling left for her he might find it in his heart to forgive her.

Sinjun shrugged. That simple, careless act dashed any hopes Christy might have harbored.

"You're my wife. I have a right to know what you're hiding before I send you back to Glenmoor. Having a wife in London will restrict my lifestyle. I'll appoint another bailiff to look out for my interests and keep tabs on you. I don't ever want to hear that my deceitful wife is cuckolding me with another man."

"What about the annulment?"

"Forget the annulment. You belong to me whether you're in London or at Glenmoor."

"Please let me return to my lodgings, Sinjun. I promise not to disappear. One hour, that's all I ask," Christy begged, desperate to return home to nurse her son. "When I return, I'll explain about the letter and . . . and everything else."

Sinjun stared at her, one dark brow arched upward. "Another lie, wife?"

Christy shook her head. "Not this time, Sinjun. Trust me this once."

Christy held her breath, aware of the struggle being waged inside Sinjun. She knew she'd given him no reason to trust her, but this time was different. She wanted no more lies between them. He must have read the truth in her eyes, for he nodded, though he still seemed a bit skeptical.

"Very well, Christy. I'll drive you to your lodgings and wait for you inside. If you fail to keep your word, I'll drag you from wherever you're hiding. Understood?"

Christy understood more than she wanted to. She had exhausted his patience, and he'd given her all the leeway she was entitled to. "Understood."

A few minutes later they were tooling down the street toward her house.

"You don't have to accompany me inside," Christy said when they reached her lodgings.

"You've been living *here*?" Sinjun asked, scowling his disapproval at her choice of living quarters. She saw the shabby facade of the building through his eyes and realized how it must look to someone accustomed to much more.

"It's not so bad. The neighborhood is still good."

Sinjun didn't reply as he handed her down from the carriage and grasped her arm as if he expected her to bolt. He propelled her up the stairs and opened the door. Christy stepped inside, suddenly aware of the difference between the grand foyer of Derby Hall and the dingy entry hall of her own modest abode.

"Christy!" Effie cried, rushing down the stairs to meet her. "Gavin told me about his lordship and we've been worried sick. What happened? How did ye—"

Effie's words halted in mid-sentence as Sinjun stepped around Christy.

"You remember Lord Derby, don't you?" Christy said, jumping into the void.

Effie bobbed a curtsey. "Good day, yer lordship."

"Show Lord Derby into the parlor, Effie, and serve him some refreshment while I ... pack my belongings."

"But Christy, I've already packed everything ye've brought from Glenmoor."

Christy pretended not to hear as she pushed past Effie and mounted the stairs.

Sinjun was convinced Christy was hiding something ... or someone, the Cameron chieftain, perhaps? Hadn't Effie said she'd already packed? He waited until Effie left the drab parlor before acting on impulse and following Christy up the stairs. He paused on the top landing, frowning when he heard soft crooning coming from one of the rooms. He followed the sound to a closed door, one of three on the upper floor. Not bothering to knock, he turned the knob and barged inside.

What he saw was almost too much for his mind to grasp. The color drained from his face, and he staggered backward against the door. Christy was seated in a chair before the window, holding a bundle in her arms. His gaze riveted on the bundle; it was squirming and making slurping sounds that sounded suspiciously like ... a baby suckling. Stunned, he lifted his gaze and met the challenge in Christy's green eyes.

"Whose baby is that?" He knew, oh, aye, he knew, but he had to hear it from Christy's lying lips himself.

"I can explain, Sinjun."

"I doubt that, madam, but proceed anyway."

"Would you like to see your son?"

"My son?" he repeated, clearly stunned.

"Aye, Sinjun. A wee healthy laddie."

Rooted to the spot, Sinjun couldn't breathe, much less move. He recalled all those weeks he'd mourned his dead child, and resentment filled his heart. How could Christy do this to him? Anger propelled him forward, rage made him seize the child from his mother's breast. Deprived of his meal, Niall opened his mouth and bellowed.

"Give him back to me, Sinjun," Christy demanded. "He's waited too long for his meal as it is."

Sinjun's dark gaze lingered on her naked breast. A drop of milk clung to the engorged tip, and he felt his loins clench despite his anger. With difficulty he tore his eyes away from the bountiful feast of Christy's breast and stared down at his squalling son. He opened his heart, and love found its way inside. The pure, melting kind of love he'd never experienced before. His son was the most beautiful child he'd ever beheld. Dark hair, large brown eyes, round little mouth rimmed with the residue of Christy's milk, and a sturdy little body, what he could see of it.

His child. Not dead, but very much alive. He lifted his gaze from his son and found Christy staring at him. A curious thickening clogged his throat as a myriad of conflicting emotions warred inside him. Though he wanted to flail Christy with angry words, only one word came to mind.

"Why?"

"I'll explain everything, just give me my bairn. He's still hungry."

With marked reluctance, Sinjun returned the child to his mother. The moment she put him to her breast, his plaintive cries ceased. Sinjun watched him suckle for a long, silent moment before dropping down into a nearby chair. He could find no reason beyond hatred for him that would make Christy tell him their child had died. What had happened after he left Glenmoor to change her? Where did the Cameron chieftain fit into all this?

Unwilling to upset his son, Sinjun remained silent while the lad suckled. But as soon as his mouth fell away from Christy's nipple and his eyes closed, Sinjun took him from Christy's arms.

"Where is his cradle?"

"Through the door. There's an adjoining nursery."

Sinjun settled his sleeping son in his cradle and returned to Christy, all evidence of tenderness gone from his face. He could forgive Christy many things, but this wasn't one of them. He found her sitting exactly where he'd left her, her breasts decently covered, her head bowed as if meeting his gaze was too painful.

"I'm taking my son," he said without preamble.

Christy's head shot up. "No! I won't let you. What am I to do without him?"

"I don't give a bloody damn what you do, madam. I'm no angel, but what you did far surpasses anything I've done in my lifetime."

"Niall needs me. He's still nursing. You can't take him away from me."

"Niall, is it? How good of you to give my son a Scottish name. I can do any damn thing I please and there's not a court in the kingdom that won't support me. Wetnurses aren't all that difficult to find. We'll get by just fine without you."

"Don't you even want to hear my explanation?"

He fixed her with a steely glare. "Not particularly. You conspired to keep my son from me, that's all that matters." He turned to leave.

"Wait! Niall doesn't know you. He'll miss me. Please, Sinjun, don't do this. Let me go with Niall. I'll be his nanny. You can pretend I exist only to care for my son. I'll perish without him."

"Go home to Scotland. The clan needs you. Take Calum for a lover. Let him get a baby on you."

"I despise Calum!" Tears flowed down her cheeks. "Almost as much as I'll despise you if you take Niall from me. Maybe if you'd let me explain—"

"It's too late for explanations."

Sinjun silently railed at himself for letting her tears affect him. He should take his child and to hell with Christy. But the look on her face cut through his defenses. He supposed it wouldn't hurt to let Christy nurse her son until he was weaned. Then he'd ship her back to Glenmoor where she belonged.

"Get Niall ready," he barked. "We're leaving immediately."

"Thank you," she whispered, dashing away her tears with the back of her hand.

"I'm not doing this for you, Christy. You're right about Niall being too young to be separated from his mother, so I'm allowing you to stay with him for now. You can live in my home until Niall is weaned."

"Sinjun, if you'd only listen—"

"I may be in a mood to listen some day, but not now. Get Niall while I inform Gavin and Effie of my decision. After they deliver your belongings to

Derby Hall, they can either return to Scotland or become part of my household. It's up to them."

Christy watched him walk away. His shoulders were stiff, the tension in his body palpable. She knew he had every right to be angry, but the arrogant knave should have listened to her explanation. What a fix she'd gotten herself into. The very thing she'd feared had happened. Sinjun wanted his son but didn't give a damn about his son's mother.

Effie burst into the room, interrupting Christy's morbid thoughts.

"Och, Christy, what are we going to do? Lord Derby said we were to deliver yer belongings to his townhouse. He told us we could either return to Glenmoor or enter his service."

"Sinjun is claiming Niall," Christy said, biting her lip to hold back her tears. "The only reason he's taking me along with him is to nurse Niall. He hates me, Effie, just as I feared he would."

"Why didn't ye tell him the truth? He should know that ye lied to save his skin."

"He wouldn't listen."

"I won't leave ye, Christy. Neither will Gavin. Someone has to look after ye and the bairn."

"I wouldn't ask it of you, Effie. 'Tis entirely up to you."

"We've already decided. Yer The Macdonald. Ye need us. Now, ye'd best get yerself and Niall downstairs. His lordship is waiting."

When she reached the bottom of the stairs, Christy found Sinjun pacing the hall. He gave her a curt nod and took the baby from her arms. Christy held tight, but Sinjun's stern look prompted her to accept his authority . . . for now. But he wasn't dealing with a weakling, and Christy wasn't as willing to accept his terms as she'd let on. She grit her teeth in frustration as he ushered her out the door and handed her into the carriage. When he placed Niall into her arms, she hugged him close and thanked God that she and her son were still together.

Derby Hall was three times the size of the modest house she'd rented, but Christy wasn't impressed with the sumptuous appointments and elegant rooms. It wasn't Glenmoor. Comfortable and unpretentious, Glenmoor was home, and she yearned for the heather-covered hills and green valleys. She wanted to raise Niall far from London's stink, where he could run free over the land that would one day be his.

"I'll see about hiring a nurse for my son," Sinjun said as they climbed the stairs to her chamber.

"No need," Christy replied. "I'd rather not have strangers taking care of my son. Effie and Gavin have decided to remain in London. Niall knows Effie, and she's a wonderful nursemaid."

"I suppose she'll do," Sinjun acquiesced. "She and Niall can occupy the small room across the hall from yours. Gavin can stay in the carriage house with my own coachman. They'll be paid suitable wages."

"Thank you," Christy said. "Since my presence seems to offend you, I'll try to keep out of your way."

Sinjun sent her a sour look. "I'm not sure how I feel about you right now so 'tis best we avoid one another for the time being. I will see my son, however, whenever I wish. I'll either inform Effie or visit his room when you're occupied elsewhere."

"Am I to be confined to my room?" Christy asked, not sure she understood him.

"Of course not. I'm no monster. You may come and go as you please. I'll see that you are provided with an allowance to spend as you wish. You may charge whatever you like at the modiste of your choice. No matter how I feel about you, you're still my wife. When you return to Glenmoor, you'll be properly provided for."

"What about you, Sinjun? What kind of example will you set for your son? Will you continue along the path to destruction you've set for yourself? Drinking, gambling, whoring, are those the qualities you want your heir to remember you by when you're gone? Lord Sin might be a fine name for a rogue, but 'tis hardly acceptable for a father."

Sinjun sent her a chilling glance. "How dare you preach to me! Your whole life is built on fabrications. You've not told the truth since the day we met."

"I can explain all that."

"I'm not interested. I'll let you settle in now. I'm rarely home for dinner, so I suggest you dine alone in your room. I'll instruct the staff. If there's anything you wish, inform Pemburton. He runs things around here."

Christy spent the rest of the day settling into her new living quarters. She directed the placement of Niall's cradle in his room and asked Pemburton to provide a cot for Effie. Peggy brought her lunch, and after she fed Niall and put him down for a nap, Pemburton asked if she'd like a tour of the house. Christy had no idea whether Sinjun would approve and she didn't care. If she was going to live here she might as well get acquainted with her surroundings.

The staff was far more accepting than Sinjun had been. In fact, they were downright friendly. Mrs. McBride, who it seemed had been with Sinjun forever, expressed her hope that the master would settle down now that he had a family. Even staid old Pemburton kept grinning at her, as if expecting her to perform miracles. And everyone, down to the lowliest maid, was enthralled and delighted with Niall.

Sinjun's townhouse was magnificent. Each room was richly furnished and sparkling clean, due mostly to Pemburton's supervision, she supposed. Christy was more than a little surprised to learn that Sinjun's chambers adjoined hers. She hadn't noticed the cleverly concealed door. She gave a small, deprecating laugh, knowing that door would never be used. Sinjun didn't need her in that way. He had women aplenty to satisfy his lust. She was here merely to nurture his son. He had made it clear that when she was no longer necessary to his son's well-being, he would ship her off to Glenmoor.

Dinner arrived on a tray that evening. Christy barely touched it though it looked and smelled delicious. It wasn't food she yearned for, it was Sinjun's love.

Sinjun made his usual rounds that night. He went to White's, found nothing to interest him, attended a fete given by the Hamptons, and ended up at Brooks, where he sat in for a few hands of whist. Toward midnight, when most considered the night just beginning, Sinjun was sober as a judge and bored out of his skull.

Truth to tell, it had been an effort to tear himself away from Niall tonight. Everything about the boy intrigued him. That he'd had a part in producing so perfect a human being boggled his mind. That Christy had intended to deprive him of his son still rankled. He couldn't look at her without being reminded of her duplicity.

And to think he had once fancied himself in love with her. He'd been eager to return to Glenmoor after Sir Oswald's trial, and then that damn letter had arrived. He should have listened to Christy's explanation, he supposed, but he couldn't bear to hear more of her lies.

On his way home he decided to stop in at Almacks and partake of the buffet. It had been a mistake. Lady Violet accosted him the moment he walked in the door.

"Sinjun! I hoped you'd stop in tonight," she gushed. "Are you aware that Lord Fenton and I had a parting of the ways? I'm free again, and quite eager to renew our friendship." She leaned close, so close her cloying perfume assaulted his senses. "Fenton couldn't compare to you as a lover. No one can."

Sinjun stared at her, not the least bit tempted. "I'm married, Violet, or have you forgotten?"

Violet shrugged. "I really don't care, do you?"

Sinjun's eyes took on a curious light as he pictured his innocent son lying in his cradle, and suddenly he cared very much. Having a father steeped in debauchery was not the legacy he wanted to leave his son. Perhaps it was time for Lord Sin to retire.

"Actually, I do care," Sinjun said. "Did you know I had a son?"

"With your wife?" Violet asked, clearly stunned.

"If you're insinuating my son is illegitimate, you're wrong. Niall is legitimate," Sinjun informed her.

"But how—"

"Surely I don't have to explain the mechanics to you, my lady," Sinjun said with a hint of sarcasm. "If you'll excuse me, I see someone I must speak with."

Sinjun could feel Violet's eyes boring into his back as he walked away. There was really no one he wanted to talk to, it had just been an excuse. He wanted to go home. He felt a sudden need to look upon his son's sleeping face. A terrible thought occurred. What if Christy had taken Niall away? Should he have set guards on her? He'd never let her take his son away from him. Never!

A short time later Sinjun let himself into the house. He was taken aback to find Pemburton waiting up for him, something he rarely did anymore.

"This is a surprise, Pemburton," Sinjun drawled. "Is something amiss?"

Pemburton sent him a censuring look. "Lady Derby dined alone in her room and retired early. Hardly a proper homecoming for a bride."

Though Pemburton said nothing more, his displeasure was evidenced in the angle of his head and the stiffness of his thin shoulders. Sinjun's first inclination was to take Pemburton to task for his temerity, but his staff had been with him so long that he supposed he shouldn't be surprised by anything Pemburton said.

"You forget, Pemburton, Christy is hardly a new bride. We've been wed over fifteen years. Certainly long enough to have a son together."

"As you say, my lord," Pemburton sniffed. "Shall I help you undress?"

"I'm perfectly capable of undressing myself," Sinjun returned shortly. "Good night, Pemburton."

"Good night, my lord. Oh, should you care, Lady Derby didn't eat a bite of her dinner tonight."

Sinjun started up the stairs, wondering how Christy had won the staff's loyalty after being in his home less than twenty-four hours. His steps slowed when he reached her door, pausing when he saw a thin line of light escaping from beneath it. He hadn't expected her to be awake and almost made the mistake of turning the knob and stepping inside.

Instead, he turned toward his son's room across the hall. Then he remembered that Effie shared Niall's room and thought better of awakening her at this late hour. He continued on to his own chamber.

Once inside, his gaze kept straying to the door connecting his chamber with Christy's. Deliberately he turned away and undressed. He donned his robe and walked to the sideboard for a nightcap. He reached for the decanter. His hand wavered, and he spun around to stare at the connecting door. Compelled by a force stronger than the beat of life inside him, he walked slowly to the door and turned the knob. It opened noiselessly, and he peered inside.

His gaze found Christy immediately, and his body jerked in violent response. She was seated in a chair before the hearth, nursing their son, her alabaster breasts gleaming palely in the firelight.

Chapter 15

Sinjun dragged in a slow breath. Desire, raw and explosive, shot through his body and hardened his loins. A groan caught in his throat when Christy moved Niall from one breast to the other, exposing both full white mounds to his hungry gaze. He watched his son's mouth latch onto the nipple, his tiny hands kneading her tender flesh as he suckled. Sinjun swallowed convulsively. His shaft surged upward against his stomach as he imagined his own mouth suckling her, his own hands fondling those perfect breasts. The truth was, he wanted her, craved her, had to have her.

How was he expected to resist so fetching a woman when all he had to do was walk into the room and take her? She was his. They had been married for many years. So what was stopping him? The answer to that question was not as simple as it sounded. Why had Christy come to London if she intended to keep his son from him? Why did she want him to believe his son had died? Nothing made sense. Perhaps, he thought again, he should have listened to her explanation when she'd offered one.

He watched, enthralled, as Christy stood up and shifted a sleeping Niall to her shoulder. The top of her nightdress slid down, clinging precariously to her hips. Firelight turned her body a shimmering gold. She appeared more ethereal than human; a goddess whose mouth spewed lies, he thought bitterly. Frustration rode him ruthlessly when she left her chamber and walked across the hall to Niall's room.

He couldn't move, couldn't think beyond the throbbing in his loins as he waited for her to return. He was still standing in the same place when Christy reentered her chamber. She had adjusted her nightdress back over her shoulders and fastened the ties holding it together with neat little bows. He had to forcibly restrain himself from advancing upon her when she crawled into bed and pulled the covers up to her neck.

Still throbbing, still needy, Sinjun fought down his clawing lust and returned to his chamber. He jerked off his robe and stretched out naked on the bed. He truly did try to sleep, but desire still thrummed through his body and his erection throbbed painfully. He spied the brandy decanter on the sideboard and found himself suddenly in need of a drink. He rose and poured a generous portion into a glass, tossing it down in one swallow. It slid smoothly down the back of his throat, the heat nearly as potent as the burning in his loins.

He poured another, then another, but sleep eluded him. He wanted the woman in the adjoining chamber as desperately as he had ever wanted anything in his life. The more he drank the more reasons he invented for making love to Christy, until he convinced himself it was something he had to do. Tossing back the last drop of brandy in his glass, Sinjun donned his robe and walked somewhat unsteadily through the connecting door. He didn't bother tying the sash as he stepped into Christy's bedchamber.

His gaze fastened on the bed. The cozy fire dancing in the hearth cast enough light for Sinjun to make out the outline of Christy's slight form beneath the covers. Determination firmed his jaw as he approached the bed. For a long time he stood over her, staring down at the bright halo of hair visible above the bedcovers. His hand was unsteady as he reached out to touch it. Abruptly he drew his hand back. Tenderness had no place in his heart for the woman who had lied and manipulated him, he told himself. All he wanted was her body. He removed his robe and tossed it aside.

Christy awoke with a start and lay very still. She wasn't alone. She had no idea what had awakened her—a sound, a familiar scent. She opened her eyes and peered into the darkness from beneath a crescent of lashes.

He stood by the bedside, flames from the hearth casting a bronzed glow over his naked body and reflecting off his ebony hair. She swallowed the lump forming in her throat as her startled gaze slid over him. His eyes were heavy-lidded with desire, his mouth taut with determination. An intriguing combination of shadows and light played over the muscular contours of his body and the hardened ridge of his arousal. A slow heat warmed her skin.

"Sinjun. What are you doing here?"

"This is my house, remember?"

She sat up, pulling the sheet up to her neck. "How could I forget?" Her thoughts scattered. Did Sinjun's presence in her chamber mean he wanted them to have a real marriage? Did he suddenly realize he loved her, needed her, couldn't live without her? Or did he simply need a woman and she was handy?

The bed ropes protested his weight as he pulled the sheet from her nerveless fingers and stretched out beside her. His body felt warm against hers, and the skin across her breasts tightened in anticipation. She tried to control her response but was utterly defenseless where Sinjun was concerned. Then she caught the scent of brandy on his breath and realized he was drunk.

"You're foxed."

"Not *too* foxed," he assured her.

"I thought you said you wouldn't ... we shouldn't ..."

He pulled her roughly against him. "I've changed my mind. You're mine, Christy, and I need a woman."

Christy had hoped for something more, anything but the casual sex he offered. She wanted to deny him, to tell him to go to hell, to find another woman, but she couldn't. To her everlasting shame, her traitorous body needed him.

He cupped her bottom and pulled her against his hard body. She felt his thick sex prod between her legs, and she sucked in a shallow breath. He stared at her parted lips a long moment, then his mouth swooped down to claim them. She tasted his brandy-scented breath and felt herself drowning beneath the overpowering intensity of his hunger. She didn't want this to happen, not this way. She wanted Sinjun's love, his regard, not his lust. Not that lust was a bad thing when love was involved, but love had yet to find its way into Sinjun's heart.

He whispered her name against her lips; she felt herself softening, her body melting. How she had missed him. Missed this. She sighed with pleasure when he cupped her breasts and raised them to his mouth. He suckled her gently until her milk began to flow. Abruptly he raised his head and stared intently at her breasts. She looked down and saw a drop of milk clinging to her taut nipple.

"Do you know I was jealous of my own son when I saw him suckling at your breasts?" he drawled.

Christy fought for breath, surprised by his bald statement. "Why are you jealous? You don't even like me."

He chuckled. "I like your body. Pleasuring women is what Lord Sin does best."

Christy winced, hurt by his callous words. "Conceited wretch. Lord Sin can go to Hades for all I care." She shoved against his chest. "Leave me alone."

Sinjun's face hardened. "Are you going to deny me?"

A glance at Sinjun's inflexible features made her want to lash out at him. "Damn you, Sinjun! Where is your heart? What about love?"

"Love?" The word seemed to stun him. "Love means nothing to Lord Sin. Love is a fairy tale, Christy. Some might take love seriously, but I consider it a fantasy, reserved for innocent children like Niall."

"At least you admit to loving your son," she said quietly.

"Aye, Niall is too young to lie to me." He sighed and pulled her closer. "The lack of love between us doesn't mean we can't give each other pleasure."

Christy said nothing as the pain inside her became unbearable. She ached for Sinjun, for the unrequited love she bore him, and she ached because she would never know his love.

"Do you feel nothing for me?"

"I remember . . ." Abruptly he fell silent, as if fearing he would say something he'd regret later.

"What do you remember?" Christy prodded.

His expression hardened. "All your lies, the fabrications, the duplicity, those are the things I remember."

"Go away, Sinjun," Christy said on a sob. Of all the things he could have said, those words hurt the worst.

"Soon, but not now."

His hands meandered down her thighs, and when they rose again they brought the hem of her nightdress with them, baring the silken whiteness of her limbs to the firelight. She gave a cry of dismay when he lifted her shoulders from the mattress and whisked the nightdress over her head, tossing it into the corner.

"You're very good at seduction," she said on a shaky sigh. She couldn't think with his heat searing her, his scent surrounding her, filling her, teasing her senses.

"We were always good together," he whispered against her lips.

His mouth closed over hers. He kissed her deeply, roughly, demanding a response she tried to deny and failed. Her mind spun dizzily, her body was aflame. A trembling cry escaped her lips when his mouth left hers to trace a fiery path down her body. When he eased her thighs apart, she braced herself for his entry, and was shocked when his head dipped down between her legs, his mouth nuzzling the bright triangle of curls. Her hips arched upward, into the heat of his mouth as his tongue flicked and swirled around the tender folds and swollen peaks. A cry wrenched from her throat and she surged upward into the most intimate of caresses. He explored the sleek, sensitive depths thoroughly, probing deeply, then laving the hardened bud of her femininity until shivers ran down her spine and desperate need vibrated through her.

He played her like a skilled musician, building toward a shattering crescendo. A flick of his tongue, an intimate caress, again and again, until she was trembling violently. He held her firmly against the heat of his mouth, driving her to that lofty place where she no longer had control of her body. It was his to do with as he pleased, to lead, to guide, to send soaring upward on multihued wings of splendor. She clung a blissful moment to the edge, then tumbled over.

Clutching the sheets in her hands, she rode the waves of pleasure shooting through her body as Sinjun crouched over her, watching, his erection pulsing against her belly. Pleasure was still vibrating through her when he spread her legs and drove deeply inside her. He was thick and full; her muscles clenched tightly around him and he groaned his appreciation. He wasn't gentle, riding her hard and fast. She arched upward, moving with him, against him, the sheer heat of their bodies and his hard thrusts propelling her toward a second climax. A sound arose, a cry that came from deep in her throat, and she shattered.

Sinjun drove on, his expression intense, his concentration total. Bands of ropy tendons popped out on his neck and shoulders. A fine sheen of perspiration covered his body. After several deep thrusts, he stiffened, groaned, and spilled his seed hotly inside her. Long minutes passed as he held himself rigidly over her, pumping everything he had into her. Then he collapsed and lay still.

Flushed with sweet languor, Christy accepted his weight until she feared her lungs would collapse, then she pushed against his chest. Sinjun stirred and slowly eased himself away. He lay down beside her, saying nothing, not even looking at her, the breath whooshing from his lungs in short, explosive gasps.

Limp and sated, Christy stirred and looked up when Sinjun left the bed. His face, clearly outlined in the firelight, was hard and expressionless, but it was the look in his eyes that made the breath catch in her throat. They blazed with an emotion that defied logical description. Without uttering a single word, he rose from the bed, picked up his robe, and returned to his chamber.

Though outwardly Sinjun showed little emotion, turmoil roiled inside him. Dammit, he wanted Christy. No matter how he fought it, how hard he tried to convince himself he'd be better off without her, his body refused to listen. He wanted to stop the constant ache that gnawed at him, the tormenting desire driving him. He should have sent her to Glenmoor immediately, he knew that now. It wouldn't have been difficult to find a wetnurse for Niall. He'd been a fool to let her pleas move him. Though her lies had nearly cost him his son, he hadn't the heart to separate mother and child.

Bloody hell! She was driving him mad. He wanted her gone. He wanted his old life back. The way it had been before Christy had come to London and disrupted his lifestyle. The only good thing to come of their affair was his son, and he'd be damned if he'd let her raise him in the Highlands with those savages she called kinsmen.

Sinjun remained polite and withdrawn during the following days. Most days Christy didn't see him at all. Clearly he was avoiding her, for he visited Niall only during those times when he knew she wasn't with the babe. It was painfully obvious to Christy that he regretted making love to her. The only explanation she could give for his breach was that he'd been drunk. His long absences from home proved that he wanted nothing to do with her.

One day Lord Blakely came to call. Pemburton showed him into the back parlor used for informal visits, and Christy hurried downstairs to greet him.

"Are you all right?" he asked, his brow furrowed with concern. "I went to your lodgings and learned you had left rather abruptly. I didn't betray you, dear lady. I steadfastly refused to tell Sinjun where to find you, but obviously it didn't matter, for he found you on his own. He didn't hurt you, did he?"

Not physically. "He didn't hurt me. Sinjun isn't a violent man. How did you know I'd be here?"

"I suppose it was a natural assumption." He searched her face. "You *are* all right, aren't you? I hope you're here because you want to be."

She studied her hands, contemplating her answer. "I'm here because I was given no other choice."

"I know Sinjun is angry with you but—"

"He has every right to be angry. If you haven't spoken with Sinjun lately, then you don't know the entire story."

"I know about the Cameron chieftain. Sinjun told me that much."

"Sinjun doesn't know everything, no one does," Christy said cryptically. "I was referring to our son. Mine and Sinjun's."

Rudy's fine brow wrinkled. "I'm sorry about the child, my lady. I have it on good authority that Sinjun was quite looking forward to fatherhood. The child's death was hard on him, and he cast himself headlong down the path to perdition to forget."

"I wasn't honest with Sinjun," Christy explained. "Our son—"

A child's plaintive cry wafted through the house, stopping her words in midsentence. Rudy's head shot up, and he stared at Christy, his eyebrows raised in question.

"I . . . well, you may as well know the truth," Christy began. "Our child didn't die. I lied to Sinjun for reasons of my own."

"Good God! No wonder Sinjun is upset. I cannot believe it of you. What did you hope to gain?"

Christy flushed. Though she didn't want Rudy to think badly of her, she had no intention of explaining. Sinjun was the only one due an explanation, and he didn't want one.

"It's between me and Sinjun," Christy said, "and he isn't in the mood to listen. When he learned about Niall he threatened to keep my bairn in London and send me back to Glenmoor. I begged him to let me stay with my son and he agreed. That's Niall you hear crying. 'Tis time for his feeding."

She turned to leave. He placed a restraining hand on her arm. "I cannot believe you'd lie to Sinjun about something like that without good reason. Would you care to tell me about it?"

Tears of gratitude filled Christy's eyes. Embarrassed by the show of emotion, she buried her face in her hands and quietly sobbed. Rudy was beside her instantly, pulling her gently into his arms, soothing her as one would a hurt child.

"I wish Sinjun were as understanding," she said on a trembling sigh. "He refused to listen to my explanation."

"I'll listen, Christy. May I call you Christy?" Christy nodded. "Whatever you tell me will remain between the two of us."

"Isn't this cozy. How long have you two been carrying on behind my back?"

Rudy's arms fell away as he whirled to meet Sinjun's hard glare. "Sinjun. You could have at least announced your presence."

"In my own home? Not bloody likely. I suppose you have an explanation. What are you doing here?"

"I was worried about Christy."

"Christy? Are you referring to Lady Derby?"

Furious, Christy stepped between the two men. "Stop it! Lord Blakely was concerned when he learned I'd vacated my house. You two are friends, you shouldn't be arguing like this."

"All I want is an explanation I can believe," Sinjun said, setting her aside. "From Rudy," he added meaningfully. "I'd be a fool to believe anything that came from your mouth."

"Now see here, Sinjun," Rudy said pugnaciously. "That's no way to speak to your wife."

"Did my *wife* tell you she lied about our child? I have a son, Rudy. And he's very much alive."

"She told me. She also said you were too hardheaded to listen to her explanation. May I make a suggestion?"

"No, you may not."

"I'll have my say anyway. Christy is unhappy."

"How astute of you to realize that, though I cannot imagine why she should be."

"Dammit, Sinjun, I've never known you to be so stubborn."

"Tell me," Sinjun said with a sneer. "Would you forgive a woman who has fed you a pack of lies? Keep out of this, Rudy, 'tis none of your business. And keep away from Christy."

"Sinjun, please listen, you're accusing Lord Blakely falsely. You're the only man I want." God, she hadn't meant to say that, it had just come out. She may as well have saved her breath. The determined set to Sinjun's jaw gave mute testimony to his inflexibility.

Rudy picked up his hat and cane. "I'm sorry, Christy. Give Sinjun time, he'll come around. I can tell you care about him. Should you need me, send word around to my townhouse."

"Good-bye, Rudy," Sinjun said without taking his eyes off Christy.

Sending Sinjun a disgusted look, Rudy strode from the room.

Christy started to leave but Sinjun stepped in front of her. "Are you so hungry for a man that you'd work your wiles on my friend?"

She glared at him. "Perhaps I was hungry for company," she retorted. "Lord knows you haven't said a word to me since..." She flushed and looked away.

"I was drunk," Sinjun returned shortly. "I should have known better. I..." Whatever he was going to say was lost when Niall's lusty cries echoed through the house.

"He's hungry," Christy explained.

"Go feed my son. He needs you," Sinjun said, his expression softening.

Christy sailed past Sinjun, her narrow shoulders stiff. "Gladly. At least someone in this house needs me."

Her parting shot did not go unheeded by Sinjun. Nor had the intimate scene he'd interrupted between Christy and Rudy. Sinjun hated the notion that his best friend intended to cuckold him, but he'd been riddled by jealousy from the moment Pemburton had mentioned that Christy was alone in the back parlor with Lord Blakely. If Christy was trying to make him jealous, she was succeeding. She belonged to him, dammit! Whether or not he chose to resume an intimate relationship with her made no difference.

Sinjun strode slowly up the stairs to his chamber, his thoughts returning again and again to the intimate scene he'd walked into. As long as Christy resided in his household she had to follow his rules. Perhaps it was time to introduce his wife to society, he mused. He could think of no better way to let all his friends know that Christy belonged to him, that she was off limits to any man with seduction on his mind. He brightened. Aye, that's exactly what he would do. Introduce his wife to society and make everyone aware that he wasn't a lenient husband who overlooked his wife's infidelities.

Sinjun heard the murmur of voices coming from the nursery and knew he'd find Christy inside. He pushed the door open and barged inside.

"My lord," Effie said, moving protectively in front of Christy to shield her from Sinjun's view. "As ye can see, yer bairn is feeding right now. Come back later."

"Leave us, Effie, I wish to speak to my wife. In private," he added, fixing her with a steely glare.

Effie stood her ground, until Christy gave an imperceptible nod. Then Effie scooted out the door, closing it softly behind her.

"I thought we finished our conversation downstairs," Christy said.

"I forgot to mention, we'll be attending Lady Dempsey's ball tonight."

"You want *me* to attend the ball with *you* tonight?" Christy gasped. "Won't having a wife on your arm cramp Lord Sin's style?"

" 'Tis time the *ton* met my wife. For years I've used you to fend off women with marriage on their minds, and it's time now to prove to society that you truly do exist."

"I'm sorry, I can't leave Niall."

"That's no longer a valid excuse, Christy. Do you think I don't know what's going on in my own home? Niall has been sleeping the night through. He no longer needs night feedings."

"Why do you want to drag me out into society?"

Sinjun's gaze drifted down to her breasts, where Niall still suckled contentedly. The sight of his son nursing at Christy's breasts never failed to enthrall him. He imagined his own mouth tasting her, his own tongue lapping at her nipple, and he went immediately hard. He turned away and adjusted his coat over his all too visible erection before he answered her question.

" 'Tis a wife's duty to accompany her husband if he wishes her to do so. No other explanation is necessary. I hope you have something appropriate to wear."

Christy lifted a sleeping Niall to her shoulder and hastily covered her breasts. "I'm not going. What if someone recognizes me as Lady Flora, your former mistress?"

"Let me handle that. What time does Niall have his last feeding?"

"Nine o'clock."

"Perfect. I'll be waiting for you in the drawing room at ten."

Christy chafed indignantly at Sinjun's high-handed manner. She had no idea where she stood with him. He wanted her. He didn't want her. He had avoided her for days. Now he was acting the perfect tyrant, demanding that she attend a social function with him. Never would she understand her complicated husband.

Perhaps it was best that she didn't.

Content after his last feeding, Niall was sleeping blissfully as Peggy helped Christy into another fancy ballgown she'd brought with her from Glenmoor. Fashioned of emerald green satin, the low-cut Empire bodice was trimmed in crystal beads. The skirt, banded with beige lace, fell in graceful folds from the ribbon tied just below her breasts.

"His lordship will be pleased," Peggy said as she adjusted the neckline of Christy's dress. "You're very beautiful, my lady."

His lordship be damned, Christy thought sourly. Being paraded around on the arm of her rakehell husband wasn't her idea of a good time.

"Thank you, Peggy. If you'll hand me my wrap, I do believe I'm ready."

Sinjun wasn't prepared for the dazzling beauty who walked into the drawing room a short time later. Oh, he was well aware of Christy's beauty, 'twas what had drawn him to her that night she'd posed as Lady Flora. But that was before Niall, before her body had matured and her sexuality had been awakened. Sinjun instinctively knew that every woman attending the ball tonight would pale in comparison with his wife.

It came as no surprise to Sinjun that he still wanted Christy. No matter what she had said or done in the past, she was in his blood. Just looking at her made him go all hot and hard. If he hadn't promised the hostess he'd attend the ball, he'd turn Christy around and march her back up the stairs to his bed.

He composed his features and said coolly, "You look quite fetching, madam."

"And you look handsome as always."

He offered her his arm. "Shall we go?"

"If we must, my lord."

A crush of carriages was lined up before the Dempseys' townhouse on King Street off fashionable St. James Square. The marquess's carriage waited in line to discharge its passengers. When their turn came, Sinjun and Christy descended and entered the mansion. They left their wraps with a maid and joined the procession upstairs to the ballroom.

"Derby, quite a crush, what?" a man standing on the stair above them said. "I told Huxley we should have gone to Boodles instead."

"No women at Boodles," Huxley said. "Besides, as I told Ashford, the food is better here."

"Indeed," Sinjun acknowledged.

Both men were staring intently at Christy, obviously waiting for an introduction. When none was forthcoming, Huxley said, "Gossip has it your wife is in town. Did you know someone has placed a wager on the betting books at White's concerning that very subject? There's even a wager that you got an heir on your wife."

"The devil you say!"

"Aye, 'tis true. Some of the wagers are quite hefty."

Amusement colored Sinjun's words. "And how did you bet, Huxley?"

Huxley grinned at Christy. "Lord Sin bringing his wife to London? Never. As for begetting an heir with a savage Scotswoman, it sounded too far-fetched to me. Lord Sin has a reputation to uphold, after all. I went with the odds."

"I say old man, are you going to introduce us to your latest paramour?" Ashford asked. "She looks familiar. Do I know her?"

"Indeed you do not," Sinjun insisted in a voice that brooked no argument. "Gentlemen, permit me to introduce my wife, Lady Derby. I hope you didn't wager too steeply for I do indeed have an heir. His name is Niall, and he's all of six months old. A handsome little fellow if I do say so myself. My dear, these two somewhat addled gentlemen are Lord Huxley and Lord Ashford."

Both men had the presence of mind to murmur appropriate greetings and bow over Christy's hand. They appeared enormously relieved when they reached the entrance to the ballroom, where they could hurry off.

"That enlightening bit of information will spread like wildfire in less time than it will take us to make our way to the buffet table," Sinjun said.

Why did he sound so pleased? "Is that what you wanted?"

" 'Tis time my wife was introduced to London society. Besides, I am inordinately proud of my son."

Soon they were besieged by people, all insisting on being introduced to Lord Derby's wife. Christy's head was in a tizzy—so many faces, so many names. She knew some of the ladies present must have been intimately involved with Sinjun at one time or another, for their smug smiles suggested more than friendship.

During the course of the night she danced with Sinjun and several of his friends, smiling until she thought her face would crack. When Lord Huxley tended to hold her too close during one of the dances, Sinjun was suddenly beside her, dragging her from Huxley's arms into his own. From then on he rarely allowed her out of his sight.

Sinjun found it difficult to remain civil to the gossipmongers and others he had once called friends. They prodded and probed and insinuated until he could stand it no longer. The last straw came when Lady Alice, on the arm of her latest lover, intercepted them and asked Christy point-blank if she intended to overlook her husband's infidelities during her stay in London.

He almost laughed aloud when Christy said, "I intend to overlook anything that poses no threat to me."

He dragged her off to save her from Alice's venom, but in truth he suspected she could hold her own with anyone. She was, after all, the Macdonald chieftain, laird of the clan.

"Where are we going?" Christy asked when Sinjun suddenly pulled her from the ballroom and down the stairs.

"Home," Sinjun said curtly. All the men slavering over her had driven him to distraction. The *ton*'s interest in his wife annoyed him excessively.

"Wait here while I summon the coachman."

Christy was standing at the door when Sinjun returned a short time later with the coach. He handed her inside, closed the door, and rapped on the roof to signal the driver. Wheels spun and the coach rattled off down the street.

"I've waited all night for this," Sinjun growled as he pulled her roughly into his arms. "You're mine, Christy Macdonald, don't ever forget it, no matter how much the *ton* fawns over you, and tonight I'm going to prove it."

Sinjun had never looked more like Lord Sin than he did at this moment. He was the most exciting man she had ever known. Her body ached for his touch, her heart pined for his love.

Chapter 16

∽✧✧✧∾

Christy's last remaining thoughts fled as Sinjun plucked her from the seat and settled her on his lap. His hands seemed to be everywhere. Beneath her skirts, skimming her legs, touching her intimately in places that set her blood afire.

"Too . . . many clothes," he muttered. "Can't get them . . . off . . . I need to . . ."

"Sinjun! We can't. The driver."

He appeared not to hear. "Need to . . . bury myself . . . inside you."

His hot looks and arousing words were doing strange things to her insides. She shoved her skirts down, but he yanked them back up. Then he grasped her waist and lifted her astride him. She felt his thick shaft slide inside her, and a moan slipped past her lips. She hadn't even been aware that he'd unfastened his breeches. Then all thought ceased as he began to thrust and withdraw, piercing her deeply as he grasped her hips, adjusting her to the heavy thrust and drag of his shaft.

A startling heat swept through her as he pulled down the bodice of her dress, freeing her breasts to his mouth. He suckled her nipples, first one then the other, eliciting a ragged sigh from her. When he pressed his hand between their bodies and massaged the hard little button protecting the entrance of her sex, shivery heat roared through her and a raging current carried her upward. Her climax seemed to go on forever, so volatile she wasn't aware of Sinjun's shout as he released his seed inside her. She was aware of nothing but unspeakable pleasure. Then he lifted her away and pulled down her skirts.

"We're nearly home," he whispered.

"Oh, God, what will the coachman think of me, of us?"

"We're married, for God's sake. He'll just think the *ton* are strange people who prefer a coach to a bed, if he thinks anything at all."

The coach ground to a halt, and Christy gave a little cry of distress as she pulled her bodice firmly in place and smoothed her skirts down. Before she was ready, the door opened and the coachman pulled the steps down. Sinjun descended first and lifted Christy down. Christy averted her face away from the coachman as she hurried up the front stairs. She gave a sigh of relief when Sinjun fitted the key in the lock and ushered her inside.

Christy hurried off to check on Niall, ashamed of the way she had responded to Sinjun. Had she no pride, no shame? He was using her and she knew it. Unfortunately love made one do foolish things.

Sinjun, wearing nothing but a silk robe, was waiting in her chamber when she entered.

"Undress," he ordered crisply as he shrugged out of the robe.

Christy stared at him. "You're insatiable."

"Are you complaining?"

"There were dozens of women at the ball tonight. Did none of them spark your interest?"

The look he gave her was fiercely possessive, wildly passionate. "Aye. One did. She's standing before me, wearing too many clothes."

The rest of the night passed in a sensual blur. Sinjun's ravenous kisses were just a prelude to the splendor that followed. Their naked bodies mated, clung, exploded in unmatched passion two more times before the sun peeped through the curtains. Christy was sleeping soundly when Sinjun left her bed.

She awoke hours later to the sound of loud voices in the foyer. She made a quick toilette, but by the time she fed Niall and descended the stairs, the visitors she had heard had moved into the study. She approached the door and reached for the knob. The door was ajar. She paused with her hand on the knob when she heard her name mentioned.

"Is it true, Sinjun? I just returned to Town and happened to stop in at White's. Gossip has it that you're living in connubial bliss with your wife. What in bloody hell is going on?"

"If you'd stay in town longer than a fortnight you'd know what was going on, Julian," Sinjun retorted.

"What is Christy Macdonald doing in London?" Julian demanded to know. "She was the one who wanted the annulment."

"There was no annulment. I never filed the document."

"You deserve better than Christy," a female voice interjected.

Sinjun's sister, Christy thought, recognizing the voice.

"There's something neither of you are aware of," Sinjun retorted.

"I saw Christy several weeks ago," Emma revealed. "I warned her to stay away from you. I told her she'd only hurt you again."

"You saw her?" Sinjun asked, astounded. "When? Where? Why didn't you tell me?"

"She was working as a seamstress in a shop I often frequent. You can be sure I had the owner discharge her straightaway. I didn't tell you because I thought you were better off not knowing."

"And so he was," Christy said as she pushed open the door and walked into the room. "I had no intention of telling Sinjun I was in London."

Julian stepped forward. "We met once, Lady Christy, under quite different circumstances. We were all under the misapprehension that you were Lady Flora, Sinjun's mistress of the moment."

Guilt rode Christy. Julian's stern features and censuring words lent her little comfort. She knew immediately that Julian was not a man to cross. "I apologize for that."

"Indeed. I feel there's an explanation for all this confusion but I vow I cannot think of one. I'd like to think the death of your child affected your sanity in some way, and that you finally came to your senses. Have you come to London to ask Sinjun's forgiveness?"

"How dare she!" Emma charged. "Sinjun owes her nothing after the way she hurt him. She doesn't deserve to be pardoned."

Christy winced. Emma's words hurt.

"Would you care to explain, Christy?" Sinjun asked.

"Would you believe me?"

"No, but they might."

"Then I have nothing to say. If you'll excuse me, I have duties elsewhere."

"Nay, stay here." He strode to the door. "Don't any of you leave until I return."

"What in the world," Emma said, sending Christy a disgruntled look. "I don't know why he puts up with you."

"That's enough, Emma," Julian chided. "Obviously there are circumstances neither of us are aware of."

Niall, Christy thought with despair. *They don't know about my bairn.* When they found out, they would hate her as much as Sinjun did.

When Sinjun returned a few minutes later with Niall in his arms, a hush fell over the room. Emma was the first to speak.

"Sinjun, that's a baby!"

"Aye, my son. His name is Niall. He's six months old."

Julian sent Christy a look so filled with reproach that she had to look away. "Is that the same baby you were told had died at birth?"

"As you can see, he's very much alive," Sinjun said.

Her violet eyes ripe with resentment, Emma rounded on Christy. "Oh, no, how could you lie to my brother about a child's life?" She reached for Niall, and Sinjun placed him into her arms. "He's adorable," she crooned, gazing lovingly into his tiny face. "He's the picture of you, Sinjun. You must love him a great deal or you wouldn't allow his mother into your home."

Sinjun sent Christy a look that sent despair racing through her. He would never forgive her, but

if she ever doubted his love for his son, his words
soon set her straight. "I adore Niall. I didn't think
it possible to love another human being the way I
love my son."

Christy flinched. She knew Sinjun didn't love
her, but did he have to rub it in?

"So where do you go from here?" the ever practical Julian asked. "I heard you introduced your
wife to society last night. Does that mean you intend to have a real marriage?"

"Christy will return to Scotland soon," Sinjun exclaimed.

"You'll never take Niall away from me, Sinjun,"
Christy vowed. "He's all I have."

"Oh, look," Emma said, clearly enthralled by her
nephew. "He's fallen asleep."

"I'll take him up to his room," Sinjun said, holding out his arms.

"Let me," Emma implored. "He's so sweet."

"I'll show you the way," Christy offered, eager
to escape the censure clearly visible in Julian's hard
gaze.

Christy preceded Emma up the stairs. When she
reached Niall's room, she opened the door and followed Emma inside. Emma placed the lad carefully
in his bed, then turned to Christy, her dark gaze
probing relentlessly for the secrets Christy had
tried to conceal.

"I don't think you've told us everything," she
said quietly. "Sometimes another woman sees
things men don't. You love Sinjun. I can tell by the
way you look at him. What haven't you told us,
Christy? When I look into your eyes I see pain and
disappointment, and . . . aye, fear. Who do you
fear?"

Was she that obvious? "You're very astute for one so young."

"I'm nineteen," Emma replied. "My brothers, like all men, can be dunces at times. I've changed my mind about you. I think you need a friend. At first I was too angry to realize there was more involved here than met the eye. I hope you'll trust me enough to confide in me."

Christy truly did need a friend, someone besides Effie, who tended to think the worst of Sinjun because he was English. But trusting Emma was no easy task. If Sinjun had refused to listen to her explanation, why would Emma believe her? She had done nothing to earn the trust of Sinjun or his family.

"What is it, Christy? I know something is bothering you. There has to be a good reason why you told Sinjun his son hadn't lived past birth."

Worn down by Emma's persistence and needing desperately to unburden herself, Christy motioned Emma away from Niall's bed. "Come into my room. I don't want to awaken Niall."

Seated next to Emma on the bed, Christy stared down at her hands and said, "I told Sinjun that our bairn had died to save his life."

Emma's eyes narrowed, apparently unconvinced. "Sinjun's life was in danger? How is it he didn't know?"

"While Sinjun was in London for Sir Oswald's trial, Calum Cameron threatened Sinjun's life should he return to Glenmoor. Calum wanted me for himself, or rather, he wanted the power that belonged to me. He thought he could have what he wanted by killing Sinjun and marrying me. I did what I had to in order to keep Sinjun from returning to the Highlands."

"So you wrote him a letter telling him you wanted to wed Calum Cameron."

"Aye, but I wasn't certain that would be enough to keep him away. Then I remembered the writ of annulment Sinjun had brought to Glenmoor for my signature, and I tried to convince Calum that once the annulment was signed and sent back to Sinjun, he would dissolve our marriage, leaving me free to marry Calum."

"Did Calum believe you?"

"No. Then I suggested that I tell Sinjun our bairn had died at birth, for then there was no reason for him to return to the Highlands."

"It worked," Emma said softly. "He was devastated. The child you carried meant a great deal to him. I never thought I'd see the day Sinjun would willingly retire Lord Sin, but I swear he would have, had your letter not arrived. Why did you come to London?"

"Calum was becoming impatient. Assuming that my marriage was no longer valid, he intended to force me into a handfast marriage and send Niall away to be raised by strangers. I couldn't allow that. God must have heard my prayers, for Calum was wounded in a raid shortly before the ceremony. I fled to London while he was recovering from his wounds.

"I knew Sinjun would hate me if he discovered I'd lied about Niall, so I tried to keep out of his way. Then you told me about Sinjun's race toward self-destruction and I had to see him, to learn for myself what my lies had wrought." She flushed and looked away, recalling the night Sinjun had discovered her identity. "Unfortunately he saw through my disguise and eventually learned about Niall. He hates me. He wants to take Niall away from me," she said on a sob.

"Did you explain all this to Sinjun?"

Christy gave a bitter laugh. "He refuses to listen to my explanation. Lord knows I tried."

"I'll tell him," Emma said. "He'll believe me."

"No! Promise you will say nothing about what we discussed here. Sinjun needs to hear this from me. I want him to believe me, to trust me. If he doesn't have faith in me, then we have no future."

Emma took her hand. "You love him very much, don't you?"

"Is it that obvious?"

"To me it is."

"Have you ever been in love, Lady Emma?"

"You're my sister-in-law, please call me Emma. And no, I've never been in love. Perhaps I will never marry. I compare all men with my brothers, and they don't measure up. Men my age are too immature, and those older are usually looking for a drudge for their motherless children or a brood mare to give them an heir. Some are only interested in my fortune."

"I'm sorry."

"I'm not," Emma said brightly. "Maybe someday I'll find the right man. Is there anything I can do to help you and Sinjun?"

"Thank you, but no. Just unburdening myself has helped. Until Sinjun is ready to hear my explanation, there is nothing anyone can do."

Emma looked pointedly at the bed, her eyebrow arched inquisitively.

Christy flushed clear down to her toes. "I'm good enough for *that*. He just can't seem to forgive the lies and deception that have plagued our association from the beginning. I know I was wrong and pray that one day he will forgive me."

"I'll pray for that, too," Emma said, giving her a hug. "I must go now or Julian will be wondering what's keeping me. May I come back to see Niall?"

"Any time," Christy said warmly.

Alone in the study, Julian was taking Sinjun to task.

"I vow, Sinjun, you do tend to surprise me. Not long ago you were well on your way to perdition. Now here you are, a father and husband. Have you forgiven Christy?"

Sinjun's mouth flattened. "No, I haven't forgiven her. The only reason she's living in my house is because Niall is too young to be separated from his mother."

"Are you sure that's the only reason? Are you saying you have no real marriage?"

Sinjun sent him a mocking grin. "Oh, it's real enough, if you're referring to the sexual aspects of marriage. Christy is a beautiful woman, and she *is* my wife." He made an impatient gesture with his hand. "Dammit, Julian, call me a fool, but I still want her."

Julian grinned. " 'Tis obvious you love Christy." Julian ignored Sinjun's snort of derision as he blithely continued. "A pity you wasted the first fifteen years of your marriage on mistresses and wild pursuits. Had you and Christy gotten together sooner there would have been no need for lies or subterfuge. Think of all the years you've squandered earning your reputation as London's finest wastrel. Lord Sin, indeed. Rake, scoundrel, reprobate. Those are but a few of the names you've collected over the years, Sinjun." He shook his head. "What a waste."

"Maybe I've changed," Sinjun allowed. "I have a son now."

"And a wife," Julian reminded him.

"That remains to be seen."

"Did Christy offer a satisfactory explanation as to why she lied to you about your child? What about the Cameron chieftain?"

"Bloody hell, Julian, leave off. If you must know, I'm in no mood to hear Christy's explanation. Perhaps one day I'll listen, when I can do so objectively."

"You know what I think, Sinjun?"

"I don't really care, but I suppose you'll tell me anyway."

"Your feelings for Christy are stronger than you care to admit. I recall how excited you were about having a child, and how eager you were to return to Christy and pick up where you left off."

"Things have changed. I'm not sure how I feel about Christy now."

"Another word of advice. Take care of Niall. He'll inherit my title one day."

Sinjun frowned. "What the hell are you talking about? You're still young. One day you'll wed and have your own son."

Julian's gaze drifted away. "No, I'll never wed."

"Your intended wife died over two years ago. The time for mourning is over. Find another woman, Julian. I know you have a mistress, maybe more than one, so you're not indifferent to women."

"I loved Lady Diana very much," Julian acknowledged. "You didn't know what was going on because you were oblivious to everything except maintaining your reputation as a rakehell. Diana and I became intimate. She was carrying my child when she died in that carriage accident two days before our wedding."

He paused, his eyes narrowing into glittering slits, his voice shaking with barely controlled violence. "It was no accident, Sinjun. She was riding in *my* carriage. I was supposed to be inside, not my innocent Diana. I should have died that day."

Sinjun stared at Julian as if seeing him for the first time. Julian was right. He'd been so immersed in hedonistic pursuits that he'd been oblivious to Julian's pain following the accident.

"Why would anyone want to kill you? Does it have anything to do with your penchant for disappearing for long periods of time? You've been mighty secretive these past few years."

Julian helped himself to brandy from the sideboard, fortifying himself with a long sip before answering Sinjun's questions.

"I'm working for the government, Sinjun. Have been for years. My trips are directly related to whatever undercover work Lord Pitt considers worthy of my talents. I have been onto something important since before Diana's death, so I suppose I'll be leaving London again soon."

"Bloody hell, Julian, this is astounding! Why have you taken on such dangerous work? You must resign immediately."

Julian's expression went cold as death. "I won't stop until I find Diana's killer. The man who killed her is still out there. Someday I'll come across him, and when I do, he'd better be prepared to die."

Sinjun was stunned by the dark menace in Julian's voice. He'd known Julian and his betrothed had been close, but he'd never suspected how

close. Suddenly all Julian's unexplained absences
made sense.

"I don't know how long I'll be gone this time,"
Julian continued. "If something unforeseen should
happen to me, I want your promise to see that
Emma marries well."

"Damnation, Julian—"

"Your promise."

"You have it."

"You'll inherit, of course, then your son after
you."

Sinjun was appalled by Julian's sense of fatalism.
"This conversation is moot as far as I'm concerned.
You're going to live to a ripe old age, and when
you do meet your maker your eldest son will inherit."

Julian's hand came down on Sinjun's shoulder.
"I'm counting on you, Sinjun."

"What are you counting on him for?" Emma
asked as she glided into the room.

"To do what's right for Christy and his son," Julian improvised.

Emma sent Sinjun a penetrating look. "My sen-
timents exactly."

"It's time we were off," Julian said, gathering his
hat and cane. "Don't forget your promise, Sinjun.
And think about what I said."

Sinjun stared after Julian with renewed respect.
He'd had no idea his brother was involved in dangerous work. But then there had always been a
scent of danger about Julian. Aye, a dangerous
man, Sinjun mused thoughtfully. And a potent enemy.

Christy made Niall her priority during the following days. She took him on outings in the park

and for carriage rides. He was crawling now, requiring extra attention. The wee lad readily recognized his father, holding out his arms to be picked up whenever Sinjun entered his line of vision. Sinjun seemed to revel in his son's adoration and spent a great deal of time in his company.

The relationship between Christy and Sinjun remained awkward. Whenever Christy caught him staring at her with a puzzled expression on his face, she wondered if he was trying to decide where she fit into his life. She waited impatiently for Sinjun to ask for an explanation of the lies she'd told him and was disappointed when he appeared indifferent to anything she had to say on the subject.

Though their daytime relationship was strained, their nights were everything a wife could ask for. Sinjun came to her each night, making passionate love to her. Sometimes more than once. His ardor never faltered, no matter how distant he'd been during the day. With the room blanketed in darkness, he whispered love words to her. He called her sweetheart and other intimate names that melted her bones. When she awakened the following morning, Sinjun was always gone. And so the days flowed one into another. But since Sinjun never mentioned sending her away, Christy began to hope things would work out between them.

Sinjun decided that his son should be christened, and that the christening should be a grand affair. Plans were immediately undertaken to make it a huge event. Emma and Julian were to be his godparents. Christy had no objections and threw herself into the planning.

The day before the christening, a surprise visitor

arrived at Derby Hall. Rory Macdonald, looking haggard and exhausted after a ten-day ride from Glenmoor, nearly collapsed on the doorstep when Pemburton opened the door to him. He asked for Christy and was shown into the back parlor.

Fear laced through Christy when she heard that Rory had ridden all the way from Scotland to see her. Nothing but trouble of the worst kind could have brought Rory to London.

"Christy, thank God I've found ye," Rory said, jumping to his feet when she entered the parlor.

"Did you receive my letter?" Christy asked. "I sent it with a messenger after I moved in with Sinjun."

"Aye, that's how I knew where to find ye."

"What's amiss, Rory? Is it Margot? Or your bairn?"

"Nay, lass. I have a fine braw son. We named him Angus after yer grandsire. Margot is well. We were married by the priest when he made the rounds a few weeks ago."

"The news must be grievous to bring you to London."

"The Cameron chieftain is feuding with the Macdonalds and Ranalds and has drawn the Mackenzies to his cause. They've already fired several cottages and stolen livestock. The clan needs ye, Christy. We canna fight without our laird to give us heart."

"What's this?" Sinjun asked, strolling into the room. "Pemburton said we had company from Scotland. 'Tis good to see you, Rory. Are the clans fighting among themselves again?"

"Aye, that's the gist of it, yer lordship."

"I assume Calum Cameron is the instigator."

"Aye, right ye are."

"What do you expect Christy to do about it?"

"The clan needs their laird," Rory explained. "The feud is getting out of hand."

"I'll send word to the garrison at Inverness," Sinjun said. "English soldiers are in the Highlands for the purpose of keeping order among the clans. If there's fighting going on, they'll put a stop to it."

"No!" Christy protested. "The Englishmen don't care who they kill. Macdonalds or Camerons, 'tis all the same to them as long as they stop the fighting. I won't have my kinsmen killed by English butchers."

"Bloody hell, Christy! What can one woman do that an army can't?"

"They're my clansmen, Sinjun. They need me. Perhaps I can talk some sense into Calum." She sent him an anguished look. "I have to return to Glenmoor. You do understand, don't you?"

"Rory, Pemburton is stationed in the foyer. Have him show you the way to the kitchen. I'm sure you must be starving. Christy and I will settle this and let you know what we decide."

Rory sent Christy a bolstering look and rose immediately. "Aye, I could use something substantial in my stomach."

"This is nonsense, Christy," Sinjun said once they were alone. "I refuse to let you place yourself in danger."

Christy assumed a defiant stance. "You can't stop me, Sinjun."

"If you persist with this, I'm going with you."

Panic raced through Christy. She hadn't forgotten Calum's threat. She had a strong suspicion that this feud was being waged with a specific purpose in mind. Calum still hadn't given up on her. She knew exactly what Calum was doing. He was using a clan war to lure Sinjun to Glenmoor so he could kill him. She loved Sinjun too much to let that happen.

"No, Sinjun, your presence can only make matters worse. You know Highlanders have little use for Englishmen."

Sinjun's eyes narrowed. "What are you proposing, Christy?"

"I propose to leave immediately for Scotland. Gavin and Effie can accompany me and Niall. I'm sure I can stop this foolishness without bringing English soldiers to Glenmoor. The disaster at Culloden isn't far from the Highlanders' minds. The situation could be explosive, resulting in bloodshed. Do you want that on your conscience?"

Sinjun's expression turned stony. "What did you say?"

Christy went still. "About what?"

"There is no way I will allow you to take my son into a potentially dangerous situation. You don't want me to go with you? Fine. But if you persist with this folly, my son stays in London with me. Is that clear?"

"Sinjun, you can't mean—"

"Every word I just said." Sinjun's voice softened. "Despite everything, I can't stop myself from caring about you." He ran his hands up her arms and slowly brought her into his embrace. "I don't want you involved in your clansmen's squabbles. I cannot make my meaning any clearer, Christy. Stay here and let our relationship develop. I've been thinking that the time has come for me to hear your explanation. Tell me, Christy, make me understand why you wanted me to think Niall had died at birth."

A groan of frustration slipped past Christy's lips. After all the weeks of waiting for this opportunity, why did Sinjun want an explanation now? It wasn't the right time. He might insist upon confronting Calum, and that would be a mistake.

"I'm sorry, Sinjun, there isn't time. There's so much to be done. Niall has to be made ready for the trip and—"

His eyes glinted dangerously. "Haven't you heard a word I've said? Go if you must, but Niall stays here. 'Tis your choice, Christy. If you return to the Highlands, you go alone."

Chapter 17

In that timeless void between one heartbeat and the next, Christy felt her world crumble beneath her feet. "Sinjun, don't make me choose. I'm The Macdonald. Grandfather trusted me to do what was right for the clan when he named me his heir."

Sinjun's eyes narrowed into glittering slits. "You have a son who needs you."

"Do you think I want to leave Niall behind? 'Tis you who are forcing me to leave without him."

He pulled her against him. His eyes seemed to blaze as he lowered his head and kissed her. His kiss was harsh, demanding, as if the sheer force of his will could change her mind. She felt him grow thick and harden against her and wanted desperately to yield, but she knew where her duty lay.

She whimpered a protest as Sinjun swept her into his arms and carried her from the room, past a pair of giggling maids polishing the woodwork, and up the stairs. The door to her chamber stood open, and he carried her inside, slamming the panel shut with his boot heel. Then he slid her down his body until her feet touched the floor.

"Sinjun, what—"

He reached behind him and locked the door. "I'm going to make love to you, Christy. I want you to remember what you're leaving behind, because once you leave this house you'll never enter it again."

Despair rode Christy. Surely Sinjun didn't mean what he'd just said. He wouldn't keep her away from her bairn, would he? He wasn't a cruel man. He'd spoken in anger, hadn't he?

"I will return, Sinjun, never doubt it. Niall is my life. I will remain in the Highlands just long enough to settle the feud between the Camerons and the Macdonalds. Don't you understand, Sinjun? I am The Macdonald."

"And I am your husband."

"You're English. That makes all the difference in the world. My kinsmen will listen to me, they respect me."

"Go then, Christy, but you'll carry the memory of our last time together with you."

He reached for her, and Christy couldn't have resisted had she wanted to. This was Sinjun, the man she loved. Though he insisted he would deny her her son if she left, she refused to believe he meant it.

He grasped her bodice in both his hands and would have rent it down the middle had Christy not grasped his hands and pulled them away.

"I'll do it."

His eyes were watchful as she peeled away her dress and laid it carefully over a chair. Her shoes and stockings went next. When she would have left on her shift, he grasped the hem and pulled it over her head. Then he undressed himself, tossing his clothes aside haphazardly.

Christy looked her fill, admiring the width of his shoulders, the taut flesh stretched across his belly, his rampant manhood. He was magnificent, every glorious inch of him. He was Lord Sin now, fiercely predatory, powerfully seductive. Her gaze riveted on his arousal, rigid and brazenly erect, rising majestically between the columns of his thighs. She flushed and looked away.

"Don't turn away, sweetheart," he said hoarsely. "We've always had lust between us, that was one thing we could always count on. You want me, don't try to deny it."

He traced the shape of her breast with a blunt finger, and she shivered. "I've made no secret of the fact that I want you, Sinjun. I've always wanted you, even when you professed to hate me."

Sinjun made a harsh noise in his throat. "You have a strange way of showing your affection. Your web of lies and deception make me wary of anything you say."

Christy's throat thickened with tears, but she refused to let them fall. Everything she'd done had been for a good reason. "Perhaps you should leave now and let me prepare for my trip."

"Oh, no." He glanced down at his erection, then grasped her hand and placed it on his turgid flesh. "This isn't going to go away."

Her hand closed around him. Sinjun spit out an oath, swept her into his arms, and carried her to the bed. "You may be laird of your clan but you'll always belong to me. I'll not divorce you, Christy Macdonald. Though you'll never become a part of my life if you decide to leave, no other man will ever have you.

"I never wanted a wife, if you recall. We'll go on as before. You'll remain in Glenmoor with your kinsmen and I'll take up where I left off before you arrived to make a shambles of my life.''

''What about our son?''

''Niall will want for nothing. He's my heir. He'll always have a father to see to his welfare.''

And a mother, Christy silently vowed. ''Can we not discuss this?''

''The time for talk is long past. I can think of far better things to do with those lush, lying lips.''

Sinjun pulled her against him. If he couldn't move her with words, perhaps he could show her with his body that she belonged with him and Niall in London. The Highlanders could go to hell for all Sinjun cared. His mouth seized hers in an ungentle kiss that spoke eloquently of his harsh disapproval, of his need. His breath rasped through his lungs, heavy and labored. There was a primitive pounding in his loins, in his head, in his blood. Desire swelled thick and hard in his shaft and stirred his body.

When her arms locked around his neck and pulled him closer, hope blossomed in his chest. Had she changed her mind about leaving? He secretly gloated as Christy arched beneath him and melted into his kiss. With their bodies locked together, Sinjun let her wildness seep through to him. He wanted to give her pleasure, so much pleasure that she'd remember it for the rest of her days, no matter what the future held for them.

He filled his hands with the generous bounty of her breasts, teasing her nipples with the heels of his palms as his mouth took hungry possession of hers. He deepened the kiss with his tongue and felt grim satisfaction when she groaned into his mouth. Though reluctant to leave such rewarding territory, he slid his lips down the slender column of her neck. He heard her suck in a gasp when his mouth closed over a tender nipple. He suckled her gently, until her milk began to flow, then he left his feast for the tempting lure of more intimate parts.

He felt her shiver as his lips traced a flaming path down her stomach. Spreading her legs wide, he placed them over his shoulders. When he parted the silken fleece protecting her womanhood with a blunt fingertip, a slow hiss escaped through her teeth. And when that same blunt finger found her moist, dew-drenched center, she cried out his name.

But it wasn't enough. Sinjun wanted to hear her scream with pleasure. He watched her face as he slid a finger inside her. She appeared transfixed, her eyes glazed, as if waiting for him to take her to the next level. Happy to oblige, he placed his mouth over the hard nub at the juncture of her thighs and sucked it into his mouth. Her fingers tangled in his hair and she arched up into the hot cavern of his mouth as his tongue slid wetly over her and his fingers tormented her.

She was panting, writhing, sobbing, but still he continued, each lash of his tongue bringing her closer to sweet oblivion.

Her breath escaped in a scalding rush. The rough velvet of his tongue was driving her mad with divine, tormenting ecstasy. Again and again he tasted her, driving her higher with each torrid stroke. Her fingers tightened on his shoulders as his hands cupped her bottom and brought her deeper into the heat of his mouth. Her body was awash in pleasure, trembling, silently screaming for him to release her.

Then he did. She felt the contractions begin deep within her core as piercing rapture turned her body into a mass of sensitive, quivering flesh. She heard someone scream, shocked when she realized it was her own voice she'd heard. On and on it went, until she collapsed inside and went limp.

Slowly she floated back to reality. Her eyes opened, glazed and unfocused. Sinjun sat on his haunches between her legs, his eyes midnight blue and smoky, his shaft still rigid and thick. His expression was strained and darkly intense.

"Put me inside you, love." His voice was heated and raw, as if his control was hanging by a frayed thread.

Meeting his scalding gaze, she took him into her hands and brought him to her core. A gust of expelled breath whispered against her cheek as he slid inside her. Her arms crept around him and clung, mutely urging him deeper . . . as deep as he could go, until he had no more to give.

She stared up at him; he was embedded to the hilt inside her, his arms braced on either side of her head. His muscles corded and bulged as he began to move. Slowly at first, as if he wanted to draw out the pleasure. Then, as if driven by an emotional upheaval, savage urgency overtook him and his hips pounded a frantic rhythm, grinding, churning, rekindling the flame inside her.

Snared in the same wild frenzy, Christy scored his back with her nails as he thrust forcefully, again and again. Her blood caught fire. She was being torn apart, twisted and swirled in a tempest of erotic pleasure, reaching for rapture with each surge of his shaft inside her center.

Sinjun knew he was dying. Those tiny, trembling contractions he felt inside her milked his shaft, bringing him closer to the edge of fulfillment. He caught her wail of ecstasy in his mouth, her spasms spurring his own, and then all thought fled, leaving nothing but the hunger driving him and the woman in his arms. His body stiffened; a ragged cry ripped from his throat and his seed erupted, hot and scorching, from his body into hers.

Unable to speak, much less breathe, Sinjun waited several long minutes before he was able to move. His heart was still pounding against his ribcage when he lifted himself off and away, settling next to her on the bed.

"Do you still want to leave, love?" he whispered into the tense silence.

"No," Christy said on what sounded suspiciously like a sob. "I never want to leave you, Sinjun, but I have to. Try to understand my position."

"What about your position as my wife?"

"I'll always be your wife. You must know that. Leaving Niall is ripping me apart. Please reconsider your ultimatum. I swear I'll keep Niall safe for you."

"You're not taking Niall and that's final." His voice was grim with determination, thick with anger. "We've gone through this before, Christy. I haven't changed my mind. I was hoping you'd change yours. The only way I'll let Niall leave is if we all go to the Highlands together."

"That's out of the question," Christy argued. "The situation can be solved without English interference. I already explained that bringing English soldiers to Glenmoor will cost innocent lives. I'll leave Gavin and Effie behind to see to Niall's welfare in my absence."

"Blast you!" Sinjun spat. He was beyond understanding, beyond patience, beyond caring. He leaped from bed, gathering his scattered clothing and muttering imprecations beneath his breath.

"Remember one thing, madam. Whatever happens now is your doing. You cannot blame this parting on me. 'Twas your choice to leave Niall."

"No! Blast *you*, Lord Derby, for not understanding a damn thing about Highlanders. Leaving Niall behind is not my choice. I am not abandoning my son. I *will* return to him and I *will* be with him, no matter what you say."

"Like hell!"

She continued on as if he hadn't spoken. "Trust Effie to find a wetnurse for Niall."

Bitterness dripped from his words. "Anything else?"

She searched his face, then looked away as if the sight of him was painful. "There's one more thing you should know before I leave."

He yanked on his breeches and shirt, impatient now to get as far away from Christy Macdonald as possible. He'd done everything but get down on his hands and knees and beg her to stay, and he had too much pride for that.

"What is it? Make it fast, my patience is exhausted."

"I know you don't care, but I feel compelled to say it anyway. I love you, Sinjun. I've loved you for a very long time. There, 'tis done. Take care of my bairn."

Speechless, Sinjun stared at her. Was this another of her lies? Why would she tell him such a thing now? "I sincerely hope you don't mean that, Christy."

He picked up his boots and headed for the door. With his hand on the doorknob, he paused and grinned at her over his shoulder.

"Perhaps I put another babe inside you today."

His laughter followed him out the door.

"I love you, Sinjun," Christy whispered into the cold emptiness of the room. "Feeling as you do, I pray God you *haven't* put another bairn in my belly."

Christy left the following morning after an emotional parting. Niall was too young to understand and waved her off with a gurgle of laughter. Christy couldn't have left if she hadn't known Niall would be in good hands. She even delayed her leaving until Effie found a wetnurse for her son. The baker's daughter had just given birth to a child and had abundant milk to spare. Her husband had been injured in an accident, and she eagerly accepted the wages Sinjun offered.

Betsy agreed to move into the townhouse with her son and injured husband in order to be on hand for Niall's feedings. It wouldn't be for long, Christy thought, for Niall was already accepting mashed foods and nursed less frequently.

Christy didn't expect Sinjun to be on hand to bid her good-bye, and he wasn't. Truth to tell, she didn't think she could bear to see him.

"Go with God," Effie said as Rory - handed Christy into the coach and four that would carry them to the Highlands. "If anyone can prevent bloodshed between the clans, 'tis ye, Laird Christy Macdonald. Dinna worry about Niall. I'll keep him safe for ye until ye return."

Gavin echoed Effie's promise and warned Rory to take care. Christy knew the journey was not without danger, for there was always the threat of highwaymen and accidents. Fortunately Rory was well armed. He had two flintlock pistols hidden beneath the seat and a claymore beside him. And, of course, the dirk he carried in his boot.

Much to Christy's relief, the only enemy they encountered on the road was the incessant rain that pounded down upon them. She felt sorry for Rory, who was perched high in the driver's box, bearing the brunt of the cold, raw rain while she huddled inside the jostling conveyance beneath a blanket. Twice the wheels became mired in mud and she was forced to leave the coach while Rory worked to free them.

The disreputable posting inns offering shelter for the night left much to be desired. Christy sometimes found herself sharing a room with up to four women while Rory made do with a pile of straw in the stables.

Christy missed Niall desperately. Though she had bound her breasts tightly to stop the flow of milk, they still ached. She couldn't ever recall being so uncomfortable. The journey to the Highlands was made even more miserable by the enforced solitude she had to endure. The empty hours gave her ample time to dwell on those last moments she'd spent in Sinjun's arms.

If only she could have made him understand that she took her responsibility to her clansmen as seriously as she took her responsibility to Niall. Leaving Niall behind had been the hardest thing she'd ever done. Had Sinjun not been so adamantly opposed she wouldn't have had to leave her bairn behind. Her greatest fear now was that Sinjun would not let her become a part of Niall's life when she returned. After peace was restored in the Highlands, Christy planned to explain everything to Sinjun and hoped he would understand and forgive her.

A wave of relief washed over Christy when they crossed the border into Scotland. The rainy weather finally gave way to blue skies and sunshine, and Christy grew excited when she saw heather blooming on the hillsides. She heartily disliked London, with its sooty buildings, crowds, and stench of raw sewage. One day, she vowed, she would bring Niall home and raise him in the invigorating, clear air of the Scottish Highlands.

They spotted the pall of smoke hanging over Glenmoor village before they reached it. Christy's heart plummeted when she realized what it meant. Rory stopped the coach at the top of a hill while Christy hung out the window, staring with dismay at the smoke curling upward from burning cottages.

"We must get down there," Christy cried. "They may need help."

Shouts of welcome heralded their arrival as the coach rolled into the village.

" 'Tis The Macdonald!"

"The laird has returned!"

"Praise God!"

The first thing Christy noticed as she stepped down from the coach was that every able-bodied man carried a weapon—either claymore, pistol, dirk or stout stick. She gazed beyond them and saw the frightened faces of women and children peeping out from the doorways of those cottages not consumed by fire. When they saw Christy, they rushed out to greet her.

"What happened here?" Christy asked.

Big Murdoch Macdonald stepped forward. "The Camerons and Mackenzies," he spat. "They came at us at dusk. We turned them back, but they still managed to burn down two more cottages."

"Any dead?"

"Nay. Three wounded, not seriously, and two

children trampled in the melee. They'll recover."

"And the Ranalds?"

"They're having the same problems we are. The Ranald chieftain said half their herd have turned up on Cameron land."

"We'll rebuild," Christy said.

"We're glad ye've returned, Christy," Murdoch said. "Maybe ye can talk some sense into the Camerons. Clan wars have always divided the Highlands, but rarely among allies. I canna understand it."

Christy understood. Only too well. 'Twas Calum's way of repaying her for fleeing. He knew she'd return once she learned what was happening to her kinsmen—had counted on it, in fact. But he couldn't make demands on her this time. She was a married woman, Sinjun hadn't gotten the annulment, and her son was safe with his father. She'd make Calum understand there was nothing to gain and everything to lose from this senseless feud. Once he understood the dangers involved should war break out in the Highlands, things would settle down and she could return to London and make things right with Sinjun.

"If anyone needs lodging they're welcome to stay at Glenmoor," Christy offered.

"Thank ye, Christy. Those women and children without homes will be glad for yer offer, but the men will remain in the village to prevent further pillaging."

Christy left a short time later, determined to put a stop to the feud before it involved every clan in the Highlands and erupted into a war requiring the intervention of English soldiers.

* * *

Margot flew out the door to greet Christy before the coach rolled to a stop at the front entrance of Glenmoor.

"Where is yer wee laddie?" Margot asked as she embraced Christy warmly.

"I had to leave him behind. Sinjun wouldn't allow me to bring him."

"Ah, lass, 'tis sorry I am. Dinna worry, he's in good hands with his sire. I'm glad Rory found ye. Yer letter reached us a few days before he left for London. We were surprised to learn ye were living with his lordship. What happened?"

"I'll tell you later. Go greet your husband. Rory has missed you and his wee laddie something fierce."

"No more than I've missed Rory," Margot said. "I'd best greet him before he feels neglected. We'll talk later, Christy, after ye've rested."

"Aye, I've yet to meet your bairn," Christy said.

Walking into the house was like greeting an old friend, Christy thought as she entered the main hall. Glenmoor may not have been what it was in its glory days, but it was still home. Mary came from the kitchen and threw her arms around Christy, bemoaning the troubles that had plagued them since Christy had left.

"I intend to take care of things, Mary," Christy said, returning her kinswoman's hug.

"Where is yer bairn, Christy? I canna wait to start spoiling the wee darling."

"I left him with Lord Derby," Christy explained. She put on a bright smile to conceal her breaking heart. "Sinjun thought the Highlands were too dangerous for his son."

Mary pulled a wry face. "Englishmen! Bah! Yer

room is all ready, lass. Go take a rest, ye must be exhausted."

"I am, but before I do, I should warn you that I invited the homeless crofters to move into Glenmoor until their homes are rebuilt. Glenmoor has plenty of empty rooms to spare."

"Aye, I'll see to it, Christy. Go on with ye, now."

Christy mounted the stairs on wooden legs. She couldn't recall when she'd been so tired. After a good night's sleep she'd be better able to cope with the situation at Glenmoor. The bed looked so inviting that she flopped down fully clothed and closed her eyes. Margot arrived a few minutes later to show off her son.

"I've brought my wee Angus," Margot said, sitting on the edge of the bed and holding the tiny boy up for Christy's inspection.

Tears formed in Christy's eyes as she took Angus into her arms and cradled him against her breast. "He's a fine braw bairn, Margot."

"Ah, lass, dinna cry," Margot said. "I know ye must miss yer own wee laddie something fierce. Lord Derby was wrong to make ye leave him behind. Yer letter dinna explain much, only that his lordship learned about his son and that ye were living with him in his townhouse."

"Sinjun was angrier than I've ever seen him when he discovered he had a living son," Christy explained. "He wanted to take my bairn away from me and banish me to Glenmoor."

"Ye dinna mention the annulment. Are ye no longer married to Lord Derby?"

"We are still very much married. For some unexplained reason Sinjun failed to file the annulment with the courts. It's been difficult. I finally convinced him that Niall needed me and he let me stay. I don't know what's going to happen now," she said on a sob. "Sinjun thinks I care more for my clansmen than I do for my bairn."

"What did the English bastard do?"

"He told me if I left London I'd never see Niall again. He doesn't understand, Margot. No one but a Highlander can understand why I had to leave."

"Dinna he want to come with ye?"

"Oh, aye, but I told him his presence here would only aggravate an already explosive situation. I couldn't let him come, Margot! I love him too much to risk his life."

"So ye do love him," Margot said sagely.

"Even though I know he hates me, there is a bond between us that defies explanation. 'Tis something I feel in my heart. The attraction that drew us together is still as strong as ever. Sinjun recognizes it but refuses to acknowledge it."

"If he doesna, he's a bigger fool than I gave him credit for," Margot said. "I'll take wee Angus to his bed so ye can rest. Will we see ye at dinner tonight?"

"Aye. Ask Rory to send riders to the Macdonald and Ranald strongholds. They're to summon the chieftains to Glenmoor for a meeting tonight. We must decide on a way to stop this senseless feud."

"Calum Cameron isna going to be satisfied until he has what he wants, and we all know what he wants," Margot muttered as she left the chamber.

Christy's clansmen crowded into the hall, waiting for the laird to speak. Christy gazed into their hopeful faces and knew how much they depended on her to end this senseless feud between allies.

"We dinna want to fight our own clansmen," Murdoch Macdonald shouted over the din of the crowd. "We want our sheep and our cows back, and our families safe in their houses."

"I know what you want," Christy said, raising her hand for silence. " 'Tis why I've returned from London. I've already dispatched a message to the Cameron and Mackenzie chieftains, asking for a meeting of the clans at Glenmoor four days hence. If this feud continues, lives will be lost. You've already suffered the loss of livestock and homes."

"Aye, and we're prepared to retaliate in kind," Rory said, garnering a roar of approval. "The Macdonalds are no cowards."

"Before you do anything, I intend to make a plea for peace. Wait four days," Christy pleaded. "If no agreement can be reached, we'll decide what to do next. The last thing we need is a full-blown clan war, and I think the Camerons realize that bringing British soldiers to the Highlands would be disastrous for everyone."

"We'll wait, Christy," Murdoch said, speaking for the Macdonalds. "But if the Camerons attack our village again, we willna sit on our hands."

"Fair enough," Christy agreed. "You must defend yourselves. Return to the village. Set patrols to guard the livestock and remain alert. I'm hopeful that once The Cameron receives my message he will call a halt to the attacks."

The crowd dispersed. Even Rory left to take his turn at patrol duty. Christy and Margot remained alone in the hall.

"Perhaps I should have asked Rory to stay," Christy mused.

"Calum willna attack Glenmoor," Margot predicted. "He wants it too badly to destroy it."

"Aye, 'tis my belief, too."

*　　*　　*

All was quiet during the next two days. Neither the Camerons nor the Mackenzies replied to Christy's invitation to meet, and she began to fear they would defy her. At least they hadn't renewed their attacks or stolen any more livestock. A tenuous hope for a peaceful solution sprouted in Christy's breast. She began to think that her return to Glenmoor had encouraged the quiet that had prevailed for the past two days. She went to bed that night feeling that everything could be worked out.

Her dreams for peace among the clans were shattered when she awoke in the darkest part of the night to the terrifying feeling that she wasn't alone. Her worst nightmare became reality when the swath of moonlight piercing through the window revealed the hulking form of Calum Cameron looming over her bed. She opened her mouth to scream, and immediately a rag was stuffed between her teeth.

"Did ye ken I wouldna come for ye? Ah, lass, ye wound me deeply. I waited a long time for ye to return to the Highlands."

Christy reached up and pulled the foul rag from her mouth.

"Dinna scream if ye wish to avoid bloodshed," Calum warned. "I'm not alone, lass, and this is a household of women and children."

"How did you get in?"

" 'Twas easy enough."

"What do you want?"

"Why, ye, of course."

"Neither my husband nor my bairn are in the Highlands for you to hurt," Christy maintained. "Lord Derby and I are still married. I refuse to go anywhere with you."

Calum laughed softly. It was not a comforting sound. "It doesna surprise me that his lordship dinna get the annulment. I dinna care about the cursed Englishman or his brat. I'm taking ye anyway."

"I told you, I'm a married woman."

"Since when has that stopped a Highlander? Wife stealing is a time-honored tradition. I wanted to marry ye, but if I canna, I will steal ye. After I put my bairn in yer belly ye'll belong to me. Yer English husband willna have ye once I've plowed in his furrow."

"You're mad! Glenmoor belongs to Lord Derby. He'll drive you off the land."

"I dinna need Glenmoor to control the clans. I'll have ye. Ye'll abide in my stronghold and bear my bairns."

"No!" Christy cried, leaping off the bed.

She was no match for Calum's superior strength. He had but to reach out to bring her into his brawny arms. The breath slammed from her chest as he tossed her over one gigantic shoulder. Her struggles hurt no one but herself as he carried her from the chamber.

"Remember, lass, not a whisper if ye wish to prevent bloodshed," he hissed.

As he carried her down the stairs and out the open front door, several silent shadows followed in his wake, confirming his words that he wasn't alone. Christy knew Calum too well to ignore his warning. Though she wanted to scream at the top of her lungs, she fought the urge.

Of all the scenarios Christy imagined, being stolen by Calum had been the one she had never considered.

Chapter 18

Sinjun was at his wit's end. For three days Niall had done nothing but cry for his mother. Neither he nor Effie had been able to comfort the unhappy boy. And despite the wetnurse's best efforts, the child wasn't eating well. As a last resort, Sinjun sent for his sister. He remembered Emma's calming effect on Niall the last time she'd visited, and he prayed she could work the same kind of miracle on the discontented lad.

How could Christy have left? he wondered bitterly as he paced the room with Niall in his arms. Her lack of responsibility toward her child was yet another sin to add to Christy's growing list of irresponsible acts. Though he tried not to think of her at all, his traitorous mind refused to obey. He recalled with pleasure bordering on pain their last hours together. He remembered her wanton response to his loving and wondered if her passion had been feigned. She'd told him she loved him. Sinjun didn't believe it. She wouldn't have left him and Niall if she loved them. Obviously her clansmen meant more to her than her own family.

Niall's lusty cries jolted Sinjun back to the present, and he wished Effie hadn't gone to the market this morning. But truth to tell, even Effie's devoted attention failed to fill the void of Christy's absence.

Never had Sinjun been so glad to see anyone when Pemburton arrived with Emma in tow.

Emma knew by the frantic expression on Sinjun's face that something was amiss, terribly amiss. "What's wrong with Niall?"

"Thank God you've come," Sinjun said with heartfelt relief. "Do something. He's been like this for three days."

"I came as soon as I received your message. Is Niall ill? Where's Christy?"

"Gone," Sinjun said with such passionate venom that Emma was instantly wary.

"What did you do to her, Sinjun? Christy would never leave without her son." She held out her arms. "Here, give him to me."

Sinjun passed Niall over to Emma. Though Niall didn't stop crying, his screams abated to a bearable level. Emma cooed to him a few minutes, then spoke to him in low, reassuring tones. She was rewarded when Niall's pathetic sobs turned into sporadic hiccups, then stopped altogether. As Emma continued to croon to him, he lay his head down on her shoulder and fell asleep, his somber little face wet with tears.

"He's asleep," Emma said. "Poor little lad was exhausted. I'll carry him up to bed. Wait here, Sinjun, I want to know exactly what you did to Christy to make her leave."

Sinjun was sipping brandy from a crystal snifter when Emma returned. He saluted her with the glass and took a hefty swallow.

"Is that necessary, Sinjun?" Emma asked reprovingly. "Drinking will solve nothing."

"Believe me, I need it." He tipped his head and drained the goblet. When he reached for the decanter, Emma snatched it away.

"What happened?" Emma was determined to get to the bottom of this even if she had to butt heads with her obstinate brother. She'd done it before. He knew how tenacious she could be when she put her mind to it.

"I told you, Christy left."

"I repeat my question. What did you do to her?"

Sinjun sent her a disgruntled look. "Not a damn thing. I tried to convince her to stay, but she was adamant. I even tried to change her mind by refusing to allow her to take my son with her. You saw the results. She left anyway. Obviously those savages she calls clansmen mean more to her than her son."

"I'm lost, Sinjun. Start from the beginning. Christy must have had a good reason for leaving."

"You sit, I'll stand," Sinjun said as he began to pace. "It all started when Rory Macdonald arrived from Scotland. The Camerons and Mackenzies are feuding with the Macdonalds and Ranalds. 'Tis all so senseless. I understand none of it. Rory insisted Christy was needed at Glenmoor to stop the fighting."

"She *is* their laird."

"Whose side are you on anyway? I offered to go with her, but she said my presence would aggravate a volatile situation. She refused the offer of English soldiers to keep peace because she feared innocent blood would be shed."

Men are such dolts, Emma thought. Didn't Sinjun realize Christy wouldn't have insisted that he remain in London if she didn't have a good reason? She couldn't really fault Christy for not telling Sinjun about Calum Cameron's threat to his life, but deep down she felt Sinjun had a right to know.

"I never thought Christy would leave Niall," Sinjun continued. "I was wrong."

"You're often wrong, Sinjun," Emma chided. "Christy loves Niall. If you weren't so dense you'd realize that she loves you, too."

Sinjun sent her a startled look. "What makes you such an expert on my marital status? I thought you didn't like Christy."

"Christy and I had a long, rewarding talk that day Julian and I visited, the day we learned about Niall. I discovered many things about your wife during the course of our conversation. She's a wonderful mother. I understand she's done things that are difficult to forgive, but she had a reason."

He made a rude sound deep in his throat. "I suppose she told you why she lied to me and tried to deceive me."

"As a matter of fact, she did."

Sinjun regarded Emma with disbelief. To his knowledge, Emma and Christy had only shared a few private moments. How had Christy made such a loyal friend of Emma in so short a time?

Hands on hips, legs spread wide apart, Sinjun glared at Emma, his face composed in stern lines. "If you know something I don't, you'd best tell me."

"If you hadn't been so stubborn Christy would have told you everything you needed to know. Instead, you treated her like someone beneath your contempt and threatened to take Niall away from her. What a hypocrite. All the time you professed to hate Christy, you were bedding her, weren't you?"

Sinjun regarded Emma with more than a little shock. "Emma! You're too outspoken for your own good."

"Oh, pooh, Sinjun, don't be such a prude. These are modern times. I know more than you give me credit for. Now, will you kindly answer my question?"

"You don't deserve an answer. What passed between me and Christy is private. I suggest you tell me what you know before I turn you over my knee for a well-deserved spanking."

Emma bristled indignantly. "I'm much too old for that. But I'm going to tell you anyway because I believe you should know the sacrifices Christy made in your behalf. Where should I start?"

"From the beginning. Why did Christy lie about Niall? Why did she demand an annulment when it was the last thing I wanted? The last thing I thought *she* wanted?"

Emma took a deep breath and repeated the story just as Christy had related it, leaving nothing out. Sinjun's face turned from outright disbelief to cautious acceptance as the tale unfolded.

" 'Tis true, every word," Emma vowed when she finished speaking. "I believed Christy, and so should you. Why else would she leave her child behind? To prevent you from going to the Highlands, that's why. She feared for your life and did what she thought right to keep you safe."

"Why didn't she trust me to take care of myself?" Sinjun argued.

"Perhaps because she knows Calum Cameron. You've said yourself that Highlanders are a breed apart."

"Aye. They're savages who steal from their neighbors and fight among themselves. They think nothing of taking what they want."

" 'Tis my understanding that Calum wants Christy," Emma hinted slyly.

A terrible rage seized Sinjun. "He can't have her! Christy is mine. Bloody hell! If he lays one finger on her I'll kill him."

Sinjun began to pace, his tortured mind awhirl. Everything was perfectly clear now. All the pieces of the puzzle fell into place. Calum had started the feud for a reason, and that reason was to bring Christy back to the Highlands where he could get his hands on her. What a stupid fool he'd been not to listen to Christy's explanation when she'd been willing to give it. All he'd been interested in was punishing her for deceiving him.

Despite his low opinion of Christy, however, his need for her had never waned. Guilt plagued him. Christy had welcomed him in her bed, aware that he was using her. If that didn't prove her love, nothing did. Would she ever forgive him? Had his arrogance killed her love for him? He prayed it was not so, for he knew now what he'd been denying since the day Christy had entered his life.

He loved her.

Loved his own wife before he knew she belonged to him.

"What are you going to do?" Emma asked.

"Go to Glenmoor. No telling what Cameron has in mind for Christy. She has three days' head start. With any luck I won't be too far behind her. I'll travel by horseback, 'tis faster."

"You can't mean to go alone!" Emma said, aghast.

"Aye. Christy was right about English soldiers.

There is much unrest in the Highlands right now. Bringing soldiers into the fray could ignite a potentially explosive situation at the cost of innocent lives."

"I beg you, Sinjun, talk to Julian before you leave. He's away right now but should return in a few days. He'll send men to accompany you. Not soldiers necessarily, but men trained to fight."

"Do you think I'm incompetent? I realize I've wasted most of my life in idle pursuits, but things are different now. I'm perfectly capable of handling this on my own. Besides, I can't wait for Julian to return. Can you and Aunt Amanda stay here with Niall while I'm gone?"

"Of course. I'll send a maid to inform Aunt Amanda of the arrangements."

"Effie and Gavin will remain behind to help. Thank you, Emma, I don't know what I'd do without you."

"Take care of yourself, Sinjun. I couldn't bear it if anything happened to you or Christy."

"Stay out of trouble, hoyden," Sinjun said affectionately as he placed a tender kiss upon her brow.

Emma's eyes sparkled mischievously. "Staying out of trouble is boring. Plenty of time after I'm married, should I ever decide to take a husband."

Sinjun rolled his eyes heavenward, wondering if a man existed who could handle his spirited sister. "Just try to behave while you're taking care of my son."

"I'd never do anything to hurt Niall. I love him too much."

Sinjun left immediately to prepare for his journey to Scotland.

*   *   *

Christy paced the length of the room and back, frowning at the locked door. She was a prisoner. How could she have let this happen? At least Calum had left her alone after he'd locked her in the room. At first she feared he'd try to force himself on her, but he'd merely locked the door and left her to fret and worry in solitude.

The room was neat and clean but small in comparison to her chamber at Glenmoor. The room was on the second floor, too high from the ground for her to jump from the narrow window. She knew there were other Camerons in the house, for she heard voices and sounds of activity below. Tired of pacing, she sat on the edge of the bed and pulled a threadbare blanket over her nightgown. She wondered what her kinsmen would think when they found her missing and prayed they wouldn't act precipitously and launch an attack before she had a chance to talk some sense into Calum.

She'd been stunned to realize how easily Calum had gotten into Glenmoor. She shuddered to think what would have happened had Sinjun been there. He would have been slain in his bed, without a chance to defend himself. No matter what happened to her, she knew she'd been right to keep Sinjun away from the Highlands. And though she hated to admit it, Sinjun had been right to keep Niall safe in London.

Christy heard a commotion outside and rushed to the narrow window. What she saw chilled the blood in her veins. The Macdonalds and Ranalds, armed with a variety of weapons, were gathered in the courtyard. Facing them were Camerons and Mackenzies, all armed to the teeth. Christy's heart leaped into her mouth when Rory stepped forward, looking as fierce as an ancient warrior.

"Release our laird," Rory demanded.

Calum came forward to meet Rory. "What made ye think we have The Macdonald?"

"No one but ye would kidnap her from her bed. 'Tis a terrible thing ye did, Calum Cameron. If ye dinna return her unharmed, there will be bloodshed. Are ye willing to place yer kinsmen's lives in jeopardy?"

"The laird willna be harmed," Calum promised. "I've done nothing that hasna been done before. Ye all know that wife stealing is a time-honored tradition. Once I put my bairn in her belly her husband willna want her back. Ye have the word of The Cameron that she willna be harmed."

"Bring Christy out," Murdoch said, stepping forward to lend Rory support. "We dinna trust ye, Calum Cameron. Yer giving us no choice but to fight for our laird's freedom."

Christy heard every word and knew what would happen if the Camerons and the Macdonalds clashed. Lives would be lost, women and children would suffer without the support of their men should they perish in battle. She couldn't allow it. Leaning out of the window, she cupped her mouth and yelled at the top of her lungs to the angry men congregated below.

"Macdonalds! Ranalds! Heed me!"

" 'Tis The Macdonald!"

All eyes turned upward to the window. Calum's expression was murderous as he yelled, "Get back, Christy. This is between me and yer kinsmen."

"No! I am The Macdonald. My kinsmen trust me to do what is right for them."

"Speak, Christy!" Murdoch shouted. "If ye tell us to rid the world of Camerons and Mackenzies, so be it."

"There will be no bloodshed, Murdoch," Christy called down. "I'll handle this on my own. Go back to your homes. Rebuild your cottages. You have nothing further to fear from the Camerons, isn't that right, Calum?"

Forcing Calum's hand might not be a good idea, but her kinsmen were treading on dangerous ground. A full-scale clan war could go on for years, resulting in serious repercussions for future generations. This was all so senseless. As for wife stealing, it had been done in the past and would continue as long as clans feuded, but she wasn't about to let Calum have his way in this.

Calum was silent so long that Christy feared he intended to ignore her challenge. She was all but ready to give up and try reasoning with Calum on another level when he finally deigned to answer.

"Go back to yer homes. I have what I want. Ye've nothing more to fear from the Camerons as long as ye recognize me as yer leader. Old Angus was wrong to think a weak woman could lead the clan. I was the natural choice but he passed me by in favor of his granddaughter. The time is right now for me to claim leadership."

An anguished cry rose up from the Macdonalds and Ranalds as they grasped their weapons and started forward, prepared to do battle to protect their rightful laird.

"No! No fighting," Christy cried. "Everyone, go home. Let me settle this in my own way. There will be no bloodshed today on my account."

An ominous silence fell as the Highlanders digested Christy's words. Some of the clansmen still held out for a battle, but the voice of reason finally prevailed as Murdoch took matters into his own hands.

"Verra well, we'll honor our laird's wishes and leave, Cameron, but ye havena heard the last from us. Lord Derby will be notified immediately. He willna forgive yer insult to his wife. Wife stealing may be a tradition in the Highlands, but 'tis a crime in England. As much as I dislike the English, they still rule our land."

"No one rules Camerons," Calum shouted. "I'm warning ye. Keep Lord Derby away from Glenmoor if ye value his life."

"I agree," Christy called down to her kinsmen. "Bringing Lord Derby to the Highlands would be a mistake. Go back to your homes and let me handle this."

Amid much grumbling and no little amount of disappointment, the Highlanders dispersed, each clan returning to its own stronghold. Calum glared up at Christy; she met his furious gaze with cool disdain. He might think he had the upper hand now, but he wasn't going to get away with this. Somehow she'd find a way to foil his plans and return to her husband and son.

Moments later Christy heard footsteps pounding up the stairs and braced herself for Calum's anger. She heard the metallic scrape of the key turning in the lock, and then the door burst open. Calum strode inside, his face as dark as a thundercloud.

"Ye made a fool of me!"

"You *are* a fool, Calum Cameron. Neither the Macdonalds nor the Ranalds will submit to your leadership. If you continue this folly you'll bring more trouble upon yourself than you can handle. The Highlanders haven't forgotten their defeat at Culloden. Perhaps you are more anxious than I to bring English soldiers to Glenmoor and let them impose their will upon us."

"I thought ye hated the English bastards who killed our parents as much as I do. Now look at ye. Yer an Englishman's whore."

"I've been Lord Derby's wife since I was seven years old," Christy claimed. "You know I had no choice in the matter."

"Aye, wife in name only until ye sought him out in England and played the whore with him. Did ye think I dinna know what ye did and why? Ye wanted his child to preserve yer precious Glenmoor. Yer no longer one of us, Christy Macdonald."

"Then let me return to England, to my husband and bairn. You cannot force yourself on me, Calum, for I will not let you."

Calum gave a bark of laughter. "How do ye propose to stop me?"

Grasping her waist, he pulled her against him and jammed his mouth down on hers. His kiss was angry, punishing, without a hint of tenderness. When he thrust his tongue into her mouth, Christy gagged and shoved him away, wiping her mouth with the back of her hand. "You're disgusting!"

His expression turned ugly as he thrust a fist into her face. "Yer a woman. Do ye think ye can stop me if I wanted to take ye?" He took a menacing step forward. "Once I put my bairn inside ye ye'll soon settle down to being my woman."

Christy gave him a smug smile. " 'Tis a little late for that. I'm already carrying my husband's bairn."

Calum unclenched his fist and backhanded her across the face. Stars burst inside her head as she spun around and crashed to the floor.

"Yer lying!" Calum stalked her, his face mottled with rage. Christy scooted out of his way.

He grasped her shoulders and dragged her to her feet. "Don't touch me!"

The blanket she'd clutched to her neck fell away. Her fine lawn nightgown left her all but nude and vulnerable to his piercing gaze. He stared at her a long time, then ripped the nightgown from neck to hemline. Long, draining minutes passed while he stared at her.

"Ye dinna look like yer carrying a bairn."

Christy made a grab for the blanket and pulled it around her nakedness. He didn't stop her. " 'Tis too early to show." In truth, Christy had no idea if she was carrying Sinjun's bairn. She hadn't conceived up until the day before she left London, but their last time together could have changed that.

"The bastard! I willna be cheated, Christy Macdonald. I think yer lying. I can wait. But if I find ye've lied to me, I'll plow ye until I'm sure there's a bairn in yer belly."

"Over my dead body," Christy said venomously. "You'll never touch me, I swear it."

Calum regarded her through narrowed lids. "Yer death might gain me everything I want with less trouble."

"It will also precipitate a full-scale war and bring English soldiers to the Highlands."

"A rebellion is inevitable. The time is ripe."

"Culloden happened a long time ago. 'Tis time to let it rest. Return me to Glenmoor and all will be forgiven."

"I dinna need yer forgiveness," Calum spat. "Nor do I want ye while yer carrying an Englishman's bairn. Doesna it bother ye that yer husband has more mistresses than I have kinsmen?"

Christy flushed and looked away. "Leave Sinjun out of this."

"He will come to no harm as long as he remains where he is."

"You don't want me, Calum, admit it. You're jealous of my authority."

"I willna deny it. I wanted to marry ye, to help ye lead our clansmen, but now I must settle for having ye as my mistress."

Christy's shoulders stiffened. "Haven't you forgotten something? Once Sinjun learns what you have done he'll come for me." Though she preferred that he remain in London where it was safe, her heart told her that Sinjun would fight for what he considered his.

"I hope he does," Calum said. "We'll be waiting."

"What if he brings soldiers from the garrison at Inverness?"

"All the better." Calum turned to leave.

"Wait! I need something to wear."

"In good time, Christy Macdonald, in good time."

To Christy's delight, Margot arrived the following morning with a bundle of clothing. Calum had gone off to tend to his herd and Margot had raised such a fuss that Donald Cameron, who had been left behind to mind the stronghold, had let her see Christy rather than put up with her haranguing.

Margot rushed inside the room and hugged Christy fiercely. "I brought ye something to wear."

"Thank you. This blanket leaves much to be desired."

Margot's concerned gaze slid over Christy. "Did the bastard hurt ye?"

"No, and I won't let him. I'm just a means to an end to Calum."

Margot looked unconvinced. "Calum said he intends to put his bairn in yer belly so yer husband willna want ye."

Christy gave her a conspiratorial smile. "I told him I was already carrying Sinjun's bairn."

"Are ye?"

Christy shrugged. "No, but it has bought me time. Calum is serious about giving me his bairn, but he can't do it if I'm already pregnant."

"Be careful, lass," Margot warned. "Calum Cameron is an ambitious man. Ambitious men are dangerous. Are ye sure ye dinna want us to send word to his lordship?"

Christy bit her lip in consternation. She'd like nothing better than to have Sinjun help her out of this mess. Perhaps she'd been wrong all along not to inform Sinjun of Calum's threat against his life. Had he listened to her explanation when she'd tried to give it, she wouldn't be in this situation now.

"Perhaps you're right, Margot, but I've wronged Sinjun in so many ways that I seriously doubt he cares what happens to me."

"Why dinna ye let him decide for himself?"

Christy heaved a despondent sigh. "Very well, Margot, have it your way. Send word to Sinjun. But as long as he has Niall, I can't see him caring one way or another about my fate."

"Ye might be surprised," Margot said cryptically.

Their conversation ended abruptly when a glowering Calum barged into the room and ordered Margot out.

Chapter 19

C lan Macdonald and Clan Ranald were crowded in Glenmoor's main hall when Sinjun entered the following day. His gaze sought out Christy, and when he failed to find her, a shiver of apprehension slid down his spine. Rory was speaking, and everyone appeared to be listening as his voice rose on a note of anger. Sinjun paused at the edge of the crowd to listen.

"One of us must go to London for his lordship immediately," Rory asserted. "No matter how much we canna abide Englishmen, Lord Derby has proven he's not our enemy. He's our laird's husband and lord of Glenmoor. He deserves to know what is going on."

Rory's words set Sinjun's heart to pounding. Had something happened to Christy? His expression darkened, and his hands clenched into fists at his sides. If Calum had hurt her, he would pay dearly.

"There's no need for anyone to go to London," Sinjun said, advancing into the room. Immediately a path opened up for him. "As you can see, I am here. Someone had better tell me what's going on. Where is my wife?"

"Sinjun!" Rory cried. "Praise be, ye've come. How did ye know?"

"What am I supposed to know, Rory?"

"I canna soften the blow for ye so I'll put it bluntly. Calum Cameron has Christy."

Sinjun's eyes went as cold as death, and his expression revealed a ruthlessness few had ever seen. "How?" That one word conveyed a wealth of emotion.

"No one seems to know exactly how Camerons got inside the fortress. No men were present. They were in the village, protecting their homes and livestock. When Christy turned up missing the next day, everyone knew Calum was responsible."

"When did all this happen?"

"Three nights ago."

"And you've done nothing but talk about it?" Sinjun roared. "Bloody hell! Are you all cowards?"

Murdoch stepped forward, his face tense with rage. "The Macdonalds are no cowards. We armed ourselves and went to confront the Camerons the next day, prepared to fight for our laird."

"Calm down, Murdoch," Rory cajoled. "His lordship doesna know what happened. Let me explain. We were ready to use force to rescue Christy but she pleaded for caution. She said she hadna been harmed and wanted to handle the situation without bloodshed."

"And you believed her? Bloody hell. Christy is a woman. What can she do that an entire clan of armed men cannot?"

Murdoch drew himself up to his full six feet six. "She is our laird. Old Angus trusted her and so do we. We couldna go against her wishes."

"What are Calum's intentions? He must have taken Christy for a reason."

There was much shuffling of feet and clearing of throats before Rory took it upon himself to inform Sinjun of Calum's plans for Christy.

"Scotland, particularly the Highlands, is a country of traditions. One of those traditions continues to thrive despite laws against it."

A coldness seeped into Sinjun's bones. "Get to the point, Rory."

"Wife stealing. To this day feuds that began with one chieftain stealing another chieftain's wife still exist."

"I care nothing about feuds and clan wars. Christy is *my* wife. No one has a right to steal her. What does he hope to gain?"

"He believes that making Christy his mistress will gain him the authority he needs to start a rebellion against the English. Power is all he's ever wanted. He intends to—"

His words stumbled to a halt. "Say it, man!" Sinjun bellowed. "Tell me everything."

"Calum intends to put his bairn in Christy's belly. He knows yer too proud to take her back after the deed is done."

"Bastard! Bastard, bastard, bastard!" Sinjun ranted. "I'll kill him."

" 'Tis good ye're here," Rory observed. "We've been discussing different ways in which to handle the situation. Christy doesna want bloodshed, but we can see no peaceful solution."

The thought that Christy had spent three days *and nights* as Calum's captive made Sinjun's blood curdle. While the clan wasted time here debating methods of retaliation, Calum could have already forced himself on Christy.

"I could send to Inverness for soldiers," Sinjun offered as a possible solution. "But it might result in innocent bloodshed," he added, discarding that idea as quickly as it was born.

"Aye. Christy agrees that bringing English soldiers will do more harm than good," Rory returned.

"Then we must do this on our own," Sinjun said grimly. "Each minute Christy remains Calum Cameron's captive is one minute too long."

"What do ye propose?" Murdoch asked. "Ye can count on us, yer lordship."

"And the Ranalds," the Ranald chieftain added, stepping forward.

"First, we'll call a meeting of the clans. Macdonalds, Ranalds, Mackenzies and Camerons," Sinjun explained, "and demand Christy's release."

"Ha! We already tried that," Murdoch scoffed.

"Aye, but I might be able to change their minds. Listen closely, here's what I intend to do."

The clansmen crowded close as Sinjun laid out his plan. He had no idea if it would work, but there were too few options that didn't call for bloodshed. If all else failed, he would have no choice but to bring English soldiers to Glenmoor.

Messengers were sent out immediately, inviting the Camerons and Mackenzies to a meeting with the Macdonalds and Ranalds. Before the men left, Sinjun cautioned everyone to keep his arrival at Glenmoor secret in order to make their plan succeed.

The messengers returned several hours later. The Mackenzies had agreed readily enough to a meeting of clans, but the Camerons had balked at first. But once they realized they had to either agree to the meeting or risk censure by the Mackenzies, they gave grudging approval, stipulating that the meeting should convene at the Cameron stronghold.

Sinjun approved of the meeting place and sent Rory back with their terms. Christy was to be present at the meeting. It took all of Rory's considerable persuasive powers to convince Calum to agree.

"Why should I agree to yer terms when I hold the power?" Calum argued. "As long as the laird remains in my custody ye can demand nothing."

"Ye might lose yer Mackenzie allies if ye dinna let the laird attend the gathering of clans. She is yer overlord."

"She is my mistress," Calum stated baldly.

"She is yer laird," Rory persisted.

"Verra well," Calum spat. "Have it yer way. We'll meet right here, in the courtyard, at noon tomorrow."

"So be it," Rory said curtly.

"Dinna think to change my mind," Calum warned as he turned his back on Rory.

Calum barged into Christy's chamber minutes after Rory left. She shot to her feet, her eyes wary as she watched him approach. "I heard voices outside. What's going on?"

"Yer kinsmen are demanding a gathering of clans."

"Did you agree?" She tried not to show her excitement lest Calum turn contrary and refuse the request.

"The Mackenzies agreed so I had no choice. But it willna change anything. Ye were promised to me by yer father at birth. Ye should have never wed that English bastard."

"I was promised to you before Culloden. Both

our fathers died that day, and with it the plans they made for us. The king seized Glenmoor and gave both me and my lands to Lord Derby. Accept it and let it go."

"Never!" Calum vowed. "If I canna wed ye, I'll have ye as my whore."

"Sinjun will—"

Calum made a chopping motion with his hand. "Think ye yer husband will bestir himself to come to yer defense? 'Tis likely he'll find himself another woman to bed and forget all about ye."

Christy feared Calum was right but refused to give in to despair. "When is this gathering to be held?"

"At noon tomorrow. They want ye to be present at the meeting, though I'm against it. 'Tis likely they want to see ye've not been harmed. If ye give them any other impression, woman, ye'll suffer for it."

"You haven't harmed me, Calum, just deprived me of my freedom."

"Once I have proof yer not carrying a bairn, I'll make ye my mistress." He turned to leave. "Sleep well, Christy Macdonald."

I'll never be your mistress, Christy vowed as she made ready for bed. She'd been an optimistic fool to think she could talk sense into Calum. She knew now what she had to do and steeled herself for the coming confrontation. With all the clans gathered in one place, she would find no better time to give Calum what he wanted. She had no choice but to abdicate her position as laird in Calum's favor. Once she did that he'd have no reason to keep her.

Feeling better than she had in days, Christy climbed into bed and drifted off immediately. Sometime during the night she was awakened by a ravaging pain so deep that it felt as if she were being ripped apart. She missed Niall. Missed him with every fiber of her being. Though her milk had long since dried up, she felt his loss in the aching emptiness of her breasts, in the hollow void of her barren arms. A sob caught in her throat as she pictured his wee face. Did he still remember her?

Christy's thoughts turned to Sinjun. She'd had long hours during her captivity to consider the things she would have done differently were she given a second chance, and she wondered if she could ever make things right between her husband and herself. She had erred in so many ways. When she'd first arrived in London she'd had no intention of falling in love with her immoral husband. Everything she'd heard about him had indicated that he was devoid of character, thoroughly decadent, a rake, a man who changed his mistresses with his linens. But at the time none of that mattered. All she'd wanted was an heir for Glenmoor.

It had never occurred to her that she'd fall in love with her husband. She'd hurt him, yet he was still gentle with her. His love for his son was unconditional and his family meant everything to him. And he had a good heart.

During the following weeks she thought he had begun to care for her, and then she had shattered what happiness might have been theirs by telling him their bairn had died. They still might have had a future together, however, had she not left him and Niall in London and rushed to the aid of her kinsmen.

Distraught and remorseful, Christy finally fell asleep. But her dreams were not placid ones. They invaded every part of her body. She dreamed of unspeakable passion, of nostalgic lust, of unrequited love. After a fitful night, she awakened pale and exhausted.

Sinjun was dressed in a crisp white shirt, Macdonald plaid, and Highland bonnet, sporting a cocky feather, pulled low over his brow. He joined the Highlanders gathered in the hall to break their fast. If he felt uncomfortable baring his knees and lower legs, he gave no indication. He was dressed like a Highlander and was surprised at the pride he took in that fact.

"No one is to make a move without orders from me," Sinjun reminded them as he rose from the table and tossed down his napkin. "I don't want Christy hurt. Calum is a loose cannon, no telling what he'll do if cornered. Are we all agreed?"

A chorus of ayes followed his short speech. "Arm yourselves. We won't go like lambs to a slaughter."

Sinjun strapped on a sword of fine Toledo steel. Unlike the unwieldy basket-handled claymore preferred by the Highlanders, Sinjun's sword was a finely honed rapier, lighter and more deadly when wielded with precision. It was a weapon in which Sinjun was skilled, having taken lessons for many years from the masters.

At Sinjun's silent nod, the Highlanders filed out the door, their faces grim, each man ready to fight should it come to that. They were as loyal to Christy as she was to them.

Christy stood in the Cameron courtyard awaiting the arrival of her kinsmen. The Mackenzies had arrived earlier and were conferring with Calum. They appeared uneasy, and Christy didn't blame them. Calum was so determined to seize power for himself that some of his own kinsmen feared he had gone too far.

Christy gazed out over the moors as the sound of music floated to her on an errant breeze. They came. Almost two hundred strong, Macdonalds and Ranalds, all dressed in their distinctive plaids and bonnets, marching across the heath to the mournful wail of bagpipes. Her heart swelled with pride. These were her clansmen, each and every one prepared to die for her should she request it of them. Teeth clenched, jaw firm, she silently vowed that not one drop of blood would flow on her account.

Calum's allies lined up in the courtyard, plaids swinging in the breeze, weapons clenched in sweaty fists. Calum stepped forward. Murdoch, an elder of Clan Macdonald, strode forth to meet him.

"State yer business, Murdoch Macdonald," Calum said.

"Release The Macdonald."

"She is my mistress. Christy has already shared my bed."

A wounded sound escaped from Christy's bloodless lips.

"Bastard!" Rory cried. If Murdoch hadn't held him back, he would have launched himself at Calum.

"Release our laird or prepare for battle," Murdoch repeated.

"Why? Her husband willna have her now so I will keep her."

Christy saw the danger. One move toward weapons and a battle would ensue. She couldn't allow that to happen. Shoving aside Camerons and Mackenzies, she positioned herself between them and her defenders. "No bloodshed," she pleaded.

"I have a solution." She whirled to face Calum. "I have a proposition for you, one you won't be able to refuse."

"Verra well, lass, state yer proposition," Calum said dismissively, "but dinna think ye can gull us with words."

"All the clansmen who call me laird are gathered in one place."

"What are ye getting at, woman?"

"Only this. I no longer wish to be laird." Though she said it with conviction, her heart was sadly burdened. Breaking her grandfather's trust was painful, but she could think of no other way to prevent bloodshed. Christy turned to address the assembled crowd.

" 'Tis my wish that you accept Calum Cameron as the new laird of the clan. In return, he must agree to release me without a fight."

The Macdonalds and Ranalds brandished their weapons amid shouts of protests. Christy had no idea her words would cause such an uproar and feared a battle was inevitable as both sides moved toward one another with grim purpose.

Suddenly a man pushed and shoved his way through the angry crowd. He wore the Macdonald plaid and distinctive bonnet. His white shirt was stretched tautly across his broad shoulders, and his plaid barely covered his knees, revealing muscular legs firmly planted against the earth. The dirk stuck in his belt looked lethal, but not nearly as deadly as the rapier belted at his waist.

Christy's startled gaze flew to his face. The breath caught painfully in her breast when she looked into Sinjun's dark, menacing eyes. She heard Calum spit out a curse and realized she wasn't the only one who recognized the Marquis of Derby. She made a move toward Sinjun, but Calum reached out and brought her roughly against him.

She felt Sinjun's hard gaze sweep over her, and she nearly buckled under the heavy weight of his intense scrutiny. Was he angry with her? She knew he had to have heard Calum's bald-faced lie about having made her his mistress and wondered if Sinjun believed it. What was he doing here?

"Release her," Sinjun ordered. "There will be no deal. Christy Macdonald is now and always will be laird. No one can take that from her."

Calum brought his dirk from his belt in one smooth motion and pressed it against Christy's neck. "Where is yer pride, Englishman? Dinna ye ken? Christy is my whore. I put my cock inside her."

Christy saw a muscle jerk in Sinjun's jaw and realized that his control was swiftly eroding.

"Christy is my wife," Sinjun declared fiercely. "Let her go now or prepare to defend yourself."

"Yer a fool, Englishman. No Highlander would risk his life for another man's whore," Calum sneered.

"We are all willing to risk our lives for the laird," Rory shouted, brandishing his weapon.

"Hold!" Sinjun ordered. "Before you wield your weapons, consider the consequences. The English garrison at Inverness isn't so far that they wouldn't hear of the fighting and come to investigate. Is that what you want? Other clans will rise to your aid. The situation can escalate into another war, bringing destruction and death to the Highlands.

"The Crown will not tolerate an uprising. Soldiers will come by the score, there will be many deaths. You'll lose your homes, your friends, your loved ones. Are you willing to give up what freedom you have now for one man's ambitions?"

The Camerons and Mackenzies traded nervous glances and shifted restlessly as they considered Sinjun's dire prophesy.

"Dinna listen to the English bastard," Calum exclaimed as he pressed his blade deeper into Christy's neck.

Sinjun saw a drop of blood on Calum's blade and was seized by a raging fury. She looked so pale, so fragile; he feared Calum had hurt her in ways that didn't show. If Christy's life had not been at stake he wouldn't have hesitated to attack the coward. Instead, he continued taunting those men allied with the Cameron chieftain.

"Surely you remember Culloden. You've all lost loved ones in the battle, some of you were made homeless when your lands were confiscated by the Crown. If you follow the Cameron chieftain you stand to lose everything you've gained since Culloden. Aye, I am English, but one day Glenmoor will belong to my heir, Christy's son, and I don't want to see any part of it or its people destroyed.

"Go back to your homes, Mackenzies. Have done, Camerons. This matter can and should be settled between me and Calum."

"Stay and fight!" Calum screamed when he saw the Mackenzies start to melt away. One by one they turned and left the courtyard, until only the Mackenzie chieftain was left.

"The Englishman is right, Cameron," he stated. "We canna afford to lose our sons, fathers, or brothers in another war. I dinna mind stealing my neighbor's livestock, but killing our own clansmen is wrong. My kinsmen stand firmly behind the Macdonald laird."

So saying, he turned and followed his kinsmen back to his own stronghold, leaving Calum standing alone with his kinsmen, who had already shown their unwillingness to bring mayhem to the Highlands by withdrawing a respectable distance from their chieftain.

"You've lost, Cameron," Sinjun observed. "Very carefully, remove your blade from Christy's throat."

" 'Tis just you and me, English dog," Calum snarled as he removed his dirk from Christy's throat and sent her hurtling toward Sinjun.

Christy stumbled, then hit Sinjun full tilt, knocking them both to the ground in a tangle of skirts and legs. Air hissed from between his teeth as he fought to regain his breath. Then, from the corner of his eye, he saw Calum leap forward and raise his claymore. Sinjun had little time to think, much less react, as his arms came around Christy, rolling with her a heartbeat before the sword hacked a groove into the ground where they had lain scant moments before.

Immediately a dozen Macdonalds leaped to his defense. As many Camerons stepped forward to meet them. Fearing an out-and-out battle, Sinjun pushed himself free of Christy and helped her to her feet, shoving her toward Rory for safekeeping. Then he drew his rapier.

"This is between you and me, Cameron. Let's keep it that way. Do you have the balls to meet me one on one?"

"I have more balls than ye, Englishman," Calum snarled. "That pretty sword of yers is no match for my claymore." He glanced at his kinsmen, who were still poised for battle and awaiting his orders.

"Back away, Camerons, while I teach his lordship how a Highlander fights."

Sinjun motioned the Macdonalds away, and a space was cleared for the combatants.

"Sinjun! No!"

He heard the terror in Christy's voice but ignored her as he concentrated on Calum, assessing his weaknesses and his strengths as they circled warily. Calum made the first move, feinting for Sinjun's gut. Sinjun easily sidestepped. Then the battle engaged in earnest with a series of thrusts, lunges, and evasions. Calum's delivery was frenzied, fueled by anger. Sinjun's moves were calculated and deadly accurate.

Blood was drawn. Sinjun bled from a shallow slash on his arm, and Calum sustained a thigh wound. Neither opponent had been badly hurt yet. Calum hacked away with his claymore, putting all his strength behind it, while Sinjun found openings and lunged in for vulnerable spots. Sinjun didn't want to kill Calum, though he knew that Calum would have slain him with little remorse.

Sweat rolled into Sinjun's eyes, and he dashed it away with the back of his hand, smearing blood across his brow. His arm was beginning to tingle, and he realized he should end this soon, before Calum got in a lucky blow. He turned aggressor, feinting and slashing, while Calum could do little more than defend himself against Sinjun's flashing rapier.

It soon became apparent to the spectators that Lord Derby was no novice at swordplay. Obviously Calum realized it too, for he tried to regain the offensive with several hacking strokes. But he was powerless before Sinjun's superior skill. Employing a deft movement that was faster than the

eye could see, Sinjun sent Calum's claymore flying
out of his hands. With a twist of his wrist, Sinjun
pressed the deadly point of his rapier into a vulnerable spot beneath Calum's chin.

"Ye've got me, ye bastard!" Calum snarled. "Go
on, kill me."

Sinjun was sorely tempted. Calum had touched
Christy, taken from her what was Sinjun's alone,
and he deserved to die. Sinjun firmed his jaw and
flexed his wrist.

Suddenly Christy came flying at him, her eyes
softly pleading. "Sinjun! No! Do not kill him."

He spared her a startled look. "You want him
alive? After what he's done to you?"

"It's not . . . you don't understand. Do not kill
him, Sinjun, please."

With marked reluctance, Sinjun slowly lowered
his rapier. "Very well. He can keep his miserable
life, but only if he kneels at your feet and swears
fealty before his clansmen."

Calum looked ready to explode. His face was red
and swollen, his eyes narrowed, and Sinjun feared
he was going to refuse. "Well? What will it be,
Cameron? Death or fealty to the laird?"

Calum's gaze flitted about wildly, finally coming
to rest on his claymore, lying some distance away.
Sinjun promptly kicked it out of his reach.

"Ye bastard! I choose to live," Calum spat as he
knelt clumsily in the dust at Christy's feet.

"Say the words," Sinjun demanded.

"I swear . . ."

Suddenly Calum slumped over, and when he
straightened he had a dirk in his hand. Before Sinjun could bring up his rapier, Calum hurled the
dirk by its tip, straight for Sinjun's heart. Sinjun

ducked, but not fast enough. The dirk struck him in the middle of the chest. He heard Christy scream, then everything went blank as he dropped to his knees and keeled over on his face.

Chapter 20

❧❧❧

"Will he live?" Christy asked anxiously as she stared into Sinjun's white face. He was so pale, so utterly helpless, that Christy feared Mary's considerable healing skills would not be enough to save him.

"Yer man has the devil's own luck," Mary said. "If his shirt button hadna deflected the point of Calum's dirk he'd be dead now. 'Tis a miracle the sword point dinna pierce his heart or puncture a lung. Regardless, his lordship is a verra sick mon. I've done all I can for him. 'Tis up to God whether he lives or dies."

"He's not going to die!" Christy said fiercely. "Were Calum not dead I'd kill him myself for what he did to Sinjun."

"Calum Cameron brought shame upon his clan. No one blames Rory for ending his miserable life."

"I thought Donald Cameron would demand Macdonald blood for his brother's death, but Donald is a wiser man than his brother," Christy replied. "He took his clansmen in hand before blood was shed and knelt before me to offer the clan's fealty. For the first time in a very long time I feel as if friction between the Camerons and Macdonalds has finally been laid to rest. We Highlanders have enough problems with the English without fighting among ourselves."

Mary pulled the sheet up to Sinjun's chin and patted his shoulder. "Och, and that's the truth, lass."

"Go get some rest, Mary, I'll stay with Sinjun."

"Are ye sure?"

"Aye. I couldn't sleep while he's like this anyway."

Christy pulled a chair up to the bed and took Sinjun's lax hand into hers, willing her own life into him. She sat beside him all day and into the night, refusing to leave when Margot offered to take her place at Sinjun's side. She wanted to be the first person Sinjun saw when he awakened.

Fear was Christy's constant companion during those long hours. She had no idea how Sinjun would feel about her when he came to. Did he believe Calum's claim that she was his mistress? What had brought him to the Highlands? He must have left London shortly after her own departure to reach Glenmoor within days of her own arrival.

Christy left Sinjun's side but briefly during the following three days. During that time he remained comatose and feverish. Mary dosed him with tea made from mandrake root for pain, and she spread marigold salve on his wound each time she changed his bandage. She also prepared an herbal mixture, which Christy patiently spooned into his mouth, to ease his fever. Then she dutifully massaged his throat until he swallowed.

On the fifth day Sinjun opened his eyes and spoke his first word since being wounded. "Christy . . ."

Incredible joy surged though Christy when she heard him whisper her name. "I'm right here, Sinjun."

Though clouded with pain, his eyes were clear and lucid. "How long . . ."

She placed a finger over his lips. "Don't talk. Save your strength. You've been like this for five days, but you're getting better."

Sinjun stared at her, concentrating on her words. She squeezed his hand and he squeezed back, indicating that he understood. He searched her face. She looked exhausted. Had she been sitting with him the entire five days? She'd been through too much; he didn't want her to jeopardize her own health by playing nursemaid. His mouth worked noiselessly a few moments before he was able to form the words he wanted to say. But he was so tired he didn't know if he could stay awake long enough to make his wishes known.

"Christy . . ."

"Aye."

"I don't want you . . ." The effort to complete the sentence defeated him. His words fell away, and his eyes fluttered shut.

Despair settled over Christy. She understood perfectly what Sinjun was trying to convey. He was trying to tell her he didn't want her. Pain kicked her in the gut. She had lied to him too often for him to believe that nothing had happened between her and Calum. Oh, God, what was she to do?

Another day passed before Mary pronounced Sinjun out of danger and well on the road to recovery. Christy felt as if a great weight had been lifted from her, but she was now faced with a far greater fear. Once Sinjun recovered from his injury, would he sever all ties with her and refuse her access to Niall?

Sinjun showed moments of awareness throughout the day, and Christy waited for him to bring up the subject he'd briefly referred to the day before. She found him awake when she entered his room to feed him some broth Mary had made for him.

"How do you feel?"

"Like . . . bloody hell. What . . . happened?"

"Don't you remember?"

"Vaguely."

"You beat Calum fairly in a duel and gave him the choice of swearing fealty or accepting death. He knelt at my feet as if to swear fealty, but grabbed his dirk instead and stabbed you. The button on your shirt deflected the blow away from your heart but the wound was still a grave one. You were very lucky, Sinjun."

"Who do I have to thank for saving my life?"

"Mary, mostly. She knows a great deal about healing."

He stared at Christy in rapt silence. She fidgeted beneath his probing gaze, wishing he'd just come out and say what he was thinking.

"What is it, Sinjun? Is something wrong?"

"You look exhausted. Are you well?" He massaged his temples. "I can't seem to think straight. I seem to recall . . ." His voice faltered. "I thought I told you I didn't want you . . ."

She placed a finger against his lips. "Say no more. I know what you're going to say."

He looked confused. "You do?"

"I don't wish to discuss this now. You're too weak yet for a serious discussion. I know exactly what you're trying to tell me, Sinjun, and one day soon we'll talk, but not now."

"You're not making sense, so perhaps you're right. I'm not thinking clearly enough to understand you. Just tell me this. What happened to Calum?"

"Rory killed him. If he hadn't, Murdoch would have. It turned out all right, though. Donald is the Cameron chieftain now, and he's not as hotheaded or as ambitious as Calum. There will be no more feuding."

Christy realized Sinjun hadn't heard her, for his eyes were closed, and his chest rose and fell in an even cadence. She tiptoed from the chamber and closed the door behind her.

"Ye can't be serious, lass," Margot argued as Christy stuffed clothing into a valise.

"I can't wait any longer, Margot. The only reason I stayed this long was to make certain Sinjun was going to recover. He said nothing to indicate he wants me or cares about me."

"Has he told ye he doesna want ye?"

"Aye. He said the words loud and clear. Once Sinjun recovers and returns to London, I'll be barred from entering his house. I'll never see my son again."

"What mischief have ye hatched now, lass?"

"No mischief, Margot. This is survival. I can't live without Niall. I'm going to London and that's final."

"Where will ye and Niall go?"

"I don't know, but I'll think of something. Sinjun won't look for us forever. He's easily distracted in London. A new woman. A gambling hell. The races. He'll soon pick up where he left off, racketing around town with a new mistress."

"Are ye sure, Christy? Did ye ever find out what brought Sinjun to Glenmoor?"

"I . . . there wasn't time. I have to do this, Margot, for my son's sake. He needs me, and I need him."

"Do ye love Sinjun?"

Christy gave a bitter laugh. "Love him? I'm head over heels, for all the good it does me. I've hurt him, lied to him, deceived him. How can I expect him to forgive me? He'll never understand my loyalty to my clan, for he's never taken responsibility seriously. It's not that he shunned responsibility, it's that he simply could not summon enough interest to care about anything except his own pleasure. Few legitimate pursuits held his attention for long, unless they earned him some form of wicked delight."

"Ye judge him harshly, lass."

A tear trickled down her cheek. "Don't you see? I have to judge him harshly else I wouldn't be able to leave him. That's how much I love him. I'm almost packed, would you ask Rory to bring the coach around?"

"Aye, I'll tell him."

"Margot, wait. I regret taking Rory away from you and Angus again, but it won't be for long this time. I'll send him back as soon as I reach London."

"What am I to tell his lordship?"

"The truth. Tell him I missed Niall. There's nothing more he needs to know."

"Will ye send word when ye settle some place?"

"Aye. Don't worry, Margot, Niall and I will be just fine. This time I won't make the mistake of staying where Sinjun can find us."

"God go with ye, Christy."

* * *

Sinjun was restless and strangely disturbed. He hadn't seen Christy all day and hoped it was because she was resting. She'd spent too many hours caring for him, and it showed. Her face was pale and drawn, and the fragile skin beneath her eyes was bruised with dark shadows.

Both Mary and Margot had bustled in and out of his chamber at various times, but neither seemed inclined to stay and chat. He supposed he wasn't the best of patients. He was so weak that he couldn't accomplish for himself even the most menial of tasks, which was embarrassing in the extreme. Though the thought galled, he feared he was in for a lengthy recovery. He hated to leave Niall without either of his parents for so long a time, but there was no help for it. When he and Christy returned to London, they would start over and become a real family.

Taking on responsibility was new to Sinjun, and having a son had changed his entire outlook on life. It didn't matter to him that Calum had forced himself on Christy, for he knew it wasn't something she had wanted. He prayed that one day she could forget that terrible ordeal. Christy had been unwilling to discuss what had happened between her and Calum, and Sinjun couldn't wait to tell her it didn't matter to him. He even understood now why she had left London against his wishes.

He understood a great deal, thanks to Emma's enlightening lecture. He and Christy had a lot to resolve if they wanted to salvage their marriage, but Sinjun felt their future happiness was worth the effort.

Sinjun felt somewhat stronger the next day and

waited anxiously for Christy's visit. He felt the first stirrings of misgiving when Margot, instead of Christy, brought his breakfast of broth and gruel.

"Is Christy ill?" he asked after he dutifully swallowed the spoonful of gruel Margot offered.

"Nay."

He swallowed another spoonful. "I can feed myself."

"Yer not strong enough yet."

"Bloody hell! Will you stop pampering me? Where's Christy? Tell her I want to see her."

Margot's lips thinned. "She isna here."

"Not here!" Sinjun tried to rise, but pain and weakness forced him back down. "Where is she?" he asked more reasonably.

"She missed her bairn."

Sinjun felt as if his world had been ripped apart. "Are you saying Christy went to London? Without telling me?"

"Yer as quick-witted as ever," Margot said dryly.

"Did she leave a message for me?"

Margot shook her head and tried to shove another spoonful of gruel between his clenched teeth. Cursing, Sinjun flung her hand aside. Gruel splattered everywhere.

"Bloody hell! Take that damn gruel away and bring me something substantial to eat. The sooner I regain my strength the sooner I can leave this bed."

"Yer stomach canna handle it."

"Blast my stomach! Blast this entire household and blast my wife! How could one small woman cause so much turmoil in my life? Christy has been nothing but trouble since the day she walked into that masked ball in London. She's intrusive, contradictory, maddening."

" 'Tisna an unusual feeling for someone in love," Margot observed.

Sinjun spit out a curse. Love! What good was love, when his headstrong wife defied him at every turn? When he caught up with her he'd shake her until her teeth rattled; he'd blister her beautiful bottom . . . he'd make love to her until she couldn't walk. He knew exactly why she had left so abruptly for London. She intended to take his son and disappear again. Bloody hell!

Sinjun's recovery progressed far too slowly for his liking. A fortnight passed before he could move about without undue pain. Another week elapsed before he felt strong enough to leave Glenmoor.

Christy reached London without mishap, surprised to find Emma and her aunt in residence at Sinjun's townhouse. Even more surprising was the warm welcome she received from Sinjun's sister.

"Christy!" Emma squealed. "You're home! Niall will be so glad to see you. Where's Sinjun?"

"Sinjun is still at Glenmoor," Christy said, returning Emma's exuberant hug. "I need to see Niall first, then I'll explain everything. I hope he remembers me."

Niall was shy at first, but it wasn't long before the familiarity of his mother's voice broke through his reticence and he was clinging to her as if he never intended to let her go.

"I've enjoyed taking care of him, Christy," Emma said. "Effie has been a big help, and so has Gavin. Niall's not nursing much now, so the wetnurse moved back into her own home. She only comes in the evenings for his bedtime feeding. Oh, look, the little lamb has fallen asleep on your shoulder."

Christy's tears flowed freely as she patted Niall's

back and crooned to him. "I can't bear to put him down." She eased into a rocking chair and cradled him in her arms. Emma pulled up a stool and sat at her feet.

"What happened at Glenmoor?" Emma asked eagerly. "Where is Sinjun? Why didn't he return with you?"

Christy knew she owed Emma an explanation but feared Sinjun's sister would condemn her as Sinjun had. She dragged in a steadying breath. "Sinjun suffered a grave wound. I remained with him until I was assured of his recovery."

Emma shot to her feet. "Wounded! By whom?"

"Calum Cameron. The Cameron chieftain kidnapped me from my bed and kept me locked in his house. He intended to make me his mistress and claim leadership of the clan. He assumed Sinjun wouldn't want me after he . . . after he defiled me."

Emma's mouth flew open. "How terrible for you!"

"Highlanders play by their own rules," Christy explained. "Most husbands refuse to take their wives back after they've been ravished by their captors."

"But that's so unfair," Emma argued.

"Aye, but 'tis how the system works despite the fact that most stolen wives are unwilling victims."

"Sinjun isn't like that," Emma insisted.

"Calum Cameron bragged to Sinjun that I was his mistress."

"Were you?"

"No. Had Calum taken me by force, I would have found a way to end his miserable life. Whether or not it was true didn't matter; Sinjun believed him." A sob caught in her throat. "Sinjun doesn't want me, Emma."

"Oh, pooh, that doesn't sound like Sinjun at all. He knows why you lied to him about Niall. I explained everything. I'm sorry I had to break a confidence, but the situation called for it. Why do you think Sinjun arrived at Glenmoor when he did? He was worried about you."

Christy's heart soared. Could it be true? "Sinjun couldn't have arrived at a better time, though he paid dearly for it. His life hung in the balance for more days than I care to count. But he's well on the road to recovery now, thank God."

"Why aren't you with him?"

"I told you. Sinjun doesn't want me. I had every reason to believe he intended to cut me out of his and Niall's life once he returned to London, so I decided to take matters into my own hands."

"Did you discuss this with Sinjun?"

"He was very clear when he told me didn't want me. What is there to discuss?"

"Obviously you misunderstood," Emma contended. "Sinjun loves you. Why do you think he left Niall and rushed off to Glenmoor? You didn't see him before he left, Christy. He was so worried and so anxious to get to you he refused to wait for Julian's help. I know my brother. Even if Calum had forced you it wouldn't have made a difference to Sinjun. His life is far from exemplary."

"That's not the same and you know it. Society has different standards for men and women."

"Aye, I know it too well," Emma huffed. "One day someone is going to set London on its ear. All that aside, you can't leave, Christy. You owe it to Niall to try to save your marriage. Do you intend to run the rest of your life? That's what will happen, you know, for Sinjun won't rest until he finds you."

Christy remained thoughtful, mulling over

Emma's words. Sinjun *had* come to Glenmoor, and he *had* rescued her from a dangerous situation. His courage had healed the rift between clans, and he had suffered a grievous wound on their account.

Could it be true? Had she misunderstood Sinjun? He'd been very ill. Perhaps she had wrongly interpreted his words because of her own guilt. How could their marriage work when she deserved so little of Sinjun's trust?

Miracles did happen, however. If Sinjun truly loved her as Emma said, then a chance for happiness existed, for *she* loved Sinjun beyond all reason.

"I'm not going to let you leave, Christy," Emma said with firm conviction.

"I cannot bear to lose Niall."

"You *do* love Sinjun."

"With my whole heart and soul."

Emma sighed dreamily. "I wish to experience a love like that just once in my life. Julian is already talking about finding me a husband."

"He won't force you to wed someone you don't approve of, will he?"

"He says not, but he doesn't want me to end up a spinster." Her chin notched upward. "I won't marry any man I'm not in love with. But enough of me. Leaving now would be the biggest mistake of your life."

Christy would give anything to believe Emma. It wasn't too farfetched to believe that Sinjun loved her, was it? Dreams sometimes came true, didn't they?

"Aye, I'll stay, Emma, though I may live to regret it."

Sinjun arrived in London without mishap. It had been a long, difficult journey, given his recent in-

jury and diminished stamina. He had refused both
Murdoch's and Rory's offer of company and undertaken the journey alone.

Sinjun couldn't bear the thought of going to his
own empty house, so he reined his tired mount
toward Julian's townhouse. He wanted to speak to
Emma anyway, in the unlikely event she knew
where Christy had taken Niall.

Sinjun didn't believe for a minute that Christy
had come to London simply because she had
missed Niall. His gut told him that he'd find Derby
Hall deserted except for servants. He had no idea
why Christy had left him again. He thought he'd
made it clear that he didn't care what Cameron had
done to her, but his memory was still fuzzy about
what he'd actually said to her. It hadn't been the
best time to engage in serious conversation. Obviously he'd said something to send her fleeing.

Sinjun dismounted, looped his reins around the
iron fence post, and climbed the front steps to
Mansfield Place, Julian's elegant townhouse. His
first knock brought an immediate answer. Julian's
dignified butler held the door open as Sinjun strode
inside.

"Good day, milord. Lord Mansfield is not at
home, but Lady Emma is in the drawing room with
her aunt."

"Thank you, Farthingale. I'll see myself to the
parlor."

"As you wish, milord."

Sinjun paused in the doorway, not surprised to
see Emma pacing the room in great agitation and
expounding animatedly to Aunt Amanda, who
nodded her head from time to time in placid agreement.

"What can be keeping him, Aunt?" Emma exclaimed. "Oh, how I wish Julian wasn't off on one of his mysterious trips. He'd know what to do. What if Sinjun's wounds were more serious than we were led to believe?"

"Worried about me, Emma?" Sinjun said, strolling into the room. "As you can see, I'm fine."

"Sinjun!" Emma cried, throwing herself into his arms. "I thought you'd never get here." She held him at arm's length and studied him with a critical eye. "You don't look fine. You're pale and far too thin. Christy told us you had been wounded."

"What else did Christy tell you?" Sinjun asked harshly.

Emma gave him a quizzical look. "Have you been home yet?"

"No. I couldn't bear the thought of an empty house waiting for me. Strange, it never bothered me before."

"Have you dismissed the servants?"

"You know darn well what I mean." He searched her face. "Do you know where Christy took Niall? How could you let her take him away?"

"Sinjun, you're overwrought. Sit down, I'll ring for a bottle of Julian's best brandy."

Sinjun plopped down into the nearest chair, leaned his head back, and closed his eyes.

"Are you sure you're well, dear?" Aunt Amanda asked solicitously. "Shall I send for a physician?"

"I am fine, just tired," Sinjun assured her as he accepted the snifter of brandy Farthingale had brought him. "I'd hoped to find Julian home. I may need his help finding Christy and my son."

Emma and Amanda exchanged knowing glances over Sinjun's bowed head.

"Julian hasn't returned yet," Emma said. "I'm

really worried about him. He's been gone longer than usual and no one has heard from him. I'm concerned about the mysterious business that calls him away so often."

"He'll turn up soon," Sinjun predicted.

"Go home, Sinjun," Emma advised. "You look exhausted."

"I don't want to go home to an empty nursery and no wife. But you're right, Emma, I am tired. My problems are none of your concern." He tossed down the brandy and heaved himself out of the chair. "Good night, ladies."

"You should have told him," Amanda scolded after Sinjun had left.

Emma sent her a mischievous smile. "I'd like to see Sinjun's face when he walks into the house and discovers Christy and Niall." She clasped her hands together and sighed. "Isn't it romantic? Do you suppose a handsome prince charming will come along and sweep me off my feet?"

"Wishful thinking, my dear," Aunt Amanda chided. "Women have to be practical. You'll marry someone notably suitable. Someone with good bloodlines who knows how to handle both your fortune and his."

Emma sent her an enigmatic smile. *Not if I can help it*, she silently vowed. *If I marry at all, the man can be a peasant as long as I love him. He will sweep me off my feet and pledge his undying love. I won't settle for a stodgy duke or earl in need of a brood mare.*

Since the hour was late and he was tired, Sinjun went directly home. Unfortunately he couldn't find his key. He knew Pemburton was sleeping, so he rapped sharply on the front door to awaken him. It seemed like forever before Pemburton opened the door, wearing a nightshirt and loosely belted robe that flopped around his bony ankles and skinny feet. A tasseled nightcap, tilted at a comical angle, sat atop his head of sparse gray hair. Sinjun wanted to laugh but knew his dignified butler would be offended.

"Welcome home, milord," Pemburton intoned dryly.

Chapter 21

"**T**hank you, Pemburton," Sinjun said as he started up the stairs. "I'm exhausted. A hot bath and something light to eat wouldn't be amiss."

"Very good, milord," Pemburton said, as if the demand for a hot bath and food at so late an hour was perfectly normal.

Weary beyond words, Sinjun wasn't in the best of moods. Had he been more himself he wouldn't have come straight home. He would have gone to one of his clubs or to White's and sought out a willing female, but frankly, even if he were up to it he wasn't interested in another woman.

Something totally unexpected had happened to Lord Sin since Christy Macdonald had brazenly thrust herself into his life. He had fallen in love with his wife and gained a son he adored. Would he ever see them again? What in bloody hell had made Christy flee Glenmoor in such a damn hurry?

Sinjun paused before the nursery door, tempted to open it, if only to gaze at the small bed where his son had once slept. But the disappointment of walking into an empty room dissuaded him, and he continued on to his own chamber.

Inside his chamber he went immediately to the brandy decanter sitting on his dresser and poured two fingers into a crystal goblet. Drink in hand, he walked to the window and stared into the dark street below, his thoughts bleak. A sleepy-eyed servant arrived to lay a fire in the hearth, distracting Sinjun from his morose thoughts. Shortly afterward the tub arrived, followed by pot boys carrying buckets of hot and cold water. Sinjun undressed and sank down into the water, sighing blissfully. Pemburton arrived with a light repast of meat, cheese, bread, and fruit. He pulled a small table close to the tub and set the tray down.

"Is there anything else you require, milord?"

"Go back to bed, Pemburton, I can see to myself. Just set the brandy decanter on the table before you leave."

Sinjun picked at the food, deciding he wasn't hungry after all. He refilled his goblet with brandy and sipped quietly. But even the heady taste of brandy palled after a while, and he set the glass down, tilted his head back against the rim of the tub and closed his eyes.

Christy awakened abruptly from a deep sleep, roused by the sound of activity coming from Sinjun's chamber. He had finally arrived! She had waited so long for him to return, and now that he had finally arrived she couldn't stop trembling.

Oh, why had she listened to Emma? What if Sinjun turned her away? What if he sent her back to Glenmoor without Niall?

Plagued by demons of her own making, Christy decided there was only one way to discover the answers to all her questions. Sinjun's chamber was separated from hers by a door. She had but to walk through the door to learn her fate.

She'd make him understand how much she loved him, she vowed as she climbed from bed and padded barefoot to the door. Gathering the tattered remnants of her courage, she cracked open the door and peered into Sinjun's chamber. The room was dimly lit by a cheery fire that popped and snapped in the grate. A tub had been set up before the hearth. All she could see of Sinjun was his head resting against the rim and his arms stretched out along the sides. He appeared to be sleeping.

Startling Sinjun awake didn't seem like a good idea. Then her gaze wandered to the bed, and a mischievous smile stretched across her lips. No matter how often she and Sinjun argued, their bodies were always perfectly attuned to one another.

Sinjun didn't stir as she tiptoed past the tub, nor did he appear to hear the whisper of cloth as she removed her nightgown and climbed into bed. Then she settled down to wait, her body thrumming with anticipation.

Time hung suspended, moving forward only when Sinjun finally stirred and rose majestically from the tub. The breath lodged in Christy's throat as he toweled himself dry before the fire. He was thinner than she remembered, but his body had lost none of its appeal. Her body swelled with desire, clamoring with the need to touch, to kiss, to feel. His back was to her. Her lips went dry, and she licked moisture onto them as she stared at the hard mounds of his buttocks, recalling the feel of their supple tautness beneath her hands.

He turned around, and Christy stifled a groan. Even at rest he was generously endowed. Aroused, he was magnificent. She held her breath and froze when he tossed the towel to the floor and approached the bed.

The bed sat in a shadowed corner, untouched by the dying flames in the hearth. She felt the mattress dip as Sinjun lowered himself onto the bed, and she heard him sigh as he pulled the covers up to his waist.

A sweetly scented puff of air touched Sinjun's face as he shifted on his side. Another breath whispered across his cheek, and he sucked in a startled gasp. With shaking hands he reached across the bed, and touched warm, supple flesh so familiar, so beloved, that his heart leaped with joy.

"Christy?"

He found her face, cupping it in his strong hands, cursing the darkness that concealed her beautiful features. His heart thudded against his ribcage as he ran his thumb over her lips and guided her mouth to his. She kissed him back. It was potent, heady; the heat and taste of her teased his senses and filled him with unbearable need. He kissed her again, and yet again, thoroughly exploring her mouth with his tongue as his hands roamed over her lush curves.

All past lies and deceptions disappeared as if they had never existed. He wanted to hold her like this in his arms forever, to feel her softness against him, to fill her with himself and never let her go.

"Don't be angry with me," Christy whispered when he released her mouth.

"Why did you leave Glenmoor?"

Her voice trembled. "You said you didn't want me."

Sinjun reared back, stunned. "When did I say that?"

"I . . . I could have misunderstood."

"Obviously," he said dryly. "I was so confused after you left I didn't know what to think. Margot said you missed Niall, and I could understand that. What I couldn't understand was why you left without telling me. I feared you would take Niall and flee. I was mad. Damn mad. Mostly at myself because I was too weak to stop you."

She touched his face. "I love you, Sinjun. I have always loved you."

"No more lies, Christy."

"No more lies, Sinjun. I want to tell you about Calum, and what happened while I was his captive."

He placed a finger against her lips. "I don't care what happened. You're mine. I had you longer than he did."

"But that's what I'm trying to tell you! Calum never had me, not in the way you mean. He was lying. He wanted you to think he'd ravished me. He knew you wouldn't want me after he'd . . . he'd defiled me."

"He was wrong, Christy. I'd want you no matter what he did to you."

"Truly?"

"Truly."

She gave a happy little sigh. "Emma said you followed me to Glenmoor because you feared Calum would hurt me."

"Emma told me you lied about my son because you wanted to protect me from Calum Cameron. It appears we owe Emma a great deal for her failure to keep confidences."

"Emma talked me out of leaving, but I've been

so afraid. I feared you would send me back to
Glenmoor without my bairn."

"How is my son?"

"He's wonderful, and looks more like his father
every day. He's eating solid food now and crawling. He'll be walking soon. He missed you, Sinjun."

"No more than I missed him. And his mother,"
he added meaningfully. "Don't ever leave me
again, Christy."

"Or? . . ."

"Or I'll tie you to the bed and make love to you
until you're too exhausted to move, much less
flee."

She made a purring sound in her throat and
snuggled against him. "Every night I dreamed of
being in your arms again. Are you sure you're recovered?"

"Why don't we find out?"

He kissed her temple, her brow, then worked his
way down the slope of her cheek to her mouth. He
lingered over a kiss before moving his mouth to
the rapidly beating pulse in her neck. Her scent
intoxicated him, fueling the fire burning inside
him. He struggled to pace himself, but it had been
so long that he found control beyond him.

His mouth found her breast. His dark head bent
to cover a nipple with his lips, drawing it into his
mouth with heated pleasure. His hands caressed
her, roaming freely over the curves and valleys of
her body as his tongue circled damply around her
taut nipple.

A spear of heat spiked through her, coiling in her
belly and setting her blood afire. His warm breath
against her flesh sent shivers of anticipation racing
down her spine as her hands moved restlessly over
him, unable to get her fill of touching.

"You're the only woman I'll ever want, Christy Macdonald."

The husky sound of his voice was a caress, his warm mouth upon her as potent as the stroke of his tongue against her nipple, and she trembled. She must have been mad to think she could survive without this special man in her life.

"You're the only man I'll ever want, my Lord Sin."

"Just Sinjun. I've repented."

His hand swept over her belly, coming to rest at the bright curls between her legs. His fingers slid through dewy flesh, opening her, stroking the inner folds, now wet with her love juices, until she burned beneath his touch. A thrumming began low in her stomach. Her nerve ends were so raw she lurched and cried out when his mouth replaced his fingers. A new fire ignited when she felt his tongue thrust deeply into her moist passage. When he dragged his thumb across the throbbing nub of sensitive flesh, she lost all semblance of control.

"Sinjun! Please!"

She quivered, straining upward against him, pressing herself with artless ecstasy against his mouth, reaching for elusive release. A soft sob tore from her throat. Then ecstasy tore through her in a shattering, tumultuous explosion.

"Sinjun! Oh, God, how I love you! Come inside me. I've waited so long."

He raised to his knees and knelt over her. She felt the tenseness of his sweat-slicked muscles and spread her thighs wide to receive him. A log in the grate hissed and spat, and in the ensuing flash of light Christy caught a glimpse of his eyes, heavy-lidded with passion, glowing like brilliant embers beneath a fringe of dark lashes. His teeth were bared, and his expression was stark with concentration.

He was so beautiful he took her breath away. She was distracted from his face when she felt his thick shaft prodding against her stomach. Her fingers curled around him, taking his hot shaft in her hand, slowly moving it up and down his hard length. Once, twice, again, then she heard his breath hiss through his clenched teeth.

"You're killing me, sweetheart."

His voice was raw, as if he were riddled with pain. Heart clamoring wildly, she knew instinctively that his control was dangling by a slim thread. She brought him to her entrance and he slid inside.

"Thank God," he whispered fervently. "Hold me, love, hold me."

Her arms slid around his warm, damp skin to hold him close as he moved forcefully between her legs. He kissed her roughly, thrusting deep and hot inside her. She cried out, overcome by sweet ecstasy. It had been so long . . . so very long. He caught her cry in his mouth as she dug her fingers into the taut muscles of his back, urging him on with soft little noises she had no idea she was making. He moved inside her with strong, relentless strokes; she arched upward into the hard thrust of him, wanting more, demanding everything.

Someone was whimpering. It was immediately silenced when he covered her mouth with his, but the whimpers continued inside her head. He drove into her with relentless fervor, his engorged shaft sending pleasure washing over her in hot, scalding waves.

Half-sobbing, she clung to him as he climaxed strongly inside her. He groaned and rested his forehead against her cheek, panting to catch his breath. After a while he rolled to one side and brought her against him.

"Do you forgive me?" Christy whispered into the silence of the chamber.

"It's probably going to take a lifetime."

"I never wanted to lie to you. I couldn't let you return to the Highlands and become Calum's victim, so I did what I thought best to save your life."

"It's all right, love, truly. I *do* understand, though I would have preferred that you told me the truth and let me decide what to do about Calum. Speaking of Calum, how did you keep him from . . . bedding you? I wouldn't have given up so easily."

She laughed and said archly, "Calum isn't Lord Sin. Seriously, though, jealousy and ambition were eating him alive. When we were children we were expected to marry, but Culloden changed all that. Calum thought that making me his mistress would give him the power to control the clans."

"Did Calum think I was going to do nothing while he used my wife?" Sinjun asked harshly.

" 'Tis a rare husband who will take his wife back once she's been compromised by another man. Wife stealing often results in a feud that can last generations."

"I must be that rare husband, because I wanted you back no matter what Calum did to you. You haven't told me how you kept Calum from bedding you."

"I told him I was carrying your bairn. It dampened his ardor, just like I hoped it would."

Sinjun reared up on his elbow. "Are you? Good God, Christy, am I going to be a father again?"

"I don't think so."

"Would you like to?"

The breath caught in her throat. "Would you like another bairn?"

" 'Tis time Niall had a little brother or sister."

"What about Lord Sin? Aren't you going to miss him? Won't the *ton* miss him?"

"I like to think that the legendary Lord Sin abdicated his title at the height of his illustrious career. He'll always be remembered as a profligate rake. As for the *ton*, I don't give a damn what they think. London no longer holds the same appeal it once did. I've learned to appreciate moors covered with heather, craggy mountains and sparkling lochs. The Highlands is a good place to raise our children."

Tears of joy filled Christy's eyes. "Are you saying what I think you are? Are you sure you're willing to forgo the pleasures of London society for country living? You know how remote Glenmoor is, how unworldly compared to decadent London."

"I love you, Christy. You wouldn't be happy living in London. Besides, the clan needs their laird. I'm not saying we won't visit London from time to time. What I'm trying to tell you is that I no longer feel the need to maintain the same lifestyle Lord Sin found essential to his well-being."

He grinned. "Won't Julian be surprised? He's been trying to reform me for years."

"I can't remember when I've been so happy," Christy sighed. "I nearly lost my mind waiting for you to return to London. I feared . . . I thought . . ."

"That I would turn you out of my house?" Sinjun drawled. "That was never my intention."

"I'll not submit meekly to a beating," Christy teased playfully.

He chuckled. "I never thought you would, 'tis why I never considered it. Not my fierce Christy.

I'll settle for your love." He pulled her against him, his hands caressing her breasts, her hips, his lips teasing her ear. "Shall we make a little brother or sister for Niall?"

"It might take a very long time."

"I've got all the time in the world. If Lord Sin is going to retire, he'll need to practice his skills frequently so he won't become boring."

"You'll never bore me, Sinjun. Just don't stop loving me."

"Loving you is my destiny. I should have realized it when that seven-year-old hellion I married kicked me in the shin and stuck her tongue out at me."

They loved and slept and loved again, for the rest of their lives.

A Taste of Paradise

CONNIE MASON

When lovely Sophia Carlisle stows away on a ship bound for Jamaica, she hardly expects to find Christian Radcliff at the helm. She and the captain have a turbulent history, which involves the breaking of her heart and the death by duel of his best friend. Now they will be forced to share a cabin, and if Christian has it his way, a bed. But Sophia finds herself forgetting the past and giving in to temptation. No man can arouse her senses as the swashbuckling captain does, and she has no use for prudence or propriety when in his kiss she can find…*A Taste of Paradise.*
